THE DISRUPTIVE PHYSICIAN

A NOVEL

ALAN ALTMAN

First Edition 2023

The Paper House Publishing
Toms River, NJ 08753
www.thepaperhousebooks.com

DEDICATION

To all the great physicians, past and present, who dedicated their lives to learning, teaching and being advocates for every patient they cared for. With specific gratitude to Drs. Daniel Present, Richard Mahler, Mark Friedman and Merle Bolton, who exemplified what being a physician should be.

ACKNOWLEDGEMENTS

Writing a first novel can take a lifetime; mine almost did. A special thanks to **my late Uncle, Mario Puzo**, who told me "write what you know."

To my wife Suzanne, thank you for having the patience to encourage me along the way while keeping me nourished with your baking wizardry.

To my son, Alex, an author whose writing skills are becoming legendary, thank you for providing the old man with so many ideas and great edits, and bearing with me till the last sentence was complete. And thanks to you and your wife Missy for taking the burden off my shoulders everyday as our company works to improve the patient experience.

To my daughter Erica, who has accomplished so much, thanks for your love throughout the ups and downs of life, and for you and James providing the joy that four grandchildren bring to me every day.

To my youngest son Nick, golf pro turned college educator, thanks for your love and honesty, and for sharing with me, thankfully in retrospect, some of your past adventures. Thanks to you and Jeanne for much laughter and fun, always a day brightener.

To Angela Pneuman, an accomplished author and great teacher, thank you for your steadfast belief that this was a journey worth taking and for mentoring me while reviewing the manuscript's many revisions. I would never have finished without your guidance.

To Mike and his team at The Paper House, thanks for doing all the work to get this in good form and published, something I could never get done on my own.

And finally, to Tomas, my rescue cat, thank you for 15 years of companionship and mutual caring, and for giving me comfort and pain relief by "purring me on" to stroke your soft, smooth coat.

CHAPTER ONE

Physicians are many in title but very few in reality.
– Hippocrates (460?-377? B.C.) The Law, I (tr. by Francis Adams).

The physician strives for the good as the artist strives for the
beautiful, each pushed on by the admirable feeling we call virtue.
– Honore de Balzac (1799-1850)

Six in the morning is the only time to hold an outdoor meeting on a June day in the California desert. The sun creeps up the horizon to the east, dazzling the sky with violent orange and yellow streaks. White clouds hang suspended like puppets on a brisk blue backdrop. On a Wednesday morning in a park a block from the hospital, thirty middle-aged souls gathered for the monthly meeting of the Palm Springs Chapter of FWP (Frustrated Working Professionals). Dressed in shorts and running gear, sipping from Starbucks or bottled water, the disgruntled mob chattered happily. Misery loves company. Accountants, lawyers, a disproportionate number of teachers, one younger woman in skintight shorts and a revealing top that suggested an older profession; they all sat in the grass or on a towel around the water fountain that served as a podium for the speaker of the month.

Margaret Janowitz, a squat fortyish lady with soft brown hair and a bellowing voice, commanded the group's attention.

"I'll like to call this meeting to order and introduce a founding member of our society whom you all know, especially those who have had a colonoscopy, Dr. Don Strader. Don has so graciously agreed to serve as moderator this morning. Don."

To light applause, Dr. Strader strode to the water fountain. Tall, fit, speckled gray hair, a straight-lined face marking his sixty years, tailored jacket and tie; all who knew him recognized that he had interrupted rounds at the hospital to attend the meeting. Strader panned the group with a friendly yet confident gaze, nodding in acknowledgment.

"Glad you all could make it. This is the part where I'm supposed to

1

say, please turn around so that I can recognize you, but I'll leave the shop humor alone. And don't let Margaret mislead you. I didn't volunteer to speak today; it's my turn. This is the thirty-fifth monthly meeting of FWP, and we have grown from three to the crowd you see around you. The rules remain the same, the moderator speaks for three minutes about issues in his or her profession, and then it's open discussion. We might not solve problems, but we sure can vent."

The assemblage murmured its approval.

Strader's voice grew solemn.

"Last week I witnessed a murder, and there was nothing I could do about it."

****

An hour later and a block away, hidden under a yellow protective gown, Dr. Strader placed his stethoscope on Mr. Alvin Wright's chest and heard a heart pounding at one hundred twenty-five times per minute. His blood pressure was dangerously low at eighty-five systolic. He served as the central conduit for an IV line, cardiac monitor probes, a Foley catheter, and an abdominal wound drain. A disruptive beep from the IV's alarm monitor annoyed the doctor. Empty.

Strader's gloved hand slid behind Mr. Wright's neck and gently leaned him forward.

"Alvin, we'll be done in a second. Breathe in and out for me."

The old man puffed in shallow, anxious spurts. Strader gently lowered him back and pressed the control button to raise the head of the bed. He patted Alvin on the shoulder. "I still have to tune you up a little before I get you out of here, Alvin, but it'll happen." He glanced again at the beeping monitor and empty IV bottle, angrily discarded his gown and gloves, and left the room.

The ICU was Grand Central Station crazy. The metal food tray cart obstructed half the floor space. Two aides delivered tea, clear juice and green Jello to four of the five ICU rooms. At seven A.M. the nursing station buzzed with a shift change and nurse sign-out chatter. Arriving and departing nurses shared a familiar weariness fostered by twelve-hour shifts.

Lucy Abrigo, RN, all of twenty-five, unbroken despite working all night, glanced up and saw Strader approach.

"Uh, oh," she cautioned her colleagues, "Darth Vader's here."

2

"Who has Mr. Wright in room two?" Strader said, staring them down.

"Me," Donna Curci softly replied. She was a crumpled, heavy-set nurse with tired eyes. She had heard it all before.

"Do you have anything against him?"

Nurse Curci shook her head, half looking up at him.

"Then why does it seem you are trying to kill him? His pump was just beeping away when I got here. No fluid for three hours. His BP is already down, heart rate up and now we'll have to watch for kidney failure."

Curci mumbled, then stopped. Silence. Finally, Lucy Abrigo spoke up.

"It's been a crazy night, Dr. Strader. Three transfers and two admits. Donna's been killing herself just keeping up."

The nursing crew looked at Strader, their expressions a common plea for a reprieve.

"Did you call the nursing supervisor?" Strader said.

No response. At the rear corner of the nurses' station a hospitalist, Dr. Kwon, cringed as he feverishly typed his note in a patient's computerized record. He raised his eyes just enough to catch Strader's iron glare, and then he couldn't disappear, no matter how hard he lowered his rail-thin body into his chair.

"Dr. Kwon, is it right for me to bring this up? To ask staff if they called the night supervisor when they were too busy to complete their required work?"

Kwon barely nodded.

Strader turned to Donna. "Did you call me to notify me that you couldn't adequately take care of my patient? Did you call the patient's family?"

Silence.

"Well, before you go home to have a nice day please hang a new IV bottle— and check the drip rate. It's thirty CC's an hour too fast."

Dr. Strader sat down at a computer terminal, studied the nurses' notes, the vital sign graphics and lab results, then picked up the patient's paper chart and unsheathed his pen. He dated his note and methodically printed in large, bold blue ink Mr. Wright's vital signs, Fluid input and output, his physical exam findings, current medications, assessment, and plan. He read it over. He wrote orders in the computerized order sheet module, and under the computer's progress note section, he typed in "Please see organized note in written chart." He pulled out his iPhone and took one photo of his note and one of the orders he wrote, his thoughts now protected if the hospital computer system went down.

He strode for the exit, then stopped and turned to the nurses still laboring over the morning report.

"What's destroying medicine is the widening gap between what is acceptable and what is accepted." As he spoke, he could feel his neck turning red. "I'm the kind of guy who accepts responsibility and demands accountability."

Once the door to the ICU was safely closed behind him, there were a few nervous twitters.

"I'm the kind of guy— who's an A-hole," said Sean Brooks, a young, head-shaved nurse in tight scrubs and a stethoscope. "I'm the kind of guy—who's a bully. Call the nursing supervisor— right. That Bro is living in the 1980's. Donna, we know how hard you work— you can't do everything. What a bastard."

Dr. Kwon's youthful frame reappeared from behind his computer. He shook his head and muttered loud enough for the nurses to hear, "Disruptive, disruptive doctor."

Lucy Abrigo, RN, wasn't too sure. She checked to ensure the new IV had started and Mr. Wright's vital signs weren't bottoming out. She'd hang around for an hour off the clock and check his lab results to be certain Donna's omission hadn't caused kidney damage. Fourteen hours and still on the job.

****

By eleven o'clock, Strader had finished rounds and performed six screening colonoscopies. He welcomed a short break in his schedule, after which he'd return to the GI lab for his final case, involving the removal of large colon polyps from a patient referred to him by another gastroenterologist. The bigger the polyp, the bigger the risk of bleeding or perforation; the bigger the risk of a malpractice suit. Strader enjoyed tackling these complex cases; they challenged his clinical judgment as well as his hand-eye skills, and the reward for a successful procedure was high, saving the patient from an operation where part of the intestine would have to be removed. And get paid two hundred dollars to boot from Medicare. He beelined for the hospital cafeteria and sure enough there was his old buddy, GP Joe Morales, tan and relaxed in his Tommy Bahama shirt, manning his corner table.

"Morales, remember when the nurses used to get us coffee when we came into the ICU?" Strader said as he sat down. "Now they won't even give my patients IV fluid. Mr. Wright, you know the one I told you about with sepsis and hypotension? They left him dry for about three hours."

"And I imagine you tactfully discussed this lapse privately with the offending party?"

"You know me."

"At least you're a specialist. I step foot in the ICU, and they ask me, "What the fuck do you want? After forty years."

Strader grinned. "Yeah, we've been off the pedestal for a while." He sipped coffee while casing the cafeteria, his eyes darting from scrub-clad techs to admins in suits to several white-coated pharmacists. He counted two exhausted nurses and eleven relaxed retired docs, still able to eat for free. Everyone except the docs was texting. "Remember when we would sit right in this corner, you, me, the surgeons, Doc Wichter, some of the G.P.s, the OR nurses, that cute ICU head nurse— Jill? We'd get all ramped up on a pancreatitis case or a toxic shock. We'd talk medicine, we'd talk about how we were going to help those patients. And we'd listen."

"I know we talked about Jill. Pretty and a great nurse. She covered my ass more than once. It made me feel better, and made my patients feel better. Angel... And for me, help was always welcomed. But that was then, Don, we were young Turks. You're still going strong, but I'm just riding out the string. And I'm kinda glad, given how things have changed. But bottom line, we have to live in this world now."

Strader said, "My guy— in the ICU no less— getting nothing but air through his IV for three hours. He could have had an air embolism and could have died. Bad enough his heart rate jumped about 40 points. In the ICU! I know they're understaffed, and they work hard, and they put up with jerks like me and incompetents like— you know. Then I read in the papers and in the New England Journal about healthcare for all and the family-centered medical home. I can't even get sugar water into poor Mr. Wright in the ICU. It's all such bullshit."

"Don, I'm older than you. Shit, I may be older than penicillin. I've been just Doc, a GP who did surgery and OB, a primary care physician, and a provider. Now I'm pretty much the same as a nurse practitioner or P.A. Soon I imagine I'll be team-member Morales. But I'm still me and I still do my thing. Remember what the New York Health Commissioner said in the late 1980's? About the AIDS crisis? When he was trying to set up a needle exchange program? One thing he said stuck with me, 'You'll never find a political solution to a health care problem.' You can only do so much."

"I haven't even said anything yet about a horrible case I wandered into last week. I just want some fucking IV fluid. I know those nurses are overworked. Trying to get more staffing from administration is like looking for ice cubes in the desert. The CEO is so tight when he walks, his ass squeaks. Every single time we've approached him for more staff or new scopes it's a no--he's like a kid guarding his piggy bank. Accounting trumps accountability. I just want someone to give a damn." Strader's pager cut them short and he headed back to the GI lab. When finished, he sprinted across the street for his office, only twenty minutes late, arriving by the back door to avoid running the waiting room gauntlet. He grabbed a fresh long white coat, gave his nurse the high sign to get the exam rooms filled up, and waded in.

****

Three hours later, Kayesha, coal-black eyes and skin contrasted against Wednesday green scrubs, phone cradled on her neck, scanned the waiting room in front of her. Four more patients—with Doc Strader, that could mean two hours. She glanced up at the clock – 4:20. That clock never told a good story – maybe they should take it down. To her right, two stacks of charts threatened to topple on Tiny T--Linda Tortaventi. Tiny, with her own cordless phone cradled to her ear, scheduled an appointment on her computer screen while transferring the top chart from the left to the right pile. The charts teetered, and Tiny grabbed a bunch, slid from her chair and began wedging them into the stuffed ceiling-high metal cabinet forming one wall of the office.

"No, Mrs. Bernard, it's NEXT Thursday at 2:00, not tomorrow. No—2:00. Yes, Mrs. Bernard, I know that some of the doctors use the internet, but so many of our patients are older." Tiny shrugged her shoulders as Kayesha gave her the 'get off the phone' look, since two other lines were ringing. "Yes, I'll mention that to Dr. Strader. He always tries to be on time. We'll see you next week. Yes, that's next Thursday at 2. I have to run now. The doctor needs me. Bye, Mrs. Bernard."

Tiny glanced at the clock, hit another call line, and spoke as she zipped from the business office to Dr. Strader's consulting office, a seldom used luxury these days. She pulled a freshly laundered white coat from the oak armoire and hung it on the antique oak coat rack adjacent to the doctor's roll-top desk. All his diplomas and certificates on the wall— why didn't he move them to the exam rooms? He always switched to a new coat every

6

afternoon at four, said it helped him for the daily home stretch, kept him fresh. Tiny gazed out the second story window at the still palm trees protecting them from the afternoon sun, allowed herself ten seconds of quiet, sighed deeply, closed the doctor's door, and returned to the fray.

Kayesha put a call on hold, spun her swivel chair to the left and took Mr. Oliver's chart from Dr. Strader. The doctor dictated their visit right in front of Mr. Oliver, an older man dominated by square black-rimmed glasses and a shining, perfectly round bald head. The patient beamed as the doctor gave him a final pat on the shoulder and disappeared into his office.

"Kayesha, he said I don't need a colonoscopy for ten years. I'll be eighty-six. God willing."

"Oh, you'll make that easily. I hope I'm still here, the way he's working me to death." With that, Kayesha took the chart and Mr. Oliver's co-pay and slid back to her center position guarding the business office window to the waiting room. Mr. Oliver left reluctantly, trading the cool of the air-conditioned office for the sweltering heat of the late afternoon desert sun.

Kayesha clicked off the phone's hold button as she watched a new patient sort through the waiting room's reading material. Not a Barnes and Noble spread, but a neat set of plastic brochure racks: Hepatitis C, Living with IBS, Crohn's and Colitis Foundation, GERD, and the two largest racks, Obesity and Lifelong Exercise. Unsatisfied, the patient, a businesswoman based on her tailored pants suit, approached the window Kayesha was guarding while working the phone.

"I'm back, Tara. Now when do you want that scheduled?" Kayesha studied her computer calendar and simultaneously kept track of the waiting room and approaching woman. The room itself was comfortable—six upholstered Queen Ann chairs, an oak bench and a rich blue rug—memories of an easier, better time. In the corner were eight folding chairs, in regular use these days with the endless patient traffic. Kayesha finished her call, acknowledged the woman at the window, and in one motion reached below and pulled out two new choices for the woman to peruse, a Wall Street Journal editorial entitled "Obamacare and You" and last week's People magazine, featuring "Brad and Angelina, what lies ahead?" Kayesha had lugged the magazine from home knowing full well that she'd never have a minute to look at it. The woman grabbed People like it was a lifeline, nodded thanks, and returned to her chair.

****

At six forty-five, after he was sure that Tiny was safely on her way home, Strader locked up the office and carried a stack of unfinished charts down to his leased grey Buick. A clear violation of his "no chart leaves the office" rule. He drove across the street to the hospital, ran in to see that Mr. Wright was stable, and headed home. He felt tired, but nothing unusual. It actually had been a fairly straightforward day. Now it was Wednesday night. No tennis or racquetball. Dinner? He had options. He drove around to the ER entrance to see if Angie Franklin, his favorite nurse, was finishing a day shift. Angie was his oasis in the desert, attractive, competent, and a decade younger than him. She'd been his sole female companion since his wife Rosemary died four years ago. Angie saw things the way he did. And they could talk shop and other things, less now about Rosemary, who Angie had known well. But tonight, her car wasn't in the lot. That narrowed it down to his frequent eat-alone options, take-out deli, pizza, Chinese, or just go home and seeing what's there. He still had all those charts to dictate and Tomas to feed— home it was.

As he opened his door, Tomas, his twelve-pound grey and white stray cat, was already purring and rubbing up against his leg. Strader ramped up the AC; the place was an inferno. He picked up Tomas and enjoyed rubbing the cat's head against his palm along with the accompanying throaty serenade. He plucked a handful of Friskies from the small kitchen cabinet and put it and Tomas on the kitchen table. For himself, he found a box of rigatoni and a can of San Marzano tomatoes. Pasta, a tired man's best friend.

After changing to shorts and a tee shirt, he boiled water in a large Farberware pot; he'd sent his daughter the good stuff— the All-Clad set—after his wife died. He'd tried to cook with it, but he kept seeing Rosemary at the stove. He watched the news as he prepared his sauce, coating the frying pan with virgin olive oil, browning onions, adding salt, pepper, basil, parsley and tomatoes. He mixed with his mother's old wooden spoon and tasted freely. He dropped a pound of rigatoni into the boiling water; he'd be set for tomorrow as well. He drained it al dente. Pictures of his son and daughter surrounded the TV on an antique oak table, and his two grandchildren took center stage. It was way too late to call them back East. He ate with gusto, the meal a welcome distraction from the thoughts that had clouded his day.

At nine o'clock, interrupted only twice by non-emergent calls from the answering service (although he should be relieved that Mrs. Erichsen's heartburn was gone), he sat at his well-oiled antique oak desk, Tomas in his lap, and dictated his charts. After each dictation, Tomas would raise his head and Strader would rub it with the warm recorder until the purring reached ten decibels. Tomas dropped his head back down. Strader put the dictated charts in front of his door so he wouldn't forget to bring them back in the morning. He read one of twenty unread journals stacked neatly at his feet and showered.

By ten fifteen he was in bed, Tomas on his chest as he zipped through three chapters of Lee Child's Worth Dying For. The book dropped from his hand, and reading light still blazing, he fell asleep.

****

The jarring ring of the phone on the nightstand failed to elicit even a raised eyebrow from Tomas, still blanketing Strader's chest. On the second ring Strader, careful not to move his feline bedmate, reached up and answered, noting it was two fifteen in the morning. It was the answering service.

"Sorry to bother you, Dr. Strader, but it's the ER."

"Put them through." Strader was already sliding off the bed, leaving Tomas curled up and cozy on the pillow. Like a fireman his clothes were jump-in ready.

"Dr. Strader, it's Angie. I'm sorry to wake you up but we have a thirty-eight-year-old Spanish-speaking belligerent male alcoholic with a major upper GI bleed. He's thrown up at least two units since he's been here. His BP is starting to dive, eighty over forty, pulse is one forty-five…."

"I'm on my way." Strader lifted Tomas and slid the comforter under him before putting him back in the bed and giving him a gentle head rub. Tomas purred and settled back in. "Angie, I know you called…"

"I called the GI bleeding team forty minutes ago and they're on their way."

"Who's on call for them?"

"Gil Morgan."

"Means you'd better get ready to help."

"I'm cleaning up my desk as we speak."

"Thanks, Angie. See you in five."

Strader fled his condo for the cool black night. As he sped the three-wood and five-iron distance to the hospital ER, he enjoyed the view of the top of the tram snug among the lofty Santa Jacinto mountains, illuminated by the quarter-moon. Even after twenty-some-odd years, the serenity of the desert night soothed him, particularly before a tough ER case. Thirty seconds after reaching the ER, the calm was gone. As he scrutinized the patient, Mr. Enrique Ramos, Strader threw on a yellow paper-cloth preventive gown over his coat, donned gloves, cap and booties. A nurse and aide were trying to restrain the unkempt Mexican male dressed in a yellow wife beater and tattoos, covered in his own blood, cursing in Spanish. His blood pressure topped out at seventy systolic, heart rate one hundred sixty. Strader thought he might crash. Where was the GI bleeding team? The special nurse and tech were nowhere in sight. As he tried to listen to the battling patient's chest and heart, a torrent of blood shot from Ramos's mouth and scored a direct hit on Strader's chest and face. Strader helped the nurse and aide secure the restraints to keep the patient safe and on his left side on the ER gurney while wiping his face with moist gauze pads. Strader craned his neck to find Angie at her desk completing the records of two patients who were headed home. Angie was a looker in her late forties. He liked to call her "pert, pertinent and impertinent." He was pumped about their upcoming July 4th picnic date.

"Angie, where the hell is my team? I'm going to lose this guy. Page Gil Morgan stat and get his ass in here. Get me four units of whole blood stat and put six units of packed cells and two units of fresh frozen plasma on hold. You may have to do this case with me."

"Blood's on its way. I'm paging now. Whatever you need, we'll get it done."

"Thanks, Angie, you are my comfort." Her posture straightened and her eyes smiled as she worked.

Strader opened the IV wide to maximize the volume of fluid being infused. The patient, still conscious, was now two wide open pupils amidst a blood-covered, weakened body. His wrists were tied to the bed with soft restraints. He lay on his left side, and the fight in him was ebbing—a young wild man staring at his own death.

"No se preocupre, todo esta bueno," Strader said, attempting to reassure the man in broken Spanish. "De pronto de le una poca medicina para hace sueño, y en cinco minutos completar." A Spanish-speaking

10

LVN smiled as she came to get a Spanish consent form signed with the patient's X. Strader was quizzical. "I think I told him not to worry and soon we'll put him to sleep and be done in five minutes."

"Something like that," said the LVN.

Several more minutes passed before Gil Morgan, R.N., thin, clean-cut, at six-one a shade taller than Strader, sauntered in, pushing the Bleeding Team emergency cart, alone. With Angie's help, within five minutes they had Mr. Ramos very minimally sedated, on his left side, a plastic mouthpiece taped in place. His blood pressure was ninety systolic with IV fluid running freely through one IV and packed blood cells through another. Strader and Morgan were gowned and gloved. Gil informed Strader that the GI Bleeding team tech never responded to the call.

"What do you mean they never responded?" Strader said, threading the nine-millimeter diameter endoscope through the mouthpiece into the mouth and down the esophagus.

"What I said," said Gil.

Strader watched the lumen of the esophagus in front of the tip of the scope on the TV monitor set up on the other side of the bed. His left hand held the handle of the scope and he felt his fingers deftly play their music as they had done thousands of times before, simultaneously clearing the scope tip with water while blowing air into the esophagus to keep the lumen from collapsing on the scope. With metronome precision, his right hand torqued the shaft of the scope to keep the lumen in view. Spurts of red blood were billowing from the gastric antrum, the area of the stomach just before it entered into the duodenum. He manipulated the scope tip and it winded snakelike until it was directly over the bleeding site, an ulcer. The patient started to wake up.

Without looking up Strader said, "Gil, give him one more mg. of midazolam. Just one. He's on the brink and I don't want to lose him." He shot a quick glance at Gil, who to Strader looked uncomfortable, as he slowly gave Ramos the drug.

Strader injected some water through a small catheter directly into the ulcer bed, washing away the blood and exposing a raw bleeding vessel underneath. Strader kept the scope tip in perfect position without ever looking at the scope handle or buttons— his fingers worked autonomously yet in synchrony, like the string section of an orchestra.

"All right Gil, give me some epinephrine, 1:1000, for injection. Then we'll put on a couple of clips."

Gil's hands slowly loaded the catheter with epinephrine and threaded it through a channel in the top of the scope. Strader sensed that some-

11

thing was wrong as he took over, advancing the catheter until it exited out the tip of the scope in the stomach. He manipulated the scope tip so that the catheter was directly over the ulcer. The patient began groaning and moving. Strader nodded his head and Gil advanced the needle outside the catheter tip. Strader quickly inserted the needle directly into the blood vessel and injected epinephrine until the area blanched. When he was satisfied he nodded again and Gil withdrew the needle. Strader removed the catheter.

"All right, let's put on some clips."

Gil squirmed. "I didn't bring any clips from the lab."

Strader never took his eyes off the TV monitor as he felt his neck redden and a storm begin to swirl in his head. "I have to clip it, or at least use a thermal device, or it will re-bleed. You know epi alone is inadequate. Give me the heater probe, then."

"Sorry doc, the heater probe's back in the lab, too. I'll run right over and get it. Do you want the clips or the probe?"

Strader banged his right hand on the bed. The patient was sleepy but arousable.

"It's two thirty in the morning. This guy could bleed out at any time; he could throw a berserk and bite through the scope. You know you should have everything on the emergency cart when you set up. For Christ's sake, you've been doing this for years."

"Well what do you want, clips or heater probe?" A touch of impatience tinged Gil's voice.

"What the fuck do I want?" Strader turned and locked eyes with him. "Both. I want both. Every time – both – here- in three minutes. On the cart. And I don't ever want to be in this predicament again. You check the cart before you set up. For a bleeder, we need a bicap probe, epi, heater probe and clips. If you can't do it, you can bet your ass I'll get someone who can."

Strader watched Gil suspiciously as he took off for the lab. Gil wasn't stupid and he was usually competent. Strader knew Gil was going through a divorce and custody battle over his young boy. He was always anxious to leave work, early if possible, which Strader chalked up to his family problems. Strader tried to be sympathetic but over the last few weeks he had to admonish Gil for lapses several times, once in front of the nurses in the ICU. But this was so blatant. And after that case a week ago.

Another small river of red gurgled from the patient's mouth. The TV monitor showed solid red. Strader emptied a syringe of water through the scope's irrigating channel and when he cleared the tip, he could see the ulcer spurting again. He filled the catheter with epinephrine again and rapidly threaded it through the scope, positioning the catheter over the bleeding vessel once more and advancing the needle tip again into the ulcer bed.

"Casi terminado. We're almost finished my friend. Almost finished." The blood pressure was back down to seventy systolic.

"Angie, I need you, now."

CHAPTER TWO

At nine fifteen the morning of the Frustrated Working Professionals (FWP) meeting in the park, following a brisk two-mile jog, shower and breakfast at Will Reed's eatery, Greg Gilliam Esq. visited the office of Dale Rupert Hendrickson III, CEO of Palms Hospital. Hendrickson frequently threw Gilliam mundane legal work that even a paralegal couldn't screw up. This morning, Gilliam was visibly excited. He was going to cash in.

"Hi Joanna, is the boss busy? I've got important news for him."

The trim executive secretary smiled, texted a message and sent it on. Within seconds she read the reply.

"Go right in, Mr. Gilliam. Mr. Hendrickson is always happy to see you."

Gilliam lowered his head to safely traverse the doorway into the CEO's private chambers. With its waxed hardwood floors, built-in cabinets, and picture window facing the mountains to the west, the office was larger than most urban apartments. Behind a pompous custom-designed mahogany desk sat the CEO. "Just-call-me-Dale" Hendrickson was an unhappy administrator who appeared precisely his stated age of forty-seven. His head was stylishly bald, his presence diminished by a growing paunch incompletely hidden by the black vest he wore daily. In twenty plus years of the usual hospital administrator's nomadic journey, he had put in three-point-four years in a ladder of jobs until he reached CEO at the Palms. This was his dream job: smaller town, no one looking over his shoulder— as long as the hospital made its nut each year, which was becoming increasingly difficult. If he lost this job, it was all downhill. No hospital hired failed CEOs. He remained seated as Gilliam lowered himself into the winged back chair fronting the desk.

"Greg, always good to see you. What can I do for you today?"

"It's what I can do for you. You know that FWP group that meets monthly?"

The CEO nodded.

"Well today, one of your doctors, Don Strader, as much as said that a murder was committed in your hospital last week."

The CEO leaned forward, both hands gripping the desk. "What?"

"He said that he witnessed a murder last week but couldn't do anything about it. Everyone knew he was talking about the hospital. I was sitting next to that old malpractice lawyer, Vialotti. I thought he was going to get up and run to the morgue to check the corpses before the meeting was even over."

"Did Strader say anything else?"

"He didn't have to. Everyone knew what he meant. No, after that he spent most of his time talking about accountability and always doing the right thing and some other sanctimonious bull. But a murder? I think you should throw him off the staff. Who's going to come to a hospital where murders are occurring?"

"A murder? Here? That's preposterous."

The CEO wished he'd been spared this morning's gossip. That's all it was, gossip from a giant incompetent. But he'd have to deal with it anyway. He texted Joanna. 'Get Appel over here, stat.'

Three minutes later the CEO and Gilliam were joined by P. Roger Appel, hospital attorney. Appel was average in every imaginable way except for his head, which was sized for a much larger species and outlined by remnants of frayed brown hair. After failing to distinguish himself in the private world, he found his niche as a lawyer with Palms--his third and hopefully final stop. Sixty and cruising, Appel hoped to spend the next five years at the Palms and then retire. His dark blue suit was neither freshly pressed nor wrinkled. White shirt and tie even in the summer.

Gilliam filled him in on Doc Strader's outburst, concluding with his own legal opinion.

"Roger, it's an open and shut case. Libel. Let's sue the bastard, ruin him like he's trying to ruin the hospital."

Appel looked past Gilliam to the CEO. He shook his head.

"Greg, there's no lawsuit here. Inferred libel is impossible to prove." He turned in slow motion to the CEO. "Dale, is this the guy you wouldn't mind getting rid of??"

The CEO marshaled his thoughts and nodded slowly.

"Strader has been a gnat on my ass since day one. He always is critical, always wants more. More nurses in the ICU, more free meals for patient families, more educational programs, more-more-more. His bitching cost the hospital close to a million bucks in the increase in nursing staff alone. And cost me a whole year's bonus. The nurses don't even like him, administrators hate him, and some of the medical staff avoid him if they can. If I ran the hospital to please him we'd have no margin--we might as well fold up. And you and I would be working at an urgent care center somewhere in Fresno. The more I think about it— yeah, I want this guy out, I really want him out. Make my life much easier."

Appel's pale greying eyebrows flirted with his forehead. "Mine too. He's been disrespectful to me, turned the docs against me, got this ridiculous physician's bill of rights passed by the Medical Staff, citing freedom of speech. A real troublemaker. But there's no legal case to pursue." He paused, paced, and rubbed his hands together. After a minute he nodded. "Let's do something that we control. We get him out as a disruptive physician."

"We haven't had one of these since I've been here," said Dale. "What's involved?"

"I'll have to pull the by-laws, but if Strader has been a pain in the ass, we dig around a bit, get a list of harassment or other charges, maybe bring in his murder statement as a peripheral event, and initiate a medical judicial review. We pick the docs we want on the jury, pick one doc to present the charges and represent the hospital, Strader picks a doc to serve as his lawyer, and we get the trial done in thirty days. If they find him guilty, he's out without much recourse. Not only that but it gets reported to the State Medical Board and gets recorded in the data bank. It will pretty much flush his career down the toilet. Nobody will hire a disruptive physician. All risk, no reward. I'll go through the by-laws and get the details."

Gilliam piped in, "How about if they don't find him guilty?"

"Trust me, they will."

Dale was not a trusting soul, having butted heads with doctors for two decades, frequently on the losing end. He buzzed Joanna again. "I need the Chief of Nursing and Alyce from Risk Management in my office in thirty minutes. And bring me a copy of the medical by-laws."

Joanna knocked and entered, then handed the Medical Staff By-laws to the CEO. "I've scheduled your meeting in thirty minutes." She interpreted the CEO's facial gesture and tugged on Gilliam's arm. "Come with me, Mr. Gilliam. I believe we have a minor matter we'd like you to look at for us. And these fellows will be tied up most of the day." Joanna led him away and closed the door. Both the CEO and Appel waited until Gilliam was gone.

Appel said, "Dale, my advice to you as CEO is to let us handle all the details. I'll keep you up to speed as we go along but you'll be above the fray as far as the Medical Staff knows."

"Christ, Roger, it's my hospital and my job that's on the line. Strader's an asshole, yet they say he's one of our best docs. He's been around a long time. But his ask list never stops— just this week he sent me a petition signed by all the GI docs and nurses to have a new fluoro unit in the GI lab and an anesthesiologist assigned full-time to that unit. He threw in a request for two more nurses in the ICU, permanent sitters on call. He must think he's at Walmart. I'm not springing for any of this shit. We've got to make our margins."

"Exactly why I don't want you to seem directly involved. I've handled these judicial reviews before. It's all in the setup. As long as we set things up right, it's basically a sure thing. I've never had one go wrong."

Dale walked to the window and gazed at the majestic grey-brown peaks of San Jacinto to the west as if wisdom etched in the rock would be revealed to him. No such luck. He turned back to Appel.

"We'll do it your way, Roger. But I need to be in the loop at all times."

"Every second. Now let's go over these bylaws together."

****

Exactly one-half hour later, Appel was joined by Alyce Wagner and Samantha Porter RN in the conference room down the hall from the CEO's office. Now pushing forty, Ms. Wagner had climbed up the ladder at Palms Hospital over a fifteen-year period from the assistant secretary in the medical staff office to her current position as Risk Management VP. Short brown hair presided over a thin, hawkish face and thinner body, giving her the impression of being much taller than she actually was. Accessorized only with narrow-rimmed glasses, she could have been CIA. Some people are hard to miss; Alyce was hard to see. She knew her job and did it too well. When Ms. Wagner let herself eat lunch, it was alone. Ms. Porter was twice Alyce's girth, and twenty years had passed since she left clinical nursing for administration. Five years ago she was named the Chief of Nursing at Palms. Ebony-faced, with grey hair contrasting with bright red lipstick, she ran her department well enough to appease the CEO and Governing Board without antagonizing the Medical or Nursing Staff. An average day found her on the wards or ICU for forty-seven minutes; most of her time was devoted to meetings, lunch, and hospital politics. While not a health care pioneer, Samantha didn't hesitate to put her stamp on things dear to her, including elevating the position of nursing in the hospital pyramid.

18

The three sat around the large conference room teak table, a bottle of water, pad and pen marking their designated positions. With Appel sitting opposite the other two, he looked at his newly created notes.

"The CEO and I thank you for coming on such short notice."

CHAPTER THREE

Three blocks north of the hospital, in a neat one-room law office, Frank Vialotti, Esq. plowed through the Internet in his typical Clydesdale style. Beatrice Jones, his tolerant secretary for thirty years, culled the past week's local papers. Frank the Bank, as he was known in the trade (we'll make them empty out the bank for you), searched for all deaths, all hospital deaths, obituaries, etc. He focused on three patients who had died at the hospital. Baby Espiranza, stillborn – bad baby. Clark Restom, a 91-year-old with a fractured hip and pneumonia and Florita Dominguez— age 45, who died after a short illness. Florita Dominguez, bingo.

"Bea, I found her. Florita Dominguez, and only 45. Those bank vaults are opening."

Bea's still trim figure was highlighted by her white cotton sun dress as she peered through fashionable reading glasses. "What did she die from?"

"If I'm right then it's not just what did she die from, but who caused the what?"

Bea's left eye twitched, an involuntary anticipation of the eyestrain of another hunt and chase for a bonafide malpractice case. She was actually proud of her boss, even with his eccentric style. He was smart, a bulldog, and he had principles. They had turned down hundreds of cases over the years, even winnable ones because Frank wasn't convinced that the doctor had committed malpractice. And Frank had lost uncountable time and money, trying good cases where the odds were stacked against him because of a doctor-friendly jury or a powerful expert witness for the defense. She peered at him over her glasses. He wasn't tall or handsome; he had no silky grey hair or fashionable suit. But he had an energy about him that rivaled a hummingbird's, and he didn't fear working himself, or herself for that matter, to death. Every workday was an adventure.

"What do you need me to do?" she asked.

"Give me a minute, Bea, to— collect my thoughts." Frank's way of saying he didn't know. And this was a unique setting for him. There's been no complaint. The family hasn't come to him. There's been nothing in the papers or news about any wrongdoing— all he really had was Dr. Strader's offhand remark at that meeting and his own intuition. He had no legal right to review any medical documents, and he didn't know if he could approach the family. Strader had taken wonderful care of his wife, even though she lost her fight against pancreatic cancer, as they all do. So he couldn't really approach him…

"Bea, please pull up the rules on solicitation."

Two minutes later they were on his screen.

Rule 1-400 Advertising and Solicitation

(A) For purposes of this rule, "communication" means any message or offer made by or on behalf of a member concerning the availability for professional employment of a member or a law firm directed to any former, present, or prospective client, including but not limited to the following:

(1) Any use of firm name, trade name, fictitious name, or other professional designation of such member or law firm; or

2) Any stationery, letterhead, business card, sign, brochure, or other comparable written material describing such member, law firm, or lawyers; or

(3) Any advertisement (regardless of medium) of such member or law firm directed to the general public or any substantial portion thereof; or

(4) Any unsolicited correspondence from a member or law firm directed to any person or entity.

(B) For purposes of this rule, a "solicitation" means any communication:

(1) Concerning the availability for professional employment of a member or a law firm in which a significant motive is pecuniary gain; and

(2) Which is:

(a) delivered in person or by telephone, or

(b) directed by any means to a person known to the sender to be represented by counsel in a matter which is a subject of the communication.

And on and on for several boring pages, even for a legal mind.

Frank and Bea both were familiar with the rules of solicitation, as they were early users of TV for advertisements for Frank's legal services. Frank glanced through the current legal prohibitions. He always chuckled at:

> (4) A "communication" which is transmitted at the scene of an accident or at or en route to a hospital, emergency care center, or other health care facility.

Language crafted to stop the true ambulance chaser in his/her tracks. Fuck them. His eyes narrowed and his lips tightened at the preceding line:

> (3) A "communication" which is delivered to a potential client whom the member knows or should reasonably know is in such a physical, emotional, or mental state that he or she would not be expected to exercise reasonable judgment as to the retention of counsel.

He thought out loud, as always, offering Bea a look into his train of thought. "Her family just lost this 45-year-old woman, so I have to presume they are in a heightened emotional or mental state. I can't go knocking on their door or even call or write. How can I help right the scales of justice? This is a dilemma, Bea, of enormous proportions." Frank retreated to his grey metal desk and cushioned chair. Three files were neatly placed on the right, leaving him room on the left to think. He scribbled on his legal pad, drawing stick figures of the deceased Florita, Strader, and Doctor or Nurse X or whoever it was that took poor Florita from her loved ones so prematurely. The hospital was a circle surrounding Doctor/Nurse X, and below was the park and all the meeting attendees from that morning, including Frank. He drew a line from the meeting to Strader's figure and connected Strader through the hospital circle to the perps.

He read the passage about forbidden actions for attorneys in this setting -- again --and again.

> (3) A "communication" which is delivered to a potential client whom the member knows or should reasonably know is in such a physical, emotional, or mental state that he or she would not be expected to exercise reasonable judgment as to the retention of counsel.

His untamed eyebrows arched as he slowly nodded.

"Beth. See if you can get a look at the Bereavement list from the funeral. And get an address on poor Mrs. Dominquez and her family. I need a bridge."

CHAPTER FOUR

Five o'clock felt like midnight for Strader. Getting through a full day after being up all night was for interns and residents, like in his day, but now they had banker's hours and he was still doing it. When the staff shuffled him out the office door, he was tempted to go straight home, but guilt guided his Buick across the street to the hospital. He stopped in the bathroom to douse his face in cold water, a transient rejuvenation. Next stop, ICU and Mr. Ramos.

Five was usually an excellent time to round in the ICU; the nurses knew their patients well and were busy tidying things up for the seven o'clock change of shift, the evening visitors hadn't yet arrived, and most emergencies had been identified and resolved. Not today. Strader entered the ICU and was rocked by the din from Ramos's room, where a beleaguered nurse Abrigo looked like a hockey goalie protecting the net. She was guarding Ramos's bed against a pack of visitors, their coarse shouting piercing the closed door. The other nurses ignored the commotion. Strader spoke to the walls just before he joined Abrigo, "That's why there are rules in the ICU— only one visitor at a time." He entered the fray. Abrigo was drenched in sweat as she guarded the space between an agitated Ramos and his guests. Ramos was thrashing against the soft restraints that were tied to his bedrails as he yelled in Spanish. Strader thought the crowd was either trying to get his restraints off or slip him some street medicine. He sized them up as he stepped in front of Abrigo to form an imperfect shield. Three muscular loudmouths, early 30's, tattoos peeking around white wifebeaters, one definitely high; behind them a quiet, cleanly dressed fortyish couple supporting a short, more elderly woman with sad, wet eyes. Strader wanted to grab the punks and throw them out of the room with a kick in the ass as a bon voyage. *But let's get real*, he thought—only one easy way to turn this.

"Quién es la madre?" he asked.

"I speak English." Mrs. Ramos was small but her voice carried strength. "My son is not a dog to be tied up. You are his doctor?"

Strader walked through the crowd and took the woman by her hand, leading her to her son's bedside. It wasn't her fault. He placed her hand on the hand of her son, who momentarily became less crazed.

"Nurse Abrigo, please escort the rest of the visitors to the waiting area. Now." He looked to Mrs. Ramos, who nodded her head and the pack dispersed after zinging a few final threats, following the grateful nurse. Once they were gone, Strader took advantage of the quiet to access his patient. Blood pressure was stable, heart rate not too bad at 116, the NG tube was clear, and 400 cc of urine in the Foley. No active bleeding. Good. He listened to the chest, heart and palpated the abdomen. Ramos didn't fight him. Satisfied, he turned to the mother.

"Mrs. Ramos, your son has made himself very sick. He is bleeding from the inside and almost died last night in the emergency room. I was able to stop the bleeding but it may start again. All of these tubes are necessary to give him medicine and make sure he is all right. He is not in his right mind, from alcohol, maybe drugs— I don't know yet. I do know that if he acts crazy and pulls out his tubes, he is likely to bleed again and maybe die. That is why we restrained him, to keep him from hurting himself and to protect the nurses."

"But he is quiet now. I am here. I will stay. I am his mother."

Strader felt for her. She was not being defiant; she was being a mother with a mother's conviction that she could help her child. He knew better. With one hand, she held her son and with the other, she reached out for Strader.

"Please, doctor, please?"

Strader scrutinized the monitors above the patient's head, the clear yellow gastric contents coming from the NG tube and the fluid input versus output chart. He donned a pair of gloves, turned off the NG wall suction, held a paper towel in one hand, and in a single smooth movement, removed the nasal tape and pulled the NG tube out, taking care not to dirty the bed linen. He discarded the tube in the biologic basket.

"I think he'll feel better with this out and he'll be more comfortable. Okay, here's what we'll do. His nurse has other patients and can't be in here all the time. You must stay in the room with him. If he's quiet for an hour, we'll free one of his hands; if he's still quiet in the morning, we'll free the other one. I'll try and get a nurse or aide, what we call a 'sitter,' to stay with you in the room. But if your son doesn't cooperate, we'll have to do what's necessary. Like I said, your son is very sick, and he may still die."

"Gracias, doctor. Thank you." She held her head high, never letting go of her son's hand. A woman of dignity. A mother who has endured and will find the strength to endure more.

Strader nodded to her, then left the room and spoke with the charge nurse.

"Millie, I'm writing an order for Mrs. Ramos to stay with her son. No other guests for now. Six people in an ICU room? Nuts. That's why we have rules. I want a sitter to be in the room at all times with them for at least 24 hours and probably more. If he's quiet I'll write to take off one restraint and we'll reassess in the AM."

"Doctor Strader, I don't think they'll be able to get a sitter for us. They don't like to have sitters in the ICU since we're already staffed with one nurse for every two patients. And you know a visitor can't stay in the room all night."

"That's fine if we were staffed one to one. But we're not. I took out the NG for now. If Ramos pulls out his Foley and IV, there is going to be a shit-storm in there. Tell the nursing supervisor that if she doesn't find a sitter she can come down and help out. When we have a competent sitter and Ramos is under control, we can ask his mom to go home."

Strader typed his orders in the computer, wrote his detailed note in the progress note portion of the chart, snapped a picture of his note on his iPhone so it wouldn't be lost, and left, escorted by Millie's good riddance stare. He checked the time— 7:10 on his ancient Bulova, 7:02 according to his iPhone. He always kept his watch a few minutes fast, but he couldn't fool the iPhone. He smiled to himself— he couldn't stay on time if he was that crazy scientist in "Back to the Future." Just plug along and do the best you can, and don't take shortcuts along the way. Not in medicine. A weary look at his messages: two consults for the morning, one call back for tonight, Mrs. Lewis. He dialed her number as he headed for the Doctor's parking lot.

"Hello, this is Dolly Lewis." She spoke with a thick New York accent between old age breaths, her tune strangely pleasant to Strader. He always took the bait.

"Hello, Dolly, this is Dr. Strader, Dolly…"

"Oh, Dr. Strader, it's so late. You didn't have to call back tonight. I'm just having problems going – you know– potty."

"Dolly, I just saw you yesterday in the office, and you were fine. You don't have to go every day. Drink your water, eat your Raisin Bran, and you can always take your Milk of Magnesia. And if you haven't gone by the third day you can take an enema. You'll be fine. Don't make yourself crazy."

Crazier, he thought.

"Okay, I'll try. And I'll call you tomorrow to let you know.."

"Sure. Goodnight, Dolly."

Well, there was his female entertainment for the evening. He passed the few lingering BMWs and Range Rovers, careful not to touch their still burning hot surfaces. He winced as he opened his car door handle and settled in the driver's seat, the heat transiently feeling good on his back before transitioning to a hot beach day, uncomfortable burning. The AC burped a blast of warm air before gradually cooling. Strader inched his car forward, looking both ways before making the right turn towards Palm Canyon Drive. It was street fair night, and he'd park and grab a taco from his favorite street vendor. He didn't notice the black Audi that followed him.

Parking was always a bitch on street fair night, and Strader luckily found a spot near the O'Donnell Golf course, three blocks away. He removed his suit jacket and tie and hustled toward Palm Canyon Drive, where traffic was closed until ten. The sun inched toward its bed behind the San Jacinto mountains; the sidewalks still bubbled and the air remained singed.

The crowd was hot but relaxed. Strader looked out of place in pants and a button-down shirt; shorts, tank tops and sandals were the norm for the hundreds walking in the street. He responded cordially to several patient and hospital staff shout outs as he made his way to and from Toro's Tacos stand. He enjoyed each bite of his spicy pork taquito.

He recognized Alyce Wagner, passing, and forced a half-nod but she didn't seem to recognize him. Strange. He finished eating and headed back towards his car for the short trip home.

CHAPTER FIVE

Friday marked a week since the murder of Florita Dominguez. As he drove toward the hospital, Strader caught the sun blowtorching the eastern horizon behind him while dissolving the deep grey shadows of the mountains in front. On the last day of a very long week, he took solace in the upcoming weekend off call. His night had been interrupted only twice by calls from the ICU about Mr. Ramos, and Strader was grateful that he didn't have to leave his bed. Practice was a grind, a trudging along rather than a walk. Somewhere along the years what was once an interesting, challenging or unusual case, a "fascinoma," had morphed into a community doc's nightmare, an invitation to a missed diagnosis, sleepless nights, a bad outcome, malpractice suit and financial ruin. The fact that he had never been named in a malpractice case lent both a sense of satisfaction and foreboding. He knew all the legal buzz-words and tips to help avoid a lawsuit: physician-patient communication, appropriate documentation, informed consent, and establishing a positive relationship. Most patients won't sue their doctors even when an error leads to serious harm. He had read that the type of harm, not blameworthiness, was the most accurate barometer for being named in and losing a malpractice case. Permanent disability fosters malpractice suit success. And Florita Dominguez was dead.

As he drove toward the hospital, he thought of Florita. She came into the ER that prior Friday morning in severe pain. Very fat, very sick. She was jaundiced with a pulse in the 140s, her systolic blood pressure barely 100. Her abdomen was diffusely tender, and she guarded against any touch from his gentle, probing fingers. The lab and CT scan confirmed his impression, acute pancreatitis from a gallstone that had fled the gallbladder only to get stuck in the common bile duct, causing a backup of pressure and release of pancreatic enzymes into the pancreas. The result was intense inflammation and tissue destruction. A critically ill patient from minute one. To stabilize her vital signs and restore the volume of fluid that had left her circulation to sequester in her abdomen, he had poured in copious amounts of IV fluid, a liter in the first hour and five hundred cc's hourly since. He cultured her blood and started antibiotics, even though he knew this was controversial. Ironic how medicine works. Every ten years the evidence changed. In this case, antibiotics, which used to be standard therapy for severe pancreatitis, were now considered of little or no benefit and no longer strongly recommended. He had read all the studies and wasn't convinced. Besides, she had a stone stuck in her bile duct, which could cause infection, called cholangitis, so by his reasoning, a strong reason for antibiotic therapy. Morphine had helped with the pain and she was more comfortable but still seriously ill. He had two choices: watch and wait to see if the stone passed the bile duct spontaneously to exit into the duodenum and travel harmlessly through the gut, or intervene with a scope and endoscopically pull the stone from the duct. He made his choice. The right one under the circumstances. And now she was dead.

Sweat lined his brow even before he exited his car in the hospital parking lot, his thoughts plagued by the preventable death of Florita Dominguez.

****

An hour later he finished his note on the improving Mr. Ramos, unobtrusively snapping his iPhone pic of it for posterity. The ICU was unusually calm. He looked around. Two empty beds; to the wards or the morgue, he always wondered. But not his worry. And with him being off this weekend, he felt almost relaxed. To his left, Dr. Dylan Hafner pecked away at the ICU computer terminal. Hafner was young, mid-thirties maybe, with short hair, clean shaven, sparkling white coat, white shirt and striped tie. Strader thought he looked like one of the actors portraying doctors on TV, trying to lure patients into one insurance plan or another. Strader was intrigued that this guy looked the same at midnight as he did during morning rounds, always neat, always working. They had shared several tough cases over the three years since Hafner arrived at Palms Hospital, and although they had productive exchanges in their chart notes, Strader thought that maybe they had exchanged ten sentences during that time. But Strader never saw Hafner talk to anyone. He came, did his work and moved on. Straight, gay, Christian, Jew, conservative, liberal— place your bets. The word around the nursing station was that he was single but not a player, strange for a beach boy from San Diego. But it didn't matter— his work was impeccable, his decision-making well-reasoned and evidence based. And he provided current references on all his consultations, something that nobody else on staff did. Even Strader had stopped listing references. None of the referring docs would look at them anyway. This young guy was still doing it pure, doing it right. And for some reason the nurses, the politics, the mediocrity around didn't seem to bother him. Strader couldn't figure him out. They nodded to each other and Strader left for the GI lab. Five procedures, four colonoscopies, an upper endoscopy, and he would be done for the morning. He glanced at his watch. 7:55. No time to see Doc Morales in the café. Florita Dominguez returned to his brain, followed by that dreaded autonomic release of cold sweat.

****

At exactly eight o'clock that morning, all players were assembled in the CEO's office with Mr. Appel presiding in the CEO's planned absence. Seated in front of him were eager Alyce from Risk Management; Ms. Porter, Chief of Nursing; Dr. Randy Robertson, hospital-based ER physician and current President of the medical staff; Dr. Thad Spencer, a non-medical staff primary care physician friend of Appel; and Joanna, the CEO's secretary, pen and paper at the ready.

Appel read aloud to the group:

"The privilege of medical staff membership requires universal cooperation with physicians, nurses, hospital administration and others to avoid adversely affecting patient care. Harassment is. prohibited by any medical staff member against any individual physician, hospital employee or patient on the basis of race, religion, color, national origin, ancestry, physical disability, mental disability, medical disability, marital status, sex or sexual orientation. Any form of sexual harassment is prohibited. Information about the competence, performance or conduct of a medical staff member may be provided by any person. If information deemed reliable indicates a member of the Medical Staff may have exhibited behavior thought likely to be contrary to the medical staff bylaws, unethical, deleterious to the safety or quality of patient care, or below accepted professional standards, a request for an investigation or action against such member may be initiated by the chief of staff, a department chair or the medical executive committee."

Appel looked up at the group. "Today we must confront a serious matter involving the actions of a doctor you all know, Don Strader. Recently, new complaints have been filed about Dr. Strader's conduct. Investigation of these complaints established adequate evidence to lead the Medical Executive Committee at an emergency meeting last night to support a recommendation for his immediate summary suspension. Dr. Strader has been found to be a disruptive physician. His behavior threatens the delivery of quality care within the hospital and his statements may cause sick members of the community to avoid seeking care at the hospital, undermining their health."

Ms. Porter vaulted up.

"Mr. Appel, are we talking about Dr. Strader here? Just about the best doctor in this hospital? Who actually cares about doing things right?" She was formidable, the oldest of ten children who over twenty-eight years worked her way up from unit secretary to Director of Nursing. Her eyes bore the sadness of reality as they met Appel's.

Appel nodded.

Ms. Porter continued. "He's a bit loud and crass at times, but he's no threat to good care, at least as I see it. You sure you've got your facts together?"

A prepared Appel fired back. "Director Porter, no one is saying that Dr. Strader isn't a good doctor. Disruptive physicians are very often good doctors. But being a good doctor is no excuse for bad behavior. There is no place at Palms Hospital for anyone who mistreats others and disrupts them from delivering the best care. And based on the evidence, much provided by your own nursing staff, Dr. Strader has to go."

She *shrugged. 'I get complaints about lots of docs all the time, some legitimate, some not. I also get complaints about the food, staffing, social services, pretty much all legit. So Doc Strader is far from being alone here. We've— I've talked with him about things in the past, but I don't know of anything recent that's come up."*

Appel continued. "Dr. Strader has often been openly critical of our nurses, our hospital staff and even other doctors. He has continually made unreasonable demands on this administration for items for which we just don't have resources to provide."

"Like more nurses." Ms. Porter couldn't help herself.

Appel avoided her glare as he read from his notes. "He has said directly to nurses that they are trying to kill their patients and recently told the entire community that we were murdering patients here at the hospital. We have tried in the past to counsel him and put up with his remarks but enough is enough. The hospital by-laws must be followed meticulously in

32

any action against a medical staff member. Let me spell out the process for you. We have received a written request for an investigation of Dr. Strader's behavior as it relates to specific instances of verbal harassment to hospital staff as well as comments made outside the hospital that are deemed disruptive. This led to the initiation of an investigation that was undertaken by Dr. Robertson, President of the Medical Staff, assisted by Alyce Wagner of Risk Management. They have completed their preliminary review and have provided their comments and recommendations in writing. Joanna…"

Joanna distributed a one-page letter to each of the attendees. Ms. Porter eagerly took hers and poured through it.

The letter read:

"We were requested to conduct an investigation into the alleged disruptive behavior of Dr. Donald Strader. We reviewed Dr. Strader's personal file and interviewed several members of the nursing staff, administrative and medical staff, as well as allied medical personnel. There have been two specific recent incidents involving Dr. Strader that we find incompatible with the harmonious functioning of the hospital. On one occasion, Dr. Strader accused a nurse of trying to kill a patient and on another occasion, Dr. Strader cursed abusively at a nurse for not having the precise equipment that Dr. Strader wanted. This behavior pattern is consistent with prior occurrences that resulted in the doctor being counseled. Finally, Dr. Strader recently went on record as saying to the community that a murder had taken place in the hospital. Based on our findings, we recommend that Dr. Strader be immediately suspended from the hospital and that his clinical privileges be revoked. This recommendation is consistent with the hospital bylaws, which call for a summary suspension 'Whenever a member's behavior is such that immediate action be taken to protect the safety or health of patient(s) or to decrease a significant or imminent likelihood of harm to the health, safety or life of any patient or other person'."

Ms. Porter had heard nothing of these incidents and suppressed her desire to crush the letter into a ball and throw it at Appel's face. She looked at the others in the room. Dr. Robertson and Alyce looked at each other with satisfaction. Dr. Spencer was a tough one to read, and Joanna was her usual professional self. Appel gave them another minute to finish reading and let things sink in.

Appel continued. "This group will serve as a committee that will remain in place until the matter is completed. Dr. Strader will be given a letter today with the specific charges against him, suspending his privileges. He will be helped to find coverage for his hospital patients, and he will then be escorted from the hospital. He will no doubt file a letter of appeal and will be afforded a formal judicial review, a trial of sorts, the details of which we will provide to you soon. This entire matter will be resolved within thirty days and we anticipate that he will be permanently removed from the medical staff and that a report will be sent to the California State Quality Board. Any questions?"

Ms. Porter growled, "Mr. Appel, you're starting a bad thing against a good doc…"

"Samantha, I certainly didn't start this," said Appel. "If you are biased and want to be removed from this committee, just say the word."

"No, I'll stay. I'm good," Ms. Porter said. *Someone had to stay and see where all this is flowing.*

"Any other questions or concerns?" Silence. "I'll take that as a unanimous approval by this committee to proceed. We will keep you informed. Thanks for giving up your time in the hospital's best interest."

The group filed out. Appel motioned Alyce and Dr. Robertson to wait. When it was just the three of them, he asked, "Where do we stand?"

Alyce, always the good soldier, glanced at her iPad notes. "Dr. Strader has finished his rounds, is doing cases in the GI lab, and he should be done by eleven. He has a full office this afternoon and is not on call this weekend. We can paper him when he leaves the GI lab. That will start the clock ticking and the next move will be his."

Appel nodded. "Good. We'll provide him with the letter when he leaves the lab and have security walk him off campus. Who'll give him the letter? Dr. Robertson, it may be best if you do it as President of the medical staff."

Randy Robertson, fifty, had manned the ER at Palms hospital for almost twenty years. He was generally quiet and agreeable, and preferred to avoid confrontation. He was tall and thin with a round face and flat grey hair that was geometrically unsettling. Perennial black prescription sunglasses effectively shielded his piercing grey eyes, even indoors. The medical staff considered him a good doctor. When Randy called to say a patient needed admission, the docs gave little pushback. Randy had used his talents to secure the coveted emergency room contract several years ago—now he chose his own work schedule, shared in the earnings of the other ER docs, and had job security as long as he held the contract. The downside was the damn contract; if he didn't play ball with the hospital administrators and the Board, he could lose everything. So he played ball.

"You know," Randy said quietly, "This may be better handled by Alyce presenting him the letter. Less confrontational than if I did it."

Alyce was willing and eager. "I'm happy to do it."

Appel nodded. *Of course, she was.*

****

Three hours later in the GI lab, Dr. Strader washed his hands, changed from his operating frock to his suit, and spoke with Mrs. Klein, who was awake following her colonoscopy.

"Mollie, everything went fine. You had two small polyps that I snipped off. My office will call you on Tuesday with the pathology results, but I'm sure everything is fine. We may not have to do this again for ten years, five at the least."

"You're kidding me. You mean you're done. I was waiting for you to start."

"The miracles of medication. It minimizes any discomfort and gives you a brief period of amnesia. We're done and I have the evidence to prove it. The nurse will give you a printed report with photos when you leave. If you have any questions just call the office."

Alyce Wagner ambushed him as he left.

Strader remembered seeing her, the Risk Management rep, at the GI Lab almost immediately after Florita had died. He assumed that this was a follow-up to that incident. Competent woman. Always seemed to be doing her job.

"Morning, Ms. Wagner."

"Dr. Strader." She handed him the letter.

"Is this about the lady who died last week?"

"Please read the letter."

As he read it his face reddened, eyes narrowed, and his jaw muscles clenched. "Are you kidding me? Are you fucking kidding me? Whose sick joke is this?"

Ms. Wagner shook her head and stood her ground. An uneasy moment passed. "I'm sorry that I had to be the one to convey this to you. The hospital census this morning shows that you have four in-patients." She removed a paper from her pocket. "Lancaster, Cerros, Wright and Ramos. You'll have to get coverage for them for the time being. We'll assign a hospitalist to care for any that you can't get coverage for."

Strader re-read the letter. Control yourself, he thought. You're shaking. Control yourself. Deep breath.

35

"Ms. Wagner, this is pure bullshit." He looked down the corridor and there was no one in sight. He tried to lower his voice. "Disruptive physician, bullshit. Leave my patients to someone else, no way. You hear me? No fucking way. It's not going to happen. Mr. Lancaster is very sick with severe ulcerative colitis; he may need his colon removed. I can't trust his care to anyone else. I'm not going to trust his care to anyone else. Ramos was virtually dead two days ago. No way." His voice quivered a bit.

"I'm sorry, Doctor, but the rules are the rules. We have to find someone to substitute for you, and then you'll have to leave the hospital."

"This whole thing is such bullshit. There isn't a better doctor in this hospital. I've been here for over 20 years, making this hospital money. I want to see Randy Robertson, and the CEO."

Several staff and visitors now walked the corridor and turned toward them to match faces to the loud voices.

He was surprised that she still stood her ground, unfazed. Was that the hint of a smirk on her face?

She said, "As I told you, Dr. Strader, this decision was made by the Executive Committee and approved by the Board. There's nothing I can do to change it. I'm sure you can figure out who could best fill in for you on each of your patients. You can make any calls from the administrative office or from your own office outside the hospital. At this point you will not be able to re-enter the hospital until this matter is concluded." Two uncomfortable security guards emerged from around the corner to herd him away.

Strader was stunned. This couldn't be happening to him. Were they going to physically throw him out of his own hospital? He wasn't going to let this happen. He felt his eyes twitch and his muscles freeze. His legs felt heavy, he couldn't move. People in the corridor were staring at him.

"Sorry Doc," the two guards said in unison as they led him off.

CHAPTER SIX

"Doc, you want us to cancel the office?" Kayesha didn't know what else to say. To her, he looked sick in an angry, shocked way, like if you lost a family member.

"How many do we have?"

Kayesha did a quick count. "Eleven, counting two new ones. I can reschedule all the follow-ups except Mrs. Kiley and move up the new ones. Get you finished by 3:00."

Strader looked at his watch.

"No, I'll see them all but I need you to start working on canceling all the procedures scheduled at the hospital for next week— better make that two weeks until I see how things unfold."

"Okay. The first two are here already. Mrs. Kiley showed up at 11:45 for her 1:00 appointment. She said, 'Just in case you were early.'"

"Just what I need. Better get her in a room and get the next one ready as well. Maybe we can get out on time today."

Strader moved down the hall to his private office, changed into a fresh white coat and looked out the window to the west. The faceless mountains were grey and somber, beaten down by the hot desert sun. But they were still there, taking all the punishment nature dished out but not yielding. There was a lesson there for him. He scanned the horizon for a final ten seconds and headed for the exam room that housed Mrs. Kiley.

"Good afternoon, Doctor Strader," cooed Mrs. Kiley, a soft voice in an old body. "You look well."

"The important thing Jean is not how I look but how you feel." Strader wasted no time in taking her blood pressure and pulse and reporting the results. "BP 136/70, Pulse 72— good enough for a teenager." He held her shoulder with one hand and efficiently listened through his stethoscope at her chest and heart. He leaned back a bit so that he could see her face and eyes. "Absolutely amazing. Just as good as an eighteen-year-old, only you can drink legally."

"You know, one of these days, all these lies are going to catch up with you when this old lady finds herself in the hospital." Jean sat up a bit straighter and a smile creased her eighty-two-year-old face.

"Nonsense. I expect you to write my eulogy when I kick the bucket. You're good for another 50,000 miles, at least. Now, what brought you in today? Any specific problem?"

"Whatever it was, you've sweet-talked me into forgetting it. I'll have to make another appointment when I remember."

"You know I'll see you whenever you need me, but the next few weeks are going to be crazy for me and the practice, and I'm not going to be able to see patients in the hospital and possibly in the office. So if you need me, call me through the exchange. Call after 5:00 and tell them that I'm expecting your call. This way they'll put you right through to me."

"Is everything all right with you, doctor?"

"I'm fine. Just a couple of things have cropped up, that's all. Now you call me if you need me." He gave her an affectionate pat on the shoulder and excused himself.

At six o'clock he was finished in the office. He had signed out all his cases to the doc covering him for the weekend, Dr. Rubin, a competent gastroenterologist with sound clinical judgment and a pleasant bedside manner. He told Rubin of his situation, and Rubin agreed to cover all his inpatients as long as necessary. They would talk daily. Strader felt relieved— he could concentrate on beating this suspension.

****

Two hours later he sipped a Diet Coke, shared his couch with an unconcerned Tomas, and painstakingly read the letter. The thick Medical Staff Bylaws of the hospital sat on the neighboring brown end table. He spoke to himself as if this would clarify the problem and offer a timely solution. Somewhere in the distant past he had read that by speaking and hearing rather than just reading, the brain became more involved in the subject at hand.

"Let me read this one more time. Disruptive behavior— three incidents— accusing a nurse of trying to kill a patient— never happened. Cursing at a nurse for not having the precise equipment that I wanted— the only thing I remember is yelling at the GI nurse when I was scoping Ramos in the ER— he should be fired, not complaining about me. And the mislead-

38

ing, oblique reference to my comments at the FWP meeting— all bullshit."

He read the rest slowly, silently.

"The privilege of medical staff membership requires universal cooperation with physicians, nurses, hospital administration and others to avoid adversely affecting patient care. Harassment is. prohibited by any medical staff member against any individual physician, hospital employee or patient on the basis of race, religion, color, national origin, ancestry, physical disability, mental disability, medical disability, marital status, sex or sexual orientation. Any form of sexual harassment is prohibited…

"Reliable information indicates you have behavior reasonably likely to be detrimental to patient safety or to the delivery of quality patient care within the hospital; contrary to the medical staff bylaws and rules or regulations; or below applicable professional standards,"

"Based on our findings, you are immediately suspended from the hospital and all your clinical privileges are revoked, consistent with the hospital By-laws. Summary suspension is necessary 'Whenever a member's behavior is such that immediate action be taken to protect the safety or health of patient(s) or to decrease a significant or imminent likelihood of harm to the health, safety or life of any patient or other person'."

Strader's hands shook and his jaw tightened as he read the rest, which summarized his options if he chose to appeal the suspension. He dropped the letter on the end table and put Tomas on his lap, petting the soft fur of his only comrade. He slumped a bit on the couch, roughing up the cat's head with his caress. Tomas purred, pushing his face toward his owner's hand. Rubbing, purring, rubbing, purring.

"Tomas, you'll let me do that all night, won't you?" More purring. Strader's grimace softened as he reached for the bylaws book, careful not to disturb his cat. "You lucky little devil, Tom. I'll spend the next two hours reading this boring stuff and you'll just stay on my lap. You are one spoiled guy. But you're my guy."

He opened the book, marker in one hand and Tomas's head in the other. Fifty pages and three hours later he put the book down, carefully moved the sleeping cat to a pillow on the couch and stretched to his full height. He took a quick trip down the hall to the restroom, and when washing his hands, he acknowledged his face in the bathroom mirror.

He was the same bastard he'd always been. This wasn't about being a disruptive physician. Shit, he'd done more for the hospital and cared more about doing things right than anyone. The way he was trained he didn't have a choice. This was all about Florita Dominguez, all about what he said when he opened his big mouth at that meeting. Well, they were fucking with the wrong guy.

CHAPTER SEVEN

For Frank Vialotti, Friday evening was also all about Florita Dominguez. His casual white tee shirt, thick shades, black shorts and sandals obscured his motive as he ambled up and down Florita's street in North Palm Springs. Near her reported address, a modest but well-kept green stucco house of the fifties, he spotted two couples and a small boatload of kids devouring juicy red Slurpees as a homage to the lingering heat, even at eight-thirty. *Frank* retraced his steps quickly to the corner 7-Eleven, bought a Slurpee and hurried back towards the group. Frank slowed as he approached them, nodding as if they were neighbors while he slurped. He raised his sno-cone and stopped.

"Tough to beat the heat, ain't it? Even with this." No response. He smiled at one of the children, a small Mexican boy with Slurpee-enhanced red lips and mouth.

"He seems to be enjoying it." Frank waited, a little anxious at the lack of neighborliness.

After a minute, a squat woman of no more than thirty wiped the boy's face and held him in front of her as he swayed back and forth, intent on finishing his cone. "Si," she said. "Demasiado calor. Too much heat."

Frank breathed easier. He couldn't figure out who the leader was so he spoke to all of them through her. "I heard about poor Mrs. Dominguez. Pobre Florita. So young. Someone should pay for her death. The family should get lots of money."

One of the men stepped forward. He looked a bit older than the rest, maybe fifty, thin, black mustache, live green-brown eyes, a long shirt, long pants, and a red bandana. *No doubt a gardener*, thought Frank. A man who worked hard for his money.

The man spoke. "Quien es?"

Frank didn't miss a beat. He handed the man his card.

"Someone who wants to help. When the family is ready, just call." With that, he walked on, glancing back as he crossed the street. The men examined the card as the whole group retreated into the house that formerly belonged to Florita Dominguez. Frank suppressed a fist pump and turned the corner, smiling for the first time that day.

****

Saturday morning Frank was at his office, alone with a desk cluttered with law books and folders of active cases. He opened his legal guidelines binder. Haven't had a good malpractice case in a while, he thought. He quickly browsed through the outline.

Number one – the doctor has a legal duty of care to the patient, a duty to abide by a certain level of care, by virtue of the doctor-patient relationship. Care that a reasonably competent, prudent physician would administer under similar circumstances. *He'd have to find out all the doctors involved in this case. Probably all the nurses, anyone involved. And of course the hospital.*

Number two – Breach of this duty. There was a failure to abide by the standard of care. *He'd need some medical experts here. Could be big bucks to spend. A definite problem.*

Number three – Causation. As a result of the breach of duty the patient was harmed. *Well, she went in alive and now she's dead. Lots of harm. If he was right, Doc Strader said she was murdered. He had to get to Strader to find out what he knew.*

Number four – As a result of the harm, there were damages including physical, psychological, economic or other. He hoped *she had a good paying job*, much higher damages than if she was a stay-at-home wife.

Frank closed the book. Duty, breach, harm, damages. Now he had to be patient and wait for the call from Florita's family. He'd give them three days.

****

Strader picked up the Saturday Desert Son awaiting him on his driveway and returned to his condo. Coffee in hand, he put out Tomas' breakfast, one half can of Friskies prime filets of beef with fresh water to wash it down. Tomas was always a bit lazy on the weekends when Strader was off call, so it took a shaking of the treat package to bring him to the kitchen.

He popped up on the kitchen counter, stretched out slowly, turned his butt to Strader and waited for the inevitable body massage. But Strader had seen the morning headlines and ignored him.

"Long-time doc suspended from Palms Hospital- claims of 'disruptive physician.'"

Strader read Patty Beam's reporting of alleged multiple episodes of disruptive behavior, including false accusations and cursing the staff. She wrote that the information was obtained from anonymous hospital sources. She noted that she contacted the hospital administration. The statement they released to her and the press was the following:

"Palms Hospital is dedicated to protecting, preserving and improving the health of its patients and the residents of the Coachella Valley. Whenever information is received about activities that have the potential to adversely affect the health of even a single person, the hospital takes this very seriously. Allegations of disruptive behavior by Dr. Donald Strader are currently under investigation by the hospital, and a resolution is expected within thirty days. In the interim, Dr. Strader will not be admitting or caring for any patients at the Palms Hospital and affiliated facilities." Dr. Strader could not be reached at his office phone for comment.

The hospital tipped her off. He thought about firing off a letter to the Editor but for what? He read the article a second time before throwing the paper down. Tomas jumped. Strader walked back and forth in his kitchen, mumbling to himself before picking up the home phone and dialing.

"Hi, dad. How are you? We're just getting ready to take the kids swimming." His daughter, a thirty-three-year-old rising lawyer in Philadelphia, always conveyed her message in opening remarks: "We're busy dad, what's up?"

"Your dad is in a mess. They've suspended me from the hospital. It's all over the papers. Calling me a disruptive physician, all kinds of bogus charges."

"Hang on dad. —Hey kids, sit down for a minute. Watch a Sesame Kids on your iPad.—Okay Dad, what kind of nonsense is this? You're the best doctor in the whole town, probably the whole country."

"I'm putting the pieces together. A couple of weeks ago there was a case I admitted that got botched by another doc and the lady died. I was really upset and stupidly made an off-hand comment at that Frustrated Professionals group meeting that I go to. I think that the hospital got wind of it."

"What did you say?"

"I don't really remember the exact words but I think I said that I witnessed a murder and there was nothing that I could do about it."

"Did you mention the hospital specifically or any names?

"Stel, I'm getting old but I'm no idiot. The short answer is no, I didn't."

"Then they can go screw themselves. That's no crime and no reason to get thrown out of the hospital. What's next?"

"That's why I called. I'm going to appeal and there's going to be a judicial review. I don't know if you remember but a few years ago they went after Doc Morales because he used a pocketknife to remove a patient's suture rather than wait for a sterile suture removal kit. I think that the staff couldn't find one, the patient was anxious to leave, and Doc had a teeming office waiting for him. So he used his own pocketknife. Nothing happened to the patient but the nurses were furious. They put him through hell, a judicial review, which he survived. Your mother kept us both sane. I remember she told him that the patient would have let him use a Samurai sword if it helped him get out of the hospital. Made him laugh out loud, but he was scared. Stel, the rules haven't changed. It's like a hospital trial without having to follow state or Federal law. The hospital picks someone, usually from the medical staff, to represent them against me. I pick a doc from the staff to be my advocate, and we each present our case in front of a jury of my peers, most likely other doctors from the staff. I haven't gone through all the details yet. But as of now, I'm out of the hospital and can't admit any patients there."

"Dad, I'm not worried. You'll find a way to win." A little bit of sarcasm crept into her voice.

"You know you're always right." Then, "You didn't do anything wrong, did you?"

"I've bitched like I always do from time to time, trying to make things better for my patients. Sometimes I'm not diplomatic. But sometimes diplomacy works poorly as a tool, particularly in the hospital where too many of the staff work their hours and go home."

"Kids," Stella interrupted, "I said Sesame Street. Gina, play one that your brother will like too. Thank you. Sorry dad. But how do you want me to help? Do you need me to be your ghost lawyer on the side? I'd be happy to do that for you, show you that lawyers sometimes can do good things."

"I may take you up on that but my immediate business is to pick a doc on staff to represent me. I thought of old Doc Morales, you know, Uncle Joe. Everybody knows him and he still commands some respect. But I'm just not sure he's the right one for something like this. It needs to be handled with precision so that if they screw me, I can find a way to take them to civil court. I just don't know."

44

"Dad, I don't think he's the best one. He's still old school. He still expects that people will do the right thing in the end. I don't think he'll feel the need to put in the work that you'll require. You need to find someone who's very smart, very conscientious, and who values being a doctor like you do. Who can think outside the box. Someone who you respect and who respects you. Does such a person exist there?"

"I think I have the guy if he agrees. I have to do a bunch more paperwork and then I'll call him. Thanks, Stel, you're a great help. You're a lot smarter than your father and maybe even your mother, may she rest in peace."

Strader cradled the phone, picked up Tomas from the couch and let him outside. Opening the sliders in the small living room led to a linear greenbelt with a great western mountain view. Tomas loved to roll in the still-green grass and chase anything that moved. He would constantly chew on a particularly long, thin-leaved plant, a prelude to throwing up his recurrent hairballs. Dr. Doug, as everyone called his vet, said that cats do that to help prevent them from getting their stomachs obstructed by a massive hairball. Tomas never strayed far from the sliders, and over the years Strader felt comfortable leaving him alone outside. Tomas had it too good at home to be adventurous and he'd eventually come in by himself. Watching him roll and stretch and blink at the sun, so at ease with his world, Strader longed for an earlier day when he too was in sync. Even the chaotic early days of training brought comfort with incremental knowledge and experience. Then it was just about the patient and not about administrative pressures and bureaucracy. Practice was hard and there were family and personal sacrifices, but the basis of it was as simple as Tomas rolling in the grass. You talked to a patient, examined him or her, knew whether they were sick or not and got them better if they were. He loved being that doctor, the one who put all of his effort into making sick people healthy. It was challenging but satisfying.

If they were well, you told them so. No chronic fatigue, no fibromyalgia. Not even pain management, a complicated, partially politically induced mess legislating the right of all to be always pain free. Pain, the sixth vital sign— so subjective. Strader was old school. Start low and go slow, know your patients well enough to understand their pain symptoms in the context of their whole life. He remembered his rheumatology mentor during residency, whose adage was "if your rheumatoid arthritis patients are pain free, you're giving them too much steroids." Of course, in those days it was largely steroids and aspirin, not these newer biologics. But no opiates. Now people with arthritis, chronic back pain—and a slew of part-

45

ly psychologic issues— are commonly prescribed narcotics, suffer untold side effects, and must deal with addiction. Many of these people did not have cancer or severe illnesses but were led down this path by well-intentioned but short-sighted do-gooders. In the good old days, you lived with pain, with sickness, and got by. Days long gone. And now the tragic case of Florita Dominguez, a death from too much pain medicine given too quickly, although not by his direction or his hand, threatened his career.

Tomas lazily looked up with those crazy lantern-yellow eyes. Strader knew the drill. He took the plastic cap off his underlining marker, showed it to Tomas then threw it maybe 50 feet away. Tomas leaped up, tracked it down, grabbed it in his mouth and retrieved it, dropping it at Strader's feet. They replayed this several times. Strader pocketed the cap and passed back through the sliders to his living room. He had work to do. Tomas continued to sun himself, alone on the grass in the summer sun.

Well, not completely alone. Fifty yards down the greenbelt, shaded by the palm trees silhouetting the development's tennis courts, Alyce Wagner took pictures of the cat, the condo, and the greenbelt. And she took notes, voluminous notes, of a man playing fetch with his cat.

Inside, Strader was getting it all together. He printed a second copy of the relevant material for his case. He included the letter of suspension with the listed charges and a separate page of notes he made regarding any moments of friction with any hospital personnel that he remembered. He copied the relevant parts of the medical by-laws that dealt with complaints, procedure and corrective action. He included the process of the judicial review proceedings. He also scanned all of the material into a PDF file that he could send to his daughter or anyone else who became involved in the case. He finished with his recollection of the comments he made at the FWP meeting and included the name of Florita Dominguez. He formulated some ideas for his defense based on his long career, his work in the hospital, and the actual by-laws he was accused of violating, but he didn't write them down. Too early. He read everything one more time and felt he was ready to make the most important call of his career, the call to his potential advocate, the young, squeaky-clean Dr. Dylan Hafner.

CHAPTER EIGHT

Strader admired the clarity, brevity, and utility of Dylan Hafner's website. There was a secure area for patients to log into, an appointment page, general office information with Hafner's office address, number, fax, and office hours, specific disease information sheets for patients as well as information sheets promoting exercise and proper diet. Professional and functional. It looked just like the one that Strader's twenty-six-year-old son, Will, had made for him years ago for a school project. That one even had a chat area that Strader was going to use for his Crohn's disease patients. But he was always so busy that he put it off from season to season, disappointing his son. And then Rosemary got sick. In the tumult of illness that culminated in her death, the website project also died.

Crazy how an unrelated website rekindled harsh memories of bad days. Will had paused from his nomadic journey to nowhere, returning home to help his mother and fight with his dad. Will was really the only source of friction Strader had with Rosemary, other than her soft entreaties for Strader to enjoy his life more than he showed. Strader was furious when Will dropped out of Boston College to "find himself," with his declaration that college and formal education were useless and a vestige of a time when content was not readily available to consume online. No need for math or science when you had real life to feast upon and you could look up anything. Yeah, Strader thought, why study when you can watch Survivor or Lost? And only God and, Strader suspected, Rosemary knew what Will was up to, how he was surviving, earning a living. Strader at times had accused Rosemary of funneling Will money budgeted for some household or recreational use, but she always shut him down with a "Don, what do you care where the money goes as long as we stay on budget. You're way too involved with your mistress, anyway." She had called his practice his mistress for twenty years, since the early days. And she would go on and lecture him about his son. "You know, Don, it's not a direct path for everyone like it was for you. Your son has to find his own way. And he

47

will." And she wasn't swayed a bit by Strader's hard-work, toe-the-mark spiel.

Tomas rubbed against his leg but for once was rebuffed, if just for a minute. Strader knew that Tomas was really the sole joint enjoyment shared with his son during those days. While Strader taught Tomas to fetch the hi-lighter cap, Will taught him to lie in wait behind a sofa or chair and jump out when Strader walked by, startling him. Somehow, he taught the cat only to do this with Strader and not with Will or Rosemary. They all got a kick out of this, an infrequent time for the three of them to smile, not counting Tomas. Tomas really became Will's cat, until Rosemary died and Will disappeared back east again. He called his dad infrequently to find out how Tomas was faring and expressed sorrow that he couldn't see his cat more, the dig not lost on Strader.

****

Hafner's office was closed on Saturday. Rather than work his way through the answering service obstacles, Strader paged him at the hospital. He responded almost instantly.

"Good morning. Dr. Hafner here." Hafner's voice was as youthful and crisp as his appearance.

"Uh, good morning," Strader choked. "Dr. Hafner, it's Don Strader, you know, Dr. Strader."

"Oh, hi." If there was any tension in Hafner's voice it was undetectable. "What can I help you with?"

Is it possible that he didn't know? Strader assumed that the news of his suspension was all over the hospital.

"Well—this is quite awkward for me. I don't know whether you've heard anything, but the hospital decided to suspend me yesterday, and it's kind of a long story, but I certainly can use your help."

Hafner's reply was unemotional, even keel. "I heard a bit this morning making rounds. Something about you being a disgruntled—no, a disruptive physician. That's never been my impression of you."

Strader allowed himself a chuckle. "Disgruntled, yes, disruptive, I don't think so. Anyway, I have to appeal the suspension, which will lead to a judicial review. I'm not sure you've ever been involved in one of these…"

"No, I haven't."

"Well, it takes the format of a trial without strict rules of law. The hospital picks a jury of my peers and a colleague who will act as the plaintiff's attorney in trying to see that I stay booted out of the place. They usually present their case first. I have an advocate who serves in essence as my attorney, the defense attorney, who rebuts their case and helps me put on my defense."

"Wow, Perry Mason comes to Palms Hospital. What a waste of time and what a burden for you. But how can I help?"

"I'd like you to be my advocate. You're the one person on the staff I feel I can trust to work with me to win this thing. I don't know you except for the cases we've shared at the hospital, but those interactions are enough for me to know. I'm sorry to drop this on you, and I'll be disappointed, but I'll certainly understand if you say no."

"Don, may I call you Don?"

"Sure."

"And Dylan works for me. Before I commit, can we meet and go over the particulars? I would like to know what I'm getting myself into."

****

Fifty minutes later, Strader closed the drapes over the sliding doors to shield his condo from the afternoon sun. He exited the front door but blocking his path to his adjacent garage were two cameramen, a once white KQRS TV truck, and a familiar TV face pointing a microphone at him. He didn't remember the reporter's name, John or James or something that started with a J. Strader figured him at about thirty-five, too stocky for his tight golf pants and tapered polo shirt. Arrogant. An ill-fitted shark lurking for its kill. His strident voice was clear, his diction precise.

"Dr. Strader, Jonathan Strick, KQRS. What can you say about the hospital suspending you?"

Strader turned his head from the cameras and mike, and tried to create a path to his garage door.

"No comment." *Fucking vultures was what he should say.* He kept walking and was forced to push one cameraman out of his path to reach the garage door.

"Doctor, they threw you out of the hospital for being disruptive. Is that true?"

"I'll make it easy—one answer to all your questions—no comment. Now show some decency and respect for my private property and get

49

out of my driveway before I call the property manager and have you removed."

Strick put the mike down at his side and motioned his crew to stop shooting.

"Then is there a time when we can sit down and you can tell your side of the story?"

Very convincing. The spider to the fly. But Strader was born sixty years ago, not yesterday.

"No comment." With that, he entered his garage door and was on his way to see Dylan Hafner, rattled but with a semblance of control.

Strader found Hafner in a back booth at Las Casuelas, a Mexican bar and restaurant along Palm Canyon Drive, the main road in downtown Palm Springs. Las Cos, as the locals called it, was busy from noon till at least ten at night, and often became boisterous as the evening wore on. Hafner's pressed, white collared short-sleeve shirt was unblemished by the salsa and chips he was enjoying. He waved, and Strader sat down across from him, glancing around to ensure no familiar faces were nearby.

"Look," Strader began. "I'm sorry to have to ask for your help. But they're trying to ruin me and ..."

"Hey, when I have a tough GI case I reach out to you, so fair's fair. What's going on?"

Strader laid out the whole story, choosing to begin with the serving of the suspension letter by Alyce Wagner and weaving his way back in time to the FWP meeting and the death of Florita Dominguez the preceding week. He produced the letter.

Dylan digested it slowly, then looked up to the older doctor and spoke, slowly and unemotionally. "We can explore the Florita case as we go along. For now, let's just say that your comments at the meeting started this ball rolling and that the hospital administration is behind it. Let's accept that as a given and not lose sight of it, but what's relevant is that we dissect the charges, respond factually, and use the bylaws to our advantage. From a probability standpoint, it's pretty simple. We define our goal, measure the variables involved and the expected outcomes, and strategize to maximize our chance of success."

Strader nodded. "The goal for me is pretty clear, to take these bogus charges and shove it— I'm a gastroenterologist. I know I'm not the most sensitive or ingratiating person in the world, but I've always acted in the best interests of my patients."

Dylan shook his head. "Don, I don't think you're maliciously disruptive or that you jeopardize care at the hospital. But that's not the point. I'm not the jury. This is basically a probability problem. Once we know who the judicial review panel is, we can figure out the likelihood of you being found innocent of these charges with that panel. Since the hospital picks a five-person panel, let's assume one or two will be sympathetic to you. We need three. Our main job will be to make that happen and improve the probability as close to one as we can to remove this burden." Dylan leaned across the table and continued in a low but firm voice. "Don, what I'm telling you is that we'll get into the details and do whatever it takes. The first order of business is to memorize this letter and the bylaws and draft a letter of appeal that we'll have delivered first thing Monday morning."

****

By three o'clock they sat around a glass table in the living room of Hafner's mid-century Alexander home, a neat two-bedroom house on a block filled with similar style houses. Some were fenced while others, including Hafner's, were separated from the road by dirt and well-worn desert landscaping. A comfortable house from a more comfortable time. Hafner sipped an Arnold Palmer while Strader nursed a lemonade. They were each armed with a copy of the suspension letter.

"They're using three specific incidents," Strader said. "They're saying I accused a nurse of trying to kill a patient. That was an ICU case where the nurse let the IV run dry for three hours. I was sarcastic but didn't actually accuse her of anything other than not appropriately caring for my patient. The second incident is my cursing abusively at a nurse. That was really strange – I was scoping a bleeder in the ER in the middle of the night and the GI nurse didn't have a heater probe or bi-cap on the GI bleeding cart. "

"Is she new?"

"That's what's a bit crazy. It's a he, not a she, and he's been doing this for years. And he was acting so nonchalant and almost antagonistic when he told me he didn't have what I needed. And the guy was bleeding out…"

"Almost like he was trying to get your goat?"

"I don't know why he would. We've worked together for years and taken care of multiple bleeders. And coming so soon after the Florita debacle. I don't know…"

"We'll think about that one." Dylan made some notes on his copy of the letter. "And the third?"

"The third I'm sure, is a reference to that FWP meeting I was telling you about. The letter says that I made a disparaging comment about the hospital at a public meeting. What I said was that recently I witnessed a murder and there was nothing I could do about it. Bad choice of words, but I never mentioned the hospital."

Dylan said, "And that was the Florita Dominguez case?"

Strader nodded.

Dylan continued, "We'll get to that later." He read from the suspension letter, 'These actions have resulted in our decision that you are immediately suspended from the hospital and that your clinical privileges are revoked. The medical staff bylaws require summary suspension in your case…" He read the rest silently. "Wow, you appear to be an imminent threat to the lives of all around you."

Strader shook his head back and forth as Dylan finished. "What unbelievable bullshit."

"That's what we have to prove," said Dylan. "My first thoughts are that in the two nursing staff incidents, you were responding to what you and any concerned physician would regard as negligent nursing care, for whatever reason, that placed your patients in immediate danger of clinical deterioration and death. Your response was, shall we say, a bit coarse, but you had to make a strong point."

Strader nodded. Nurse Porter would probably have been more than a bit coarse with him in response but she'd take care of it for both sides. He felt more at ease. *He'd made the right decision in picking Dylan.*

Dylan placed the letter on the table and completed a yoga-like stretch and thoughtful yawn. "The murder statement is both more and less of a problem, at least as I see it. You never mentioned the hospital and you never reported any murder. But why would a witness to a murder have no options on the table? And why would a silent witness go public at a group gathering?"

Strader started to answer but Dylan held his hand up.

"Don, if the judicial review jury interprets that statement as influencing their patients and other community members to avoid Palms Hospital, then we have a problem with appearance if not fact. That may wind up being our toughest obstacle in this forum since it doesn't follow strict rules of law. We'll have to figure out the probability of this being a club against you, and decrease that probability to zero. Maybe some kind of free speech or First Amendment approach, I don't know. I don't think we have any disparagement rule in the by-laws. Maybe this won't even come up—it's nothing the hospital wants to go public—the stuff they fed to the media was about you being disruptive, not about any murder. They want to destroy you without impugning themselves. And they weren't specific in that charge. When it's time we'll work our way through it. Right now, we have to draft the request for a hearing. We have to send it to the medical executive committee with a copy to the Governing Board. Since they've suspended you, we can waive the waiting period of at least thirty days for preparation and move it up as quickly as possible."

"Let's do that. I want to get this behind me ASAP. Should I write the request?"

"No, I'll take a crack at it and call you in a couple of hours. Let me make sure I have your cell."

Strader felt that Dylan was finished for the moment. They exchanged cell numbers, and Strader twice had to clear his throat.

"Dylan, all I can say is thanks…for taking this on."

"No problem. And you know, if something like this ever happened to me, I'd probably be coming to you. I remember how you helped with that necrotizing pancreatitis case. He wouldn't have made it without you making the right calls on drainage and surgery." The two shook hands, and Strader left.

****

Dylan checked the time. 4:30. He opened a new document and typed.

"Dr. Robertson, Chairman of the Medical Executive Committee, Palms Hospital
cc: Mr. Robert Fornay, Chairman of the Board of Directors, Palms Hospital
Re: Hearing Request for Don Strader M.D., FACP

Dear Dr. Robertson,

I have received written notice of suspension of my privileges at Palms Hospital, dated June 20, 2014. On that day, I was physically escorted from the hospital campus. Pursuant to the hospital medical staff bylaws, I hereby provide you with notice of my request for a hearing to contest this suspension and the false assertions that my behavior is such that immediate action be taken to protect the safety or health of patient(s) or to decrease a significant or imminent likelihood of harm to the health, safety or life of any patient or other person'. I waive the need to have at least thirty days to prepare for the hearing that will follow. I await your prompt response so that I can proceed at the earliest possible date.

Respectfully submitted,
Donald Strader MD, FACP

Dylan saved the letter, read it twice, and sent it as an attachment to Strader for his review. It was now 4:50. He would contact Strader at 7:00 to get his feedback. That gave him two hours, enough time to play.

CHAPTER NINE

Dylan popped on a red Los Angeles Angels hat, shades, faded jeans and a tee shirt. He locked his front door, walked briskly to his garage and jumped on his Yamaha Galaxy Blue Raider cycle. He ripped out of the driveway and headed downtown, hands and legs burning, forehead sweating under the punishing sun, grateful the trip was only six blocks long.

The Spa Casino was a well-established venue owned and run by the Agua Caliente band of Cahuilla Indians. The tribe actually owned fifty percent of all the land in Palm Springs, divided in a checkerboard pattern. The Spa and its sister casino, Agua Caliente in Rancho Mirage, were the Agua's financial jewels. The outer face of the Spa was a soft southwestern yellow with blue awnings and trimming, the architecture substantial without a Vegas complexity.

Inside, the cool dimness was unsettled by the variegated slot machine lights and marred by the smells of cigarettes, cheap perfume and sweat. Dylan made his way past aisles of penny and nickel slots operated by young workers and ancient women, each killing time and pocket money—or savings. He always marveled at the disparate crowd. An old white-haired woman methodically hit the Max Bet button on the Quick Hit machine while her young Mexican caretaker minded her walker and provided occasional encouragement. A heavily tattooed burly man in black shorts and a black tee shirt slept at a quarter Sopranos slot. A bevy of women clutched their glasses of White Zinfandel in one hand while cheering on their friend, who had just hit a spin on the Wheel of Fortune. The spinning wheel ignored their screams for "a thousand—a thousand" as it rested cozily on twenty-five.

As Dylan passed the bar, he noted Holiday Grove smiling and waving to him.

"Joe, Joey, Joseph, over here."

Trapped, he smiled back and joined her. Holiday was a bright, beautiful, late-twenties blonde with everything going for her. She knew him, as did the gambling crowd, as Joey. Tall as Hafner in her red Jimmy Choo flats, she filled out her green halter and white shorts admirably. Holiday was rumored to be a high-end escort. Hafner had trouble believing that. He had seen her a few times at the casino but never leaving with anyone. She was always surrounded by a cadre of wealthy suitors, but then again, she was a beautiful woman. She always seemed to be having fun while staying in control of the situation. Hafner slid onto the adjacent bar stool, noticing the eyes of surrounding patrons fixed on the woman. He spun his stool till he directly faced her.

"Holiday Grove, when I look at you, each of my eyes is jealous of the other for the beauty it beholds."

She laughed. "A bit of the blarney in you, eh."

"Not one word." Well, not about that, he thought.

"I don't buy that, but it's nice to see you. What's going on?"

Don't ask, he thought. He said, "just another day." She was unnervingly beautiful up close. She locked eyes with him and smiled. He felt sweaty, a bit awkward. He wanted to keep the conversation going.

"Holiday, by the way, what's your real name?"

"Crazy as it seems, it's Holiday. I was born on December twenty-fifth and my mother objected to the name Christmas, although she's always said I was the best gift she ever got. How about you? Joey can't be your real name." Her eyes twinkled. She intertwined their arms.

Did she know? He didn't remember ever seeing her outside of the casino. Weird that he felt an urge to actually tell her who he was. He offered, "My story is pretty lame. We'll talk some more some other time. I have about an hour to make rent money." He extricated his arm from hers.

Her full lips pushed out and her green-blue eyes narrowed, but then she laughed. "I look forward to it."

He doffed his baseball cap, "Great. See you around." He couldn't figure out how someone who had so much going for her could hang around the casino, let alone be an escort. He thought of Julia Roberts in "Pretty Woman" and how she wasn't even in the same league as Holiday Grove. Someday he'd find out her story.

Hafner cruised to the high roller room, which featured several card tables and five-to-one hundred dollar slots. Saturday afternoon in June was not a traditional poker tournament time, and the video poker slots would have to do. He nestled at a Game King video poker machine that was shielded from other guests. A large, dark-haired Native American woman, at least twenty years his senior, sat three machines away from him and forcibly banged away, muttering under her breath with each losing hand.

Dylan didn't have a player's card and didn't believe in getting "comped," the casino's compensation of a meal or free casino play based on the amount of money a gambler bet. A great way to pay $100 for a ham sandwich. A loser's folly— not for him. He slipped two one hundred dollar bills into the money slot and selected five card draw as his game. He checked the pay tables on the machine. It was a 9/6 machine, which meant he got nine for one on a full house and six for one on a flush. Fair. Dylan played expert poker, and the payback on this five-card draw machine was 99.54%. For every dollar he played, the machine statistically would return 99.54 cents, giving the house about one-half of one percent advantage. Theoretically, if he played an infinite number of hands, he would be expected to lose forty-six cents for every one hundred dollars bet. Dylan disliked giving anything away, as evidenced by his choice of Jacks or Better over more volatile video poker games, such as Double-Double Bonus Poker, where the pay back was under 99%.

He loved Texas Hold-em the best when he played against live players and could factor into the game the number of players playing and their personal traits and play styles, whether conservative, bluffing or reckless. So much more challenging and more fun. The probability of winning varied with the location of his seat at the table, the amount of his chip stack versus the others, the money in the pot and whether a prospective bet was able to get pot odds, the probability of winning with his initial two hand cards and how that changed with the three card face card up flop (these cards being used by all players staying in the pot), and the subsequent fourth or "turn" card and the final fifth or "river" card. And Joey was a math genius; he loved the mathematics of anything from poker to medicine to almost anything in life. Life was math with a probability of death being one, or 100%. He had to reckon with that probability daily in his medical practice, and he relished trying to beat it. Playing at a machine rather than against live players was a simple math exercise, like doing his times table. The odds of getting a Royal Flush were one in 40,000, four of a kind, one in 423, four aces, one in 5,760, and so on. He hit max bet and the first hand came alive. A pair of sevens and three discards. He kept the pair. His mind cranked out the numbers even as he hit the deal button. *Odds of turning one pair into two pairs is one in six, into three of a kind one in nine, of getting four of a kind one in three hundred sixty.* The three replacement cards were an Ace, Jack and nine. No luck. Chalk up one for the house. His play was mechanical, more the typist than the pianist. No emotion, no extraneous gestures. Just max bet, math, card selection and deal. Hand after hand.

Twenty minutes later and two hundred dollars to the good, thanks to one hand of four Aces and several nice fill-ins for flushes and a full house, he was bored. His mind drifted from the spice of Holiday Grove to the troubles of Don Strader. *The hospital brought the charges; they got to pick both the presiding or hearing officer and the judicial review jury, which they would stack in their favor. And if he and Strader objected to anyone on the jury or to the hearing officer the final decision was made by that same hearing officer. A stacked deck. The hospital had the right to keep adding charges along the way, too. Strader had a history of verbally standing up for patient rights and patient care, no doubt ruffling feathers. Then there was this whole murder witness mystery business. And what did Strader have? Him, Dylan Hafner, internist and part-time gambler. The odds were not looking good. He rolled a pair of imaginary dice. Strader was going to need some luck and with high probability, something else.* Hafner peered back at his smooth face, shades and cap reflecting from the slot machine's glass. *Whatever it took, they'd just get it done.*

CHAPTER TEN

Appel had converted the CEO's videoconference room into a War Room. The elongated brown composite table with central burnt orange inlay seated fifteen. The high-backed orange swivel chairs stood uniformly upright as if at attention in a military ceremony. At one end was a 56" sleek, black HD monitor. Appel stood at the other end reflectively as his committee members took their seats. It was Monday, June 30th—106 degrees and summer was just waking up. Appel mused over the events of the last ten days: Strader's suspension, the choice of Hafner as his advocate, and their request a week ago for an accelerated hearing and a detailed list of all charges supporting documents and witnesses that the hospital would call. *Well, they'd get all that and more. Appel would paper them to death.* He smiled when he thought of the Medical Executive Committee's rejection of Strader's request for reinstatement and Strader's assertion that he did not provide any imminent threat to a patient. The Med Exec Committee's plurality of hospital-based docs had voted en bloc against Strader in the mindful presence of CEO Hendrickson.

Alyce Wagner had been invaluable to Appel. She helped develop recommendations for the hearing officer and judicial review panel that would be endorsed by the startup committee now assembled before him. Once they won this case, he'd have to talk to the CEO about moving her up the ladder.

He glanced down at his notes as the group filed in: Alyce Wagner, Ms. Porter, Dr. Robertson, Dr. Spencer, and of course, Joanna. Appel made eye contact with each of them as he scanned the room, but only Ms. Porter defiantly returned his stare. Appel dropped his eyes to his notepad and spoke.

"Thank you all for participating in this uncomfortable but necessary project. Things are moving along and today we are going to select the Judicial Review Committee, the group of peers that will act as jury. I want to give special thanks to Alyce Wagner for her diligent work. Thank you, Alyce."

Alyce peacocked in her chair and smiled broadly.

"Dr. Robertson, a special thanks to you as well for taking the time to work with us on this difficult task."

Robertson tacitly nodded. His knee jumped rhythmically as he sat to the far left of the assemblage, a man anxious to leave the building.

"As the startup committee you have one function today, selecting the Judicial Review Panel, the group that will hear the facts from both sides and render a decision. The Bylaws require that the Panel include at least three members of the medical staff who will gain no direct financial benefit from the outcome, and who in essence, have played no part in the process up until the present. It's okay, however, for the member to have knowledge of the matter. We can choose from members of the active medical staff, other staff categories, or doctors who are not members of the medical staff. One member must have what the Bylaws calls 'the same professional licensure as the accused and may include an individual practicing the same specialty as the member.' All others should have M.D. or D.O. licenses. I would suggest we select a five-person committee and designate one of them as the chair, as called for in the Bylaws."

Samantha Porter spoke up. "Mr. Appel, do you have copies of the part of the Bylaws that deals with this so we can review it before we select anyone? You know, just for our own clarification."

The sentence wasn't out of her mouth when Alyce double-stroked her laptop and the relevant Bylaw was shown. It took a few moments until all had read it.

Dr. Robertson broke the ice. "Just as you described, Mr. Appel." His hand was tapping a pen as his knee kept jumping. "How do we go about picking the— uh—jury—committee?"

No one spoke. Appel nodded to Alyce, who projected a list of nine names, including those of Dr. Robertson and Dr. Spencer, the doctor who was not on the medical staff.

Dr. Spencer, a wiry, respectfully dressed, middle-aged primary care physician who worked part-time at the Desert Aids Project, scoured the list and frowned. In a voice an octave too low for his size, he spoke for the first time, addressing Appel. "Based on your Bylaws, my name should come off, as should Dr. Robertson's."

Robertson gleefully nodded his agreement.

Spencer continued. "That leaves, let me count them, seven candidates. For those of us who've never experienced a judicial review, can you tell us about how many meetings this will entail, over what time, and when will these meetings typically take place, during the day or in the evening?"

Appel smiled as he regained the floor.

"In cases like this one, where there is a summary suspension, we do everything we can to expedite the process so that the doctor can have his privileges restored if that is the decision that is reached. We'll pick the jury, as Dr. Robertson put it, plus a hearing officer, and we'll send out the letter with the complete list of charges and potential witnesses along with a hearing date, which we anticipate being a week from today. We'll accommodate Dr. Strader if he asks for a delay to do any necessary homework. Usually, the hearing will be concluded after three meetings, each spaced up to a week apart. The hospital will present its case just as a plaintiff would in a civil case. Dr. Strader and his advocate Dr. Hafner will be able to cross-examine the witnesses as they see fit, and then Dr. Strader and Dr. Hafner will present their defense. Once both parties rest, the jury will make its decision, which will be sent back to the hospital board for its approval."

"A big time commitment, particularly for a private practitioner," said Spencer. "Maybe we should focus on those in the list who are in large groups. Like radiologists or pathologists or other ER docs."

"Well, we can certainly find some of those," Appel said. "We already have a couple on this list."

"And what about 'the same professional licensure as the accused'?" said Spencer. "What does that mean, exactly? And how can you choose someone in his specialty that works in this hospital without it having the potential for economic gain? If another gastroenterologist participates and if this guy Strader is thrown off the staff, won't there be more work for the other gastro guy, and therefore financial gain?"

"Dr. Spencer, you should have helped write these Bylaws," said Appel. "Good points. 'The same healing arts licensure' means that the jury should be made up of doctors and not dentists or nurses. The other point, there's a potential conflict with a gastroenterologist on the jury, I don't know that we can solve that other than simply by not naming one to the group. We certainly want to be above board with this. Does anyone have any suggestions from the names on the monitor?" He shot a glance at Dr. Robertson. "Dr. Robertson? You're the Chief of Staff. Who would you pick or not pick? And why?"

Robertson thought for a moment, then carefully chose his words. "Our job is to pick five docs who would be good jurors, without preconceived notions, willing to put in whatever time is necessary to do the job right. I agree that the time commitment might be easier for those in a group practice than for someone in solo practice. Looking at your list and off the top of my head, I would have no problem with Dr. Alvarez, head of anesthesia or Dr. Klein, head of radiology. They've been around a long time and their on-call schedules should be manageable. Dr. Kalim, the hospital intensivist, spends all her time in the hospital and should have a good feel for this sort of thing— and she should have the necessary time to participate. She'd be a good choice. I'm not so sure about Dr. Morales—he's a very good friend of Dr. Strader, and although he's been around for a very long time, I'm not sure he has the stamina to undertake this."

"Dr. Robertson," said a frowning Samantha Porter, "are you saying that because Dr. Morales and Dr. Strader are friends, he shouldn't be on the jury, or are you saying he's too old to be on the jury? Which is it?"

"Neither. I'm just sayin'…" His feet were tap dancing now.

Appel took over. "I think Dr. Robertson is just pointing out things that should be taken into consideration—"

"—Like how old he is and whether he's a friend?" said Porter. "Should we only be picking young people who dislike him?"

"Whoa, Ms. Porter, hold on. That's not what he's saying at all. Let's keep this civil. No decisions have been made on any of these candidates. What I guess we are looking for are –uh – more neutral jurors without, so to speak, an axe to grind."

Samantha wished she had an axe. If she did, she wouldn't be just grinding it. *Goddamn slicky boys, that's what she was dealing with.*

Appel continued. "Let's take a look at the others on the list. I must tell you, we originally thought that Dr. Hafner would be a good juror, but now that pick is out the window since he's Strader's advocate. The next one we have listed is Dr. Sandy Meller. He's a cardiologist who's in solo practice but has a good coverage schedule so he's only on call about once every ten days. He's been around for a good many years and has a good reputation in the hospital and community. I don't know if he'd do it but he seems like a good candidate."

Dr. Robertson chimed in. "He's always been a pleasure to work with. I think he'd be a good one. Maybe even a good one to chair the committee." He avoided a quick look from Appel.

Ms. Porter thought *maybe Robertson didn't follow the script, but decided he did.*

Hearing no other comments, Appel named Dr. Carlos Rosero, a family medicine doc with a small boutique private practice. Rosero was the doctor for employee health but otherwise spent little time in the hospital. He was a D.O., about forty, tall, with pitch black hair. He was one of the few, along with Strader, who actually wore a suit and tie in the summer. The nurses perked up when he was around, but he had very few of them as patients. Ms. Porter didn't know much about his medical proficiency, but she too liked the way he looked.

"I don't really know much about Dr. Rosero," said Dr. Robertson. "His credentials have always been in order and the nurses seemed to like him… he must spend most of his time in his office. Nothing negative in his file that I know of."

Appel looked at the remaining name but didn't mention it. He glanced at his watch. "Time flies. We still have to name the hearing officer after we finish this. Based on the names submitted, can someone offer a motion with a list of five jurors with one serving as head juror?"

Dr. Spencer corralled his thoughts. "I move to nominate Drs. Rosero, Meller, Alvarez, Klein and Kalim for the jurors on the Judicial Review Panel. I move that Dr. Meller be appointed head juror."

Dr. Appel asked, "Do I have a second?"

Dr. Robertson seconded.

"We have a motion and a second. Any discussion?"

Ms. Porter declined to say anything. *They stacked it, for sure, but it could be worse. Dr. Meller was a really good guy. Nothing she could do.*

"All those in favor?"

Up shot the hands of Robertson, Spencer, and Alyce.

"Opposed?"

No one.

Porter now spoke up. "Please put in the record that I abstain, since with a medical staff of over three hundred docs I have no way of knowing that these five selected would be the best neutral jury for this case."

Appel didn't mind. "One abstention. The motion passes. We have our jury." He had to turn to hide a smirk. Once under control, he continued, "Before we adjourn, I'd like to tell you about the hearing officer selected by the Medical Executive Committee.

Dr. Spencer asked, "What role does the hearing officer play in all this?"

Ms. Porter also was interested. "Yeah, what does this person actually do?"

"The hearing officer presides over the hearing," Appel said. "He is usually an attorney who has no regular business with the hospital, the medical staff, or the involved person. His job is to ensure that both parties have a reasonable opportunity to be heard and that the hearing stays under control. He runs the hearing and rules on the law. The Bylaws state, 'The hearing officer shall decide the order for presenting evidence and argument during the hearing and shall have the authority to rule on all questions involving matters of law, procedure or the admissibility of evidence.'

In short, he runs the show. If the Judicial Review Committee wants him to participate in their deliberations or provide legal advice, he may do that, but he can't vote on the outcome."

Ms. Porter spoke. "Sounds like an important job. A real important job. Who did Med Exec pick?" *This should be good.*

"They've chosen a local attorney, Greg Gilliam. Mr. Gilliam has a private general law practice and has lived in Palm Springs for many years."

No one commented.

Appel concluded, "If there are no further questions, the order of business of this committee is complete. The startup committee is disbanded and the meeting is adjourned. Again, let me thank all of you for participating."

Yeah, right, thought Ms. Porter as she filed out behind the doctors, leaving Joanna, Mr. Appel and Alyce Wagner behind.

Joanna finished taking notes and left.

Alyce shut down her laptop and packed it in her black bag. "Is there anything else you need, Mr. Appel, before I leave?"

"No Alyce, nothing at all for the moment. I think we did well—quite well. Over the next few days, I'll need some help sorting through all of the material you've gathered so we can prepare it for the Judicial Review, but nothing more for today. And Alyce—thanks." Appel let her leave before heading for the CEO's office. *He would be pleased.*

The CEO was not pleased. He wanted a slam dunk and to him this wasn't it. He wanted to be able to count on five votes from the Panel, and to him, they had only three. He liked Gilliam as the hearing officer; he could totally control him. He knew he had the anesthesia vote, the radiology vote, and Dr. Rosero's vote. They all had contracts they wanted to keep. He wasn't sure about Dr. Kalim, the intensivist. She had a contract with the hospital but she was young, a bit too idealistic, and she was too good to have her job threatened. She could write her own ticket anyplace she wanted. And the cardiologist, Dr. Meller, was a complete wild card.

"Appel, you're killing me. My ass is on the line here. If this guy stays, between the Medical Staff and the Board, I might be the sacrificial lamb that goes. And I like it here. I let you take charge, I put my faith in you, and you promised me a— I don't even know what to call it, a conviction. Strader being thrown out. You were supposed to fix the deck. I see a lot of wild cards here, Appel."

"Don't you see, Dale, that's the beauty in it. All we need is three votes, not five. If we stacked the deck with five hospital-committed docs, we would be accused of being unfair, and at some level of appeal we could get overturned. Three votes make it look like a reasonable Panel. Why, it's artistic. Having Gilliam as the hearing officer is added protection. He gets to rule on what's admissible, which witnesses get presented, the order of presentation, and he adjudicates any issues that come up. So we have the judge and the jury, and they're going to go down thinking that at least they had a fair trial. And the Board will uphold the Panel's decision. We're in great shape on this one."

"You better do everything to make sure this isn't a fair fight, and you'd better win. If I go down, you know who's coming along for the ride."

"Don't worry, we are going above and beyond on this one. Trust me."

****

Strader, in the meantime, sat at his small desk at home, Tomas curled up on a neat stack of papers. He'd read and reread the hospital bylaws until they were entrenched in his brain, along with the charges against him and his letter of appeal and request for a hearing. He flipped to the last page of his notes with his right hand while his left thumb and forefinger played with Tomas's soft, velvety ear. Each time he stopped, Tomas would shoot him a lazy glance and the massage would commence once more. He muttered, first to himself and then aloud in a disgusted voice directed away from his cat.

"Fucking bureaucrats—administrators. Like, I don't know what's going on. This is payback for me opening my mouth in frustration, payback for wanting things done right. Disruptive physician my hairy ass. I've sacrificed my whole life—college, med school, internship, residency, fellowship, and twenty-five years on the front lines, taking care of sick people. Not a check-up doc—no—taking care of sick people. Taking responsibility for them. Only to be put through this shit." His voice had gotten loud and awakened Tomas. Strader picked him up and rubbed him under the chin, watching his eyes drift shut as he snuggled in Strader's arms.

"It's all right Tom, I know you're on my side. I was just venting— as you do sometimes when I miss getting you a treat." Strader ran through the barrage of thoughts bouncing between synapses in his brain. The suspension, getting his inpatients taken care of, being grateful that Ramos was out of the hospital and Lipshutz was recovering from his colectomy. Knowing that his office staff was competent in managing the office was a big help, and he had to see only a very few patients for the next month.

He reflexively looked at the reminder list on his iPhone. No patients today, and only four patient calls he had to make, one being his daily update with Dolly Lewis – two BM's yesterday—a good day for Dolly.

He'd talked to Morales, who thought Hafner was a good choice. The older man seemed relieved and not offended by being bypassed. He told Strader that this wasn't going to be a popularity contest, and Hafner was a very smart guy, one with a different set of eyes, younger and with clearer vision.

Hafner was obviously incredibly smart, Strader thought, and he packaged his thoughts with precision. But Strader hadn't learned much about him—he was unmarried, rode a motorcycle, and seemed to worship the god of mathematics. His slant on this case was different from Strader's, maybe more practical. Strader wanted to bury the jury in all of the good things he had done for the hospital and make them acutely aware of his reputation in the hospital and the community as a fine doctor—a doctor's doctor. Not Hafner—he called that information already factored in, like the news on a stock being already factored in by the market. Hafner had pointed out that Strader's career wasn't on a limb because he was a bad doctor—actually it was quite the opposite. Strader had the confidence to call out things that were wrong and try to have them fixed. But the gradual buildup of frustration over the years made his voice grating and his message coarse and strident. He had been tolerated for years, although his pleas most often were ignored, but when he spoke about murder, the line had been crossed. Fixated on this, he called Hafner.

"Dylan, I've been thinking…"

"Shoot."

"Isn't it ironic that they're trying to boot me and no one from administration or even the medical staff have asked me to explain what I had said, what I had seen?"

"Don, like I told you before, it's irrelevant. We need three votes out of five, that's it. We scrutinize the Panel and figure out what's required to swing them our way. It might be just showing that you were trying to improve care in the hospital…but I doubt it. They're out for blood, your blood. With that in mind, I'll do whatever I have to do. Three votes. That's it.

Stomach turning, Strader said, "Just don't shoot anyone."

CHAPTER ELEVEN

Bea shepherded five members of Florita Dominguez's family into Frank Vialotti's conference room— the same room as his office accessorized for the occasion with an additional four metal folding chairs. Frank said, "Welcome to my office and my conference room, multi-purpose I call it. One way I keep my legal costs down to better help you and all my other clients." The truth is that all of his malpractice cases were contingency cases, that is, the clients didn't pay up front and instead got a stipulated portion of the settlement money as payment. So what Frank the Bank really meant was that he was keepin5g HIS expenses down, which in no way provided any financial relief to his clients. Sometimes lawyers were just misunderstood.

Frank checked them out as they sat down, the young Hispanic couple from the night he ventured to Florita's neighborhood, a somber, fiftyish man in a gardener's long pants and long sleeve shirt, and an elderly couple dressed quietly except for the woman's turquoise bandana. Florita's husband, sister and spouse, and parents or in-laws, he thought.

"I'm so sorry to have to meet you under these tragic circumstances." Frank never sat still, as if he were imprisoned behind his desk and trying to break loose. The elderly woman's eyebrows arched as she watched him. "My Spanish es muy pobre, very poor, and I hope your English is better. Can you understand me?"

The man Frank identified as the husband spoke quietly. "We understand. For many years we lived and worked in Palm Springs."

"Great. I just want to be sure that you understand everything we talk about, and if you have any questions, anything at all, just ask. Now you need to know that we have to get Florita's medical records from the hospital. Unless Florita had a will, they won't release them to Mr. Dominguez. Did she have a will?"

Mr. Dominguez said, "No." He lowered his head.

"Of course, she didn't have a will," said Frank. "She was a young and healthy woman. What young and healthy person has a will? No one. But not to worry. We can get the medical records and we will, even if we have to go to court. But I have a way that may speed things up. Do you have Florita's death certificate?"

Mr. Dominguez nodded.

"And your marriage certificate?"

Mr. Dominguez looked at the older couple. The woman nodded.

"Good," said Frank. "Usually, they won't give you the records if you just go there. Why? Because they're hiding something—they're afraid. That's why you need me. They did something wrong, but I'm—we're gonna make it right. And we're gonna take them to the bank with this one." He neglected to disclose the fact that under California law, medical records could not simply be handed over to the surviving spouse without a court order. Details. He passed two documents across the desk to Mr. Dominguez. "First, we'll try it the easy way. You will take this letter from me along with the death certificate and a copy of your marriage license to the Hospital. You take it to Medical Records on the second floor. You take it at 5:30 in the evening, just after the day shift goes home. This letter says that someone in the family needs Florita's health records immediately and that it's an emergency, which is true. It says that if they don't give you the records, we will have to sue them; say to whomever you give this to that they will be included in the suit. Usually that will do the trick. Comprende?"

Mr. Dominguez cocked his head while slowly rubbing his hands together. "You want me to go to this place at the hospital with your letter and the other two papers and give it to them and see if they give me the records. Si?"

"Exactly. Si. But you have to go at 5:30 in the evening. Okay?"

"Si—okay."

"And I want you to sign this other paper so that if they don't give you the records, I can submit a request to the court for approval that you shall be the administrator of all her affairs. This will allow us access to the hospital. If they don't give us the records, it gives us the right to sue them. And don't worry, all of my work won't cost you even a penny until we win our malpractice case."

The younger Mexican looked skeptical.

"How much you take? One hundred percent? This man is my brother, and his wife—she dead now."

Frank turned his full attention to the man, not happy at his scowl, his muscular arms, and the defiance and distrust in his eyes. Frank smiled.

"I'm so glad that you are family, that you look after each other. My friend, the state of California has fixed the fees in this case, and it depends on how much we are awarded. The lawyer, me in this case, makes 40% of the first fifty grand we recover, and the percentage then keeps dropping so that at six hundred grand, I only get fifteen percent. So let's just say we get paid five million dollars to make up for her death, even though no amount of money will ever bring her back. You get four million and two hundred thousand dollars, I get a little over eight hundred thousand dollars, which I use to cover all the court costs, staffing costs, depositions, and medical experts, and whatever is left is mine. In many cases the plaintiff, the one who sues, must come up with the costs of the lawsuit as they occur, or else the money comes off the top once the suit is settled. For you, I'm taking all the costs out of the money that the state says I should charge solely for my legal fees. Fair enough?"

The consensus murmur was one of approval. Mr. Dominguez signed the document.

Frank moved ahead. "Now, it may take a while to get at the actual records, depending on the backlog in the court and the hospital's behavior, but one thing is certain—we will get those records, we will find out what they did to your wife, and we will make them pay."

Mr. Dominguez straightened up, resolve replacing despondence, hope displacing despair. Turning to his family, he said, "Este hombre, Señor Frank, yo creo que ayudame."

"You bet I'll help you," Frank said, *half-sure that he got the message right. "Let's get started."*

Frank pressed the old-fashioned buzzer hidden behind his desk and within seconds, Bea appeared with her laptop and sat at the ready.

"Who can tell me about Florita's sickness?" Frank began. "I want to hear everything you know."

The family looked at each other. Florita's husband cleared his throat.

Frank said, "Mr. Dominguez, tell me."

Mr. Dominguez spoke haltingly, still unsure of his English after so many years. "The night before, Jueves, Florita, she ate not so much. And she went to bed—early. She said she had pain in the stomach. She no sleep that night. En Viernes—Friday, she hurt so much, but she say I go work." He turned to the older couple. "Madre, Y que?"

The mother-in-law of the late Florita appeared to be close to seventy, with sun-creased skin and short grey hair. Her husband nudged her till she leaned forward in her chair and spoke. "Mi *inglés*, my English—she's not so good."

Frank spoke softly, supportively. "I understand, Mrs. Dominguez, go ahead."

"El día Friday Florita had too much pain. She cried. My son, my husband, both work. Solamente home era Florita, me and Maria." She nodded at the other woman in the room, a chunky bleached redhead with lively red lipstick to match, dressed in tight red pants and a low cut blouse not meant for a fifty-year old. "Maria called the 911 and the fireman and ambulance man they come."

"We went with her to the Emergencia— eight o'clock," Maria broke in. Her English was the best of the group. "We wait two hours. A nice doctor come out and tell us Florita very sick, that her gall bladder, was sick and her— how you say, pancreas, had much inflammation. She had stones from her, uh, gall bladder that moved and made serious problems for her. The doctor say she must come into the hospital, to intensive care, because she so sick. He say another doctor would do something that day to take the stone away without an operation, and she would be better. He said when she was better she would have surgery to take the gallbladder and she no get sick again. "

Frank asked, "And the doctor who you spoke to in the emergency room, did you get his name?"

Maria handed Frank a business card on which was written:

Donald Strader MD FACP

Gastroenterology and Liver Diseases

Below were his office number, fax number and e-mail address.

"The doctor that saw Florita in the emergency room, the one that gave you this card, that was Dr. Strader?"

Maria said, "Yes. Florita go into the hospital. They give her the IV and medicinas. We see this Dr. Strader later— he say that in the afternoon the test will be done by a specialist. He say that Florita was very sick but a little better. Habla en español, he was nice."

"And then?"

"We see Florita two times. She sleepy from the medicina. And she look yellow. Entoncesno more. They take her for the test and—she die."

Frank saw Mr. Dominguez wince and lower his head in sync with his sagging shoulders. The room was church quiet. Sometimes life doesn't just go on.

CHAPTER TWELVE

Riding the back of Hafner's Yamaha at seventy-five mph was not soothing for Strader. He felt his legs dangerously close to the ground with each swerve around a bend, despite Hafner's assurances and a borrowed full-face Shark Raw Helmet that buffeted the wind with minimal suffocation. At seven AM, no traffic impeded them as they snaked up Hwy 74's asphalt imprint on the lofty Santa Rosas. A narrow lane each way, on the one side a precipitous drop hundreds of feet to the speckled valley floor, on the other the cold granite mountain, stones of varied sizes shrugged off to its feet. Not just dangerous but crazy. Strader forced himself to concentrate on leaning with the bike on the turns as Hafner instructed. Hafner pulled into a lookout area where they dismounted and removed their helmets. Hafner close to the edge, Strader a careful three paces back, they admired the view of the Coachella Valley stretched out below them, dotted clusters of houses separated by broad squares of brown desert and traversed by the green stripes and white dots of a hundred golf courses.

In the early nineteen eighties, when Strader first came to the desert, there had been much more brown and less green and white, and Palm Springs had pretty much closed down in June for the summer. Those were the years when the "snowbirds," the hordes who descended on Palm Springs for the beautiful winter weather, would flee back to Chicago or Washington state or Canada if they became ill, as they didn't trust what they felt Palm Springs offered--tourist town doctors. Times changed, and within ten years, the area had young well-trained specialists and advanced hospital and outpatient facilities, and those same snowbirds would opt for the convenient and high quality local care. That's when Strader became the go-to desert gastroenterologist. He split the care of many affluent visitors with their doctors back home, never failing to communicate with them, never balking at a suggestion for a second opinion, for he knew it would invariably coincide with his own. The collaboration with others to heal a shared patient was so sacred a bond, the essence of medicine, something he couldn't bear losing—just because he was so troubled by what happened to a local patient, that he knew for less than a day.

Florita had been so sick, her face a canvas of fear painted by acute, persistent pain. He remembered calming her with news that she would have that stone removed that very day without an operation but instead a procedure called ERCP. He'd explained to her about general anesthesia for the procedure, that she wouldn't feel a thing, that Dr. Ahmad, the young doctor who would perform the procedure, had very specialized training to correct her exact problem, and that he was very skillful, more so than Strader. And now Florita was gone, unnecessarily gone. Not from her illness. Anguish set in, the Monday morning quarterbacking, the "what if..." and "If I had only..." If he had done the case himself, if he had been in the room, if Dr. Ahmad had waited for the anesthesiologist.

"Wow, you're either deaf from the ride or deep in thought," Hafner said, bringing Strader back to the present.

"I was just reliving thirty years and that recent case."

"I know, Florita Dominguez. We'll get to that. I took you away from Palm Springs so we could focus on Wednesday's judicial review, not on her."

"You want to talk here, on this lookout? I thought we were driving up and back, and we'd work at home."

"Just thought it would be a refreshing change from a stuffy room and a desk." Dylan said, taking in the striking valley view. He was awed by the natural symmetry of the flat valley floor encircled on three sides by high grey rock a hundred thousand years old, trailing off to the empty opening of the Banning Pass to the north. From this height, nature seemed only subtly marred by man's footprints. "Such a majestic place. Sometimes I bike through the National Forest and Wilderness Park all the way to Lake Elsinore and down to San Diego. Gets my head back on straight."

"It's beautiful up here," Strader said. "Just tough for me to enjoy it with all this...you know."

"I can only imagine. All right, let's head up to Garner Valley to a place I know we can talk." They hopped on the bike and sped up the mountain, past Carrizo Creek and Pinyon Pines to the undulating green expanse of Garner Valley, home to horse ranches and homes generously separated by trees and dense bush. Hafner pulled over at an unfenced green pasture sporting benches and tables.

"This is it. Just the trees and us. Great place to talk." He took off his small backpack and emptied it on the picnic table. He placed the Medical Staff By-laws next to a batch of papers on one corner while setting up a cache of grapes and bananas, two apples and a thermos of coffee. It was noticeably cooler up here at 4000 feet, probably 15 degrees lower than in Palm Springs. An energetic breeze blew by in whispers. They ate and drank and looked at each other much as two college roommates would size each other up on the first day of class.

Hafner broke the ice. "How do you want to work this?"

Strader thought for several seconds. "I don't know. Maybe we should look at each charge, including the new one, and talk them out."

"That latest one is great—that you were racist with the Filipino nurses." Hafner chuckled. "You know you're a much worse person than I would have ever thought possible. Not yet on the Hitler scale but you're closing in."

Strader shrugged his shoulders and managed a weak smile. "After reading some of this stuff, I think maybe they should throw me off a train, not just off the medical staff."

"Try not to mention that on Wednesday. Before we get into the details of the charges, let's look at the jury and hearing officer. Remember, we need three votes, we don't need a unanimous vote. Right now, I see us as having a good shot at one, and a fair shot at two. Getting that third will be tough."

Strader scanned the jury list. "I know Bob Klein and Alvarez only professionally, only in the hospital. I have no issues with either of them. A while back when we started doing more complex, invasive procedures in the GI lab, I went back and forth with Alvarez over the need for anesthesia scheduling for our procedures, but we eventually worked it out. We never get top priority over operating room cases but we do get anesthesia help when we need it-- except in Florita's case, and she's dead." He shivered. "Alvarez has been Chief of Anesthesiology for a while, and overall they provide a good – make that very good service. I think he'll be sympathetic to me and my story."

A sour-faced Hafner shook his head. "My take is different. I'm looking to see who has something to lose by voting for you and if that's the case, who would take a hit, maybe a financial hit, to see you reinserted. Here's the thing. Alvarez's three-year hospital contract is up for renewal at the end of the year. That contract is worth more than a half-a-million a year, plus complete control of his scheduling. He's fifty, has two kids still in college, and drives a Toyota. I don't see him jeopardizing his livelihood for you. I'm writing him off as one for the bad guys. I mean, would you vote for something that would take money out of your pocket?"

"Sure. I do it all the time at the polls."

"I guess you do. Probably why we're in this mess in the first place."

"How do you know all this stuff about Alvarez?"

Hafner grinned. "Friends, and Google. Anyway, take it from me, we're not getting Alvarez's vote or Klein's either for the same reason. Klein has been Chief of Radiology for eleven years. He has two years left on his contract. He's sixty, married a third time, and he lost everything he had with his last divorce and the recession. He has to work for at least another ten years to be able to retire. He has a bad back and trouble getting around. He can't do interventional stuff, and he's not a giant with CT or MRI imaging. He's getting four hundred sixty thousand a year on his contract and needs it to be renewed. So we chalk up vote number two against you, even if I'm Perry Mason."

Strader put his coffee down and rested his head in his hands. Hafner had this whole thing as a charade, and human nature would support his view. Strader looked at the dirt and saw a procession of ants laboring with breadcrumb leftovers from a previous picnic. With great discipline, they marched in line to deposit their load in the hidden ant colony, repeating their trek again and again. Strader used a twig to disrupt the line in the sand, but the ants never missed a step. Life goes on. His life would go on, no matter what, but maybe not like he knew it. He had his road blocked several times—his wife's illness, problems with his son, changes in his practice—but he was still walking the straight line until Florita came along, until they screwed up in the GI lab and he opened his big mouth.

"Alright, say we don't get Alvarez or Klein," said Strader. "That means we have to get Meller, Rosero, and Kalim."

"Yep, the trifecta. I'm still getting some info on them and working my way through them all. But Meller's a no-brainer. He's a good cardiologist, is in solo practice like us so he knows what goes on, and he has no ties with the hospital that I can find. He'll listen to your story, he'll understand. He's vote number one for us."

Strader couldn't disagree. He had a good relationship with Meller and always found him to be a stand-up guy and an honest, hardworking doc. A good clinician, too; Strader had sent some of his toughest patients to Meller and never had any complaints. "Okay, so it's two to one, hospital."

Dylan glanced at Strader with a comforting nod. "That's the red vote in the red state, the easy one." He rubbed his hands together and blew on them, even though the temperature was already in the seventies. "I'm thinking that Kalim is our vote number two."

"But she's the hospital's intensivist. She has a contract."

"I know, I know. But look at it this way—she's what, about my age, about thirty-five, she's incredible in the ICU, she pretty much always runs the show on the ICU patients."

"Yeah, but…"

"She's single, Boston trained, so we know she's fiercely independent. She can write her own ticket anywhere; she doesn't need Palms Hospital, they need her. I can't see them actively trying to coerce her and I'm betting that she doesn't feel any obligation to anyone, unfortunately including you. I think that she'll vote based on the actual events, based on my legal skills versus the other side. By the way, we don't know yet who's going to be the hospital advocate; we won't know till Wednesday night. But I'm counting on Frieda Kalim M.D. to be vote number two for us."

Strader said, "That leaves Rosero. I really don't know that much about him. He's rarely in the hospital. I think he does employee health and some private stuff. What's the scoop?"

Dylan smiled. "Carlos Rosero is the wild card in this case. And the toughest one to figure. You've seen how he looks. He's married to a rich socialite wife with no scandals or money problems that I could find online. All the nurses think he's gorgeous and he plays off that, but I haven't uncovered any escapades. He has the contract for Employee Health, but it's a part-time gig that doesn't pay much, and he doesn't do much. The nurses there run the show. He comes around once in a while just to show his pretty face. His wife is so rich that I think our boy Carlos keeps a small private practice just for show, probably taking care of some of the high society in-crowd. This way he becomes relevant, and his wife has some added power. I don't know whether he's in their camp as well."

Dylan picked up a rock and threw it toward a tree one hundred feet away, hitting it broadside. He tossed a second rock to Strader and motioned for him to take a shot at it. Strader accepted the challenge, reared back and let it fly. The rock fell short of the tree and skipped to rest just under the trunk's shadow. He shrugged.

Dylan was on target with his second rock as well. "Must be the rock. Rosero's the wild card, the key. I'm working on getting the scoop on the hearing officer, Greg Gilliam, but I haven't heard back yet."

"Gilliam," Strader said. "He's that tall, ex-jock lawyer…he goes to the FWP meetings. He was there when I spoke."

Hafner winced. "He was there? Maybe he's the deep throat. It fits. Gilliam will run things to help out the hospital and screw you but in a lawyerly way. We just have to keep our cool and get everything on the record in case we have to appeal. But from a probability perspective, it doesn't change things. The probability of getting Klein and Alvarez is zero, no matter what shenanigans Gilliam plays or doesn't play. I think the probability of us getting Meller and I'll throw in Kalim as well, will be high just based on the facts that we'll present. Still leaves Rosero as the wild card. Gilliam doesn't play a critical role here. We'll figure out Rosero's story and get his vote."

Strader scoured the ground, and picked up a round rock approximately the same diameter as a quarter. With eyes on the tree, he wound up and it slid smoothly from his hand, arching slightly, clipping some leaves as it descended. Not a bulls-eye, but he did get some tree and that was good enough for him. In the pasture beyond the tree, two grey stallions danced a western ballet, graceful and powerful across the green meadow. Strader watched them with the appreciation of a spectator for an athlete, of a bogged down human for a carefree animal. Envy gripped him.

"Any thoughts?" said Hafner. "You want to fire me, get your money back?"

Strader's face relaxed with an ever so slight smile. "No, but don't ask for a retainer."

Hafner said, "It's possible that the hospital has a stronger grip on Kalim than I think, but I've worked with her on lots of cases and she's been openly critical of the nursing ratio in the ICU, of problems with getting stats done at night, and she absolutely hates the hospital's computer system and vendor. Actually, the more I think about it, she's you with tits and better self-control."

"Thanks. I never looked so good. Yeah, her whole practice is in the hospital, so the problems must bug her more than me—she—uh—just knows how to behave a bit better."

Dylan held two fingers about an inch apart and laughed. "About this much. We'll get to see them all close up, but I don't know how much we'll learn. It depends on if the hospital preps them at all beforehand, how this guy Gilliam chooses to run the proceedings—there are lots of variables at work. But at least after Wednesday, we'll know the full case against you and their plan of attack. You'd better clear your calendar completely on Thursday because we'll pour over everything together. I have no patients in the office on Thursday and I'm signing out to my coverage for the entire day."

"I'm all yours."

Hafner looked around to confirm that they were alone and in a soft voice asked, "Now can we talk about the murder?"

CHAPTER THIRTEEN

"Her name was Florita Dominguez. She was forty-five years old. She came into the ER on a Friday morning a couple of weeks ago with gallstone pancreatitis. She had 10/10 pain, fever, shaking chills, was jaundiced, had a serum lipase of 4500, and her abdomen was distended and markedly tender. The ultrasound showed gallstones and her CAT scan showed a dilated common bile duct with stones blocking the duct. Her temp was 102 and her white cell count was about 18,000."

"Cholangitis and gallstone pancreatitis," Hafner said. "Real sick, but I'm not hearing the murder part. Sounds like she could have croaked just from her illness."

"The problem with Florita was that she was a large woman—two-ninety-five. She needed an emergent endoscopic procedure, ERCP, under general anesthesia. These cases can be challenging— we used to do them in the GI lab with just Demerol and midazolam, but in a very heavy patient it becomes difficult to move them if you have to during the procedure. It's much easier to have the anesthesiologist handle the job of safely keeping her comfortable while the GI guy concentrates on getting the stones out with the scope."

"So what did you do? What happened?"

"I've been doing ERCP's since the eighties but they aren't that frequent; maybe I do one a month now. This new doc, Ahmad, took a whole year of advanced ERCP training, and besides being young he's very, very good. I asked him to do the case for me on an emergent basis that Friday under general anesthesia and he agreed." Strader sat down and rested his head in his hands, his fingers draped over his temples as if feeling for a pulse.

"Go on."

"So, I'm thinking everything is all set up. I admitted her to the ICU and started her on large volumes of IV fluid and two antibiotics. I told the family what was going on. Florita stabilized a bit but continued to have severe pain despite lots of narcotics. I later learned from Emily, our GI unit secretary, that anesthesia was going to be tied up until nine or ten that night, and Ahmad and the GI lab nurse decided to proceed without them. They started late in the afternoon. Initially they sedated her with 100 mg of Demerol and 3 mg of midazolam. They had her up on her left side and positioned her on the fluoroscopy table, but she was still anxious, in pain, and couldn't stay still. According to the nurse's note, they gave her an additional 5 mg of midazolam in only a couple of minutes and shortly after, she became hypoxic and stopped breathing. They tried to reverse her with Narcan and Romazicon, but that failed. They called a code. I was still in the hospital making afternoon rounds and I rushed down there, hoping it wasn't her but it was. We tried everything, more reversal agents, we intubated her and shocked her maybe nine times but we couldn't bring her back. Dr. Ahmad and I went out and spoke with the family. When we came back to the lab I saw the GI nurse, Gil Morgan, speaking with Alyce Wagner from risk management. The lady hadn't been dead for more than fifteen minutes and already, risk management was on the scene."

"So a very sick lady has a bad outcome from a risky procedure done emergently. That's why they call it risky. What am I missing?"

"They gave her 8 mg of midazolam over a total of four minutes. Much too much given much too fast. They killed her."

"But you called this a murder— and you said there's nothing you can do about it. If you think this was wrong, why not go to the Chief of Medicine, or Chief of Staff, or risk management— you have lots of options. I don't get it."

"Midazolam is a benzodiazepine that reduces anxiety and causes transient amnesia, and as you know we have used it with Demerol or Fentanyl for years. It takes two to five minutes to start working and then lasts for about thirty to sixty minutes. We usually will start with about 2 mg IV, then give about 0.5 to 1 mg every two to five minutes. We never give more than 2.5 mg at a time, and that's usually given at the beginning. This lady got 3 mg initially, and then within a couple of minutes she got an additional 5 mg without even being given a chance for the initial dose to take effect. Ahmad and the GI nurse knew this—everyone in GI knows this. And yet she was essentially given what in her case, was a lethal dose of midazolam— they killed her by doing something that should never be done. Never."

"So they committed malpractice, in your estimation, an undisputed case. I know this Ahmad is a fellow gastroenterologist, but why didn't you do something? Tell someone."

"I'll tell you why. When I got the record to dictate the death summary, remember I was the admitting doctor so I had to do the death summary, I was shocked to see the computerized record. It says Florita only got 3 mg of midazolam. I knew this was wrong because I was completely blown away when I ran down for the code and saw the handwritten nurse's log note, which said she got a total of 8 mg. This was my patient— my dead patient."

"And how did they explain the difference?"

"They didn't have to. The handwritten nurse's note was gone, removed."

"Well, there's probably no need to keep it once they enter it into the computer. Maybe you were wrong. Maybe what you read as an eight was only a hastily written three."

Strader shook his head.

"How do you know? How can you be sure?"

Strader pulled out his cellphone, went to the photo icon and produced a picture of a hand-written note. It read in clearly legible cursive:

> Florita D.
> 4:52 Demerol 100 mg, Midazolam 2 mg
> 4:54 Midazolam 1 mg
> 4:56 Midazolam 5 mg

"Holy shit, you took a picture of the note? That's the GI nurse's hand-writing?"

Strader nodded and reclaimed his phone, glancing once more at the note before shutting it down.

Hafner was wide-eyed. "Batman, you just opened Pandora's box. Let me see it again."

Strader complied and Hafner read the note deliberatively. He shut off the phone and handed it back to Strader. For a moment, neither of them spoke. Strader broke the ice.

"Now I hope you can understand what I said at that meeting. The note is gone and the computer says she only got three milligrams of midazolam over five minutes. I have the photo but I'm not sure because of HIPAA that I have the right to even take that picture on my cellphone."

"Good point," Hafner said. "I keep billing records on my phone and e-mail my patients on a secure site, but I don't know about going around photographing other physician's orders. What happens if someone steals your phone or you lose it? Some non-medical person can get hold of a stranger's medical record, or at least part of one. I don't know. We have to look into that. But why not unload this whole thing on the hospital? Take it to Risk Management."

"Remember, when I came back from talking with the poor woman's family, Alyce Wagner from Risk Management was already in the GI lab talking with the nurse. She could have been managing risk right there by changing the record— how would I know?"

"Why not bring it to the Chairman of Medicine or to the President of the Medical Staff, or even the Executive Committee?"

"I thought of that, but you know in issues like this the hospital and docs usually operate in an Omerta mode, a code of silence. If I do nothing, then this is just another death in a high-risk patient— shit happens. Life for everyone else goes on. Do you think anyone in the hospital actually wants to get involved with allegations that a patient was killed and records falsified to protect the hospital and the doctor? I would be the biggest pariah in the history of medicine. Plus, I don't know that my photo would stand up legally. And who would refer a patient to a doc who just exposed a colleague to a huge malpractice risk? My career in Palm Springs would be over."

Hafner sat, hands folded in front of his face, his thumb digging into his chin just below his lip. "I see, so when they got wind of what you said at the meeting, even though they probably don't know about the photo, no, make that a definite that they don't know about the photo, they decided to ruin your reputation and your credibility and get rid of you." He paused for a minute, still thinking. "And the beauty for them is by bringing this action on so quickly, before you came forward, it will make it look like any action you take against them will be retribution and they'll discredit you further."

"And remember, this was my patient, so if a malpractice case is brought forward I'm sure to be named."

"They'll name everybody, but the hospital has the deep pocket. You weren't in the room; you didn't give the order. What will they say, that you should have been in the room? That you should have supervised the other doctor and the nurse? That's ridiculous."

"They could say a lot of things—I should have been there, I shouldn't have allowed the case to be done without an anesthesiologist, I should…"

Hafner interceded, "That's a song for another concert right now. I need to think about Florita. And you need the advice of a healthcare attorney or malpractice attorney or…"

"My daughter's an attorney in Philadelphia. Maybe I'll start with her."

"Good idea, but I don't think they're going to bring that up right away.

It opens up the whole incident, something they're going to great lengths to avoid. I could be wrong but I don't think that will surface on Wednesday, and we need to concentrate on Wednesday's session. We need an opening monologue disputing the charges and a strategy for responding to each one. Lots of work to do. I'm going to have to cancel my office for a day or two."

"Okay. My office is pretty much closed except for a few of my sickies and any office emergencies. One thing I am— available."

CHAPTER FOURTEEN

Strader was a slug when he got home. He was indifferent to Tomas's affectionate greeting, the rubbing dance in and out of Strader's legs accompanied by the soft crooning purr. He filled a tall glass with ice cubes and doused them with Diet Coke, three ounces of soda diluted by 12 ounces of ice. He had measured once, curiosity piqued by the memory of his father always ordering a soda in the candy store with "no ice, I can drink water at home for free."

He sat on his desk chair and pulled out his working folder, but he couldn't focus, his thoughts drifting from his meeting with Hafner to that moment in the GI lab and then, as so often when he sat alone, to Rosemary.

Rosemary Strader met her future husband at a rainy picnic on Jones Beach. She was twenty-three, two years his junior. A slim, dark-eyed NYU law student, she had already mastered the most challenging art form of life, balance. She was serious about her schoolwork but did not let it define her. She enjoyed outings, relationships, and was a competitor rather than a spectator in all things that came her way. The harsh rain and gusty wind on that summer day in 1982 didn't derail her intention to win the swim-and-run event at Jones Beach, and she handily beat him. His repeated joking that he'd let her win was always greeted by the pounding of her soft hands on his shoulders or chest, part of their eternal love dance. They married within a year and when the children came along, she gave up her career to stay at home. She referred to the change from a six-figure forty-hour week as a lawyer to a twenty-four/seven pro bono homemaker as a most unusual promotion that she was just thrilled to accept. To come home to her each night was Strader's joy. She always looked for the higher good; when an event she planned was thwarted by the need for her husband to make an emergency visit to the hospital, Rosemary managed to praise his efforts while creating an enjoyable Plan B. In the pre-children days, she would accompany him at four in the morning to the ER if he was called, somehow whipping up a bacon sandwich on a croissant for him to eat on the way. She sat in the car with knitting needles or a crossword puzzle doing something productive while he worked. Even after the children, right up until four years ago, when leukemia invaded her bone marrow and overwhelmed her, she would jump out of bed with him when he was called in and made sure he never left the house without coffee or an English muffin. And she made the nights he wasn't called in so much fun. They'd laugh together as she recalled the kids' soccer goals, poetry contest victories, loss of a tooth or a lunchbox. They'd talk, embrace, and her twinkling eyes led to a relaxing massage or passionate lovemaking. As the children became adults, they'd argue about Will's lack of direction; Rosemary insisted that her son would find his way. Life wasn't a straight path for many like it was for her husband. He was unconvinced but somehow was reassured by her life view. God, how he missed her.

He had made the diagnosis with horrifying clarity. He noticed her to be a little pale when she popped into bed almost four years ago to the day. His eyes had been riveted to the little red dots on her legs. Petechiae, spots caused by the failure of platelets to do their job of maintaining blood vessel integrity, resulting in tiny breaks and extrusion of red blood cells into the skin. Low platelets, a condition known as thrombocytopenia. Strader had sorted through the likely causes of conditions that caused either low or defective platelets that would result in petechiae in a middle-aged woman, saving the worst for last. She didn't have any recent infection. She wasn't taking any prescribed medication and she used no supplements or vitamins other than a multivitamin. No quinine. So, a drug related event was unlikely. She was pale, suggesting anemia as well as low platelets, suggesting that this was not ITP, an autoimmune disease that affected platelets primarily. Anemia together with low platelets could be caused by conditions such as Lupus or other autoimmune disorders, including the rare Evan's syndrome in which the body develops antibodies both to red cells and platelets, resulting in anemia and thrombocytopenia. He remembered her acquiescent expression as he touched her abdomen, his fingers looking for an enlarged spleen under the left side of her rib cage but not finding one. Not likely that her spleen was chewing up red cells and platelets. If it wasn't drugs or antibodies, then her bone marrow was the primary culprit. Either the bone marrow had failed or was being crowded out by an unruly autonomous population of primitive cells, most likely white blood cells— leukemia.

That very night he had her admitted to the hospital; had his hematologist friend perform a bone marrow exam to confirm what they saw on her peripheral blood smear and CBC. Her husband's urgency provoked both alarm and comfort. Whatever she had he would take care of. She would get the very best care, and he would be by her side. And of course she'd recover; he would see to it.

Acute myeloblastic leukemia. Strader reviewed the slides with the hematologist. He was jolted by the sheer numbers of those bullying large irregular ameboid white blood cells, with dark blue nuclei crowding out the remaining cell cytoplasm. What had fascinated him as a medical student and house officer now was repugnant. Rosemary had acute leukemia. He tried to think clinically. Genetic studies would take a few days. She didn't need to start chemotherapy immediately. He had a couple of days to organize things. Three hours later, after reviewing the literature in UP TO DATE, his bible of medical information, and after speaking with Joe Rosen, a hematologist and fellow intern with Strader years ago, his decision was made. He hired a private plane and the following day they flew to New York and the great Sloan Kettering Memorial hospital. He told his kids that their mom was sick with a blood disorder but didn't elaborate.

The care at Sloan Kettering was wonderful, the rare combination of twenty-first century expertise and twentieth century empathy. Her room was painted a cheerful green and accessorized with soft reprints of Monet's gardens and the Rouen Cathedral. But Rosemary's leukemic cells more than met the challenge of the best cocktail, Cytarabine for seven days and Daunorubicin for three days. Strader shuddered at Rosemary, requiring Daunorubicin, a drug so toxic that during his residency, the house staff referred to it as "the red death. The genetic tests came back revealing a poor prognosis; even if a complete remission was achieved it would likely last only a few months. The chances for a cure were extremely remote. In just a few days the leukemic cells marched throughout her body and the treatment caused severe infection.

She had remarked about leukemia's irrationality; if she died, all those roving cells would die with her; she likened them to suicide bombers. Strader knew that she actually had a good point there. In a leukemic crisis there are roughly ten to the twelfth power leukemic cells in the body, that's ten times ten times ten times ten another nine times. And when a complete clinical remission was achieved, when there were no signs of leukemic cells in the peripheral blood or bone marrow, there were still ten to the ninth leukemic cells in the body, but the body defenses could keep them dormant, unseen. But Rosemary never got a remission. Her body was decimated, her skin so pale and thin as to be transparent, flesh melted from her bones. She couldn't get up and could barely lift her head. Her innate spirit and being, however, were unconquerable. She still teased her husband, protected her children from the awful worry, and defended her doctors and nurses even as they could not defend her. And in that last twelve hours, when she was losing her grip on life, she told her husband she was not afraid of death, she made him get a bottle of liquor for her intern, who she saw crying as he left her room, and she asked her daughter, Stella, to look after both her husband and her son. Rosemary accepted her last hours with the same grace that had been with her all her life. Strader pleaded with her to try and hold on for her treatment to turn things around— he couldn't lose her. But she knew it was lost.

Her son Will, twenty-two at the time, thought for sure that his dad would get her better, for he had promised. Will watched his mom struggle to breathe, her arms turned to bruised pin cushions, her face so pale. His tears were part sadness, part anger. At his dad. Why didn't he level with them? Dad was always on the up and up, always on his high horse. And yet he couldn't tell them their mom was dying, give them a chance to—he didn't know what.

Just before Rosemary died, she asked her family to step out of the room for a bit so that she could rest, Strader reflecting later that she must have thought her trip to heaven would be a long one.

Her death left him bitter and joyless, more estranged from his son and devoid of her life compass. He had his practice to return to, and Tomas to take care of; everything else was amorphous, a blob of today and tomorrow and next week. Tomas. Rosemary had instructed Strader on the wet food, the dry food, the treats— all that he had to know. Tears fled his eyes as he recalled a vibrant Rosemary sitting with him at Starbucks, scooping whipped cream with her finger and treating that little grey fuzzy head peeking out from her purse.

Tomas rubbed against his leg, bringing him back to the present. He picked the cat up and stroked his silken ears. "It's been a long journey, Tomas." He swore the cat winked at him.

CHAPTER FIFTEEN

Strader needed to call his daughter. He checked his watch—11:30—that was 2:30 in Philly—the baby would be up from her nap.

"I need some legal advice," he said when Stella picked up.

"Again?" she said.

Strader fought for words. It did feel strange to be asking.

"Dad, are you there?"

"I'm here, just trying to collect my thoughts. Dylan--Dylan Hafner, the doc who's acting as my advocate, suggested I contact a lawyer for some advice."

"Dad, California law is worlds apart from Pennsylvania law and health-care law varies state by state," said Stella. The kids, miraculously, were nap-ping. "Your judicial review isn't even bound by California law based on the By-laws you sent me. And it's not like you've taken my advice in the past."

Stella's tone was such that Strader knew she was thinking of Rosemary.

He sighed. "That was different. Your mother— I thought if I could just buy a couple of more days, maybe the chemo would kick in and reverse that leukemic crisis. I didn't want to let her go; I couldn't let her go." He felt a thickness in his throat, an inability to mouth his words. It took a few seconds before he continued. "It was probably the wrong thing to do."

"Probably?" Stella sighed. "Anyway, no point in rehashing that again. Let's focus on your problem. Shoot."

Stella's voice, with its confident pitch and musical inflections, was her mother's. Likewise, her honesty and her ability to leave a bad thought be-hind. Of course, no one could capture all of Rosemary's being – she had been the perfect woman to his children and all who knew her. Maybe she had been autocratic in her handling of the house. Or not hard enough on Will when it would have served their son well. It wasn't as if they'd nev-er fought. But the good—the good was what lived on. Shakespeare got it wrong, and Strader was thankful for that.

"Dad."

His loss of focus was becoming a problem. Jolted back to reality, Strader recited the two-minute version. "I admitted a very sick lady with gallstone pancreatitis, asked a well-trained, young gastroenterologist to remove the stone via ERCP, with anesthesiologist help. They didn't wait for help and the doc and nurse did the case. The nurse gave too much medication and the patient arrested and died.

"That sounds like malpractice, but not murder."

"It gets more complicated. I ran down to help during her code and I saw the nurse's handwritten note where he was jotting down the meds as he was giving them. He essentially gave what for her was a lethal dose of midazolam."

"What do you mean? Was the dose something that would kill anyone?"

"Well, when you give this drug, you titrate it in very small amounts over time, like an initial one to two milligrams and then a milligram every three to five minutes if the patient needs it. The nurse gave her three milligrams initially, and a couple of minutes later, gave her an additional five milligrams. And shortly after that she stopped breathing."

"Why?"

"I don't really know. It was late Friday afternoon, she was probably moving a lot, and I don't know, maybe he was in a rush."

"Did the doctor order that much?"

"Here's where it gets even crazier. After the code, I confronted the doctor and he told me they only gave the patient a total of three milligrams. And when I looked around the lab for the note it was gone. Later I saw they logged three milligrams in the computer as the total dose. And another thing, while I was with the other doc talking to the family, a woman from the hospital's risk management team arrived on the scene and when we returned to the lab, she was talking with the GI nurse who gave the meds."

"Dad, maybe you misread the nurse's note. What did they say when you asked them about the note?"

"I didn't. I looked for it but couldn't find it. I saw the risk management person talking to the GI nurse— and I froze. I didn't know what to do or say. So I left."

"Well, you probably read the note wrong. It was probably a three that looked like an eight."

"You know the tip Will gave me about using my iPhone to photo my orders and notes when a patient is in the hospital, so that nothing gets lost if the system goes down?"

"Oh no, you took a picture of the note."

"I did. And there's no doubt. It's an 8."

Silence, the absence of sound, not soothing but foreboding.

"Stel?"

"I'm thinking. You've got options— let me think."

More silence. Strader patted his lap and Tomas joined him, stretching out with a yawn, snuggling while awaiting his massage.

Strader grew anxious.

"Any good ones?" he asked.

"Let me think out loud, so you don't think I left the room. First, I'm assuming the picture is definitive— the patient received too much medicine. As a direct result of this she died. That's malpractice, but not murder. They weren't trying to kill her."

"No, I'm sure they weren't… But giving that much midazolam at one time is never done. Why were they in such a rush? It was an act of grave indifference to life."

"Okay. So we have the act, and then we have some type of cover-up. They got rid of the evidence and falsified the computer record. Dad, do you know what spoliation is?"

"Never heard of it."

"The nurse might say that the protocol is simple; nurses take notes during a case so that they don't have to rely on their memory, and as soon as the procedure is over, they enter the information into the computer and discard the written note. And she'll say that that's what was done with this case."

"The nurse is a guy, Gil Morgan."

"So he'll say that's what he did, transcribed the written note to a computer entry, and then destroyed the written note."

"But I'm not so sure they have the right to destroy anything. The GI endoscopy lab does keep a paper record and I would think that it should be kept there."

"If your photo clearly shows what you say it does, and if it can be authenticated, as it likely will be, then the issue is different. There is obvious falsifying of the computer record, and the destruction of the written note that had the accurate information could be viewed as spoliation. Spoliation is when a person negligently or intentionally withholds or destroys relevant information that will be required in an action, in this case a probable malpractice case. Although this is usually used at the time of discovery, a case could be made that the nurse knew he screwed up so he destroyed his accurate note, enabling him to write a false note in the record. Again, the rules surrounding spoliation vary with the state, and I don't know what the rules are in California, but at the very least there is a negative evidentiary inference, which means that for anything that pertains to that document, a ruling will always be against the party that altered or destroyed the document. In this case, the ruling would be against the nurse."

"I'm not sure whether the cover-up was the nurse's idea, the doctor or Alyce Wagner's idea. She's the woman from Risk Management who was on the scene while we were still talking to the family."

"From a legal perspective, it doesn't matter. The nurse is the employee of the hospital, so any action would be against both the person and the hospital. But let's not get off base. We're not litigating a malpractice case. We're defending you from a disruptive physician claim. "

"That was brought because of what I said at that meeting."

"Dad, I'm not sure that they're going to want to bring this up at your trial, but they could. They don't know about the photo, do they?"

"I don't see how they could."

"If they don't know about the photo, they'll say that you're making this whole murder fantasy up because you're mad at the hospital, because you're a disruptive physician— in fact it proves their point. By the way, is there a disparagement clause in the bylaws, something that says that you agree not to say anything bad about the hospital? I didn't see one."

"I didn't see one either. I'd say no, there's not."

"So what did you do? You responded to a code, saw the note, took a picture, helped with the resuscitation efforts, spoke with the family and questioned the doc who did the case. I'm not sure HIPAA would allow you to take that picture, so you could be faced with a HIPAA violation, a violation of the patient's privacy."

"But it was my patient…"

"But not your order. I don't know— we'll need to research that. Then the next question is why didn't you do something right after that, given that you had the evidence that you had? Why didn't you?"

"I didn't do anything because I didn't know what to do. I spoke with the doc, who denied it. I wasn't sure about a lot of things. Did the doc order the full amount given or did the nurse take it on himself to push the envelope? Did the nurse destroy the note on his own or did Alyce from Risk Management actually orchestrate the cover-up. If that was the case, I sure couldn't go to Risk Management with my story. I was pretty messed up. And that's why when I spoke at the meeting five days later I said what I said. That patient died unnecessarily, and I wasn't sure what I could do about it."

"All right. I have to do my homework on this. If anyone starts talking about what you said at the meeting, say that you never mentioned the hospital by name or said anything about the hospital. For all anyone knows you might have witnessed a murder on the street and the murderer threatened that he would kill you and your whole family if you said anything. Or you could have witnessed someone killing an animal, and they slipped away before you could catch them. If they then ask you if you had witnessed an event at the hospital that you considered a murder, I want you to say that on the advice of counsel you cannot answer that question at this time."

"I'm so sorry to drop all this on you, Stella. You have your husband, kids, your law practice, plenty of worries of your own. It's just that these allegations— all I've ever tried to do was what was...."

"You don't have to tell me. But we'll get you through this. We'll have the satisfaction of making sure that everyone knows who was right and who was wrong. And hopefully some good will come of this, at least to the family of the poor woman who died. And you and I will be working together, which I really treasure. Remember what mom always said, 'there's always rain before the rainbow.'"

Strader's eyes watered and he held back a sigh. "Your mother— she could turn an earthquake into a dance class."

"All right," her voice choppy. She paused. "Dad, I think the baby just woke up." In a moment her cadence was restored. "I'll call you Thursday to see how things went. And send me that photo from your iPhone as soon as we hang up. And have a copy printed, along with the time and date it was taken. And Dad—thanks for letting me in."

****

Stella ended the call and immediately called her brother Will, three years her junior. She and her brother were so different— she tried so much to emulate her mother. Stella was a master juggler, keeping her two tots busy and happy, maintaining a productive and well-respected law practice, and yet finding time to maintain her own sanity and enjoy her marriage. She knew her mom was and would be proud of her and the way she managed her life. Mom was the original multi-tasker, raising two kids, maintaining a beautiful home, building a thriving marriage despite the time drought created by her husband's training and then practice demands, and cultivating her own artistic talents while lending a hand to anyone who needed one. And taking in all those strays, both cats and dogs. Stella remembered one of her dad's favorite activities, going around the house and counting all of the home's inhabitants, and scoring it on a small chalkboard he kept next to the refrigerator in the kitchen. And he'd yell out whenever a new record was reached. "Thirteen," he would say. "We have thirteen— a new Strader record, seven cats, two dogs, two children, and two parents. Lucky thirteen." And he'd give his wife a big hug and kiss and high-five Stella and her baby brother.

Her brother picked up on the third ring. "What's up?"

Typical Will, Stella thought. The family outlier. He should be working the 911 line— just the facts.

"Will, can you hear me? I hear a lot of traffic. Where are you?"

Will had been weaving his trail bike in and out of traffic outside of Boston's famous Faneuil Hall, finally finding an empty pole to latch his bike against. Tall and thin, he looked like a marathoner, but he wasn't.

"I just got to Faneuil Hall to grab a bite. I have a gig at Mass General, troubleshooting their pharmacy IT system. Part of an effort to decrease medication errors. Neat stuff. What's up?" He wandered the single middle corridor of the Market amidst a growing mob, enjoying the friendly competition between food shops, the sights and fragrances of the North End Bakery, Boston & Maine Fish Co., and a dozen others. The Brown Derby Deli always was a magnet for him, and today was no different. He was second in line and knew that he would order, as always, his freshly carved turkey sandwich on a baguette with lettuce, tomato and deli mustard. His mouth watered as he waited.

"It's about Dad—he's in a bit of a mess." Stella's voice was strained, unusual for her.

"Dad?"

"It's kind of a complicated story, but the gist is that one of his patients died when she shouldn't have, not through any fault of dad's."

"Yeah, but…"

"But he opened his mouth like he sometimes does and now the hospital's trying to throw him off the staff."

"What did he say?"

"Something like he saw a murder but couldn't do anything about it…I guess the inference was pretty clear as to where it took place. They're out to torpedo him, putting him through what they call a judicial review."

"Weird. They can drop him for saying that?"

"Well, they're calling him a disruptive physician, and they've found some spats he's had with the nurses where he's said some things— you know, dad."

Will took a few seconds. "How is he?"

"I think he's shaken up a bit and of course, real angry. We both know he's always been all about his patients, even if it screwed us up a little."

"You mean me."

"Us."

"Yeah, I remember running into them all the time and hearing about Dad. Saved them all…almost all."

"When will you let that go? Mom never had a real chance."

"The facts are that up to 90% of AML patients get a remission, and 27% are alive five years later. Look it up. Why not her?"

"She wasn't one of the lucky ones. That's not on dad. She had so much pain at the end… she looked forward to death, but dad wouldn't give in. I was so mad at him that last day, but she said to me "That's your father." And then she sent us all outside and died. I didn't forgive him for a while for not letting her go, and you're still pissed at him because he couldn't keep her from going."

"Well, I miss her, but not him."

"Hey, listen, empty your jug another time but he— we may need your help with some IT stuff."

"IT stuff?"

"It seems like they gave this patient too much medicine, noted it on a hand-written note, but entered a different, safer amount in the computer record."

"If they wrote the note first, that's it. Do you think they changed the computer record? If they did, there's always an audit trail that would pick that up. The hand-written note is the key."

"Well, that's gone, disappeared. The note that backs up Dad's story is gone. The only record is the computerized one. Dad doesn't think they changed it, they just entered it one time, but with a different amount."

"Then Dad's fucked."

"Well, not completely. You know how these hospital electronic record programs go down all the time and sometimes lose data?"

"Dad asked me about the problem of losing data and the medical records system going down— like a couple of years ago. He was so pissed at writing notes in the computer only to have them lost. I told him to write them on paper and have them scan them in and to take a smartphone photo of the note just in case the paper got lost. Set up a filing system for him and everything. HIPAA compliant."

"I know. Will—he took your advice. He took a photo of the nurse's note of the medications that were really given. He's got the evidence."

Will glanced around him and sought a more quiet corner before responding. "Maybe. Photos are a problem— they can be photo-shopped or manipulated. It's good but he probably needs more to prove it."

"Well, that's all he's got."

"Maybe not. Let me think about it." He raised his forefinger to let the deli man know he would pay for his sandwich in a minute.

"It would be cool to be able to help him."

"Yeah, well take care, Stel. I'll be in touch. And you don't have to tell him we spoke. I don't need him to be asking me about what I'm doing and what I should be doing—you know."

CHAPTER SIXTEEN

Tuesday, July first at 5:30 PM was the precise time picked by Vialotti for his client to enter the medical records office at Palms Hospital. Mr. Jorge Dominguez, a gardener in a demanding town, was good at following orders. After work he removed his straw hat and changed to a short sleeve, cotton shirt, and chinos. He took the elevator to the second floor, strode into the large office and stepped up to the counter, carrying documents within a thin binder provided by Vialotti. Not an ordinary binder but one accessorized with double-sided tape on the bottom. Just as Vialotti predicted, there was a single sheet of paper on the counter. Although facing the opposite way, Mr. Dominguez could read the title "MEDICAL RECORDS FOR RELEASE ONLY WITH ADMINISTRATION APPROVAL," below which were a list of names and chart numbers. He placed the binder over the paper and then lifted the binder— presto— the counter was now clean. He folded the cover of the binder back over the paper just as he had practiced in Vialotti's office. He looked around. The multiple partitioned staff work spaces were vacant. He gazed at the unprotected banks of computers and the stacks of old medical files on sliding floor-to-ceiling shelves filling the room's back and side walls. It struck him that there were no windows, that all light in the room was artificial. Two droopy rubber plants failed to add any sense of life to the room. Thinking of working in such a place made him happy that he was a gardener, nurturing life rather than documenting sickness…and death. After a minute he noticed a flat white bell on the counter and reluctantly hit it once, then a second time.

"Hold your horses, I'll be out in a minute," came a gruff adolescent voice from behind the stacks.

Almost five minutes passed before a pale young man of about twenty appeared. With unruly hair and wire-rimmed glasses, he lacked a presence that might have cautioned Mr. Dominguez. His name tag cataloged him as Gus Smith.

"What can I do for you?"

"I'm here for my wife's records."

"Did you make an appointment?"

Mr. Dominguez answered by producing the letter and documents that Vialotti had prepared for him. He handed them over to Gus, and as Gus looked them over, Mr. Dominguez took out a pen and paper and made sure that Gus saw him write down Gus's name.

Gus perused the papers. There were four of them, a marriage certificate commencing the bonding of Jorge Dominguez to Florita, her death certificate, a copy of Mr. Dominguez's driver's license and a letter from Frank Vialotti, Esq. The letter read:

July 1, 2014

To: Medical Records

From: Frank Vialotti, Esq.

Re: Release of medical records of Florita Dominguez to her husband, Jorge Dominguez.

Pursuant to the statutes of the State of California, you are provided with documents that attest to the marriage of Florita and Jorge Dominguez and the unfortunate death of Mrs. Dominguez in Palms Hospital. These documents are the prerequisites required to allow the release of the medical records of Florita Dominguez to her husband and the executor of her estate, Mr. Jorge Dominguez. You are also provided with a copy of Mr. Dominguez's current California driver's license for proof of his identity.

Her medical records are urgently required by the family. Failure to comply with this request at this time will result in prompt legal action taken against both Palms Hospital and the individual denying this request, as it will add to the family's pain and suffering during this difficult time of grief.

With respect,

Frank Vialotti, Esq.

Gus glanced up at Mr. Dominguez, acknowledging that his face matched the photo on his driver's license. He looked on the counter for the very sheet of paper Jorge had removed, and not finding it looked on the desk and floor in an increasingly frenetic dance. Sweat cropped his brow and his face flushed. Jorge stood tall and adopted the stern face that his lawyer made him practice. Gus fumbled for words that didn't come.

Finally, "I'll...be right back." And he darted off to the back room. Jorge listened; he thought he heard a phone dialed, but no talking followed. He waited patiently for eight minutes, as Vialotti had counseled, then rang the bell repeatedly, louder each time.

"Gus Smith," he called out.

A sheepish Gus emerged.

"My wife's records," Jorge demanded.

"I'm printing them off now, sir."

Two minutes later a whistling Jorge Dominguez left Palms Hospital, Florita's records in hand. Around the corner, he handed them to a smiling Frank Vialotti, who patted him on the shoulder for a job well done.

CHAPTER SEVENTEEN

Alyce Wagner scurried down the hall toward the CEO's conference room, one-handedly reviewing multiple texts on her iPhone while lugging her personalized briefcase. It was 7:59 AM on Wednesday the second, and Alyce sprinted down the final corridor to avoid being late, propelled by the adrenaline rush of the day's coming events. She slowed as she entered the conference room door where Appel, Greg Gilliam, and Dr. Robertson were already seated around the long table. She was happy to see Dr. Robertson since she had encouraged Appel to select him as the hospital advocate in Dr. Strader's case. The large wall clock recorded the time at 8:02.

Appel noted the time. "You're two minutes late, Ms. Wagner."

"Your clock is two minutes fast, Mr. Appel." She flashed him her iPhone that noted the correct time as being 08:00. "Sorry I wasn't able to make it earlier, but some things have to be handled, stat."

"Take a seat and we'll get started," Appel said. Before seating herself between Gilliam and Dr. Robertson, Alyce opened her briefcase, spread out four sets of papers and delivered them around the table. The reticent Robertson stacked them neatly, welcoming the opportunity to read rather than interact with the others. Gilliam exuberantly snatched his set from Alyce before she could place them on the table.

Appel nodded to Gilliam. "Greg, any last minute questions about tonight? As a hearing officer you play a major role here," Appel said, emphasizing the "major."

Gilliam said, "Everything's under control, Roger. The time I spent reviewing this with you and Ms. Wagner was very helpful. I'm good."

"Dr. Robertson?" Appel asked.

Robertson lifted his head up from his reading, already finished with the first two pages. "Uh, Mr. Appel, I guess I'm just supposed to follow the script. Read the opening statement you've provided, listen to Dr. Hafner's statement, take notes, and proceed with stating each charge and the evidence supporting it. It seems fairly straightforward, although I've never done anything quite like this before."

Appel reassured him. "Anxiety provoking, I know. That's why most lawyers stay out of court. Just remember this isn't a court of law and you're not the one being judged. And you'll have help." Appel nodded Greg's way.

"This is a bit different," Dr. Robertson said. "You understand that I have concerns about doing something that can harm another member of the medical staff, in this case a longstanding member, one considered by everyone to be a very good doctor. That's what makes it so difficult."

Gilliam jumped in. "Nonsense. The question isn't whether he's a good doc or a good anything, but whether he's disruptive."

"I know, but…"

"Listen, Dr. Robertson, I'm the hearing officer. I'll be the one who decides who says what and when. I got your back. You're just present-ing the facts given to you by the hospital, that's all. You aren't the one bringing this case. And you don't decide the outcome. The jury panel does that— with my instructions. No one will hold you accountable when Strader gets…booted."

Appel corrected him, "That's if the panel finds against him. There's probably just as good a chance of him being returned to the staff."

An unconvinced Robertson retreated into himself, legs forever bang-ing quietly against the table.

"Look, Randy," said Appel. "Someone from the medical staff has to present these charges and the most appropriate person is the one voted by the medical staff to be their President, and that's you. Everyone knows that you're not a troublemaker. Your job here is limited strictly to seeing that the Medical Staff Bylaws are enforced. We all know that you have no axe to grind with Strader and that you have no stake in this game."

With that last comment, Robertson tilted his head toward Appel, much as a dog does when he's trying to comprehend what his owner is really saying to him.

Appel continued, "Greg, let's nail down your role as the hearing offi-cer."

Greg referred to the sheet titled "Hearing Officer Duties" prepared for him by Alyce and Roger.

"As the hearing officer, I must have performed no significant amount of work for the hospital. Check. I mustn't benefit in any way from the ju-dicial panel's decision. Check. I decide on any requests for access to infor-mation by either Strader's side or the hospital's side. I must be impartial, and if either side challenges my impartiality or the impartiality of any of the jury panel, I rule on that challenge."

Dr. Robertson blurted out, "You get to decide whether you're impartial or not?"

Gilliam smirked. "That what the bylaws say---remember this isn't a court of law. I rule on all procedural disputes that may arise. During the trial I will make sure that everyone has a reasonable opportunity to be heard and at the same time I'll move things along efficiently. I have determined the order for the presentation of evidence. Dr. Robertson, you'll make your opening statement. That's page one of your set. I'll then allow Dr. Hafner, Strader's advocate, to make his opening. Following this, we, I mean the hospital through you, will present each charge and the witnesses and evidence supporting it. Dr. Hafner may argue or cross examine as long as I determine it is being done efficiently and in an expeditious manner, and if not, I'll take discretionary action as I see fit. I am solely responsible for making rulings as they pertain to law, to procedures or to the admissibility of evidence. If the judicial review panel desires, I will participate in their deliberations and be their legal advisor, but I will not cast a vote."

Gilliam looked authoritatively at Dr. Robertson. "I expect there to be three sessions. Tonight I will specify the nature of the proceedings based on the Palms Hospital Medical Staff Bylaws and allow opening remarks by each side and your presentation of the hospital's case. All three of our witnesses will be available to you. A week from now we will have Dr. Hafner present Dr. Strader's case with their witnesses, of which there will also be three; at least that's my current understanding. Two weeks from tonight I'll allow each side to make closing arguments, and then I will meet with the judicial review panel and allow them to render a decision. The case will be won by the side that gathers a majority of votes, in this case, at least three. That will conclude the judicial review, although either party does have subsequent remedies if the decision is appealed."

"Very well summarized, Greg," Appel said. "I'm sure this procedure is in good hands."

Randy's legs grew quieter.

Alyce had been busy listening and jotting down notes as Greg spoke. She raised her hand, forefinger up, and was acknowledged by Appel. Her eyes swept over both Gilliam and Dr. Robertson. "If there are any questions about anything, the bylaws, the proceedings, anything, you can contact me at any time. My cell number is at the bottom of page 4. No e-mails. Any correspondence should be either person to person or via the phone. As Mr. Gilliam has laid out, we should be finished with the trial two weeks from today, and Dr. Robertson, your work will be completed at that time. The panel's decision hopefully can be made on that final day, although it could drag on for a short time. Mr. Gilliam's work will be completed when the final decision is made by the panel and prepared for presentation to the Medical Executive Committee and the Board. Does anyone have any questions?"

Both Gilliam and Robertson shook their heads.

"Then we're all set for tonight," Appel said. The proceedings begin promptly at 6:00 PM; I suggest you be there at 5:30. Thanks, Greg. Thanks, Dr. Robertson." After Gilliam and Robertson cleared out, Appel closed the door and asked Alyce, "Well?"

"I think it went well."

"No, I mean, what do you think of our team? Gilliam? Robertson? Particularly Robertson."

Alyce was thrown on the defensive. Robertson had been her choice and he was clearly underwhelming this morning. "I know that he doesn't want to do this, and he'll be anxious, but he's a smart guy and he knows his contract is vulnerable if Strader wins. Did you see that look he threw you when you said he had no stake in the outcome? I think he'll be okay. Are you really worried about him?"

Appel's fierce look dissolved into a broad smile. "Are you kidding? I think he's perfect. These docs don't want anyone ramming stuff down their throats like they're regular people. They're above that, they'd revolt…in this case vote the hospital down. But Robertson's soft-spoken, very sympathetic. He's one of them. Gilliam's the asshole— he has some issues, but since he makes the rules and passes judgment on them, I can't see him hurting us. We control them, and we already have three or four votes locked up. This should be a no-brainer."

Alyce sighed. "I'm glad that you're happy. And I'll stay on top of this with you, particularly if things come out about the Dominguez case."

"Have you turned up anything more on Strader, or Hafner for that matter?"

"Nothing significant on Strader, although I have his routine down cold. I'm keeping close tabs on him but I'll focus more on Hafner depending on what happens tonight."

"Alyce, Strader and I have crossed paths over the years on a bunch of issues. He's brazen and blunt but otherwise a very smart and resourceful man. At the very least, I'd say he's been unkind to me, and I've had to let it slide. But his attitude has stuck in my craw. He fought me when I wanted all of the heart patients admitted here to have their surgery here. He insisted that docs could send their patients wherever they wanted and had the Medical Staff pass a rule that said as much. Do you know how much money that cost us? Lots. Pardon my French but I want this asshole taken down as he should be."

Alyce nodded. "We don't need troublemakers."

"I'm going to let the CEO know what a great help you've been. We'll see how things go tonight and what else we need to get ready for next week. I'm sure I'll be keeping you busy. See you here in the morning at eight…by my clock."

CHAPTER EIGHTEEN

Strader dashed up the steps to his second story office. Tiny had called him in distress; they needed him ASAP. He flung open the office door to find Mrs. Ramos and her son in the waiting room, the young man curled up on the rug, his mother standing over him. He barely moved; his breathing hardly perceptible. His eyes a deep yellow, and his skin a sickly composite of yellow and white overlaying copper undercoating. *He's jaundiced*, Strader thought, leaning down to examine him. A differential diagnosis derived from thirty years of experience cultivated by journals and textbooks and seminars launched itself from deep in Strader's brain to his ready consciousness, as if a series of cue cards were shown to him sequentially in perfect synchrony with his perceptive eyes and examining fingers. The heart and lungs were normal other than his heart rate of 124, but Strader didn't consider this crucial for such a young man. The abdomen wasn't distended on Strader's inspection, a good sign, but the liver was enlarged and modestly tender. Recalling all of the lab and imaging studies Ramos had undergone during his recent hospital stay, Strader was comfortable that what he was seeing was hepatitis, liver inflammation caused either by his prior drug use or alcohol. Testing for viral hepatitis A, B and C as well as HIV had been negative in the hospital. The risk of contracting hepatitis from blood transfusion these days was very unlikely and the incubation period was probably too short. So viral infection was unlikely. Progressive liver failure was possible, maybe from alcoholic hepatitis, particularly if Ramos had gone back to drinking, but one look up at the resolute Mrs. Ramos nearly eliminated that as a possibility. Benign cholestasis, like that seen with postoperative jaundice, seemed like a good bet. Ramos had an inflamed liver when he was hospitalized and with all the bleeding and transfusions, a tremendous load of bile pigment from hemoglobin was sent to the liver for processing, and the liver was overwhelmed and stopped processing it. The partially broken-down pigment sat in the liver cells and backed up into the circulation. Cholestasis—static bile. If Strader was right, and he was confident that he was, then Mrs. Ramos could care for her son at home, feed him with some nutritional supplements, and over time the liver would recover enough to resume its work. He would have the Visiting Nurses help and would have an ultrasound done to make sure he wasn't missing something important. Strader patted Ramos' shoulder and the young man uncoiled a bit in response. Strader got to his feet and barked out to Tiny.

"I need lab to come over here and get a CBC, PT, and CMP. You better add a type and group. Also, get a Phosphorus and Magnesium and a blood ammonia level. See if you can arrange for a stat ultrasound of the liver, gallbladder, and abdomen to r/o obstruction or ascites. I need home health to provide him with two liters of IV fluid today over four hours, D5W + ½ NaCl plus I amp MVI. Have them see him every day for the next five days and call me with his vitals and his progress. And remind me to call my coverage about him."

Strader turned to Mrs. Ramos, who had been trying to follow what he said. "Mrs. Ramos, I think your son's liver, su hígado, is sick. He needs some time to get better. I don't want to put him back in the hospital." Strader didn't say he couldn't, even if he wanted to. "We'll do some tests, get the nurses to see him at home, and get him some fluid and vitamins. No medications. Let him eat what he wants. You can call me at any time. The nurses will call me every day, and I'll call you. Bueno?" He thought about the fact that he wouldn't be available tonight when his trial started, but it should be all right.

Tiny had already used a nursing wrestling hold to hoist Ramos into a chair. Sitting up, he already looked considerably better. Like he would live.

Mrs. Ramos held his hand, her face hiding the emotion behind it. "Gracias, mi doctor. Gracias a Dios."

Strader squeezed her hand gently. *"I hope God's listening. Divine help is always appreciated, and I'm probably going to need some."*

Strader barely released her hand when the office door opened, and in strode a seething Samantha Porter. The Chief of Nursing paused at the sight of the jaundiced Mr. Ramos, who she recognized from his time in the hospital. She up-and-downed the patient and offered best wishes to him and his mother for a quick recovery.

"Excuse me but we need to speak, Dr. Strader. Now."

Strader motioned to Tiny, who left Mr. Ramos with his mom while she ushered Ms. Porter back to the doctor's consultation room. Strader followed.

"Doc, I just came from that asshole Appel's office. What did you do, sleep with his wife?"

106

"I'd rather sleep with the fishes. We've been enemies for years. He tried to control the medical staff and some of us fought him. He wanted to throw docs off the staff if the hospital statistics suggested that their patients cost the hospital too much money. They wanted to use claim and billing data without looking at the severity of illness or patient mix. So, if one doctor got consulted and wound up taking care of the sickest patients, he would obviously generate lots of expense and be at risk of being thrown off the staff. Together with the medical staff attorney and a great health-care statistician, we made him back down and look stupid in the process. That didn't endear me to him one bit. We've had other clashes. But you look so upset. What happened to you?"

She settled her large frame softly in his wing-backed chair. "Mind if I sit down? I got old nurse's feet."

"You already are. Get comfortable. Tell me what's going on."

"First of all, I have nothing to do with this trash that's going on, with this disruptive physician stuff. You and I both know you are a squeaky wheel, but we've done some good over the years and I appreciate you."

"Likewise."

"When I found out that they were using some nursing incidents to hang you, I went to Appel and told him that since I was the Chief of Nursing, I'd like to appear as a witness. After hearing what I had to say, he ordered me not to appear, said my presence would not be necessary and that the hospital had its case all ready to go. I said that you might call me as a witness and he said I wasn't on your witness list. He went on to say that if I was put on the list, I shouldn't say anything but just not show up. When I objected, he threatened my job and mentioned the importance of hospital loyalty, particularly for senior management." She moved the tip of her thumb and forefinger about one inch apart. "I came this close to givin' him an old-fashioned whipping."

Strader smiled. "I would have paid big money to see that. Listen, I really appreciate you coming over here, but I would never do anything to put your job at risk. We have a plan and I think we'll be okay. I think the good guys will win."

Ms. Porter stood up and gave Strader her best bear hug. "I don't care if I'm on the list or not. You need me, I'm there. We need all the good guys we can get, the few that still care."

They walked arm in arm to the front, like senior prom royalty. Before she left, she had one more thing to say. "Doc, you know that flat-assed Al-yce from Risk Management, she's been on me all week like a hog on slop. She's Appel's snoop. Be careful with her, I'm tellin' you."

CHAPTER NINETEEN

No malpractice. Vialotti had read and re-read Dr. Rand Paget's four-page report. Death from severe biliary pancreatitis, cholelithiasis (gallstones), choledocholithiasis (common bile duct stones), cholangitis and sepsis. Co-morbid conditions---morbid obesity.

Vialotti shouted into the phone, the sound reverberating in his small office like an echo in the Grand Canyon. "The lady is dead. The doctor says she was murdered." His shouts turned to screams. "And you're telling me that I have no case. And you're the f—expert? You're screwin' us here. You're screwin' this poor woman's family. You're screwin' me, Dr. Paget."

The voice on the other end was measured, unemotional. "I'm sorry you feel that way, Mr. Vialotti. There wasn't much to the medical records, about 15 pages in total. If you have anything more to review, I'd be happy to look."

"You already got three grand on this," Vialotti retorted.

Unperturbed, Dr. Paget continued. "Since the record was so—manageable, I showed it around the office to my colleagues. They all agreed. The woman was very sick and septic, they tried to get the stone out, they gave her the right amount of sedation, and the illness was just too much. People do die of sepsis, Mr. Vialotti."

"But the doctor said she was murdered."

"You either have an irrational doctor or the wrong patient."

The wrong patient. Oh my God, could that be? Vialotti crumpled into his chair. All of this for nothing. And three grand down the tubes. He felt crushed.

"Well, what should I do? Do you think I should get another opinion? Could you have missed something?"

"Not on this case, unless there's something missing, which I doubt. I suggest you talk to the doctor who started this, Dr. Strader."

"Well, okay, thanks. I'm sorry I blew up at you. But you know, the poor family…"

"And as you put it, the three grand. I understand. Good luck with this, Mr. Vialotti. If I can be of any more assistance, please let me know."

Vialotti banged the receiver down, missing its mark, leading to an annoying repeated buzzing. He popped it on correctly and the buzzing stopped. He hated the idea of relaying the lost cause to the family. One of the reasons he had always chosen his cases so carefully. He hated that meeting even more than losing his three grand, although that hurt as well. He wasn't a big law firm, just one guy trying to make things right. He had only one move left and he'd take it. He had to talk to Strader.

CHAPTER TWENTY

Sitting at the far end of the boardroom conference table, Strader watched each judicial review panelist arrive. Dr. Frieda Kalim, not surprisingly, was first. Strader mused she had been first at everything she ever did. A Harvard grad and a member of the first class of hospitalists/intensivists trained at the Massachusetts General Hospital. She nodded to Strader as she sat down. No emotion, no smile, no words, just a nod. All he could do was return the nod and force a collegial smile. When she looked down, Strader whispered to Hafner, who was seated next to him. "And she's one of ours?"

"A slam dunk," responded Hafner. "At least that's how I figure it."

"Remember, this is—my career—my life." Strader's voice was tense.

"Fully aware."

Klein and Alvarez trooped in together, the radiologist and the anesthesiologist, hospital men. They sat together next to Kalim without even a glance toward Strader's end of the table, trying to lose themselves in small talk.

Hafner nudged Strader. "Our two lost causes. If they look your way, offer up a big smile. No hard feelings. That'll make them squirm a bit, even though we can't turn them." Just then, the financially beleaguered Klein looked up, his sixty years clocked on a worn and sun-beaten face. On cue, Strader flashed him a big smile and Klein abruptly looked away.

Hafner took full note of this. "See that? He's voting you down, but at least he feels bad about it." An obvious tell, he thought.

"Small consolation to the man on trial. And Alvarez looks like he's taken some of his own gas." Dr. Alvarez, still in his OR anesthesia greens, his face inches from the tabletop, looked as if he was killing time between operating room cases.

"Here's the one we need," Hafner said softly as Carlos Rosero made his runway entrance, his white smile a perfect accompaniment to his dark eyes and long, wavy hair. A blue button-down shirt and perfectly creased tan slacks over Bruno Magli loafers completed the package. He looked around the room and warmly said, "Hi to everybody. I hope I can be of help."

Strader had no idea what he meant by that. Maybe Dr. Kalim did; she locked eyes with Rosero for a prolonged second and he unabashedly winked at her.

Strader said to Hafner, "This guy is George Clooney before he turned grey."

"Clooney never looked so good." Hafner kept his eye on Rosero, saw Dr. Kalim chuckle to herself and looked away. Hafner grunted and made a note in his yellow legal pad, purchased specially for this occasion.

The lead juror, Dr. Meller, was the last to arrive, still on his phone. Dr. Robertson, the advocate for the hospital, and Greg Gilliam, Esq., who would preside over the proceedings, followed shortly. Gilliam, all six foot eight of him, with the possible exception of Rosero, seemed the only one of the group happy to be there. He settled in, mid-table. Next to him sat Dr. Robertson. At one end sat the five docs of the jury panel. At the other sat Strader and Hafner. The room went quiet and there was really no need for a call to order.

Gilliam rose from his chair to his full height and spoke. "My name is Greg Gilliam. I am an attorney in Palm Springs and I've been asked by the Hospital to preside over this judicial review. I take my charge seriously and will ensure that we proceed efficiently, fairly, and equitably until we have completed our work. Dr. Donald William Strader has been charged with being a disruptive physician and his alleged actions have resulted in suspension from the medical staff while this matter is being settled. The hospital has asked that Dr. Robertson, the Chief of the Medical Staff, present these serious charges. Dr. Meller will serve as the lead juror for the doctors' panel. Dr. Dylan Hafner will serve as Dr. Strader's advocate."

The room was quiet as a Montana winter night.

Gilliam settled in his chair. "This proceeding is quasi-judicial. By that I mean that we do not have to strictly follow the rule of law and I will grant some leeway in the process, as long as it is fair and the issues brought up are relevant and warranted. Tonight, I will allow opening remarks by each side and Dr. Robertson will present the hospital's case against Dr. Strader. I understand that witnesses will be called. We will allow Dr. Hafner to question each witness after Dr. Robertson has completed his examination. If we can finish the hospital presentation, which loosely I'll call the prosecution's case, tonight, then in one week we'll have Dr. Hafner present Dr. Strader's defense. At that time, Dr. Robertson will have the opportunity for rebuttal. Week three will hopefully be the concluding session with each side presenting a summary of their position, and with the panelists reaching a verdict or decision. During the entire proceedings I will field questions from either side regarding the appropriateness of any action or statement and I will decide on the appropriateness of inclusion or exclusion. I will be the final arbiter of all process concerns by either side. Are there any questions? Dr. Robertson?"

Robertson shook his head.

Strader dropped his chin as his head shook slightly, side to side.

"Members of the jury panel?"

Dr. Meller spoke up. "Just one, Mr. Gilliam. You said this was a quasi-judicial hearing where the strict rule of law may not apply. What will be the basis of your ruling when questions arise?"

Hafner poked Strader under the table as he leaned forward to listen, pen in hand.

Gilliam tugged at his collar. "I'm a lawyer, Dr. Meller, so I'll try to see that everything is done fairly and efficiently. Since I'm the only lawyer in the room, I expect that each side might make a few—shall we say un-lawyer-like mistakes. It's my job to correct them and not draw out the proceedings. Since it does remain possible for the party that does not prevail to move outside the Medical Staff policy system to the legal system, I'll make every effort to see that errors that may lead to an incorrect conclusion are corrected.

Any other questions from the jury panel?" No response. "In that case we'll get started."

Hafner looked at his notes, raised his hand, and when not recognized by Gilliam he spoke out. "Mr. Gilliam, I have a question. I didn't want to just blurt it out but you didn't ask if we had questions on this end."

"I wasn't excluding you, Dr. Hafner, just didn't see your hand. And your question is…?"

"Just as a matter of clarification, are you getting paid to oversee this hearing?"

"It's not something I'd enjoy doing for nothing."

"I take it that's a yes. Could you tell us what you're being paid?"

"Irrelevant to these proceedings. Any other question, Doctor?"

"Just one. I've been a doc here in town for four years and I haven't had the pleasure of meeting you before tonight. I was wondering how you were picked for this job. Do you specialize in hospital law or medical staff law?"

"I'm a lawyer in good standing in the State of California."

"Congratulations." The shudder in the room was palpable. Strader was shocked at the way that Hafner was going after Gilliam.

Hafner continued. "Do you do a significant amount of work for the hospital?"

"The work I do outside of these proceedings is of no concern to you."

"That's not really true. The bylaws say— actually I'll read what they say: "The hearing officer may be a licensed attorney at law, but not be from a firm that is regularly utilized for legal advice by the hospital, the medical staff or the involved medical staff member. The hearing officer shall have no direct financial benefit from the outcome and shall neither act as a prosecuting officer nor as an advocate. The hearing officer shall act in a manner to allow all hearing participants a fair opportunity to be heard and to present relevant evidence. The hearing officer will strive to conduct the hearing efficiently and with proper decorum. …""

Hafner looked up, first at Gilliam, then at the juror panel. Dr. Meller seemed interested, Dr. Kalim amused. The others—hard to tell. "I've checked with Dr. Strader and he has no financial relationship with you, nor has he hired you for any work. There is no conflict of interest there. So Mr. Gilliam, once more I'll ask, do you do any significant work for the hospital and do you stand to benefit in any way from the outcome of these proceedings?"

Gilliam stood to his full height, his jaw muscles clenching. He thumbed through the bylaws he had brought with him. Finding the right page, he read a passage to himself, then relaxed. Turning to Hafner he replied, "Dr. Hafner there is a section a bit further down that you failed to recite, which I'll read for the benefit of all. 'The member shall have the opportunity to challenge the impartiality of the hearing officer and judicial review committee members. Any such challenge shall be ruled on by the hearing officer.'"

Hafner broke in, "Then based on your responses so early in these proceedings and in my sole capacity as an advocate for Dr. Strader, I request your dismissal as hearing officer of these proceedings on the grounds of lack of impartiality."

Gilliam glowered at Hafner and in passing, at Strader. His tone was loud and his cadence harried.

"And based on these bylaws and consistent with my authority as hearing officer, I deny that request." He sat down.

Hafner smiled, nodded to the juror panel and responded to Gilliam. "We thank you for your consideration." He dropped back in his chair and jotted a note to the sweating Strader which said, "Needed that on the record. We're good."

Strader felt his chest tighten, his pulse race, and he had an urge to bolt from the room. A mini-panic attack. He breathed deeply and slowly and managed to calm himself. Hafner *was a smart guy; Strader knew that, that's why he chose him. He just had to take a back seat and let him run with this. It made sense to show the docs on the juror panel how this was being stacked against him. This should help with Meller, with Kalim and maybe even Rosero. Keep your eye on the prize—Meller, Kalim and Rosero.* He scribbled three words to Hafner—I'm with you. Hafner jotted back—like you have a choice? Strader completed the correspondence—very reassuring.

Gilliam pierced the brief silence. "Now that we have that behind us, let's proceed. Dr. Robertson, please present your opening remarks as to the Hospital's charges."

Hafner leaned back in his chair, Strader forward in his. Let the games begin.

CHAPTER TWENTY-ONE

Dr. Randy Robertson was unfit to be a prosecutor. He made his living in the emergency room, an arena that screamed for patience and discretion in dealing with patients and their families. Collegial behavior and consistency in presenting cases to the on call doctor staff was a necessary virtue; it wasn't easy to get a doctor to leave his bed in the middle of the night to admit a less than critically ill patient. Even these days, with hospitalists in the hospital it still was a challenge to sell them a Medi-Cal or uninsured patient for admission: lots of work, malpractice risk and little monetary satisfaction.

Robertson was a respected doc and elected Chief of Staff. He held the emergency room contract; all the money came to him and he spread it around after taking his significant "taste" off the top. He also scheduled the most lucrative ER shifts for himself. The ER contract was a prize, and it was that prize that had him here at Doc Strader's trial. If he didn't do the hospital's bidding, he'd no doubt lose it. He hated being manipulated but he had no economic choice. And prosecuting Strader was even worse. Strader would always, always, answer his calls, discuss an impending case, come promptly to the ER and expertly care for the patient. He never gave Robertson a hard time about a legitimate admission, and on cases that could be handled as an outpatient, Strader always offered a solution, often initiating treatment and making arrangements to see the patient in his office the following day, even on weekends. Robertson didn't relish what he was about to do. He stood up behind his chair, cleared his throat and spoke, his eyes on his notes rather than on the jurors he was supposed to be trying to convince.

"Good evening, everyone. I'm sorry we have to spend this time after a long working day and I appreciate each of your commitments to helping in our efforts to maximize the quality of care that we deliver at our hospital. I'm also sorry that we have to consider this action against Dr. Strader."

Strader jotted "but" on his pad and Hafner underlined it twice. The fact that Robertson was the advocate against him made Strader realize that Hafner was right, that the hospital pulled all the strings on their puppets. That made Alvarez and Klein sure votes against him. He'd get Meller on the merits of his case. He was pretty sure of that. But he had to count on Hafner's belief that Kalim's independence would swing her to his side and that somehow Rosero would be persuaded as well. Rosero remained the one completely blank card. But the hospital must either know that they've sewed up his vote already, or Kalim's, or both.

Robertson's voice pulled Strader back into the moment. "The charge in this case is quite simply that Dr. Strader, while being an excellent physician, has behaved in a manner so disruptive to the hospital that it threatened appropriate delivery of care and actually posed an immediate threat to patients, staff, colleagues, and even the community at large." Robertson's voice cracked just a bit but his eyes remained laser-focused on his notes, perhaps conveying that he was only the messenger.

Strader's neck reddened, jaw muscles locked, and involuntarily the words flew from his mouth. "It's all such bullshit."

Gilliam jumped in. "Dr. Strader, you'll have your turn. But in the interim, I insist on quiet. Dr. Hafner, please control the defendant. These outbursts are likely what got him here in the first place."

Hafner, one hand patting Strader's arm, calmly responded.

"Mr. Gilliam, it's very difficult for Dr. Strader or anyone in the room to stand by idly and listen to their character be wrongfully assassinated. And your last comment displayed your lack of impartiality. I respectfully ask that you retract that remark and dismiss yourself from this proceeding."

"Hafner, I have nothing to retract and I will not dismiss myself. I have a job here to run this trial efficiently, and that requires that your client not indulge in any more outbursts. Now, Mr. Robertson, I mean—Dr. Robertson, please continue."

Hafner kept the needle jabbing. "That's Dr. Hafner, Mr. Gilliam. We're all doctors here except you and the stenographer. Dr. Hafner."

Gilliam sharply repeated, "Dr. Robertson, please continue."

Dr. Robertson swayed a bit behind his chair before moving ahead.

"I was asked as Chief of the Medical Staff to present the hospital's case, and it is solely in this capacity that I am here before you." Sweating freely, foot tapping, he went on amidst palpable discomfort.

"Tonight, I will present three witnesses to establish the disruptive behavior alleged in three different instances at the hospital. The evidence will show a pattern of intimidation, inappropriate language, and of resultant fear among the nursing staff in caring for Dr. Strader's patients that presents a clear danger to the delivery of care at Palms Hospital. This disruptive behavior has been tolerated to date but cannot be going forward. There is in addition, another action by Dr. Strader that I reserve the right to present to the panel at a subsequent time." With that, he sat down, his leg still tap dancing, wiped his wet forehead, and dropped his gaze down at his notes, looking neither at the panel nor at Strader.

Strader scribbled two words—Florita Dominguez. Hafner crossed them out and wrote—Hail Mary—won't happen.

Gilliam looked at Hafner and grumbled, "You're up."

Hafner smoothed himself out of his seat and addressed the panel, one hand resting on Strader's shoulder. First, he looked directly at Dr. Robertson.

"Thanks, Dr. Robertson, for telling us that you too consider Dr. Strader an excellent physician and that you didn't volunteer for the role you have to play in this charade." Dr. Robertson felt forced to look up and he smiled weakly at Hafner, actually pleased by the remark.

"That's not what he said," Gilliam interjected. "The panel should disregard this remark."

Hafner responded. "I thought that if the good doctor objected, he would say so himself. Wouldn't you, Dr. Robertson?"

Robertson remained quiet, his nod barely perceptible.

Hafner went on. "And these are just my opening remarks, actually my opening remark. Mr. Gilliam, if the hospital's advocate didn't object, I don't see why it would be appropriate for the unbiased hearing officer to jump in. Now, if you'll let me continue…"

Strader scrutinized the panel members as Hafner had earlier that day suggested. Notably, he focused on Kalim and Rosero, paid less attention to Dr. Meller, and ignored Klein and Alvarez. Kalim seemed a bit perturbed and was leaning forward in her seat, making a note as she listened. Strader couldn't tell if she was pissed at Hafner or Gilliam. Rosero unabashedly kept smiling and seeking Kalim's attention. Even in this setting, Strader thought. He made that his first bullet point and underlined it. Rosero—likes a challenge; would go to a Sunday convent convention looking for a Friday night marathon.

Gilliam had the last word. "The panel will disregard the defense's remark." And to Hafner, "You may continue."

"Why thank you, Mr. Gilliam. What I was going to say was that I'm sorry that you all have to give up your evening after a long day's work to participate in this charade, but I do appreciate your being here. Everyone in this room, probably even the stenographer…"

The stenographer, a courtly middle-aged woman with short hair and 3-D-like glasses looked up at Hafner and smiled, pleased to be recognized. He returned the smile and went on.

"Everyone knows that Don Strader is an excellent physician, has a paramount interest in the welfare of his patients, and demands that they be given high quality care at all times, particularly when they're sick enough to be in the hospital. Dr. Kalim, Dr. Meller, Dr. Rosero, you all provide direct patient care in the hospital and are aware of the challenges posed at times by the process, whether it be the nursing staff, scheduling, pharmacy, whatever. You, the patient's doctor, bear the ultimate responsibility for the care he or she receives, and you are thankful when things are done correctly and when the patient does well. Sometimes, we all know, everything can be done perfectly and yet we can have a bad outcome." He acknowledged the nods of Meller and Kalim.

"Medicine is not an exact science but a complex web of probabilities that determine the patient's outcome. When we, as doctors, come across a process in our patient's care that is harmful or potentially harmful, we can shrug it off or we can address it and try and improve the likelihood of it not recurring. Don Strader doesn't shrug things off. Don Strader prides himself in being accountable to his patients and his peers and demands that of those who participate in the care of his patients. He has no choice. He wants to maximize their chance of getting well. And when the process improves, it improves for all patients, not just his. For yours, Dr. Meller, yours, Dr. Karim, yours Dr. Rosero, and mine. And for that, he sits here tonight on trial for being a disruptive physician."

Hafner turned to Strader. "Don, I'm so sorry that you have to be here, that you have to defend yourself for actively advocating for your patients. And I'm sure that when the doctor members of the panel who take care of hospitalized patients hear the charges brought tonight and are given the specifics behind each and every charge, they will vote to return you ASAP to the active medical staff with all privileges intact. Especially knowing that you are devoted to your patients and to quality care, and that your actions serve only to elevate care at our hospital." And with that Hafner sat down.

Gilliam cleared his throat in a dismissive way. "Mmm. Platitudes don't work here. Evidence does. Dr. Robertson, you may bring forward your first witness."

CHAPTER TWENTY-TWO

Strader caught Alyce Wagner's half-mocking smile as she led Nurse Curci into the conference room. Risk Management behind the scenes, is unshake-able. Just like the day at the GI lab, just like with Florita. He didn't know what he had done to her—probably nothing—she was just on the other side, the hospital side. They paid her check. He had dreamt about catching her off guard, grilling her on her role in what took place in the moments immediately after Florita had died—what had Alyce been told by the nurse, and how had she responded? But in real life she was in the enemy's camp, which meant she was the enemy, and you don't talk to or try to reason with the enemy. Hafner had explicitly warned him about Wagner, telling him that it's always you against the House, and the House knows that, so you'd better as well.

Mr. Gilliam turned exquisitely deferential as he relayed his rules to the witness. "Ms. Curci, I know that you have been a loyal nurse at our hospital for many years and we are in great debt to you for your loyal and profession-al service." Hafner's eyes flashed a "give me a break" look.

Ms. Curci nervously half-listened as he droned on. She didn't want to be there; she surely didn't want to be in the middle of any fight between Dr. Strader and the hospital, particularly over the event in question. She was the one who screwed up. But after meeting with Mr. Appel, the hospital at-torney, and Ms. Wagner, she really had no choice but to deliver her coached lines. All she really wanted was to come to work, do her job, go home, take care of her husband and pets, and see her two grandkids when she was off. She had spent two decades at The Palms Hospital, almost as long as Strader, and she saw the change in him after his poor wife died. As she sat down at the witness chair opposite Gilliam and Dr. Robertson, her attempts to clear her throat sounded like a lawnmower trying to start after being idle all win-ter. She looked straight ahead, avoiding Strader and the jury panel.

"Excuse me," she managed to say. She had difficulty focusing on any-thing that Gilliam said, and remorse built up, remorse for allowing herself to be bullied and acquiescing to the hospital's demands, and remorse for having to play a part in ousting Strader, a guy who she had worked with on so many sick patients over the years. Absent was remorse with regard to her failure to provide the essential IV fluid for the patient on the incident in question; she hadn't been sleeping on the job or taking a cigarette break—she didn't even take a dinner break that night. You can only do so much. And it seemed ironic that Strader was the one always advocating for more ICU nurses.

"That's quite all right, Ms. Curci. I'm sure working those long shifts wears you down." Gilliam being so comforting. She settled in and Gilliam nodded to Robertson to start.

Dr. Robertson stumbled a bit on his script.

"Good evening Ms. Curci and thanks for coming. I too want to thank you for all your years of service. Let me see…24 years to be exact."

The good nurse nodded.

"I bet you've seen it all, being an ICU nurse for all these years."

No response but a shrug of the shoulders.

"And you've had contact from time to time with many of our doctors, including Dr. Strader."

A shrug and slight nod.

Gilliam interrupted. "Ms. Curci, we have a court stenographer recording this session. Please respond verbally, even with just a yes or no to any questions asked. All right?"

She nodded, adding a belated "Yes."

"Thank you. Dr. Robertson you can continue. Sorry for the interruption."

Robertson checked his notes and continued his teleprompter-like reading. "And I'm sure that you've taken care of hundreds, maybe thousands of critically ill patients." Robertson didn't even wait for a gesture. "And in checking your record, we haven't been able to find a single incident report, not one instance where any patient or doctor lodged any complaint about you."

A weak smile. "Uh, yes."

Hafner jumped up. "I'm sorry, but some of us have worked all day and are here pro bono. Several of us know Nurse Curci and have worked with her many times in the ICU. This proceeding is not about her. Are we ever going to get a question that relates to Dr. Strader?"

Gilliam's neck reddened and his face seemed to extend halfway down the table toward Hafner. "Dr. Hafner," he bellowed, "you're the one who is holding things up. If the train gets off track, I'm the one to get it back on, not you."

Under his breath but still, audible Hafner muttered, "At least he admits this is a railroad job." Then before Gilliam could lash out again, and looking toward Robertson, a louder "sorry."

Strader noted Kalim smiling and Rosero smiling with her. Meller was jotting down a note, which amazed Strader, since nothing really had been started. Gilliam and Hafner had firmly established a hate-hate relationship; Strader hoped that Hafner knew what he was doing, trying to expose Gilliam's bias. But why? To help get Meller, Kalim? To try and sway Rosero? To set the stage for an appeal should they lose? The sole benefit of this sideshow to Strader was a slight lessening of the pressure he felt; for that alone, he was grateful.

Robertson re-studied his notes and continued, unable to adlib from Hafner's outburst. "Well, we all know the pressures that come with working with the sickest patients in the hospital. Nurse Curci, do you remember a recent time when you were caring for a patient of Dr. Strader's, and he made some remarks to you?"

"Yes." Head down, low voice, her best shot at hiding in the room.

"And what did he say?"

Without looking up, "I don't remember exactly, but something like he wanted to know if I had anything against his patient or was—uh, trying to kill him."

On cue, Robertson raised his voice, "Trying to kill him. Did he say this in front of the patient? No, take that back, in front of the nurses?"

"Yes."

"And why do you think he asked you this bizarre question?"

"I guess it's because the IV had run out and I hadn't had the time to replace it."

"And what did you say to Dr. Strader?"

"Nothing."

"How did you feel?"

"I was very upset."

"And why was that?"

"Because I work very hard, I don't even take my breaks, and I always try and do my best. And that night we had several admissions—very sick patients, and we were playing catch-up all night long."

"And did you tell that to Dr. Strader?"

"No. Another nurse did."

"Do you remember which one?

"I think it was Lucy Abrigo."

Dr. Robertson jotted that name in his notes. Like he didn't already know it.

"So despite the fact that you were killing yourself, trying to care for these critically ill patients, Dr. Strader chose to belittle you in front of your colleagues. Was that demoralizing to you?"

Curci looked up, her eyes a sad river of unspent tears. A hushed "yes."

"And do you think it can make you more anxious in the future caring for his patients? Could it wind up affecting your nursing care?"

"I don't know. I suppose so. Yes."

On their common writing pad, Strader had jotted down "calls for speculation" wish. Hafner crossed it out and wrote, "watch."

Robertson softly concluded, "I think that's all I have for you at this time, Ms. Curci. Once again I thank you for your devotion and for many years of service to our hospital and patients."

Curci began to rise from her chair, but Hafner was quick.

"Mr. Gilliam, can we cross?"

Gilliam reluctantly had Ms. Curci sit back down.

"Dr. Hafner will now have the opportunity to briefly cross-examine the witness. Briefly."

Hafner stood up and spoke without the use of his notepad. "Mr. Gilliam, excuse me, I couldn't help but notice that Ms. Curci wasn't sworn in prior to giving her testimony. Are the witnesses sworn in to tell the truth as is done in court proceedings?"

Gilliam fetched the Bylaws and glanced at them, turning a few pages quickly, a superficial rather than studious review. "The bylaws are silent on this issue. Witnesses are not required to be sworn in. We presume honesty in these proceedings."

"Presume honesty. So are the witnesses obligated to tell the truth or not?" Looking at Nurse Curci, Hafner was quick to add, "Ms. Curci, I'm not insinuating anything about your testimony. This is the first time I've been involved in a judicial review and with Dr. Strader's career in jeopardy during this one, I'm just trying to make sure I know the rules. I'm sure you understand."

Gilliam was curt. "Asked and answered. Please proceed, Doctor." The last word was drawn out disparagingly.

Hafner took a moment to write a legal note on their common notepad. A single word. Asshole. He looked at it before deciding he got it right, then engaged Ms. Curci.

"Ms. Curci, we thank you for coming here. I'm sure it's not been easy for you to be asked questions about a doctor that you've worked with so closely in the ICU for over 20 years."

She offered only a confused look.

Hafner continued. "Do you find being here difficult?"

"Yes."

"I feel the same way. I'll try and be brief so that we can get you home. Ms. Curci, would you say that Dr. Strader can be stern and demanding at times when he has a critically ill patient in the ICU?"

"I guess so."

"Do you mean that you're not sure?"

"Um, no, I mean yes… Yes, he can be demanding."

"Can you describe to us what you mean by that?"

"By what?"

"Demanding. By being demanding."

"Um…I don't know." She remembered that Alyce had coached her to ask that a question be rephrased if she wasn't totally prepared to answer it. "Could you rephrase the question?"

Hafner scanned the juror panel before settling his gaze on the witness. He asked the court stenographer to read the conversation that mentioned demanding.

Dr. Hafner: "Ms. Curci, would you say that Dr. Strader can be stern and demanding at times when he has a critically ill patient in the ICU?"

Ms. Curci: "I guess so."

Dr. Hafner: "Do you mean that you're not sure?"

Ms. Curci: "Um, no, I mean yes… Yes, he can be demanding."

Dr. Hafner, "Can you describe to us what you mean by that?"

Ms. Curci: "By what?"

Dr. Hafner: "Demanding. By being demanding."

Ms. Curci: "Um…I don't know. Could you rephrase the question?"

Mr. Gilliam's hostility towards Hafner was becoming less occult. "Ms. Curci asked you if you could rephrase the question, not would you read back the testimony. Now, please, rephrase the question. It's been a long day for all of us."

Strader thought that was one for Gilliam's side, but Hafner was not deterred. Speaking to Dr. Robertson, Hafner said, "Well Randy, I'm not sure you're needed here. Mr. Gilliam seems to have you covered."

Robertson's expression combined squeamish with uneasiness to the point of being painful. He dove into his notes like a groundhog into its hole.

Hafner went on. "Ms. Curci, you agreed that the doctor could be demanding at times and I'm asking that you expand on that. Can you give us examples of Dr. Strader being demanding of you and how his behavior differed from the other doctors that you work with?"

She fumbled for an answer. "Right now…I can only think of the episode with the IV…there probably have been other times…I'm sorry."

"So let me make sure I have this right. As you sit before us tonight, the only example you are sure of is this recent episode where he scolded you about the IV. Is that correct?"

"Yeah, the only one I can think of now, yeah."

"Good. And Mr. Gilliam says that in all of the testimony we are given, we can presume honesty. So, I presume you are telling the truth."

"Yes, I am."

"Great. Just a couple of more questions, then. We'll make this very brief. Dr. Strader and I have reviewed the chart of the patient with the IV. The record shows that the IV had run out for three hours and a new one was only started after Dr. Strader made rounds and called it to your attention. Is that true?"

"Yes…but I was so busy that night…it was so hard to keep up."

"You know that I occasionally have patients in the ICU, and Dr. Rosero probably does as well. Dr. Meller and Dr. Kalim always see patients there, so we are sympathetic to the unreal demands of your job."

Ms. Curci's tired eyes and pallor were pleadings for mercy for ending it here.

Hafner pounced but gently. "And I'm sure that leaving IVs dry for three hours must be a rare occurrence. It is, isn't it?"

"Yes."

"Must be. I don't remember having a case like this and," looking at Karim and Meller, "I'm pretty sure you haven't either."

Both doctors shook their heads.

"So I'm not sure what the proper protocol is here. Dr. Strader has told me, and this has been confirmed, that he asked if you had relayed the difficulty you were having providing care to all your patients that night to anyone. He asked you that, seeing as you couldn't take care of his patient adequately, that is, you couldn't find time to replace an empty IV bag with a new one for three hours. What did you do? Did you let anyone know this so that the patient wouldn't be harmed? He asked if you contacted the Nursing Supervisor, the doctor himself, the family, or anyone else, and you said you didn't. Is that true"

Ms. Curci looked around for help at Dr. Robertson and Gilliam.

Robertson involved himself softly. "Dr. Hafner, aren't you being a little rough with her?" Strader could tell that Gilliam was thinking but didn't yet have an effective plan.

Hafner raised his eyebrows. "A bit rough? I'm just trying to clarify the facts and the process. I'm trying to find out what a nurse is supposed to do if the work is overwhelming and she, or he, falls behind. This issue happens to be important not only to Dr. Strader but to myself, the other doctors in this room, and on staff who place patients in the ICU because they need more nursing time and care, and most importantly, to all ICU patients and their families. So please, Nurse Curci, tell us what the protocol is for such a time?"

"I'm not sure. We all pitch in to help each other out to try and get everything done...That night things just got out of hand I guess..."

"Do you know what the Nursing Supervisor was doing that night?

"Uh, no."

"Was there a reason not to call her?"

"We try not to bother her. She covers the whole hospital and is always busy."

"Too busy to spend three minutes in the ICU and hang a bag of IV fluid?"

No answer.

Hafner asked, "Ms. Curci, in your opinion, was the danger to this patient of having a serious complication directly related to your failure to provide ongoing IV fluid as ordered for three hours or was it related to Dr. Strader bringing this failure to your attention, even if done strongly?"

No answer. Hafner looked at the juror panel.

"Well, we'll all have to draw our own conclusion on that...we're almost through here. Nurse Curci, you've been at The Palms Hospital for a long time. Have you ever been in a situation before when you failed to replace an empty IV bag for three hours?"

"Not that I remember, no." Not said with confidence.

"Then you have never previously been in this situation where an attending physician confronted you about such a failure?"

"No, I haven't."

"Then you have no first-hand knowledge of whether another physician faced with this same clinical circumstance would be more or less stern or demanding or confrontational than Dr. Strader was that night, do you?"

So anxious to be done, she quickly replied, "No, I don't."

"One final thing. As a result of this incident, it's my understanding that a conversation was held between the Chief of Nursing, Ms. Porter, and Dr. Strader and that a memo was provided to the entire ICU staff that the Nursing Supervisor was to be called immediately if there is a crisis in staffing that would adversely affect patient care and that it would be the Supervisor's responsibility to make sure that adequate staffing is always present in the Unit. Is that true?"

"Yes."

"So something good came out of this incident, after all. Something that helps you and the nursing staff and protects patients, allowing them to receive the level of care their illness require for high quality treatment. I'm glad that Dr. Strader spoke up for you and his and all ICU patients and that Ms. Porter clarified the process going forward. I thank you for coming here tonight and speaking with us." To Gilliam, "I have no further questions."

Gilliam stood up. "Dr. Robertson, anything on re-direct?"

Robertson shook his head.

Gilliam said, "Ms. Curci, I'm going to ask you to wait for another ten minutes. We'll take a five minute recess—no, make that fifteen, and if Dr. Robertson has nothing further to ask, you will be dismissed. Let's take fifteen." He jerked his head slightly and Robertson followed him out. The juror panel predictably got up and stretched. Even more predictably, Rosero buzzed around the sultry Dr. Kalim.

Strader waited till Robertson and Gilliam left before exhaling and turning to Hafner.

"You did great for a first timer. I thought you were nuts the way you went after Gilliam, but you did great with Curci."

"Good, not great. But Robertson is trying so hard not to be the bad guy that I think it's hurting them. That's why Gilliam called the break, to read Randy the riot act or give him a pep talk. The Filipino nurse is most likely next. They'll leave Gil Morgan till last, I would think.

"Dylan, I think they're going to come back with a bit more for Curci, trying to at least get something."

"For sure. What do you think they'll ask her?"

"I don't know. But something…maybe about the future, about being nervous taking care of my cases, being afraid of me…something like that."

"Agreed. I can deal with that. If she has a problem, they can assign your patient to another nurse, but you have no hard feelings and you're sorry if she felt offended in any way that night. Hopefully, the whole process of care will be improved so that problems like that won't recur. I'm not worried."

A few minutes later they reconvened. Strader saw Robertson and Gilliam come in separately. Yeah. Gilliam called to be back on the record.

Gilliam asked Robertson, "Dr. Robertson, any questions for Ms. Curci on re-direct, or shall we dismiss her?"

"Just one more question, if it's all right with Ms. Curci."

Gilliam said, "Fire away."

"Ms. Curci, one final thing. After Dr. Strader yelled at you and embarrassed you in front of your colleagues, do you think that you and perhaps some of the other nurses may be reluctant, maybe even afraid to be assigned his patients, and that this could be extremely disruptive to administering care in the ICU?"

Ms. Curci hadn't been coached for this question and took her time. Strader could see her mouth silently wording different responses.

"Ms. Curci?" Robertson asked gently.

"Maybe…yes, I think it would at least be awkward."

"Thanks. No further questions."

Hafner sprang up.

"Mr. Gilliam, I have one more question."

Dismissively, Gilliam snarled, "You had ample opportunity. Ms. Curci, you may step down. You're free to leave. And thank you for your time."

"But…"

First smile of the night by Gilliam. "Dr. Robertson, you may call your next witness."

Dr. Meller raised his hand and when it went unnoticed, he called out. "Mr. Gilliam, can I ask a question?"

Gilliam told the stenographer to go off the record. To Meller, "Sure."

"Can you tell us why you wouldn't allow more questioning?"

"Sure can. An efficient proceeding typically runs with direct, cross and re-direct. Everyone gets one shot at the pie, and one shot is allowed to respond to the cross examination. Otherwise, we could go on forever, each side asking more questions in response to the others. I recognize that we all have full-time day jobs, this is an evening proceeding, so we limit ourselves to direct, cross and re-direct. In the interest of efficiency and fair play. Question answered?"

Dr. Meller seemed satisfied. "Thanks."

Gilliam said, "Let's take a quick five minute break but stay in the room until we get the next witness in."

CHAPTER TWENTY-THREE

Precisely five minutes later, the door magically opened, and a petite, thirty-ish woman appeared just as Dr. Robertson summoned her, witness Imelda Kalaw. Dressed in a white summer dress, she strode briskly to her witness chair. Dr. Strader thought from her entrance that she had been well coached.

Gilliam was the first to greet her, his smile reminding Strader of a jack-o-lantern on a Halloween night.

"Good evening, Ms. Kalaw. Am I pronouncing it right?"

"Yes you can," bubbled the witness. Hafner and Strader exchanged a telepathic "we're going to have fun with this one" message. He saw a Kalim smile followed by a Rosero smirk.

Gilliam tried his best to lay some groundwork. "Yes we can. Dr. Robertson?"

A despondent Robertson seemed a full two inches shorter as he stood to address his language challenged nurse. He was praying that she had memorized the answers to these questions.

"Ah. Ms. Kalaw, thank you for coming this evening. The hospital has asked us to look into certain things that have happened that could be harmful to the hospital and that involve Dr. Strader, who is seated at the end of the table."

Ms. Kalaw waved and smiled at Dr. Strader, who smiled back. "Oh, I know him, Doctor Strader. Hello."

Strader offered a bemused hello in response. He couldn't predict what was going to happen here; was Robertson making his case for him?

Robertson went on. "Ms. Kalaw, I understand that you've been a nurse for seven years, and you've worked at The Palms Hospital for the last five years. Is that right?"

"Yes, five years."

"And you work the night shift, from seven o'clock at night to seven o'clock in the morning? Is that right?"

"Yes. My husband and the children. So nights, yes." It took barely one second to get that out, a Gatling gun.

Robertson spoke slowly, as if that would make the conversation more intelligible, like speaking loud to a deaf person. "We all appreciate the sacrifices you make to work and yet fill all of your family obligations. It's a unique challenge you have, moving to this country, learning English and using it extensively at work. Ms. Kalaw, have you had problems at work because of your nationality? Because you're Filipino?"

This is so awkward, thought Strader. Why doesn't he ask her if she's been called a Flip and how she likes that? Hafner really has been all over this complaint and felt good about handling it, so Strader was more relaxed than when Curci was testifying.

The tiny nurse slung her answers in rapid, high pitch, run-together sentences that apparently couldn't be cured with any pre-trial language courses, job security threats or other reprisals. "I Filipino and many nurses also Filipino where work. Everyone nice. Sometimes no understand so take more time." She seemed so happy with her job, her life, even her testimony. "So no, all is good."

"I'm glad to hear that. The reason you've been asked to speak here is to explain an episode where apparently Dr. Strader made fun of you and got mad at you because of your accent when he called your floor. Apparently one of the nurses called him about one of his patients and he returned the call but got angry and made fun of you. Do you remember?"

"Oh yes. What a time. I remember."

Patiently, "Can you tell us about it? Better yet, I'll ask you and you can answer. OK."

"Okay. You say."

"On that night, did one of Dr. Strader's patients get very sick?"

"Very sick. Yes."

"And were you the one who called him?"

"Yes, very sick. I called. Late, very late."

"And you spoke with him? Yes?"

"Yes."

"Do you remember what you said, no, uh- what did you say to Dr. Strader?"

"I said, Dr. Strader, come quick, patient very sick."

"And what did he say?"

"Not sure. He asked lots of questions."

"What questions do you remember?"

"He asked if patient was his patient. He asked what is problem with patient. I'm not doctor, that's why I call him."

"So what did you tell him?"

"Again, patient very sick. Come quick."

"And then what did he tell you?"

"He told me get someone who speak English or get Nursing Supervisor."

"And how did that make you feel?"

"I feel bad. Very bad. I just do my job—patient sick I call doctor. My English not too good but okay. You understand, right?" Like now she's remembering her lines, thought Strader.

"Yes, I think we all understand you very well. And we're sorry that this happened to you. One more question. When someone makes fun of your accent, like Dr. Strader did, and it makes you feel bad, like you said, can this be a problem in the future?"

On cue, "Yes. I afraid to call Dr. Strader for problem. All Filipino nurses afraid. We no call. Call somebody else." She was no longer smiling at Strader.

Robertson was warming up to inserting the final nail. "And could this fear of calling Dr. Strader be disruptive, and interfere with your patients getting proper care?"

Bingo. "Yes, for sure."

A triumphant Robertson finished. "I have no further questions. Thank you Ms. Kalaw, for your honesty and your help. And we all understand."

Hafner pounced from his seat as soon as Gilliam gave him permission to cross-examine.

"Good evening, Ms. Kalaw. Thanks for coming. You work on the surgery floor, don't you?"

"Yes."

"So, unless the hospital is full and there is an overflow of medical admissions, all of your patients are surgical, right?"

"They have operations. Right."

"Very good. And you know Dr. Strader is a medical doctor, not a surgeon, right?"

"If you say so…"

"No, it's not what I say. I'm asking you if you know or knew that Dr. Strader was a medical doctor and not a surgeon?"

"I no understand."

"On that night that you said Dr. Strader made fun of your language—you remember that night—about three weeks ago?"

"Yes, I remember."

"Do you remember the patient that was so sick?"

"Oh yes. I remember. He so very sick."

"What was his name?"

She was searching but nothing came out.

"Ms. Kalaw, do you remember his name, or what it sounded like?"

"Not so good with names. But I know he very sick."

"So when Dr. Strader answered your call, and from the record it looks like you called at one A.M. and he called back in two minutes, and when he asked you which patient it was that you were talking about, did you answer that he should come quick, patient very sick?"

She smiled. "Yes. Come very very quick."

"But you didn't tell him which patient, I see. And when he asked you what was the matter with the patient, how was he sick, what were his vital signs, had he had surgery, did you respond that he should just come quick because the patient was so sick?"

"Yes, he very sick. I worry."

"We all appreciate your concern. And then, when Dr. Strader asked that you get him someone who spoke English or the Nursing Supervisor, what did you do?"

"I ask Mely to talk to doctor. She English very good. And she talk with Doctor Strader."

"And when Dr. Strader made you get someone else, did this upset you?"

"Sure. My patient and I worry. I want Doctor come right away. He waste time."

"And what happened to your patient?"

"Other doctor come. He fix problem. But Dr. Strader no come."

"And what was the problem, Ms. Kalaw?"

"I upset. No remember. Sorry."

Hafner smiled at her. "It was a good thing that you saw that your patient was not doing well. The record showed that the patient had a prostate operation and his Foley catheter had gotten plugged with blood clots. Dr. Strader once had done a colonoscopy on this patient but was not involved in his hospital care during this admission. After you noted your patient wasn't well, Mely spoke with Dr. Strader, and the patient's urologist was called. The Foley catheter could not be irrigated and since the patient was recently post-op, the urologist came in and replaced the Foley himself. And the patient did well. Thanks to you, Ms. Kalaw—and thanks to Mely and Dr. Strader—and of course thanks to the urologist for coming in the middle of the night. Now is there any way that you think

Dr. Strader should have come in instead of the urologist?

"He could come and then other doctor."

"Wouldn't this delay things?"

"Not sure."

"Just one more thing, Ms. Kalaw. Do you and all of the foreign speaking nurses have to take any language course or take any English test before you start work at the hospital?"

"Yes, we all pass."

"That's great. Thank you, Ms. Kalaw; no more questions."

Gilliam promptly put it back on Robertson. "Dr. Robertson, you can re-direct now."

Robertson fumbled at his notes, choked back a mumble, and replied, "Nothing on re-direct."

Gilliam wasn't pleased. "Nothing? Uh—let's take a fifteen-minute break. I'm sure the juror panel could use one. I'll ask the witness to stay until we come back. All right, we'll reconvene at 7:40."

Hafner dashed out to the hall in time to see Alyce Wagner lead Gilliam and Dr. Robertson into a side room, Gilliam already expressing his disappointment. And Robertson was answering back, but Hafner was too far away to hear clearly. Strader caught up with Hafner in time to see a smiling Dr. Meller and an apparent sympathetic Dr. Kalim glide past them to the lounge, the hunter Rosero on their heels.

Strader said softly, even though they were now alone in the corridor, "You're doing great, Dylan."

"I didn't give away the farm, anyway. I don't think we lost Meller or Kalim so far, but the only thing impressing Rosero so far seems to be Kalim's legs."

"Good taste."

"If only you or I had big tits, this trial would be over."

Strader stuck his chest out as far as he could. "This won't do it, right?"

"Right."

Ten minutes later, all had reconvened. Robertson did not re-direct. The irked Gilliam grimly announced to the juror panel that the session was over.

"Next week we'll begin with Dr. Robertson's last witness, Gil Morgan, and we'll move to Dr. Strader's witnesses and hopefully finish them." Gazing at Hafner, he continued, "I anticipate next week that there will be no hang-ups and things will run smoother and more efficiently so that we can finish at a reasonable time. We're adjourned for tonight."

Day one of the judicial review was over.

135

CHAPTER TWENTY-FOUR

The juror panel had quickly and quietly vanished after whispered good-nights. Strader and Hafner, in better spirits, agreed to take Thursday off and disappeared in their cars. Seeing the coast clear, Appel had Alyce reconvene in the conference room with a deflated Gilliam and an ambivalent Robertson.

Appel began the interrogation. "Well, how did it go in there?"

Gilliam glanced at Robertson, knowing the first move was his own.

"Overall, I'd say it went all right."

Appel's gaze flashed to Robertson, "You agree?"

Robertson cleared his throat, tapped his legs, finally getting out, "Not great, but I think we stuck to the script."

Appel to Alyce, "Alyce?"

Robertson looked confused. Alyce hadn't even been there…unless.

Alyce caught his expression and chimed in. "Yes, doctor, we're able to listen to and view the proceedings. I'd say that Hafner scored some points, and our witnesses weren't extraordinarily impressive." Turning toward Gilliam, she continued, "I'm not sure what he has against you, Greg."

Gilliam's jaw tightened and he thrust his shoulders back. "He did challenge me on several issues, including my impartiality, and I had to respond forcibly."

"I'm not sure what his strategy is other than to try and make Strader the underdog," said Alyce. "I think he's trying to go after the three who see patients, Meller, Karim and Rosero."

"I can see that," said Gilliam.

Appel listened and nodded. "Very astute, Alyce. Watching Strader when Hafner went after Greg—he seemed surprised, and then he jotted a note to Hafner. Hafner knows which three votes to shoot for. From watching their body language, I think Meller is sympathetic, Kalim I can't read, and Rosero—he should be ours but who knows? Next week we'll present Gil Morgan, our strongest witness, and we'll be ready to deal with their defense witnesses. We'll be prepared, improved, and we'll perform."

To Robertson, he added, "Randy, you got more comfortable as you went along tonight, and I'm sure you'll be more relaxed next week. We'll create a great script, and you'll get it out there just fine. It's late — take off and get some rest. We'll meet with you Monday."

Robertson jetted out the door, closing it behind him like leaving a bad dream.

The ensuing quiet was Gilliam's calling to bid adieu as well.

And then it was two. Appel motioned for Alyce to clear her mind. He thought she seemed a bit squeamish when he mentioned their ace witness, Gil Morgan. Maybe not.

Alyce unleashed three sheets of notes, with copies for Appel. She glanced over the first page and addressed her boss.

"I don't think we scored with anything tonight. Their play is pretty obvious—Strader was doing what he had to do to make things better. The fact that he was abusive and insensitive doesn't count. Hafner is clearly separating Meller, Kalim and Rosero from the other two. Meller, I think we'll lose. We should own Rosero, given his Employee Health contract. I'd like to think we have Kalim, but I'm not sure. We need a strong finish next week with Morgan, and a good rebuttal to their witnesses. So far, it's just the nurse from the ER and Strader himself. They have the old doctor, Morales and Chief of Nursing Porter on the list…"

"She's not going to appear. We'll get to work on Angie, whatever her name is from the ER. I know what Strader is going to say—he's God's gift to patient advocacy. He does everything for his patients, and how dare we accuse him of anything bad. I've dealt with his never-changing shit over the years, including that time when he made me look bad for pushing staff loyalty to the hospital, which he said infringed on their constitutional rights. He even got the medical staff to push through an amendment to protect them in case they said something against the hospital. Most hospitals have a non-disparagement clause in the Medical Staff Bylaws; we have a physician bill of rights. What bullshit." Their history was riling Appel. His pupils were Grand Canyon-wide in the narrowed slots that housed them. Scary. His scalp and forehead gleamed with viscous sweat droplets. He was loud, almost bellicose like he was yelling at a crowd 100 feet behind Alyce. "Well, his time has come. He's going to be judged strictly on what he did, not why he did it. You don't talk down a tired nurse and you don't make fun of an immigrant. And you don't curse at a nurse in the middle of the night when you're trying to save a young man. Never. Case closed." He was breathing deep and rapidly, his chest a big accordion.

Alyce remained mechanically calm. "I'm working on it. I'll work on the nurse and Strader all week, and make sure Morgan is prepped for next Wednesday. I'll probably be out of the office most of tomorrow and maybe Friday, so text me if you need me. Will I see you here on Saturday morning? Usual time?"

He nodded. They were both spent and left without goodbyes.

CHAPTER TWENTY-FIVE

Hafner blew home, threw on wraparound shades, his "Joey" broad-rimmed cap, and zoomed to the casino. Exhilarated by the evening's events, he smiled broadly as he recalled his interactions with Gilliam and the witnesses. If the outcome was fixed against Strader, at least he'd make it close–no, he'd find a way—he'd get the three votes. But now for some fun, try his luck against the house or in a live poker game. Maybe he'd find Holiday Grove.

Hafner scanned the flashing, pinging machines, penny slots brighter, louder and more obnoxious than their dollar counterparts. A crowd of drunken automatons. Approaching the VIP bar, he was surprised to feel his heart drop as he saw Holiday, in a light blue sundress and sandals, chatting it up with a grey fox of about fifty who wore more bling than the adjacent slots. Hafner slithered away to the poker room minus a bit of verve. Only one table was active, a no limit game with multiple buy-ins. He hated this poker variant since it removed much of the skill from the game itself. If someone went all-in, bet all of their chips, and lost, they simply could buy more chips and stay in the game. It favored aggressive betting and the player with the largest bankroll. Joey said hello to the few players he knew, about faced and headed out. As he walked toward the Hi-Limit room, a soft hand grabbed his shoulder from behind and he spun around. Holiday Grove.

"Joey, you weren't planning to leave without saying hello, were you?"

"You were busy."

"I knew you saw me. I was hoping you would come and save me, pick me up and carry me off, like Superman or one of those Marvel guys."

"You did not seem to be a damsel in distress…quite comfortable, actually."

"Not inside, I wasn't—trust me."

"Well, here we are."

"Yeah, us and about a thousand losers. Sometimes…"

He broke in, "Listen, you want to do something?"

****

Twenty minutes later, he waited downstairs outside her modest two-floor apartment building while she changed into motorcycle attire. She popped out the front door like a bubbling teenager in faded jeans and a long-sleeved top, hanging on to a deep blue bag. She mounted the bike behind him, snuggled into her helmet, held on and they were off. As they sped up his favorite Hwy 74, he was immersed in her touch, her smell, her arms around his waist and her chest against his back. Every curve in the road became a sensual tryst. He drove slightly slower than usual to accommodate the distraction and prolong each subtle caress.

Near the top, he asked, "You okay?"

She heard him clearly through the helmet's bluetooth mike. "I'm fine, but can you pull over up ahead, just for a minute?"

He couldn't believe she had to pee already, but he pulled over to a thin shoulder on the naked side of the road. She jumped off and yanked free from her helmet. He watched her blonde hair flow down the side of her face, like the very edge of a waterfall against a smooth rock. He removed his helmet as she approached.

She gave him no time to get off the bike but leaned forward and nestled her soft, parted lips against his. One long kiss, God's honey, the sole connection between their bodies. So soft and yet intense. Something to hold onto. Then Holiday laughed playfully, put back her helmet, and jumped back on the bike.

For the next hour, they traversed the road's windings in the darkening night, conversing in what felt like a protective space, their own confessional booth.

"Joey, this is so beautiful. I'm glad you fell in love with me," she teased. She had the privilege and she knew it.

"If I recall, you were the one who latched on to me—on a slow night." He regretted the way that came out. "I meant on a slow gambling night for me."

"Things are not always what they seem." She squeezed him tightly. "Maybe you know what I'm talking about."

"Listen, it's your business. You don't owe me any explanations. We all have our secrets." Awkward, followed by silence. He wasn't sure what he really wanted to know about her.

Two tight curves up the hill, she said, "I'll tell you mine if you tell me yours."

He hesitated before taking the plunge. "I'm sure yours is more interesting, so why don't you start."

"Not that interesting. A poor woman trying to pay her bills."

"Yeah, and I'm an inveterate gambler trying to win the big one."

Telling her story through the confessional helmet made it easier.

"I've been back in Palm Springs for a year. Came home to take care of my dad."

Hafner said, "What's the matter with your dad?"

"I'll get to that. I moved to the east coast for college—UPenn. Graduated and started Holiday Designs, an interior design company to enhance festive times. It was starting to do really well."

"No marriage, no kids...?"

"Dated a bit, no one serious. Spent most of my time building my business."

"And...?"

Her voice was a choked-up whisper. "Just about a year ago—a Friday night—I was looking at July 4th stuff when my dad called, crying. My dad—you should have known him, a big, happy guy—crying." Her soft voice trailed off. "He said he left his car running overnight in the garage; nothing like that had ever happened before. Then it was a flood—he got lost coming home from the bank; he recognized his friends but not their names; bills somehow got lost. Fifty-eight years old, an accountant..."

He felt her shudder.

"His doctor said he had rapidly progressive pre-senile dementia—he might last two years. Dad was embarrassed, afraid and alone. So I left everything and went home. He called me baby—couldn't remember my name. Dementia was not only destroying his brain but his posture, his vitality, his self-respect, his very humanity."

"You're taking care of him at home?"

"I tried for a while, but he had these mental swings, refused to let me do stuff that needed to be done. He had to be watched every minute. His friends came by to help out, but it was overwhelming and became unsafe. I thought about taking him back east, but he'd lose his friends and be truly alone, and it would cost almost fifteen grand a month. So I put him in an assisted home for memory patients in Palm Springs."

"You did the right thing."

"I know, but it wiped me out financially. Eight grand a month, plus all the medical bills."

She became quiet, not wanting to talk about her escort job. The truth was that she had to pay the bills. She steered herself towards elderly rich gentlemen who wanted to be seen with a young beauty rather than sweat and have chest pain-inducing sex. She was beautiful and charming, and they were generous. A temporary fix till she could get her design business up and running in Palm Springs.

She held Joey tight, thinking of her dad as they sped over the now flat stretch of dark road.

He said, "Hey, you still on back there?"

She pinched him softly just above the belt line then gently rubbed it out.

He didn't object. "I'm hungry. Do you want to stop at a café up here, or do you want to head down toward San Diego?"

"San Diego? That's like two hours. We wouldn't get back till four in the morning. But hey, you're screwing this cat. I'm just holding its tail."

He pondered that for a minute, a weird visual. "You have a unique way of expressing yourself at times, but—I don't know whether I'm screwing this cat up here or down in San Diego. What's your schedule? I don't have any…anything scheduled for tomorrow except for a short teaching gig." He almost said, 'making rounds with the house staff' but caught himself in time. So what, he thought.

"I just have to see my dad sometime tomorrow."

"I'd like to meet him if he's doing okay—I mean, if it's okay with you?" Joey's ears reddened at his own words.

"He has good days and bad. Sometimes I'm Holiday, sometimes June, my mom. Sometimes I'm even Cassie, his nurse. His black nurse. Dad never was prejudiced. "

After a moment she continued.

"They've had him on two drugs, Aricept and memantine, but they haven't helped."

She nestled her head against his back and held on a little tighter. Her voice became a whisper.

"And I see him every day, tell him I love him and I'm there for him—and sometimes he looks but doesn't even see it's me. Sorry, I don't know how we got into this—hopefully you'll never have to deal with stuff like this."

"Holiday," words burst from his mouth, "I'm not just a gambler on a motorcycle."

She leaned back a bit. "You're married. I knew it."

"No, and never have been. I'm…not Joey…I mean that's not who I am. I mean…he's more of a disguised me. In my day job, I'm a doctor. An internist. My real name is Dylan Joseph Hafner. I specialize in geriatrics—I care for many people—like your dad."

"So, who is this guy Joey that I have my arms wrapped around right now going seventy miles an hour?"

"I don't really know. Maybe it's all a guilt thing where I get rid of the money I take from sick people, that is, if I actually got rid of the money. Listen, I love numbers, so I gamble. And I'm good at it. I only go at night when I'm not on call. It's not an image I want to send out to my patients and even my colleagues, so I do the Joey bit. I'm not a gambling addict or anything…I choose my spots…I actually make money gambling."

Holiday laughed out loud. "Wow, a doctor who can take care of my dad and make money gambling. I've hit the jackpot." She snuggled him more fiercely than before.

He joined in the laughter. "Past performance does not necessarily predict future performance. Standard disclaimer."

****

Two hours later, they were nestled in a small booth at an IHOP on Sports Arena Blvd. in San Diego, munching their way through a dangerously large stack of buttermilk pancakes nearly obscured by mounds of whipped butter and maple syrup.

"I think I'll still call you Joey," Holiday said. "Dylan kind of reminds me of a cross between that old Gunsmoke Marshall and a folk rock singer—I see a musician strumming on a six-gun. Sorry."

"I'll have you know that Dylan is the twenty-ninth most popular name for boys and is even in the top four hundred for girls." Joey smiled. "Well, it's actually a Welsh name and means 'son of the sea.' And here we are in San Diego, so I'm right at home. Maybe that's why I love this area so much. Sometimes I'll ride over near Sunset Cliffs, listen to the ocean, and watch the pelicans dive for food. I teach at the medical school here once a week—sometimes I spend the night in Ocean Beach. I'm supposed to make teaching rounds at the hospital at ten o'clock this morning. Medical students and interns." He stopped to devour a forkful of pancakes. "But you should talk about names. I mean Holiday—Holiday Grove."

Holiday placed her fork on her plate, signaling she was done. "Like I told you before—a Christmas— present." She watched him load another mouthful and they both smiled. *Without shades and a baseball cap, he was a clean-cut guy.* He wasn't much taller than her but she liked his wide shoulders and tight butt. He looked like a California beach guy without the tan or tattoos. But it was his demeanor, his easy confidence without being an asshole, that most attracted her. She liked this guy, at least so far, but she'd been down this road before. She fumbled a bit as their eyes stayed locked.

"Joey, I know what you think. I mean about what I do, and I want to set the record straight…"

"Hey, I'm not the law—you don't need to explain anything to me. I enjoy being with you. And hey, you're not too bad to look at either. To me, we're good. Okay?"

She said, "It's not okay. I'm not—a hooker. I keep these old guys company, make them feel still meaningful, and they help me pay for my dad's care until I can get my design business going. What I do is temporary, and it's not bad…" Her voice trailed off.

He said, "Holiday, really, I'm okay. Okay?"

Their eyes locked until she finally looked down at his plate. She hesitated, gently bit her lip and inhaled her thoughts. Neck bowed, hands clasped in front of her as if she was in prayer; her quiet was startling. Joey uncomfortably turned his fork back and forth as if he was turning his motorcycle on and off.

After what seemed far too long, she looked up and responded with a slight nod and soft smile. "We're okay. Now finish your pancakes and let's get out of here. Let's find us a beach." Now wasn't the time for more revelations.

He wolfed down what he could, paid the bill and they were off.

CHAPTER TWENTY-SIX

Wednesday was game-planning night at Alyce Wagner's one bedroom condo on the south end of town. She was concerned about round one of the Strader trial; Hafner had the upper hand against Robertson, and Gilliam's attempts to control the proceedings had been ineffectual. Still, as Appel continually pointed out, they should have four of the five votes; losing Dr. Meller was irrelevant. Karim and/or Rosero had to tow the hospital line. Comfortable in her long-sleeve pajamas, Alyce pulled up her calendar on her cellphone. Thursday was open—she'd stake out Strader's place; Friday was the fourth—the fireworks show. She'd have to spend time with Gil Morgan early in the week. He was the hospital's final witness and she felt that he knew the score; she'd cleaned things up for him after the Florita Dominguez fiasco—Dr. Ahmad didn't know anything, and Strader had been upset with her death but couldn't have evidence of wrongdoing. Gil would be fine, thanks to her. She'd work on getting more info on Strader's likely witnesses for next week's session two, Angie the ER nurse and old Dr. Morales. Appel had assured her Nurse Porter would not be called. She jotted the names down on her Visio flow diagram and connected them with small arrows, all leading to Strader. She peered studiously for a minute, lifted a glass of white wine, and smiled. The late-night local news was on, and she never missed it.

****

Appel was numbing the evening's pain with his third medicinal scotch when his iPhone Night Owl ringtone caused him to juggle his glass. His boss was the only one to invade his evenings, and 10:30 was actually an earlier than usual assault.

"I'm not really happy with our performance," said the CEO. "I just finished with the tape. I've been mulling it over—you know our asses are on the line here."

"I'm well aware of that and…"

"Aware of it? You're aware of it? Let me clue you in Rog. Docs in the hallways are stopping me and complaining about this, uh, judicial review. Since you had that reporter write about Strader in the Daily Son, letters to the editor and comments on their website favor the doc about eight to one. And tonight, I think we got a beat-down by what's his name, Traynor?"

"Hafner."

"Hafner. If I have to tell the Board of Directors that this judicial review came out in support of Strader after I went out on a limb to tell them what awful things he has done, I might as well apply to be a greeter at Walmart."

"Listen, I know that we didn't do well tonight, but we have the votes. We have the votes. We can't and we won't lose this thing."

"So you say. But I want the case to be made anyway. I want those docs to leave that trial thinking that they did the right thing. I want Strader to look like the total asshole we're saying that he is. I want him destroyed and out of our hair. And I shouldn't have to say, 'or else.'"

"Understood."

"Let's continue this conversation Tuesday morning at eight, my office." Click.

Appel pocketed his cellphone, swirled the two remaining ice cubes in his drink and downed it. A hundred thoughts collided in his brain with concussive force. He wrung his hands then hesitantly picked up his phone and speed-dialed Alyce Wagner.

****

Strader reclined in his brown leather La-Z-Boy, checked his messages and turned on the TV. He'd return Stella's call in the morning since it was already 1:00 AM back in Philly. Tomas positioned himself to afford maximal petting, metronoming his tail against Strader's thigh, and went to sleep. Strader flicked through his On Demand list, but all the baseball games were over and he couldn't handle a repetitive SportsCenter. His eyes scanned the photos above the TV—their wedding picture, the family skiing in Steamboat when the kids were small, he and Rosemary salmon-fishing in the Kenai in Alaska. He scratched Tomas's head, eliciting a purr.

He looked down at Tomas, and gently massaged his front paw, noticed his approving slight blinking. "I guess we need to get your picture up there too."

CHAPTER TWENTY-SEVEN

Frank Vialotti knew what he was up against when he called Strader's office on Thursday morning, July 3rd; he had some tricks, to be sure, but no one had The Answer.

"Dr. Strader's exchange. May I help you?"

"Yes, hi, this is Frank Vialotti. Dr. Strader has taken care of my wife. I need to speak with the doctor."

"What problem is your wife having, Mr. Vialotti?"

"This isn't about my wife, uh-it's about me."

"Is this an emergency?"

"Not a medical emergency, but it's imperative that I speak with him."

"I'm sorry, but he's not on call this weekend, and he's not admitting patients to the hospital right now. Would you like to speak with the doctor who's covering?"

"No, I need to speak with Dr. Strader." A little too much edge to the voice there. No response. He tried again. "Listen, I know that the doctor would really want to speak with me. Could I hold on and have you just try him? Let him know Frank Vialotti needs to speak with him?"

"I'm sorry. If you want, I can leave a message with the office on Monday."

"Okay. Frank Vialotti –760-323-2222. Tell Dr. Strader that it's about Florita; that's F-L-O-R-I-T-A. He'll understand."

"760-323-2222. I'll leave that message for the office. Is there anything else I could help you with?"

"No, you've been a doll." He'd wait until Monday, but if Strader picked up his message Vialotti was pretty sure it would be sooner, July 4th notwithstanding.

Vialotti thought of hitting the office early. He didn't remember whether his secretary was making it a four-day weekend or not. After so many years working with her, he had long since relinquished all things non-legal to her, from work schedules to paying the bills, salary and benefit upgrades, and equipment. He needed access to LexisNexis and to his old school law books, and that was about it. And he needed Bea. It was a little before nine; if this was a working day, Bea would be in. He walked briskly, trying to create a breeze to evaporate the sweat already on his brow and neck. After his wife died, Vialotti downsized to a small one-bedroom apartment in Palm Springs just off Miraleste, in a dark cluster of small apartments that even the Jehovah's Witnesses avoided. The office was only five blocks from home, but Frank detoured to Palm Canyon for coffee and a bagel— not like when Vivian would ply him with bacon and eggs and two slices of home-baked banana bread before sending him off to work. Passing Doc Strader's office building, Frank's path veered and he climbed the steps to the doctor's second story office. Maybe someone would be there, perhaps the doc would be in. Through the wooden shutters, artificial light peeked out. The door was open.

Tiny was filing charts in the business office when Vialotti walked in. She recognized him and dashed around to the waiting room to give him a hug.

"Mr. Vialotti, so nice to see you. How are you? How are you doing?"

Suddenly flooded with horrible images of his wife being devoured, chewed up, disintegrated by millions of large-mouthed cancer cells, Vi-alotti cringed. Coming here was a mistake. Vivian always sat on the far corner of the waiting room bench, leaving as much room as she could for others. Dignity was all that was still intact. He remembered how wonder-fully the office treated his wife—Kayesha would see her, buzz Tiny, who would lead her inside, help her on the examining table, and wait with her until the doctor came in. Give her time to make up lies about how well she was doing, had no pain, and how she was looking forward to Christmas with Frank and the kids. And she'd leave the office smiling as if she won a Go to Heaven free card: do not have pain, do not have suffering. And her reply to Frank's grilling was always the same, "Oh Frank, you worry too much. I'm in such good hands." He shuddered in Tiny's embrace, then stepped back.

"I'm alright. Staying busy—and that's why I need to see Doc Strader." His voice, far from commanding, was apologetic.

Tiny hardened just a bit. "I'll need a little more than that. How can Doctor Strader help you?"

"I'd rather talk to him."

"I need to tell him something. He's under a lot of stress right now—I don't know if you've heard what's going on in the hospital."

"I've heard. That's why I need to talk to him."

152

Tiny knew she wasn't going to get much more from him, this defiantly subdued lawyer. She remembered how Vivian would always send Frank on his way when they took her into the examining room and how relieved he was to leave. What did Vivian use to say? 'Frank, we'll call you to pick me up when I'm through. Go back to the office. Bad enough, I have one guy giving me the third degree; I surely don't need two.'

"I'll let him know, Mr. Vialotti. And either he or I will get back to you, but it might not be until Monday—the holiday, you know."

Before Vialotti could leave, from the back came a voice, "Frank, Frank Vialotti, how are you?" Two seconds later he found himself shaking hands with a weary but warm Doc Strader.

Strader continued. "What's it been, six years?"

Vialotti nodded sadly. "Six years next week."

"Vivian was a great woman, Frank. I don't remember a braver person, a better fighter. She must have loved you a lot, not wanting to leave you." A sympathetic smile.

"Yeah, Doc, they say love is blind; was sure that way with us. Anyway, that's not why I'm here."

Strader looked at him quizzically for a few seconds, then it clicked. He gave Frank a long man hug. "Oh my Lord. You heard me at the meeting and you've been reading all this junk in the paper about my fight with the hospital. You're here to see if I need any legal advice, aren't you?"

Vialotti stood dumbfounded.

"Well, I really appreciate the offer, but right now it's just a judicial re-view—no lawyers, and my daughter, Stella, I don't know if you remember that she's a lawyer, I've been bouncing things off her. Depending on how things turn out, I might need you if this results in a civil suit. It's basically a railroad job at this point—they want me to shut up and do what they think my job is. And I don't know about you, but I guess since my Rosemary passed away, I'm probably less tolerant with others than I used to be."

Vialotti looked at the floor, his cuffed pants hanging too far down over his shoes, at least according to Bea. He collected his thoughts. Not a good time for confrontation, but he was here. He did have a client to represent, he had a forty-five-year-old woman who was dead.

"Doc, that's not really why I came," Vialotti stammered, his voice two decibels more than a whisper. "I came to ask you about a case that I have about Florita Dominguez."

Strader recoiled. He searched the lawyer's face. "You know I can't talk about a patient with you. HIPAA and all that. Besides, I hardly even knew her."

They quietly sized each other up. Silence ensued. Vialotti knew what was next. Just wait him out.

Strader broke. "Well, what about her anyway?"

"I'm representing her family in a wrongful death case. You know, she came into the hospital and died." He noted pain, maybe anger creeping from Strader's eyes. He waited.

"And?"

"I had the case reviewed and the experts found nothing done wrong, nothing unusual. Nothing. But you know, I thought you could help."

"Help?" Now Strader waited.

"Doc, listen, you know I respect you. You were great with my wife. I'm not trying to come after you."

"But?"

"But I have a forty-five-year-old woman who came into the hospital and died the same day. You took care of her."

"She was very sick, Frank. If you looked at her records, you must know that."

"No doubt. But you know I was at the meeting where you mentioned a murder—and I kind of put two and two together." Waiting. Waiting. Vialotti watched Strader rub his hands together vigorously as if gloveless outdoors on a frigid night. He sensed the Doc wanted to say something, wanted to open up, like when he gave Frank the bad news about Vivian. He waited.

Finally, Strader advanced his hand to shake Vialotti's.

"Sorry, Frank. I wish I could help you. But I can't."

What Vialotti heard was not a denial but almost an admission. Something was there, something real, something bad.

"HIPAA is HIPAA," Strader said.

****

Jogging down the steps, Frank replayed the conversation in his head. HIPAA is HIPAA. He was sure Doc was implying that something had happened, something he couldn't reveal. That the Florita case wasn't a dead end. Frank stepped lively, heading for the office. They might take this to the bank after all.

Alyce Wagner had been sitting in the office building parking lot, waiting for Strader to leave, when she saw Vialotti, recognizing him from his

154

previous legal encounters with the hospital. She followed on the stairwell behind him and saw him enter Strader's office. She retreated to her perch behind the steering wheel of her car and watched. Frank's lively exit caused her concern. Was he providing Strader with legal advice? Could they have discussed the Dominguez case? But what if they did? The record was clear, and she'd made sure of that. And they hadn't gotten to Gil. The man needed his job, and couldn't afford to have his fatal mistake revealed. It wasn't possible they'd turned him. Still, she should probably report this to Appel, maybe after the weekend.

****

An hour later, Vialotti had finished recounting his meeting while literally twirling around his small office. A bemused Bea didn't try to slow him down.

"My, you are the energizer bunny this morning," she said. "But where does that leave us? Where do you go with this?"

A high octane turn and half-flip landed him in his desk chair, with his head bouncing and his mouth set like a white computer dude at a Soul Train dance. "I don't know, Bea. Somewhere. It's not what he said but what he didn't say. He said she was very sick but he didn't say there was no murder. He didn't say that I was wasting my time or that Florita did not die wrongfully. He just made a point of telling me that he couldn't tell me."

Bea sat there sympathetically, like it all made sense.

"We have to stay on the case, stay on Doc Strader," said Vialotti. "We have to dig deeper. There's something there, I know it. We have to keep working."

Bea did not like his use of the word "we."

CHAPTER TWENTY-EIGHT

Strader thought it odd that Vialotti showed up. He had obviously taken on Florita's case. A malpractice case, but why would he come to Strader? Why not Doctor Ahmad, since her death occurred in the GI lab under his direction? Strader had only responded to the emergency code, which was handled well even though the result was bad. And if this were going to be a malpractice case, Vialotti wouldn't come and talk to him about it since he, Strader, might be named as a defendant. He would be named; they always named everyone whose name was in the chart. Perplexed, he dialed his daughter on the office landline. She picked up on the second ring. The grandkids must be napping.

"Dad, what's up? How did it go last night?"

"Overall, pretty well. My advocate, Dylan Hafner, is quite a guy, and at least to me, he established that the mediator in this trial, a lawyer named Greg Gilliam, is a hospital tool. They presented two witnesses and Dylan pretty well debunked what they said."

"That's great, dad. I'm glad you let me know. What's coming up next week?"

"They have one more witness and then we present our case. Joe Morales, my character witness, Angie from the ER, the Chief of Nursing, and one or two others we might call. We don't want to drag this out but Dylan wants to get everything on the record so that we could appeal this in civil court if it doesn't go our way."

"That's smart. A bored jury in a tedious proceeding is not friendly to the side needlessly prolonging things."

"Stel, another problem just cropped up. I don't know if you remember the malpractice attorney, Frank Vialotti?"

"Frank the Tank, we'll take it to the bank. Is that the guy?"

"One and the same. I took care of his wife a few years ago. He's actually a pretty good guy…"

"I know, especially for a lawyer. Remember whom you're asking for advice."

"Sorry. Anyway, he's representing the family of that lady who died. He came to talk with me."

"What did you tell him?"

"Nothing. I told him that HIPAA prevented me from saying anything. But I'm not sure how that applies once somebody's dead."

"Me neither. I'll look it up. But why would he come to you if he hasn't filed a case and you haven't received anything? What's he looking to do? What's he looking for?"

"I don't know Stel; I just don't know. The hospital polished that record clean."

"He's looking for info off the record. A smoking gun. When was the last time you saw Vialotti?"

"It's been a few years since I took care of his wife. By the way, she died—pancreatic cancer—I was with them until the end. The only other time I've seen him has been at those monthly meetings we have in the park. He was there when I opened up my big mouth about the murder. So that's it?"

"Let me think for sec—an aggressive malpractice lawyer hears a doctor say in front of a crowd that a murder has been witnessed. What's he likely to do? Find out who died unexpectedly in the hospital during that timeframe and figure out a way to get to the family. That's what Frank the Tank did."

"Okay, but why come to me?"

"Easy. He must have gotten the hospital record and sent it to an expert, who found nothing wrong. You said yourself the hospital scrubbed the record clean. So Frank is left with an expert's bill to pay and no case—except he still has you. My guess is he'll be back."

"Well, what should I do? Should I call my malpractice carrier? That's all I need is a malpractice case, on top of everything else."

"Let me do some research on patient confidentiality after the patient dies—although it won't make much difference if he's legally representing the family. But I'll find out. In the meantime, concentrate on your judicial review, don't say anything else to Frank Vialotti, and be careful with what you say to anyone."

"Not to worry, the only one I'm seeing today is Doc Morales—breakfast at your favorite place."

"Oh, those cinnamon buns, yum. Say hello to Doc Joe from me. And open your mouth only to swallow your breakfast."

****

B. Reed's was a local favorite on Palm Canyon, north of Vista Chino, serving up plentiful portions of a varied menu. Its entryway and inner corridor featured antique Early American and English furniture. The word in town was that while Bill also ran a local antique store, he was reluctant to sell any of his unique collection. Fortunately, he was less attached to his cinnamon buns, burgers and steaks, and the restaurant did a great business.

Finding Joe Morales in the crowded restaurant was no problem for Strader; his old friend wore a palm tree-decorated bright blue Hawaiian shirt decorated with yellow palm trees. He was waving his arms like a school guard at a railroad crossing.

Strader slid into the booth. "Hi-ya Joe."

"Don." The greeting was as soft as the shirt was loud.

Joe looked down at his half-empty cup of coffee, fingers tapping his napkin to a nervous tune.

Strader said, "You must have gotten here early. Did you open the place?"

"No, you know, this place is always full and I wanted to get us a booth. I've been here maybe fifteen minutes."

"You going somewhere with the family for the fourth?"

"Nah, my son and his wife are going down to the river and we're minding the grandkids. All four of them, the oldest one seven. This may be my last meal."

"You'll be fine," Strader smiled. "Plenty of Band-Aids for them and nitro for you."

"Yeah, and the wife didn't even ask me. I wanted to go fishing. But the kids are fun—it's a good time. I shouldn't even be talking about this with all the shit you're dealing with. How are you holding up?"

"We just finished week one of my judicial review. They're trying to drop me off the staff for being a disruptive physician. It's all bullshit—the hospital wants us all to go about our business with blinders on—do the best with what they give you. Be a good soldier—no insubordination or face a dishonorable discharge. At least in the Army they held people accountable."

"I know exactly what you mean. Don't open your eyes or your mouth.

159

Don't comment about the hospital, the insurance companies, or the government. Like this Affordable Care Act—what a joke. I'm seventy years old, and I need an insurance plan with pregnancy and pediatric coverage? Fuck, I can't even open up my zipper half the time. My group rates have gone up twenty-eight percent, and when you look at the California Bronze plan, the deductibles are killers. Not to mention no doctors to speak of. And in my practice, Medicare is going to punish me, take some of my money, because I'd rather talk to my patients and examine them rather than play fuckin' video games on their electronic medical records. I mean, each visit--6 pages of bullshit to cover our ass. Do I need to ask a sixty-five-year-old marathon jock whether he's fallen down in the last year? I get dinged by Medicare for not writing down a patient's BMI but I can't get them to pay for a dietician and bonafide weight loss program? I'm happy I'm not forty, that's all." He raised his hands in the classic surrender position.

Strader nodded solemnly. "We're lucky to be old—maybe we'll even get luckier and die before the system falls apart completely. Before the accountants, policy wonks and statisticians completely ruin healthcare." He stopped at the sight of a neighboring elderly eavesdropper looking apoplectic. He lowered his voice and leaned a bit closer to Morales, who was scrutinizing the menu as if it was his first visit. "Joe, it was strange that you called me; I was just about to call you."

"I figured we should talk; maybe I can help."

"Well, Hafner, you know, Dylan Hafner, he's working as my advocate…"

"Fine young doctor."

"I agree. Anyway, we were talking about my case, and your name came up—as a possible character witness since you've known me for such a long time. I think he put your name on our list."

"I could testify that you're a character, all right." Morales seemed grateful when the waitress interrupted them. They ordered breakfast and got started with brimming hot coffee filling large wooden mugs. Morales seemed content with sipping his coffee after quenching its smoke with a liberal amount of cream, applied with three nervous pours. Strader barely touched his, watching Morales, waiting. Finally, Strader spread his hands apart, inviting more talk.

Hearing none, he spoke. "Joe, you were saying?"

Joe watched his hands add cream twice more before he knocked down two generous gulps of coffee. "I don't know. Where were we?"

"We were talking about you helping me out, coming to the review session next Wednesday as my character witness. It'll take five minutes, ten tops. No prepping; you say what you feel."

Morales sipped again, dusted his mouth with his napkin, and fingered the top buttonhole of his open shirt. His eyes darted around the large dining room as he spoke to the table. Softly. "I don't know, Don, I don't know that I could help. Remember when I went through that review because I took out someone's sutures with my pocket knife? I almost got booted back then for nothing. These guys all know who you are, what kind of doc you are, and what your intentions are. What am I gonna add to that, that you're my friend and I've only known you to do things that were good for your patients, my patients and the hospital?"

"That would be helpful, yep."

Morales shook his head and forced his eyes to meet Strader's. "But they know that already. This isn't about that, from what I've heard."

"What did you hear and who from?" Strader's voice was much louder now.

"They're saying you're disruptive. The same crew that wanted to run me over for cutting a suture. Appel, right? So I get through telling them what a great guy you are and they ask me if I ever saw you chew out a nurse or badmouth another doc, even if for some incompetent act, and what am I supposed to say? What am I supposed to do, lie?" His voice broke. "What if I screw up? What if I hurt you?"

"Listen, if you don't want to..." Strader folded his hands, leaning them on the table in front of him. He watched hungry Medicare-aged diners shuffle noisily past them, worn legs aching to be seated. Joe's face was lowered to his coffee cup, sipping without lifting. Strader waited.

Joe spoke without making eye contact. "I'm sorry, Don. It's not like that."

Strader's jaw clenched, his neck muscles tightened, anger mixed with uncertainty. Maybe Joe had a point. Perhaps they could turn his testimony around—perhaps he just didn't want to be put in the fray. Strader remembered Stella's advice. Keep his big mouth shut. The moment passed. As the waitress approached with their food, he let Joe off the hook.

"Joe, maybe you're right. I tell you what, I'll leave your name on my witness list, but I won't call you. No need for you to worry yourself over this. After all," Strader peered over the rim of Joe's cup, "what are friends for?"

CHAPTER TWENTY-NINE

The blinking flashlight of San Diego's morning sun awakened Holiday. She was alone in Joey's makeshift sleeping bag, sandwiched between over-sized towels adorned with San Diego Padres logo. Where did he come up with this stuff? Her head rested on their clothes, buttressed by a weathered Yale sweatshirt. She reached down, touching her white cut-offs and blue-and-white striped tee shirt, knotted below her breasts. Relief. She reveled in the soft tickle of the cool ocean breeze. The modest warmth of the early morning sun peeked intermittently through the 'June gloom' of grey clouds. Gulls serenaded her, accompanied by the percussion of ocean waves against rock and sand. A fitting sonata to a magical night. She stretched and reached next to her. No Joey. She lifted herself on her elbows and looked for him. He called this place Bermuda Beach, a small sandy beach surrounded by rock, accessible from a battered stairway at the end of Bermuda avenue, a block off Sunset Cliffs Blvd. Off to the right, an older woman, comfy in her tight spandex, walked her Yorkie in the sand, the tiny dog disappearing at times in the small dunes. Obviously a brave or illiterate woman, ignoring the signs that offered advice of "Unstable Cliffs, keep off," and "No dogs allowed." Holliday scanned the otherwise empty beach before being drawn to a single form swimming strongly some hundred yards offshore. She ran to the water's edge.

"Joey, Joey," she yelled. "Get in here, I'm hungry."

The lady with the dog gave her a surprising smile and a nod.

Joey heard her and swam powerfully toward the beach, bucking or riding the waves he encountered. Holiday admired his body until he reached the water's edge and darted toward her.

"No, no, don't," she laughed as he chased her. The Yorkie lady now stopped, hoping for a show. "I don't have another change of clothes."

He swept her up from behind and she twisted in his arms, the cold wetness of his embrace countered by her inner heat. Their bodies fused and their lips locked. She half-squirmed, half-rubbed against him before dislodging. Joey threw himself face down on the towel; she piled on top of him. Yorkie lady, now seated on a rock, adjusted her spandex, her dog straining against the leash to get a closer look.

Holiday nibbled and whispered in his ear. "Want to show dog lady something new?" She tried to reach around his thigh but he was flattened and pressed tightly to the towel, and sand below.

"Want to get us arrested?" He expertly flipped on top of her, pressed against her, tossed a good morning kiss on her nose and sat up. She pouted.

He checked his watch. "It's seven o'clock already. Let's dust off, change, and grab a bite. There's a Broken Yolk breakfast place about five minutes from here. I'll order you the twelve egg omelet--you polish it off, I don't have to pay."

"Didn't we just finish off pancakes a few hours ago? What's with you and breakfast?" She helped him gather up their things, and shake them out. They took turns draping each other with a towel for privacy. Spandex lady watched them walk hand in hand toward his bike. She hugged her Yorkie football-like under her arm as she slowly mounted the steps, her ample backside seeking freedom with each step. The show's over.

****

By ten o'clock breakfast was long gone. They each showered in the Doctor's lounge facilities at the University Hospital. An hour of teaching rounds ahead, and he thought it might be fun to have her accompany him. He found a long white coat for her to wear over her jeans and instructed her to button it to the top so his students could focus on the patients. Putting on his clean white coat, he was reminded that while Strader also still wore long white coats in the hospital, most everybody wore scrubs.

This wasn't lost on Holiday as they walked the corridor. She said, "I think we're overdressed."

"A few of us still respect the fact that our patients generally feel more positively when their doctors are dressed neatly and appropriately, which includes wearing this. Those who don't justify their position with the hypothesis that the more clothes you wear, the greater the likelihood of harboring bacteria that could transmit disease.

"Is that true?"

"Studies had shown that white coats and ties could carry bacteria;

stethoscopes and doctor's fingertips were even bigger culprits, carrying resistant bugs including MRSA. Handwashing between seeing each patient and wiping clean the stethoscope diaphragm (the flat piece that touched the patient's chest) were universally recommended by epidemiologists and infectious disease experts but were only casually followed by the docs. The problem with white coats and ties is that you can't wash them between patients. Apparently, the fact that scrubs are not changed between seeing patients is not a topic for discussion. In my opinion, scrubs just give a false sense of security. Besides, there aren't studies that establish Typhoid Mary-type epidemics from ties or coats. So, I wear my coat and wash my hands."

He rounded up the house staff team in the ward corridor, a straggly group of nine huddled in a wide circle filling much of the corridor. All wore green scrubs except for the senior resident, Dr. Beacon, a male fire hydrant who wore khakis and a button-down shirt. After three weeks, Hafner had them all figured out. He liked the huddle, standing format—fewer participants fell asleep than if they were seated.

"Team," he said, "Let me introduce Miss Grove. She's actually not a doctor but a designer. We're exploring ways to improve the hospital design to be more patient comforting."

A series of muted hellos followed. Hafner noted that the women seemed much more intrigued with the design pitch than the men with Ms. Grove herself. He smiled to himself that even a white coat couldn't diminish her presence; her long hair, alluring face above and toned legs below added to the mystery of her hidden body.

"Hi, everyone. Thanks for letting me tag along."

"All right," he said. "Let's get to work. Who has the first case?"

The first case was run of the mill. An old man going down the tubes after losing his wife, needing recurrent hospitalizations for congestive heart failure. He ate canned food with lots of salt, didn't take his water pill if he was going out, and missed doctor appointments, habits that recurred each time he returned home. The medical student, Ms. Lin, presented the case. The intern filling in the dosages of Lasix and ACE inhibitors. Holiday appeared mesmerized.

Hafner took over. "So this old guy lost his wife and can't stay out of heart failure. Let's divide up this case into goals, treatment, and what I call process of care. First—goals. Ms. Lin?" He recognized her look of fear that she would make a mistake. After a moment he said, "Ms. Lin? Hint—common sense applies here."

Ms. Lin whispered a question-answer, "Make him feel better?"

"Good. Let's call that reducing morbidity. So making him feel better-- reducing morbidity, improving health-related quality of life and functional status, and decreasing the rate of hospitalization. He's been a disaster since his wife died. Either she was the one who made him take his pills and go to the doctor, or now that she's gone, he just doesn't give a damn. So you'll make him feel better. What's your other main goal?" Ms. Lin's eyes darted around the group seeking help. She even looked to Holiday, who shrugged.

Hafner patiently waited.. "Ms. Lin, we're not only trying to decrease his morbidity, but also his m…"

"Mortality?"

"Perfect. We want to decrease his morbidity and mortality. And we can do this in this gentleman who has a reduced left ventricular ejection fraction. My reference for this is the 2013 ACC/AHA guideline." Turning to the second-year resident, he said, "Dr. Beacon, you can provide this to the group?" The resident was already clicking his iPhone, forwarding the reference to all.

"Done, Dr. Hafner."

"You're not that cute, Beacon, but you are my number one for efficiency. Refresh us on these guidelines."

"Sure." He rattled off the facts. "Treat acute fluid overload with diuretics, add an ACE inhibitor or ARB and beta-blocker. Exclude the presence of active ischemic disease and rigorously reduce lipids. Stop any drugs like NSAIDs that may be contributing to heart failure."

Hafner asked, "How about lifestyle modifications?"

Beacon was smooth. "I was getting to that. This guy isn't a smoker or drinker and I'm pretty sure he doesn't snort cocaine. His BMI is 23, so he doesn't need to lose weight. I'd have him weigh himself every day and increase his Lasix if he's gaining. And I'd tell him to watch his salt intake."

Hafner said. "Time for a great teaching point. What exactly would you say to the patient—let's call him by his name, shall we—Mr. Taylor—would you say 'Mr. Taylor, you should watch your salt intake?'"

Beacon's weight shifted from foot to foot, and his hands gripped together behind his back. He fired back, "No, that would be worthless. In the hospital I'd have the dietician counsel him on a low salt diet."

Hafner, "And by low salt you mean…?"

"Two grams sodium a day. I'd have her make suggestions to his diet to limit his sodium to two grams a day."

"And your reference for this recommendation?"

"I believe that this is the recommendation of the American College of Cardiology and American Heart Association."

"Close but no cigar, Dr. Beacon. In 2013 those societies actually recommended sodium restriction to less than three grams a day in patients with symptomatic heart failure. The literature doesn't support any specific level of sodium intake in these patients, so we're just guesstimating. But let's take your two grams of sodium diet. What is the most likely result from this dietary intervention? Let's give old Beacon here a break. Someone else. Let's see, whose curly hair is that behind Beacon? Dr. Hawkins. Front and center. What is the most likely result from Dr. Beacon's dietician counseling Mr. Taylor on a salt restricted diet?"

Dr. Hawkins was an intern with a crop of tight black curls that surrounded his otherwise clean face like an astronaut's space helmet. Never an eager participant in teaching rounds, he nevertheless was a promising young physician. Hafner liked him.

Hawkins said, "I want to say that he would have fewer symptoms of CHF and hopefully less frequent hospital admissions, but honestly I think you're screwing with me and that's not what you're looking for."

Hafner chuckled. The group joined in and the atmosphere was more relaxed. He saw Holiday divide her time between listening and looking at the faces around her, some leaning a bit forward to make sure they heard every word, others hiding in the weeds.

Hafner put his arm around Dr. Hawkins' shoulder. "The nail on the head. You hit it. The guidelines say to restrict the theoretical patient with heart failure to a two or three gram sodium diet. The real patient, Mr. Taylor, is ninety, lives alone, and no longer has the woman who most likely cooked every meal of his for sixty or so years. He's depressed, just going through the motions. So what will the diet recommendations result in?"

A question that called for a non-textbook answer. No response. Hafner said. "Ms. Lin, soon to be Dr. Lin, this is your patient. What will happen to him with this new diet?"

"He won't listen? Nothing will happen?"

"And that will be terrible, won't it?"

"Yes, terrible."

Hafner was energetic. "No, I'd say it's probably the best thing that could happen given the circumstances that he ignores the advice. Why?" Hafner looked around, no one meeting his glance except Holiday. He shifted gears.

"Maybe I'm being unfair. This becomes an art of medicine question, not a science question. Really not a medical question at all. Given these circumstances, if this old man goes on a low salt diet, what will happen to him?"

Silence. Hafner turned to Holiday. "How about you Ms. Grove, what do you think?"

She answered quickly. "He'd stop eating or eat less. He'd lose weight. He'd become more depressed."

"Bingo. Seventy percent of the live-alone elderly who try to follow a restricted diet wind up malnourished. So, Ms. Grove, now that you have abandoned your designer career for medicine, what would you prescribe for Mr. Taylor? Should we have Giada or The Barefoot Contessa come and cook for him? Probably cheaper in the long run than the hospital bills."

"I don't know what services are available for Mr. Taylor. Something like Home Instead, where someone could come in and provide his meals and some companionship. That might help."

"And if that wasn't available or adequate?"

"Assisted living."

"Exactly. This is exactly the place for an old, lonely guy who has a medical problem, doesn't take his meds, see his doctor or eat appropriately. Find the right place and he'll have company, take his meds, and hopefully enjoy a healthier diet."

Dr. Hawkins wasn't convinced. "I think it's terrible to take this guy out of his home to assisted living. From what I've heard, the food is lousy, the people are old and older, and he'll probably get more depressed and die."

Hafner looked through Hawkins. "Dr. Hawkins, do you do marketing or testimonials for the assisted living sector?" Hawkins threw him a look. Hafner went on. "Is this an accurate portrayal? Is Mr. Taylor going to live in solitary confinement, meals pushed under his door?"

"Not necessarily. You have to find the right one," Holiday blurted. Everyone looked at her.

"My dad is in assisted living. He has an aggressive form of dementia. I see him every day, feed him when I'm there, and the aides help feed him when I'm not." Getting a bit emotional but defiant. "At every meal the staff leads him out to the dining room. Half the time, no, most of the time he doesn't recognize me or calls me by my mother's name. But crazy as it may seem, he has a friend, a very old man named Richard, who sits across from him at a table for two, and they eat together. They say hello, eat, finish together and then return to their own lives. My dad's not quite sixty, he doesn't know me so well, but he treasures Richard. If my dad comes out to eat early, he asks the staff, 'Where's Richard'?" Her voice broke just a trifle. "So for my dad it's been good, and there's no reason why it couldn't be good for Mr. Taylor." A prolonged awkward hush from the group. Holiday covertly knocked her shoe against Hafner's. He regained the platform.

"Ok, then. Assisted living it is. And acute health care costs will go down. Hopefully he has long term care insurance or adequate savings. Ms. Lin, you should work with the case manager on this." He winked at Holiday.

****

An hour later they were zipping along Highway 15, heading back to the desert. Holiday held him tightly. They shared the scrumptious high of physical and emotional bonding achieved in fact, only by the young, and rarely at that. As they approached Carmel Mountain Road, Holiday giggled at a thought.

"Dr. Hafner, pull off at this exit and find a place to park. We have one more teaching round to finish before we head home."

Hafner took the exit and found shade under a stand of jacarandas.

CHAPTER THIRTY

Strader had known Angie for over a decade and she had successfully weathered life's storms probably much better than he. Now forty-nine, youthful in figure and face, her blue eyes shone softly against her tanned skin and mid-length brown hair. She had lost her husband in a seaplane crash in the Alaskan wilderness fifteen years ago which extinguished her love for fishing and the Alaskan outdoor world. She moved to the desert three months after the accident. Strader's late wife Rosemary and she became good friends, and when Rosemary was dying, she lobbied her husband for Angie to succeed her. Strader really liked her, enjoyed her company when he saw her in the ER or when they shared an occasional meal, but he wasn't sure if he was ready for more.

To celebrate the Fourth, they picnicked together at Palm Springs Stadium, for an evening of baseball followed by fireworks. Strader was impressed not just with her knowledge of baseball but also with her passion for the local team and the game itself. She snagged a foul ball in the third inning—her third of the season, she told him. He tactfully declined her offer of the ball despite some hidden young boy in his brain or his heart that lobbied him to take it. She yelled her share of 'strike 'em out' when Brooks Kriske was mowing down the San Diego Force batters. She shrieked in joy when Palm Springs Power's Nate Pollock scored from third on a double play grounder, the only score of the game, a 1-0 thriller. After the local's Doug Finley retired the Force in the ninth, Angie supplied Strader with final stats.

"Did you know that the Power pitching staff has allowed only one run in their last thirty-five innings pitched? And we're now 24-4?"

"Of course, I knew that."

"You should really get out more, spend more time like this."

"My practice…"

She finished his sentence for him. "Shouldn't consume you. Look at what it's getting you now, with this crazy review. Have you ever thought about teaching? The ER nurses still talk about the lecture you gave us on upper GI bleeding."

"I can't take time to travel to LA or San Diego to teach house staff. And I'm solo. It would be tough to get regular coverage. I do enjoy researching a subject and giving a lecture."

"I think you'd be a great teacher. I'd rather see you do that than take an administrative job or work for a pharmaceutical company."

His face contorted as if he were tasting a lemon. "I would never do those. As for teaching, I'd be afraid that after one session with me, my students would barricade themselves in, with me out." He allowed himself a chuckle.

She playfully punched him on his arm as they grabbed their stuff and hustled from the stands to the field. Strader helped her spread the large blanket on the outfield grass. She covered the San Diego Padres logo with a medium sized Styrofoam cooler. The lid opened just enough to allow a glimpse and sniff of the wonders inside. It was almost 8:30. The sun had settled behind the mountains to the west, the sky slowly changing, from lingering red-infused soft clouds to dark blue sky sprinkled with early white stars.

Three blankets and two rows behind them, Alyce Wagner sat alone, munching bunny-like on carrots and celery. She watched as they talked and ate. There was still enough light to snap a photo. She zoomed in on them with her cell phone camera and snapped.

Strader commandeered his second piece of chicken, enjoying the crunchy gradient texture of the crust yielding to the soft, white meat inside. He thought back to Rosemary involving him in cooking, usually on weekends when he was off call. She would guide his hand as he rolled a chicken breast in buttermilk, dredged it through egg batter and threw it in a paper bag filled with flour, shaking it till the covering was complete. She preached that food always tasted better when your hand was in the preparation. Angie's chicken was great even without his help. As he guzzled water, his line of sight alternated between Angie and the sky; he didn't mind being seen by patients or providing free consultations (a blessing if it would keep the patient out of the office or the ER) but he didn't want to hear awkward statements of support for his current ordeal. He managed a wave to Doc Morales and a thumbs up to Samantha Porter as they caught his eye in the crowd. He wanted vindication but he also wanted it to be over. Blanketed by the black sky, he inched closer to Angie.

"The chicken was outrageous," he offered. "Thanks for putting this all together for me."

"For us. I gobbled down my share, in case you weren't looking."

"Trust me, I haven't stopped looking. It's real easy to do. But—aside from all your help in the ER and everything else, I really appreciate being with you. And now—it's such a tough time for me, I appreciate it even more." The surrounding crowd helped him suppress the urge to move even closer, to …

As the fireworks show began, funnels of yellow and white explosive light sped from the ground toward the sky.

Angie leaned closer, briefly resting her head on his shoulder. "Oh Don, the show has started. For a moment, I thought it was just us."

A Kodak moment, caught by a grinning Alyce Wagner.

CHAPTER THIRTY-ONE

Mr. Dominguez did not attend the Fourth of July festivities, the baseball game, or the fireworks. He sat quietly in front of his TV, unaware of the scores of his beloved fútbol, for Saturday and most of Sunday. The initial disbelief that Florita was dead had morphed into anguish, then sadness and anger. He was a pot of emptiness, of thoughts without consequence, of white memories turned black. The rest of the family wanted revenge, and vindication; they wanted money. He wanted—nothing. He didn't want to be left alone, yet he abhorred their company. He didn't want to eat but he welcomed food for distraction rather than caloric necessity or taste satisfaction. Work was a welcome time-killer without job satisfaction. And he had always been a proud gardener who treated his grass, plants and trees like children. Now he was more passive in his work, and the joy of nurturing was absent. His steps were suddenly those of an old man. Why did the emptiness hurt so much? When would the suffocating fog of depression lift? Why had God taken his wife?

He dodged the family crowd in the living room, trudged down the back steps to his sun-drenched yard, protected by his wide-brimmed hat and long sleeve shirt. The drought resistant Buffalo grass was neatly mowed, brightened in contrast to the desert-landscaped perimeters manned by bougainvillea soldiers in bright red uniforms. He wandered the yard, trimming the few straying branches of the rounded bushes nearest the house. The doctor said they tried everything. God had promised. Nothing had made a difference. Now he was left with Senor Vialotti, who couldn't bring her back but might be able to....

The yard fully manicured, Mr. Dominguez sat on a sun-tarnished wooden chair, each so familiar with the other that they creaked in sync.

****

When the kids were small, Strader would make rounds early Sunday morning, and Rosemary would page him at the hospital when she had secured a table at Elmer's. She would order for him, and the German pancake would be just hitting the table when he scampered over. And when the kids were grown and out of the house, Rosemary insisted that they continue the tradition, at times straying to IHOP or Bit O Country but constantly circling back to Elmer's. Strader couldn't quite remember the reasoning for his transition from German to buttermilk pancakes or from a large to short stack; now it had been four years since he'd tasted either. After she died, Sundays changed; there was no need to make super early rounds; in fact, making rounds later helped to pass the day; rounds took so much longer due to necessary updates with family members and the need to track down the patients at their various "off the floor" activities. Rounds took all morning and were followed by the rewards of an Einstein everything bagel and coffee. Depending on the time of year, Sunday afternoons were spent watching baseball or football, playing handball or racquetball, enjoying a vigorous bike ride, and almost catching up on his chart dictations and journal reading.

Today he pedaled along the bike path from Palm Springs toward Rancho Mirage. His front tire hit a hole and Strader had to grip the handlebars tight to keep to his path. It was a needed break—since the hospital had removed him, all he found himself doing was reviewing material for the trial, strategizing with Hafner, and entertaining Tomas. And, too, there was Angie. She was so easy to be with. And the fireworks that followed that night, when he invited her back to his apartment, topped the chart. Maybe after this was all over…

He took the tree-lined bike path over Mesquite and appreciated the shade. The bike was a standard black mountain bike, five-speed, nothing fancy. He threw a nod to approaching riders sporting Rapha high performance gear with bib shorts and cycling tights featuring a superior chamois pad; he was not a big fan. He wore a simple, breathable tee shirt and running shorts. After caring for a young man with a severe head injury sustained in a bike fall two years ago, Strader had less reluctantly donned a slim protective helmet. When he reached Date Palm Drive, he turned to go back, figuring the fifteen-mile round trip was enough to clear his coronaries and his brain. Then his cell went off and he pulled over. Stella.

"Guess who's visiting, Dad?"

He panted, breathless, sweat suddenly burning his eyes.

"It's me, dad." Will sounded upbeat, unusual for him. "Stel has us on speaker."

It took a minute. "Wow, two for one. Funny, I just biked past Elmer's and was thinking about our Sunday morning trips there when you were young."

Stella chimed in. "Buttermilk pancakes for us, German for you, Swedish for mom."

Strader said, "Swedish. I'd forgotten. Those thin little things, they looked more like crepes. Strawberries all around them." He chuckled, "They must have been good; she never offered one to me."

Stella said, "Now I eat granola, yogurt and berries. I would kill for a big stack of pancakes but there's gluten and carbs and calories— how screwed up is that?"

"You are what you eat, Stel," said Will.

"What are you eating these days, Will? How are you doing? What are you doing?"

"Whoa, dad," Will replied. "Ease up on the inquisition. I'm fine. We're calling to see how you're doing and to give you some info."

"The sad truth is that a parent is only feeling as good as his children are doing."

"Well, then, you should be feeling great," Stella said. "Will looks great and he's got some tips for that Florita case. Before I turn it over to him— remember when I told you I'd find out about the HIPAA obligations after death? It's actually fascinating."

"Tell me."

"The broad category falls under protected health information, in this case, how the privacy rule protects the health information of deceased individuals. Guess how long this information is protected after someone dies. Dad?"

"I don't know. Ten years?"

"Will?"

"One year?"

"This will blow you away. Fifty years. This is supposed to balance privacy interests of surviving relatives with the need for historians and others to access them for historical purposes."

"Fifty years—that's crazy, but can't the family get that information?"

"They sure can. The executor of Florita's estate, probably her husband, can gain access to her information. The HIPAA excuse won't work, but all that entitles them to is the hospital record unless they bring on a malpractice suit and you have to give a deposition. There are some other rules, but they don't apply here."

Strader broke in. "So I can tell Vialotti to look again at the hospital record, and if he has a release from Florita's husband, I could theoretically tell him the rest."

Stella replied, "You could, but I'm not sure you want to right now. I'll have to look into that, but let's wait till after the judicial review is over. You're not planning on bringing this up at your trial right now, are you?"

"No, Hafner and I haven't talked about including it now, even though that's the reason these SOBs started this to begin with. Revenge for my stupid remarks." He realized he was almost shouting.

Stella said, "Dad, we can wage that war after we win this one. But Will has some ideas he wants to share with you. Go ahead, Will."

"Dad, I was thinking about the picture you have of the nurse's note and how it contradicts the official medical record," said Will. "The question is whether that lady got a total of three milligrams of midazolam like the record reads or eight milligrams like the note says. Stel said that all of the drug was given in three minutes, and that's where the problem was, too much too soon."

"That's right," said Strader.

"What size was the vial? Was it a unit dose?" asked Will.

"We usually use single vials that may have either 1 mg of the drug per mL or 5 mg per mL There are multidose vials that can be up to 10 mL in size."

"So that means there could be up to 50 mg of midazolam in a vial. What size were you using?"

"Usually, we use the smaller vials but at times there may be a shortage and we have to use a multi-dose vial."

"Well, if the nurse wrote that he gave an additional five mg and he didn't crack open another vial, then the vial had to be at least two mL and would contain a total of ten mg."

"I think we were using a big multidose vial the day before," Strader said. "I remember the nurse complaining that they had to use a small syringe and draw up only a fraction of a mL for each patient to avoid having to discard a lot of unused medication after each case. So the day before, they must have been using the five mg per mL concentration and the vials were anywhere from 2 mL to 10 mL. But I'm not sure I see…"

Will couldn't hide his excitement. "Do they do a drug count?"

"Every day."

"Great. If they do a drug count, they would have found the discrepancy at the end of that day when the lady died."

"I didn't hear of any discrepancy, and that's usually a big deal because the nurses stay until they reconcile the count with the amount used."

Will's voice rose an octave, like an excited kid. "If there was a cover-up, and my guess is there was, then the easiest way to make the drug count match would be to add a volume of saline to the vial. They probably injected saline back into the vial—if the vial had 5 mg per mL of midazolam, then they added back one mL."

"So we're screwed."

"No, not really. One thing we can do is look at the amount of meds given on average to the patients before that lady and the amount of meds given to subsequent patients who would use the same vial, if it was a multi-dose vial. The patients that used the meds after the lady would appear to have been given a larger than usual dose, since the drug was actually diluted and they were getting mostly saline."

"How would I find that out?"

"I've done computer work in hospitals to simplify inventory, sales and requisitions. We need to get the lab's records to see what size vials were being given at that time, which should be available on the order forms and the stock records. Then we need to look at the log of the patients the day before, the day of the incident and the following day, and compare how much midazolam was given between the groups. My guess is that it will show that a larger volume of medication was required for a very brief period until the watered down multidose vial was used up, and then the usage returned to the average."

"I can't get those records. I'm not allowed in the hospital, remember?"

"Maybe someone else can. Maybe Dr. Hafner? It may be possible to log on to the hospital computer and download those records as well, at least the ordering records. Or we may have to break into the GI lab."

"That's not happening."

"Will's not saying we have to do these things right now," said Stella, "only that there is an additional way to prove that your photo of the note describes what really took place. Let us work on it and you work on your next trial date…Wednesday night, right?"

Strader felt a vague gnawing in his stomach, "Yeah, this Wednesday and next Wednesday, and hopefully we'll be through. This week they present Gil Morgan, the GI nurse. I had a blowout with him in the ER.

He's also the guy who must have screwed with the medications in the Florita case. Should be an intense session. Then we put on our witnesses."

Trying to be cheerful, Stella said, "Like always, you'll do fine, Dad. This Hafner guy seems like an ace, and you'll be as well prepared as you were last week. We'll let you go now, but we'll stay in touch. Call if you need anything."

"Bye, Stel, bye Will…and thanks, both of you. Love you both." He pressed the red icon to end the call, suddenly realizing that he was soaked in sweat. He had been oblivious to the heat and to the several riders who had zipped past him. Wet and stiff but feeling better, he mounted his bike and pedaled for home.

CHAPTER THIRTY-TWO

Sickness arises 24/7, but CEO Hendrickson was a nine-to-five Monday through Friday guy, barring some gala or sumptuous dinner event that demanded his presence. Sitting in his office, the local TV news a background voice, he reflected on Strader. The CEO would not have his glorious gig threatened by the Strader judicial review. That inflexible bastard, constantly pushing for changes that dwindled operational margins. The CEO had tried to make nice—for Christ's sake, this was a community hospital, not the Mayo Clinic—and now he had the opportunity not only to rid himself of a major pain-in-the-ass but, at the same time, send a message to the others: the hospital was Mother Earth, don't fuck with her. But the first round of the judicial review was appalling to him. Christ, both his and Appel's jobs were at stake—Appel's most definitely. What made things worse was a swell of support for the doctor from the medical staff.

The word "Strader" on his TV caught his attention. As he listened, his neck hairs straightened.

To this reporter, after speaking with my friends in the community, including several nurses and physicians, Doctor Strader is a terrific gastroenterologist who first and foremost looks after his patients like a Mother Hen, even if he cackles too much while doing so. Just maybe what the medical community needs is more cacklers like him to help move our population health upward. Anyone who has spent hours and hours waiting for care in the ER or trying to find someone in the hospital to explain their loved one's illness to them surely would freely serve chicken feed to the cackler and get it back to work.

The CEO abruptly shut the TV. He grabbed paperwork on his desk that included a letter of support for Strader signed by fourteen hundred plus Palm Springs citizens, crumpled it and threw it in the trash. Who was behind that? Who was Kayesha, anyway? He glanced at his watch. Appel was due any minute. He rose and paced, stopping only to glance at himself in the mirrored wall on the side of his desk away from the door. He stood up straight—a rooster against a chicken.

Thirty minutes later, the CEO's crowing turned Appel's face red.

"Roger, this isn't the Supreme Court, it's a goddamn judicial review in front of a fixed jury. Why should I feel so nervous? I'll tell you why. That shithead Robertson presented two-thirds of our case last week, and if I were on the panel, I would vote not only to acquit Strader but to make him the President of the Medical Staff. "

"Dale, he's already been President about ten years ago; served two terms, so we don't have to worry about that."

The CEO half-wiggled, half-leaped from his chair like a salmon on a fly rod, just not as graceful. "Are you fucking with me? Is this the time to be fucking with me? Do you want to be back drawing up wills and overseeing escrows?"

"Sorry, just trying to lighten the mood. Sorry."

"I don't want sorry. I got sorry. I want success. I want this guy gone."

"Dale, no one wants this more than me. He's been on my shit list for five years now, since before you came. At one time, we tried to ensure we kept our cardiac patients at the Palm, but he had the medical staff pass some rule that gave the docs free rein to refer wherever they wanted. No loyalty—that's what I hate. Another pompous doc who feels that he owes us nothing, owes the hospital nothing. We're just here to make him money."

The CEO wasn't mollified. "What's going to happen on Wednesday? How can I be assured that I won't be witnessing another abortion?"

"First of all, remember that we've gone to great lengths to sew this thing up. We have the three votes and likely will get a fourth."

Dale started to object and Appel hurried on.

"Nevertheless, we are going for all five votes; we are going to blow him out of the water. We're spending much of today with our third witness, Gil Morgan, the GI nurse. Alyce Wagner met with him over the weekend and says he'll do very well; he's prepared. She's actually working with him again as we speak. We also have information to rebut his opposing witness, the ER nurse."

"Gilliam knows all this—and our prosecutor?"

"Gilliam knows, and the script is being completely written so that Dr. Robertson doesn't screw it up."

"And how about Strader's witnesses, his defense?"

"We're all set there...one will be detained, one will be forced to admit that Strader's a hothead, and the third one will be impeached."

"And is Strader going to take the stand?"

"That depends, Dale, on how things go; it's more their call than ours. But we hope they do. We have a plan to get him riled and to have all the jurors witness him blow a fuse. That should clinch it. We also—know, that should clinch it."

Dale started to ask something but Appel's look was enough to tell him that he didn't want to know whatever he was going to ask.

****

Down the hall, on company time, sprawled out on a wide upholstered chair, Gil Morgan RN once again answered Alyce Wagner's questions with the confidence of a cross-country runner cruising a 5k.

"I'm on call a lot for emergencies, and we deal with a lot of critically ill patients, so I don't recall all the details. I remember coming to the ER, it was late at night, and Dr. Strader was at the bedside of a bleeder."

Alyce, sitting prim and proper across a banker's desk from him, prompted, "You mean that you got there as fast as you could with one of your kids sick, and the tech on call with you couldn't be reached."

"Oh, yeah, I forgot."

"Well, don't." She looked at him, his youthful frame, amazing black hair with matching eyes. An attractive guy, but maybe not yet fully believable. "Your story for Wednesday is simple, you got out of bed in the middle of the night, didn't have a tech, you rushed to the hospital, and then this jerk starts cursing you. He gets really uptight when he has a sick patient. And he was taking it out on you. It really offended you and makes it very difficult for you to work with him."

"Yeah, I got it. But he's pretty cool under fire and I didn't have all the stuff we needed on the cart..."

"We lay that off on the tech. Say that the tech usually takes care of that."

"How about the ER nurse, Angie? I bet she'll take his side."

"Trust me, she's not going to be a factor."

"Yeah, but I still have to work with these people."

"Come on, you're being a hero, standing up for them by speaking up. You shouldn't be cursed at, simple as that."

Morgan slumped in his chair, avoiding Wagner's gaze. All he offered was a "yeah."

She pushed on. "Listen, I'm not asking you to crucify him. You can say you've worked with him for years and he's a good doc and all that stuff. But you have to come back to the fact that no matter what, he shouldn't be cursing you. You're a nurse, a husband, a father of two, and you come to work every day—to work, not to be abused."

Morgan listened, gave a little head bob while he straightened up in his chair and confronted her gaze with his own. "Yeah, I can do that—I will do that. But what if they ask me about the other case, about the dead lady?"

Alyce wasn't sure how to play him. He wasn't stupid—he was letting her know that they were in that together. Soft or tough, co-worker or boss. No, there was only one way. She stood and leaned forward across the desk, their faces separated by no more than two feet. Her voice was firm, her words clipped.

"You can tell them what you did..."

"What we did..."

"I don't remember giving that lady a single drop of medicine, much less eight milligrams. Not in my job description. You can tell them that you were the nurse, that you gave exactly the medicine that was ordered, three milligrams, it was all documented on the hospital record, and that you still feel horrible that she passed away, but she was very, very sick."

He didn't like her face, her breath, her imperious manner. But he wasn't stupid.

"Yeah, I can say that—that's what happened. Right?"

"That's exactly what happened, like the record says. Unless you want to tell them that you had to get to your kid's soccer game so you—worked too fast."

"No, I'm good with staying on the record."

"Word for word."

Morgan stood up, careful to move away from her. "Are we done here?"

Alyce came back at him, "Sit down, my friend, and let's do it again from the beginning."

CHAPTER THIRTY-THREE

Monday was a quiet day for restaurants in Palm Springs; many were already closed for the summer. Despite or maybe because of this, John's diner on Palm Canyon Drive was brim full, and Alyce Wagner was fortunate to navigate her way to a small corner table and sit down without dropping her patty melt or the turkey club she bought for Appel. He arrived a scant three minutes later, spotted and joined her in a frenetic succession of darting maneuvers to avoid the crowd. His white short sleeve shirt had a rim of underarm sweat, which could explain his chronic unwillingness to remove his blazer in the hospital. His face was redder than usual as if he had just finished a brisk trot. He half sat as his eyes traversed the diner, like an Indian guide from an old Western scanning the land for the enemy. He finally sat down facing Alyce, his eyes continuing to dart, table to table. She pushed his sandwich toward him, a little uneasy by his external distress.

"The CEO is beyond nervous. He wants us to bury Strader on Wednesday. Leave no prisoners."

"Well, I finished with Gil Morgan this morning. He knows what he has to say."

Appel, still looking around, leaned forward to keep his voice low. "Any problems with him?"

"Nothing unexpected. I think he's a little concerned about being shown up or having some conflict with some of the other nurses, like Angie."

"I assume you put him at ease."

"I did."

They both paused to take a bite of their lunch. Alyce swallowed first.

"Oh, one more thing," she added. "He brought up the GI lab case. He was worried they were going to question him on that."

"And…"

"He knows how to respond. The medical record speaks for itself.

He's certainly not going to say that he was in too much of a hurry."

"So it would be Strader's lame assertions which followed us nailing him for being disruptive versus the clear documentation on the computerized medical record, with no changes that would be detected by an audit trail review. I have to say—good job, Alyce. Good job."

Appel consumed his entire sandwich before Alyce had taken her third nibble, eating like a getaway driver waiting for his crew to dash from the bank. In a low voice with eyes patrolling the perimeter, he machine-gunned his thoughts.

"Alright, let's go through Wednesday. We start off with Morgan. He's all set, you say."

Alyce nodded. Appel continued.

"Then Hafner will put on their case. Three witnesses, Morales, Angie the ER nurse and Chief of Nursing Porter."

Alyce picked up the thread. "We're all set for Morales. And for the ER nurse, too." She pulled up the photos she had taken of Strader and Angie at the Fourth of July celebration and showed them to Appel, who shielded the phone from surrounding patrons as if someone was trying to see his hand at a poker game.

"Nice. Send them to me and we'll get them ready. You'll have to talk to Gilliam and Robertson about them, but let's wait till Wednesday morning."

Alyce nodded.

"And the Chief of Nursing? Porter? What about her? She's been against this from the beginning. A real Strader fan."

Alyce paused, fidgeting with her empty plate and napkin. "All I know is that she's not on call on Wednesday evening, Nurse Brodie is. "

"So Porter's testifying? I warned her—she's supposed to be on our team. We'll figure something out to keep her busy." His voice was up five decibels. He glanced over Alyce's head, his pupils dilated, and his face turned half-crimson, half pale-white.

A smiling Hafner, burger and fries in hand, approached their small table.

"Mr. Appel, Ms. Wagner, mind if I join you? Seats are at a premium here."

Hearing no objection, he pulled over an adjacent chair and sat down. Alyce still had some sandwich to bite into, but Appel was stymied, empty plate and fork, napkin already used.

Hafner continued, "This place sure jumps in the summer. Decent burger, fries not too soggy." He took a healthy bite while studying them, smiling all the while. "But hey, I've been so tied up between my practice and this Don Strader ordeal that I haven't been able to get down here much. It's a shame we have to waste our time with these political witch hunts, isn't it? And against one of our best doctors." Another burger bite and slow, satisfying chewing.

Appel and Wagner glanced at each other, Alyce partially protected from speaking by her dwindling lunch. But Appel remained silent.

Wagner started falteringly, "Well, it's not really…

"No need to be modest, Ms. Wagner," said Hafner. "The word among the medical staff is that the two of you are leading the charge for reasons unclear—at least to some. People frown on those who do bad things to good people."

Appel said, "Now listen here, Dr. Hafner, we just want a hospital where people treat each other with respect, you know, collegial-like."

Hafner swallowed once more, wrapping the remaining half of his burger in the tin foil it came in. "Some of us want a hospital where we can count on our patients being treated professionally and responsibly. That's what Dr. Strader wants. That's what our patients want."

Wagner stiffened her lip. "That doesn't give him the right to be a bully or act rudely to our nurses."

Hafner stood up and left with a parting comment, "Ms. Wagner, I'd rather be told, even brusquely, that I screwed up so that maybe it doesn't happen the next time than be the one who really gets screwed, you know, the Florita Dominguez's of the world. Enjoy your lunch. I have to get my Perry Mason on for Wednesday."

They watched him leave, both shell-shocked. Appel recovered first.

"He's pissed off because he knows we got the votes and he's a loser."

"But he mentioned the Florita case. Why?"

"I don't know, but if they bring it up in any way, I'll just have Gilliam crush it. One thing for sure, if Strader testifies I want to blow him out of the water; I want him to explode right there in front of them."

Alyce listened but was distracted by a heavyset lady at the table next to them, whose large straw hat and prominent cataract glasses did little to hide her anguish. She soothingly stroked her tiny Yorkie's face as it nestled on her lap, one paw bandaged with a tiny ace wrap embellished with a red bow that matched the one in its hair. Alyce's eyes sparked.

She half-whispered to Appel, "I think I found a way. Leave it to me."

CHAPTER THIRTY-FOUR

The following day, Tuesday, Hafner was performing his best Perry Mason with his sole legal client.

"Don, say it with emphasis but not with anger. With control, not emotion. Let's try it again."

Strader shrugged his agreement.

Hafner said, "I'll ask you again. You were telling us that Nurse Morgan arrived late, the patient was hemorrhaging, and when you asked for the tools you needed to stop the bleeding, he said he didn't have them."

Strader cut in on cue, "Correct. I asked for the bicap—he didn't have it—then the heater probe—he didn't have it—the hemo-clips—no can do."

"And these are standard tools that are on what you call the GI bleeding cart, aren't they?"

"Without them we can't stop the bleeding. It's the main reason we come in in the middle of the night to scope someone who is bleeding heavily, to find out what's bleeding and use our tools to stop it, to stabilize the patient, who otherwise would need emergency surgery or even die." Strader felt a bit awkward reciting this to a group of doctors, but Hafner had assured him that this was necessary in case they lost and had to appeal in a real court.

"And these are standard. There is no way that the nurse would think that maybe they wouldn't be necessary for that case."

A bit of vehemence, "No, there is no damn way—the cart is supposed to be set up each night and checked before each case. No way in hell."

Hafner shook his head. "Don, you are scoring a goal for them. We don't need the emotion, and we certainly don't need any 'damns' or 'hell.' Just factual, 'no, it's standard to check the cart and stock the cart so that it is fully equipped before each case. It's our standard of care.' That's all you need to say. And we need to ramp it up to let them know what you actually feel with a dying patient in your hands and none of your arsenal available to save them. I'll ask the right questions."

****

Ms. Wagner exited PetSmart on Monterrey Avenue carrying a small package, though she didn't have a pet. On to Home Depot, then one more stop, then home. Time to show the big boys who she was. She was amped and had to ease her foot off the accelerator as she torpedoed out of the parking lot.

****

Strader glanced at his watch as he pulled into his garage. Seven fifteen. Probably still a hundred degrees out. The six hours with Hafner were grueling but necessary. He had cleared things up in the office with a phone call, happy that he didn't have to go in. Dolly Lewis had enlightened him on her bowel activity of the day, and there were no emergencies to address. Time for a cold one, a salad, maybe watch a ballgame, and get a good night's sleep before Wednesday, part two of his trial.

He entered his condo, awaiting Tomas's clamor, but it was quiet. Strader turned the AC down from eighty-four to seventy-eight. His monthly electric bill in the summer hovered in the four to five hundred dollars range despite what he thought was prudence. Still quiet. He checked out his cat's favorite sleeping haunts, the easy chair in the living room and the bed in the second small bedroom. No dice.

"Tomas. Tomas." Strader made a repetitive clicking sound that usually grabbed the cat's attention. Nothing. "Tomas, want a treat?" He invaded the pantry and retrieved the cat's bag of Friskies Party Mix treats. He stepped into the living room area and shook the bag, creating one of Tomas's favorite crunch tunes, one that invariably drew him out wherever he was hiding. Nothing. Maybe he was outside, Strader thought, but this was not his usual routine on a hot summer day. Tomas would sit by the large window to corral the sun's rays in the morning and late afternoon but would otherwise find cooler spots to stretch out. Well, Strader mused, he was somewhere. He would come out when Strader opened the fridge.

He poured himself a large mug of Crystal Light enhanced by orange and lemon slices. Refreshing without caffeine or calories—maybe not a

190

man's drink. No sign of Tomas. Strader uneasily walked to the small cat door to see if it was stuck. No, it opened and closed freely. Strader opened the sliders to the back of the condo facing the greenbelt. The sun threw shards of light toward the valley as it ended its day.

"Tomas. Tomas." Strader caught a whiff of a strange sweet smell in the thicket that demarcated his turf from the common area ground. There was a clear area at the middle base of the thicket where Tomas would sometimes sleep, protected from the view of neighbors or predators. And there he was. Strader was relieved, but the sweet smell was stronger as he approached the thicket.

"Tomas, let's go." The cat didn't move. Strader got down on his knees, his face filling the void in the thicket. Tomas was lying in a pool of vomit, undigested pellets of dry food and sweet-smelling, green-tinged liquid debris. Muscles on his torso were twitching involuntarily. His head had a slight tremor but he was not arousable.

"Tomas, what did you get yourself into?" Strader yelled, thinking a million things at once. He breathed deeply, slowed himself down for a few seconds, then dashed to the condo, returning in less than a minute with car keys, wallet, a blanket, small bag and the kitty litter scooper. He took several quick close-up photos of the scene with his iPhone for no reason other than it might be helpful to the Vet. He wrapped Tomas in the blanket, and when he cleared the vomitus from the cat's frozen face, he was alarmed by Tomas's short rapid eye movements that indicated likely central nervous system damage. He ran to his car, placed Tomas gingerly in the passenger seat, ran back to the thicket and scooped up some of the green liquid and vomitus into a plastic bag, and was on his way. He couldn't place the smell, although it was vaguely familiar, one of those times when your senses encounter something you know you should know, but you don't.

He roared down Sunrise and fired a left on Ramon. It was almost seven-thirty, and he didn't remember whether the Vet animal hospital closed at seven or eight. Stopped at a light on Ramon, he looked at the unmoving form of Tomas, his slight head tremor the only sign of life. Breathing was barely perceptible to Strader's trained eye. Strader felt inwardly sick, numb, feelings that brought him back to Rosemary's final days. Tomas was only a cat, but he had provided so much to Strader, a companion, an affection-sharer, someone to take care of—all things otherwise missing from Strader's private life since Rosemary died.

As he pulled into the hospital parking lot he saw three cars, and the light was still on. He picked up Tomas and rushed toward the building, afraid that the doors would close before he got there.

A tired but friendly receptionist greeted him, a young, pretty, dark-skinned girl who couldn't be more than twenty and whose name tag read Victoria Marie. She peered at the blanket and Tomas.

"Oh my, what happened?" She came around the desk, scooped up Tomas and darted to an exam room.

She called back to Strader, "Come on." He was but two steps behind her. She placed the blanket on the exam table, motioned Strader to stay with the cat, and opened the door leading to the treatment and operating rooms. She yelled out, "Doctor, we have an emergency in room one. Please come stat." Turning to Strader, she asked, "Do you know what happened?"

Strader produced the baggie of the vomitus he had collected and handed it to her. "He must have eaten something that was bad. I found him in a thicket in the back of my condo—he had thrown this stuff up and was just lying there."

"Is this your cat?"

"Sure, but does it make any difference?"

"Well, if it's just a stray I'm not sure you would want us to try anything, the cat being so sick and all."

"Oh, I know what you mean—who would pay for his care?"

"Exactly."

"Exactly what?" The back door opened and a garrulous, full-bearded mountain man exploded into the room. Strader was relieved to see Dr. Doug, who had cared for all the Strader pets for the past twenty years. Raised eyebrows were the vet's sole greeting to Strader as he scooped up the near-lifeless cat. It took all of thirty seconds for him to examine the eyes, listen to the heart, poke at the belly, and go through a neuro exam. He sniffed at the cat's sweet breath. He placed Tomas in Strader's arms and examined the bag of vomitus—taking all of an additional 5 seconds. Turning back to Strader, he said, "Sorry Don, no rudeness intended. But we got to get to the quick. This baby's sick, real sick. Ethylene glycol poisoning."

A tech joined them, a middle-aged woman with an empathetic face and a competent walk.

"Jill, let's start an IV, push the fluid, and get a catheter in. Piggyback an amp of bicarb to go in slowly. We want blood, and get me a urine sample to look at under the microscope."

She complied, without questions, lifting the cat gently from Strader and taking him back to the treatment area.

Dr. Doug turned to Strader and asked, "Don, you do want us to try and save him, don't you?"

Strader nodded.

To the receptionist Dr. Doug said, "Please get me the file on Tomas Strader. It is Tomas, isn't it, Don?"

Another nod.

"Sorry to see you in this circumstance, Don. We hadn't gotten together since before Rosemary got sick. What is it four or five years? The only time I see you is at those monthly meetings in the park whenever I can make them. While Jill gets started, I need to know a few things. First, did you find Tomas in the garage?"

"No, he was in a bush at the back of my condo, facing the common area, facing west."

"And is there any place near there where someone would be working on their car, adding coolant?"

Strader thought for a moment. "No."

"And Tomas can come and go as he pleases? He's an outdoor cat?"

"Indoor—outdoor. We have a little cat door he can get in and out of. But he always stays around the back deck area and the lawn right around us when he goes out. He's always in sight when he's out."

"And there are no golf carts or any big lawn mowers that are driven where a coolant could have been given, or leaked?"

"No, it's not a golf course. There's a greenbelt about twenty or thirty yards between my condo and the next row. I'd say a pretty definite no. Why?"

Dr. Doug examined the bag of vomit and with gloves on, opened the bag and ran his hands through it. He picked out a kernel of the dry food that was in the vomitus and carefully examined it.

He asked, "What kind of cat food do you feed Tomas?"

"Uh, Friskies. I think the bag says 'indoor' something. Big green bag."

"Most likely it's Friskies indoor delights." He again looked at the vomitus kernel, cleared it off with his gloved finger and showed it to Strader. "Friskies are small and basically triangular. This is bigger and rounder. This is another brand."

"But I don't …"

"Don, this wasn't an accident. Your cat was poisoned. Ethylene glycol mixed with cat food. Dumb, they probably didn't need the food. The sweet taste and smell of ethylene glycol is often enough to have animals taste it, although the aftertaste is pretty severe. The green color is the frosting on the cake. Yeah, your cat was poisoned."

Strader was searching for answers. "Ethylene glycol poisoning—I know in people it causes seizures, renal failure and often death."

"Same in cats. The brain, kidneys, and liver all fail. Pretty common, but without the food. Usually, someone adds antifreeze or coolant to a car and spills some on the ground, or it leaks from a car's engine, or someone may leave the container uncapped and the cat gets at it. But with the food mixed in, your cat was poisoned. Any of your neighbors have a problem with him or with you?"

Strader shook his head.

"Any crazies near you? Nutty kids?"

Another shake of the head.

"Well, who has it in for him, or for you?"

Strader frowned. "Until a couple of weeks ago I'd have said no one. Now—I have a lot going on. I don't know. Can you save him?"

"Don't know. From the looks of him this must have happened about four to ten hours ago. He has some of the acute signs—vomiting, twitching, rapid eye movements and tremors, and also some of the things we see a bit later, like the drooling, severe lethargy and early coma. We can treat him but I don't know about saving him. If he survives, he'll be as good as new. We can sure try."

"What's involved?"

"We'll hydrate him up and correct any acidosis. I'll check his urine for oxalate crystals, which will clinch the diagnosis, although I'm certain it's ethylene glycol poisoning. We'll see what his kidney function is—sometimes temporary dialysis is needed. And I may want to give him some ethanol. It may be early enough for it to work, I'm not sure. It competes with the ethylene glycol for ADH and limits its activity. It's a bit old school but we don't use the new antidote, fomepizole much, because it costs way too much—in the thousands. But I've used ethanol for years, made quite a few cats and dogs drunk but happy. We'll see."

Strader asked the elephant in the room question. "How much are we talking about here, Doug? Just a guess."

"Weird isn't it, asking about the cost of treatment beforehand. In your business, with insurance, you really haven't had to do that."

"No, but now with copays rising and high deductibles and all these new biologic agents and novel therapies, it's becoming part of our daily vocabulary."

Doug countered. "I guess my big advantage is that we're always dealing in the third person. I can say to an owner it's not worth trying to save this old dog; he'd suffer and never be the same. I can even jack up the cost that would be saved if I really think it's not right for the dog or cat to be treated. I can tell them it'll be four thousand dollars and it's not going to bring him back to where he was. It's time for a new puppy or a new kitty or whatever. Hard to tell some old business tycoon he should drift off into the next world and allow his wife to take on a younger mate. That would make for interesting conversation."

"How about Tomas?" Strader fidgeted with his keys.

The receptionist knocked on the door and peered in as if on cue. "It's after eight. I'm closing up." She waved as she left, thankful she didn't have to work overtime.

"Tomas. It'll be a few hundred bucks for the visit, the IV fluid and the lab stuff. A couple of hundred more for an overnight stay. I can do an ultrasound to look for a swollen kidney and oxalate crystals, but if I see them on the urinalysis, that won't be necessary. The dialysis would be expensive but I don't know if I can get a tech in to run it tonight, and like I said, I won't use fomepizole because it costs thousands and I certainly couldn't get it tonight if I wanted to. So it'll run you about seven hundred dollars tonight, and tomorrow we can reassess things if he's still with us and responding to treatment. Or, given that he's so sick and the odds are pretty much against him, we can just let him go."

"I can't just let him go. He was Rosemary's cat, then Will's. Right now he's all that I have at home. And I'm all that he has. He's been poisoned; it's treatable—he could recover. Let's treat him."

Dr. Doug patted Strader on the shoulder. "Fine. Let's see how he's doing."

He led Strader through the exam room's back door to an area with multiple treatment rooms, an operating room, and an x-ray cubicle. To the right was a good-sized open room with four small enclosures, each housing a sick pet, three dogs and a kitten with a makeshift tunnel over its head. They stepped into the only lighted treatment room where Jill was stroking Tomas, still unconscious but now immobilized and sporting an IV and urinary catheter. The catheter bag was empty except for a few drops. Upon seeing Dr. Doug, Jill removed the scant urine, placed two drops on a slide, and slid it under an old, well-used microscope. Doug sat and peered through the scope, then motioned first Jill and then Strader to take a peek.

Doug said, "See those little crystals shaped like cigars or dumbbells? Those are calcium oxalate crystals—this is ethylene glycol poisoning." He slapped his hand hard on the counter. "God-damn crime." He scooted his chair nearer to Tomas, leaned forward and stroked his head. Tomas was breathing but was otherwise motionless except for the scattered muscle twitching. Doug swung around to Strader.

"Don, are you familiar with ethylene glycol toxicity in humans?"

"Not really. I vaguely remember seeing one patient when I was an intern, and I think there was a New England Journal CPC about ten years ago. What I told you is about all I know. Nervous system depression, renal failure—that's about it."

Doug lifted Tomas's front paw and watched it limply drop as he removed his hand. No reflex or other response when he stroked Tomas's chin. Doug shook his head.

"He's pretty deep—if the lab shows he's already in renal failure, then we may want to reconsider how aggressive to be. I don't want to lead you on a wild ride for nothing."

"When will the lab be ready?"

"Anytime now. Jill?"

"I'll check, Dr. Doug. You watch our little guy for me."

Jill walked to a table with a stainless-steel metal box containing an automatic blood analyzer. She checked the read-out status and printed the results. She gazed at them as she solemnly retrieved them for Doug. Her vibe deflated Strader. Doug reviewed the lab with sad eyes and a downward look. All Strader could do was look at Tomas, touch him, and try and prevent himself from crying. "How bad is it?"

"Don, in a cat, the BUN may be up to 36 and the creatinine as high as about 2.0 and still be considered normal or only mildly abnormal. When the creatinine rises towards five, we call it stage three renal disease and grade four is greater than five. Age and hydration all enter into our assessment. How old is Tomas?"

Strader thought back to the time when they rescued him as a little kitten. Rosemary was still well, and their son was still living at home. Strader ran the numbers.

"He's about four. Rosemary actually rescued him. She had just finished shopping at Vons. It was windy and raining and what she told me was that as she was putting the groceries in the trunk, she heard a little chirp-like sound coming from an upside-down ice cream sundae container. When she lifted it up, there was Tomas, vanilla ice cream on his little grey and white face as if someone had painted him a mustache. He knew a sucker when he saw one, so he purred right into her hand. Ten minutes later he was home with us; from then until right now." He heard his own voice break. "Sorry."

"Four is quite young for a cat to develop renal problems in the absence of some event such as this poisoning, but cats can live for years with chronic renal failure as long as their diet is adjusted and they are kept well hydrated." Doug took another look at the comatose cat before continuing. "Tomas is critical; his creatinine is 6.8, a bad sign in the evolution of ethylene glycol poisoning. We know he got poisoned this afternoon, so it's still early and the worst may be yet to come. There are several phases to treat. We're already hydrating him and monitoring his urine output, which so far is virtually nil. We've given him bicarb to treat the acidosis that comes with this. We have to watch for fluid overload, cardiac failure, and progressive neurologic depression."

"And…"

"There are actually two other things to try which may help. Jill, get my Vodka from the locker room?"

Jill was on her way. "Sure, Dr. Doug."

Doug turned to Strader. "We'll piggyback in some IV alcohol; I've done this many times."

"And if he doesn't start making urine soon—then what?" asked Strader just as Jill re-entered the room with an unopened bottle of Grey Goose Vodka. Both men watched her struggle to open it.

"If we wanted to go all out," said the vet, "we'd start peritoneal dialysis and continue it for at least twelve hours, maybe much, much longer. But I don't have an extra tech and Jill has four other patients to take care of all night in addition to Tomas, so dialysis is out."

Jill, Grey Goose in hand, said, "I can do it, Dr. Doug. I can run his IV, the alcohol drip and do the dialysis. You just have to set it up and leave instructions. It'll keep me busy but the other animals are pretty stable. I'll do it. No problem."

"Jill, all four of the others are on antibiotics; it's too much for one person. Sorry."

A forlorn Strader smiled softly at Jill. "Thanks, Jill, but I think Doug is right. Peritoneal dialysis alone is a full-time responsibility." He turned to Doug. "I did some peritoneal dialysis back in my internship days and it can't be that different. I'll stay and do it. I won't sleep if I go home anyway. Just show me what to do."

Doug thought a bit, then reached and rubbed Tomas's head. "What the hell, let's give it a try." Looking at the still largely lifeless cat, he continued, "Sure can't hurt. I'll teach you how to hook him up, and I'll stay for the first four hours to make sure everything's working right. I just better check in with the boss."

"Doug, you really don't have to stay…"

Doug ignored Strader, pulled out his cell phone and placed a call to his wife.

"Hi, Kathy. Ran into a little problem here. Don Strader, you remember Dr. Strader, Rosemary's husband? He's down here with his cat, who got poisoned—ethylene glycol—I'll tell you about it when I get home… Let's see, about midnight…What, okay, I'll put him on." He handed the phone to Strader.

Strader spoke hesitantly. "Hello, Kathy. Sorry to keep your husband at the shop."

Her voice flowed. "Don, it's so nice to talk with you. I remember Rosemary and that silly cat when it was a kitten. She'd meet the girls for lunch and open her purse and that little white and grey face would pop out, with that grey freckle on his nose. She loved that little thing to pieces. Don, I'm sure, like you, I have Rosemary in my thoughts so often. I miss her so much."

"Thanks, Kathy, that's very kind of you. She was one cat lover, that one. Listen, I'm really trying to get your husband home but he's a very stubborn guy."

"Keep him as long as you need him. He won't be much use to me if he comes home now anyway— he'll just be thinking of your cat. He'll be bouncing in and out of bed and calling the tech every five minutes." She laughed. "I'm sure between the two of you, if there's any chance of your cat getting better, it will. I'll let you go now. Tell Doug I'll see him when I see him. Goodnight."

Strader, misty-eyed, returned the cellphone to Doug.

"A good woman. Seems like you're just as bad as I was. Never much good at home if there was a sick one in the hospital."

Doug chuckled. "Never much good at home, period."

****

Thirty minutes later the vodka was slowly being infused into the IV, as an unconscious Tomas lay immobilized on his back on the surgical room's lone operating table. Jill placed a sterile white cloth over him and shaved a small area on his abdomen that Doug had marked. Strader threw on a green sterile gown over his street clothes, matching Jill and Doug. Doug used a scalpel from the surgical tray to make a small vertical incision through the shaved area down to and through the thin membrane covering the abdomen, the peritoneum. The peritoneum is a semi-permeable membrane that separates the abdominal contents from the more superficial skin and connective tissue. When fluid is placed within the abdominal cavity toxins from the blood can diffuse through the peritoneal membrane

198

and be washed away when the fluid is withdrawn and cycled with fresh fluid.

Don watched intently as the vet placed a clear polyethylene catheter through the hole he created into the abdomen and then taped it in place, securing it with a stitch connecting suture material looped around the catheter to the adjacent tissue.

"We used to run in about five hundred cc's of fluid in over a few minutes, leave it for up to forty minutes, then remove it and start all over again," Strader said. "But that was in humans and over thirty years ago. How does it work with cats?"

Doug finished cleaning and bandaging Tomas as he responded. "It's much less standardized in the animal kingdom. We usually will run in about three hundred cc's of fluid, let it sit for about a half-hour or so, then remove it and start the next cycle. Once we commit to doing it, we'll usually go at it for at least four hours, and if there is a response will continue for about twenty-four hours, give or take. Not very precise but when it works, it's pretty cool."

Jill carefully assembled the dialysis bag and tubing. The clear plastic IV fluid bag had a capacity of two thousand cc's of fluid, about two quarts. It was mounted on a tall IV stand. From the bottom of the bag, a large bore IV tube was connected to one arm of a Y connector, named because there could be two different tubes connected to a third tubing. In this case, the sterile fluid from the large plastic IV fluid bag could be unclamped so that fluid could run through one side of the Y connector and through the large polyvinyl catheter into the cat's peritoneal cavity. Once an adequate amount of fluid passed through, the IV bag fluid was clamped, as was the tubing from the other side of the Y connector, which drained into a different bag via gravity. Both sides were clamped for twenty minutes, allowing ethylene glycol toxins to diffuse from the blood into the peritoneal dialysate fluid. After twenty minutes, the other bag was placed low to the ground and that tubing unclamped. The dialysate fluid flowed from the cat to the receptacle bag, and that fluid was subsequently discarded. And the process was repeated, over and over.

Over the next three hours, Jill tended to her other patients while Dr. Doug monitored Tomas and helped Strader improve his dialysis technique. By midnight Strader was well schooled in tipping the cat a bit from side to side to help get all the fluid out after each dialysis run while maintaining a sterile technique. Tomas continued to twitch but had no significant seizure activity, and his breathing was easier. Dr. Doug had hooked up an IV to give some extra fluid and bicarbonate to reverse acidosis.

"Doug, why don't you take off for home?" Strader urged. "I'm here, Jill's here if I need her, and if something happens, I'll call you. Get some sleep so you won't be worthless tomorrow."

"Why should tomorrow be different than any other day?" Doug stood up amidst a weary creaking of an identified source. "Okay, I'll get on my way, but call me for anything; my eyes will probably be open most of the night. And Don, think of who could have done this. When we find out—I'm gonna go after the bastard."

Strader looked down at his helpless Tomas. His voice was soft, his spirit all but broken. "I don't know. I'm going through this business with the hospital, but who could do such a thing over that?" He shuddered, his hands like automatons, switching clamps on the dialysis tubing, releasing more poisoned fluid from Tomas. "For now, I'll just keep at it and report to you as needed. And Doug, thanks."

"You can thank me by having that cat of yours wake up. Night." And he was gone.

CHAPTER THIRTY-FIVE

During that long night, Strader was reminded of the struggles to stay awake on similar nights as an intern so many years ago. Sitting at the nurse's station on old KCC4 North, one of Mount Sinai's teaching service floors, drinking coffee and smoking while writing up a new patient's history and physical exam at two AM. His two companions, the one toxic, the other controversial, but there with him all the way. Those nights were pretty much the only time he smoked; if he had to pour over his orders or write additional ones, puffing on a fresh smoke was company.

"Another cup of coffee?" Jill was already handing it to him.

"Thanks. Long night."

It was 4 AM. He sipped the motor pool grade coffee and pined for a smoke. Now, thirty years since he quit, he still could feel the pleasure of drawing on the cigarette and exhaling that smooth, poisonous cloud. Company, but bad company—ironic that it was his dad's angina attack that caused him to quit rather than any of his medical knowledge.

He fought fatigue like he did in practice by speaking to Rosemary. 'Hon, your cat misbehaved, drank coolant fluid—he's really sick. Would you believe it's four in the morning and I'm in Doc Doug's place dialyzing him? But Tomas found you when you turned that ice cream cup over—he longed for her words of support and confidence that Tomas would recover. He fought back the tears of his failure with her, with Will, the pangs of loss and loneliness, as he clamped off one tube, opened the other, and sent yet another 300 cc's of fluid into his lifeless cat's abdomen.

****

At 2 PM, Wednesday, after sixteen hours of dialysis and only four hours before round two with the hospital, Tomas began showing signs of life.

Strader, exhausted, hands and shoulders sore from the endless all night work, couldn't help but weep as Tomas opened his eyes, moved his head in a slow motion, series of twists and turns, and reacquainted himself with the world. When he focused on Strader, Tomas gave a tremulous sigh and soft purr.

Strader couldn't resist the urge and called his kids, told them what happened, and that Tomas would survive. He snapped a picture of Tomas, eyes wide open, already licking his paw. He texted it to both of his kids. It felt so good to share a joyful moment.

Dr. Doug wrapped his big hand around Strader's shoulder as a small crowd of vets and techs gathered behind them, laughing. One by one, they shook Strader's hand and gave Tomas a quick rub.

"Ok, back to work, still a lot to do." barked Dr. Doug. He spoke with two of his techs before approaching Strader. "Don, renal function is almost back to normal, everything looks good. You go home and rest." Doug chuckled. "Amazing what a little alcohol will do."

CHAPTER THIRTY-SIX

Hafner spread papers in front of him on his end of the conference room table. The second hearing session was to start in thirty minutes and Strader hadn't yet arrived. Gilliam was near the room's entrance, talking with Dr. Robertson and an animated Alyce Wagner. *Always plotting*, Hafner mused. He hadn't lost his cool despite having to keep track of Strader's mental state and the risks and benefits of asking for a postponement of the session because of Strader's sleepless night. Strader made the decision for him, saying that he needed to get this done and there would be no postponement. Nevertheless, they lost precious time and couldn't review the plan and tactics for tonight's session. There was a risk, and his antenna was up.

Hafner loved to reflect: assessment, feedback, reassessment, time to think – so crucial to medicine and to life. He had a few minutes, so he reflected. First he asked himself, why were they here, on trial? The real reason of course was Strader's inopportune statement that there was a murder committed, with the assumption by many that he was talking about the hospital. The Florita Dominguez case wasn't yet ready to be dissected, at least for this hearing, other than planting the seeds when they crossed Gil Morgan.

In the hospital, Strader was disruptive. That was the charge. Hafner knew that in his own practice and almost certainly in soft-spoken Dr. Meller's as well, there was recognition of all of the hospital problems that existed on a daily basis. Some personnel didn't put the patient first, but why tilt at windmills? Bitching and moaning weren't going to move the needle upward. That's just the way it was. But Strader, like a crazed Don Quixote, would not stop jousting, would not accept substandard care, and Hafner admired him for speaking out, really, for all of them.

Hafner liked the definition of disruptive as 'to prevent something from continuing or operating in a normal way.' In the hospital setting, 'normal' was far from 'high quality' or, at times, 'acceptable.' Strader was being disruptive in a good way, trying to achieve a higher standard of care, but he was an asshole in the brutally honest and insensitive things he said when he really got going.

To Hafner, and in his calculation in the minds of Meller and Kalim, the good to the patient far outweighed the bad. If good disruptive was greater than bad disruptive, then Strader, in sum, was not negative disruptive, so not disruptive, and therefore innocent. He was counting on this reasoning to get the votes of Meller and Kalim. Klein and Alvarez's two votes for the hospital—the probability of swinging them was zero. Money talks, almost always—even in medicine.

So, as he'd anticipated from the beginning, it all boiled down to Rosero, and Hafner didn't have the data to predict a probability of getting his vote. On the plus side, the guy was married to an extremely wealthy woman, so the hospital link with the employee health position was not such a formidable obstacle. He did have a small private practice, so he should at least be aware of some of the hospital's problems that could affect his patients. He should be at least indirectly thankful to Strader for addressing them, even if in a clumsy way. On the other side, his main interest appeared to be Kalim's legs and some serious skirt-chasing. He must be a careful Casanova because Hafner hadn't heard too much gossip on the hospital floors. Rosero certainly hadn't been attentive to the proceedings last week. Yeah, his mind was likely already made up—one more against Strader.

Hafner glanced at his watch. Almost 5:50 – ten minutes to showtime. He'd have to work on Rosero's vote later. The hospital jurors were straggling in, Klein and Alvarez together, Kalim looking fresh and lovely, with Rosero panting right behind her, and Meller, still giving orders on his phone as he sat down. Strader, not looking too much the worse for wear for his ordeal, nodded to the docs while slowly marching to his seat next to Hafner. He was freshly shaved and wore a blue sport shirt and khaki pants instead of his usual suit. But Hafner noted the redness of Strader's eyes, his eyelids blinking with fatigue, trying to stay open. Although he hadn't said anything to Strader, he figured the timing of the poisoning of the cat and this evening's session was anything but coincidental.

Before Hafner could say a word, Strader offered, "I'm good. I just heard from Doug, and my cat is taking water and a few nibbles of chicken. Let's get 'em."

Hafner had his doubts. Strader's eyes looked tired, not really bloodshot but a bit glazed and slow to focus.

"Don, let's not kid ourselves. We did really well last week and they're looking to turn the tables on us. I'm sure they've got your GI nurse well prepped to describe what a maniac you were and how upset he was with your behavior."

Strader shrugged, the rise of tired shoulders almost imperceptible.

Hafner continued, "I didn't have a chance to tell you today, but I might slip in a little pearl that indirectly will help us down the line with Florita. Nothing you have to do with that. I agree that when it's our turn, we don't call Joe Morales. Meller and Kalim already know what Joe knows, so their vote won't change; Klein and Alvarez certainly won't change, and I'd have to tattoo something on Kalim's thighs for Rosero to pay attention. So say no to Joe."

Strader listened without responding. It was his decision not to call Joe. He was angry that Joe hadn't insisted on stepping up to the plate for him. He mollified himself, thinking at least he'd be spared the worry of Joe's well-meaning words twisted in further support of the hospital's case.

"That brings me to Chief Nurse Porter. I spoke to her today— they have her working what they're calling an emergency shift. I'll call her, but when they say they can't find someone to fill in for her, I'll tell her it's okay not to come. We'll have it clear on the record that she was on our list of witnesses. They chose to make her work and wouldn't find a substitute. This will be a plus for us if we have to take this to a real court and trial. I also think there is nothing she can say tonight that will determine Rosero's vote, which in the end is really all that's at stake."

"Ok." Strader swiveled his neck to peer at the jury. Who could possibly have been involved in hurting Tomas? He couldn't imagine that it was anyone now in the room. Well, at least that narrows it down. His mind was fuzzy but still working. It was 6:00.

Everyone was in place, the court reporter ready, and Gilliam called the hearing to order.

"Once again, I want to thank everyone for taking the time to participate in this judicial review. It's a substantial undertaking with a lot at stake, specifically whether the hospital can maintain an environment conducive to employee health and well-being."

Meller and Kalim and Dr. Robertson were already glancing Hafner's way. They weren't disappointed when he blurted out, "And whether it's within a doctor's right to call out practices that endanger the very patients who enter the hospital, to improve their health and well-being."

Gilliam seemed better prepared than the previous week. "Dr. Hafner, I've had about enough of your outbursts. Keep this up and you'll find yourself excused from this review, and I'll appoint another to serve Dr. Strader in your current capacity."

Hafner didn't back down. "Before you do that, you'd better find someone to rewrite the bylaws. I'm sure the hospital will not be pleased to find you preventing due process as provided by these bylaws to a physician that has served the hospital and community admirably for more than twenty years. And I'm positive the news media and the public will be eager to learn of the details of this proceeding and ALL of the directly and indirectly related issues. So why don't you assume your proper role?"

Dr. Kalim whispered something to Dr. Meller, who stood up and raised his hand. Gilliam acknowledged him.

Meller looked at his fellow jurors and around the table at the others. He spoke quietly but clearly. "We've all worked all day. We are here voluntarily and with no compensation to hear the evidence supporting the hospital's accusations and Dr. Strader's defense. That's it; that's why we are here. So can we please stop these shenanigans and get on with the next witness?"

Gilliam reddened and appeared frustrated that he couldn't hit back at Hafner, but he remained silent.

"I apologize if I did anything to delay these proceedings," Hafner interjected. "I agree, let's move forward." The last thing he wanted was to lose Meller or Kalim or alienate Rosero.

Dr. Robertson chimed in. "I agree."

Meek, Hafner thought.

Gilliam acquiesced. "Dr. Robertson, please call your next witness."

"I'd like to call Gil Morgan."

Morgan was ushered in, sporting hospital green scrubs, and took his place, agreeing to be truthful.

Robertson read from his script. "Can you please state your name, title and position in the hospital?"

"Sure," he replied, his voice distinct, deep, and clear. "I'm Gil Morgan, an RN who works in the GI lab as a GI nurse. I've been with the hospital for about eight years."

"And for those who aren't familiar with the GI nurse position, could you tell us what you do?"

"Sure." Morgan looked around the room as he spoke, first at the jurors, then eyes settling on Strader for a second before darting on.

Hafner thought this guy had been well coached, making a notation on his notepad for Don to see. 'Very even, very cool. Very sure of himself. Cocky. We'll use it.'

"I'm educated as an RN, with special training in gastroenterology. I am certified as a gastrointestinal nurse and a member of the Society of Gastroenterology Nurses and Associates."

Hafner barked, "In the interest of time, as expressed by Dr. Meller, can you please have the witness answer the question asked and not provide a CV?"

Gilliam responded, "I'm sure the panel is interested in nurse Morgan's educational background."

Hafner was quick to retort, "I'm not. The question was, 'what do you do, not how did you train.' Go on.'"

Morgan had to recalibrate and move from the script he had memorized. He did it skillfully.

"I was hired on the basis of my credentials to work in the GI lab at the hospital. I do everything from greet the patient, take their history and vital signs, put them at ease, start their IV, medicate them under the doctor's orders, and assist during the various endoscopic procedures, helping with biopsies, stents and the treatment of active hemorrhage. I'm responsible for all of the endoscopic equipment being in operational condition, and I send equipment for repairs and order new equipment when necessary. If I'm assisting with a case, I make sure the tech or I set up all the instruments and medication before the case starts and that everything is cleaned by protocol after each case and at the end of the day. Either the tech or I set up and maintain the GI cart when we have to do a case in the ER or OR, you know, for a bleeder or a foreign body. I function as the head nurse in the GI lab, so I do many different things in dealing with patients and their problems, which is why I chose this field."

Hafner jotted down 'medicate them under the doctor's orders.' He thought, *boy this guy is good. Looking so sincere at the panel and then back to Dr. Robertson.* Hafner patted Strader's forearm to reassure him.

Dr. Robertson asked, "So I take it that you have worked with Dr. Strader over these past eight years?"

Morgan: "I've worked with him and with all of the staff gastros." No rancor, no venom.

Robertson: "And how would you describe your relationship with Dr. Strader?"

Morgan: "Fine. I've learned to put up with him. He means well."

Hafner anticipated Strader's nostril flare and grunt and motioned for him to settle down and not respond. He hoped the panel couldn't see it from the other side of the table.

Robertson: "When you say, 'put up with him,' can you tell us what you mean?"

Hafner watched Morgan, the panel, and soothed an increasingly irate client simultaneously.

Morgan, smiling at Strader: "Sure. Doc Strader is a very good doc, and everybody knows that. It's just that sometimes, if things aren't going his way, he gets a bit riled and yells, saying things he doesn't mean."

Hafner interjected, "Point of order. For those of us who actually practice medicine and take care of patients, this is particularly galling. We all know that when things aren't going our way, they're certainly not going the patient's way, and if something's not being done right and it's harmful to the patient, shouldn't we as doctors be obligated to insist on getting things right?"

Gilliam's raised hand didn't stop him.

"So, Mr. Morgan, your statement omits anything about things going wrong for the patient but you focus on Dr. Strader's mindset. I guess you feel you're not only a nurse but a mind reader and psychiatrist. I move to strike Mr. Morgan's last statement."

Gilliam: "You'll have your chance to cross-examine. Motion overruled. Please continue."

Hafner jotted another note, this one to Strader. *Don't worry, we'll get him. Just stay cool.*

Morgan was still on his game but slightly less spontaneous and glib. "I mean, sometimes Doc Strader yells at us, even in front of patients. It can be very embarrassing."

Robertson: "When you say he yells at you, you mean he raises his voice?"

Morgan: "Yes."

Robertson: "In front of patients?"

Morgan: "Yup."

Robertson: "Did he ever use foul language? In front of patients?"

Morgan: "Yes."

Hafner was furiously taking notes amidst mounting concern that Strader was coming alive and threatening to erupt as his jaw tightened and redness washed over his face. "Let it go, Don. I got it." He wasn't sure that Strader could let it go.

Strader, to Hafner: "Such bullshit. I never…"

Hafner patted his shoulder to calm him down. "I got it."

Hafner thought that Morgan was mocking Strader, watching him start to squirm. It seemed clear that they wanted Strader to boil over. He had to keep Strader in line without getting himself distracted from the proceedings.

Robertson: "Can you give us a recent example?"

Morgan: "Sure. He called me in the middle of the night a few weeks ago for a bleeder. The guy was a young alcoholic who was really bleeding. Very sick. I had to rush in without my usual tech helper. When we were endoscoping the patient, we found a bleeding site, but I had to run back to the lab to get some extra equipment. Doc Strader screamed at me, called me the f-word and threatened to have me fired. I think everyone in the ER heard him, the nurses, the patients, everyone. It didn't make me feel good. Not one bit."

Strader was at the edge of his chair, loudly mumbling, "liar."

Robertson ignored him: "And what happened to the patient?"

Morgan: "I was able to run to the lab, get the equipment, and we stopped the bleeding. I think the patient did well."

Robertson: "And all of this yelling and cursing that Dr. Strader did, do you think that it's disruptive to you or anyone else being able to work with him?"

Morgan: "Sure. There are lots of nurses who don't want to take care of his patients because they're afraid of him."

Hafner jumped up: "I object. This witness is here to give testimony on his interactions with Dr. Strader, not give his speculations on the fears of others. We've already had testimony from two of the nurses. I demand that this last statement be stricken from the record and that the prosecution be counseled to avoid asking speculative questions." Hafner looked at the panel as he sat down, noting no reaction except for some note-taking by the studious Dr. Meller. Rosero had somehow inched closer to Kalim and was trying to engage her in his antics, but she was ignoring him and paying attention to the proceedings.

Gilliam: "Your objection is noted, Dr. Hafner. Dr. Robertson, please continue."

Dr. Robertson: "I'm finished with my questions."

Gilliam: "Dr. Hafner, you may cross examine the witness. Let's try and limit it to five minutes in the interest of time. After you're done, we'll take a short break. Then you can bring in your witnesses, and we can wrap up everything but final remarks and the panel's decision."

Hafner rose from his chair and began, "In the interest of justice, it likely will take me more than five minutes with this witness, so I ask the panel to be patient with me. I'm an internist, not a lawyer. I remind everyone that what is at stake here is an attempt to discredit a fine doctor who has worked for years and years in the best interests of his patients, this hospital and the community."

Gilliam looked at Robertson, then broke in himself: "Dr. Hafner, I know you're not a lawyer. This is the time to cross-examine the witness, not to make closing arguments. You'll get your chance there in the interest of justice. Please restrict your comments to the statements made by Mr. Morgan."

Hafner shrugged it off. "Thanks for the help, Mr. Gilliam. Okay, Mr. Morgan, let me get this straight. We'll get to the specific incident you mentioned, but prior to this, do you have a clear recollection of Dr. Strader yelling at you?"

Morgan nodded his head: "Yes."

Hafner: "And cursing at you, using the f-word, or maybe we should just say fuck. Do you remember him ever saying fuck to you or one of the other staff?"

"I'm, uhm, not sure."

"I'll take that as a no." And when he yelled at you or someone else in your presence, did he just yell out of the blue?"

Morgan shot a glance at Gilliam, then at Dr. Robertson, before answering: "Uh, I'm not sure...but maybe...yeah, I think yeah."

"But you just said during your testimony that he yelled when something went wrong. So should we believe what you're saying now or what you said twenty minutes ago?"

Gilliam: "Dr. Hafner, I'm instructing you not to badger the witness. You're not Perry Mason, and this isn't a formal court of law."

Hafner: "Dr. Strader and my peers on the jury panel are entitled to hear cross examination of the witness and clarification of his testimony. And that's what I'm trying to provide in what indeed is my first rodeo. So I would entreat you, Mr. Gilliam, to allow these proceedings to take place as they were written in the bylaws."

Gilliam begrudgingly: "Proceed but keep it on target, Hafner."

Hafner: "Thanks, Gilliam."

Hafner noted his exhausted client's bemused smile; maybe, on some level he was able to get a little kick out of this.

Hafner: "Now, where were we? Mr. Morgan, we were trying to make sense out of your comments. Did Dr. Strader yell out of the blue or only when he had reason to?"

Gilliam: "You are putting words in his mouth. I don't think he said that Strader yelled 'when he had reason to'...he said..."

Hafner stopped him. "That's right he said, 'when something went wrong.' I'm not sure whether Dr. Robertson appreciates you usurping his role as the prosecuting attorney for this procedure, but I certainly don't."

Gilliam: "I'm just helping move things along."

Hafner: "Be that as it may. Okay, Mr. Morgan, you said that the good doctor yelled when something went wrong. That's what happened that night in the ER with the bleeder, right? He yelled because something went wrong?"

"That's right."

"And that upset you. Maybe made you not want to work with Dr. Strader. It made you think he was a disruptive physician who should be thrown off staff. Were those the feelings that went through your mind that night?"

Morgan was more careful, a little unsure now. "It upset me. I rushed in to help and wound up getting cursed out. He didn't have to do that. I didn't really think about those other things at the time."

Hafner: "Well, you're offering testimony to determine whether or not Dr. Strader should be permanently thrown off the hospital staff, so when did these other thoughts crop up? Did something else happen? Did someone approach you? You've been working with Dr. Strader for eight years. Why now? When did this epiphany happen?"

Morgan looked down at his hands, for the moment getting no help from Robertson or Gilliam.

"Mr. Morgan?"

"I really can't say."

"You can't or you won't?"

No answer.

Hafner: "Let's approach this in a different way. You've worked with Dr. Strader for eight years and this is the first time you've been involved in an incident that's been reported, namely the incident in the ER with that GI bleeder. Is it that incident that got you so upset to come forward like this?

Morgan breathed a bit easier. "Yeah, this incident really got me upset. He shouldn't yell at me like he did."

Hafner smiled slightly and shook his head. "I agree, in an ideal world where all goes well, a bad word should never be uttered. All of us who work at this or any hospital know that the world is far from ideal. Mr. Morgan, if in your job as a GI nurse, you saw another nurse about to give blood to the wrong patient or became aware that a nurse gave too much medication to a patient, would you speak to that nurse?"

Morgan was slow with his words, again waiting for help that didn't arrive. "Sure I would, but I wouldn't raise my voice."

Hafner: "How about if they were across the room and about to do something wrong, would you yell for them to stop?"

Dr. Robertson, reacting to a stare from Gilliam, voiced a weak objection. "I think this calls for speculation and isn't what we are talking about."

Gilliam followed in a flash. "Sustained. Hafner—I mean, Dr. Hafner, you must move this along. This review is about Dr. Strader's behavior, not nurse Morgan's speculations about his own behavior. Move on."

Hafner didn't mind the response; he expected it. "Fine. I guess I was just thinking about what the perceived problem would be if someone yelled 'fire' because there actually was a fire. Which leaves me back to the incident that you say brought you here. How long does it usually take you to get to the hospital from home?"

"About 15 minutes, 20 tops."

"And that night, at two in the morning, an emergency, no traffic, you must have made it in 10 flat."

Morgan smiled, "Something like that."

Hafner held up his hand while he pulled out a small stack of papers and thumbed through them quickly. He looked up at Morgan. "Hospital records of the ER visit, the incident."

Gilliam jumped up, shaking his finger in a no-no tracing. "We cannot look at any hospital records without the written consent of the patient, even if this was a patient of Dr. Strader's. This is a HIPAA violation and you, Dr. Hafner, will be held accountable for it. There will be no such violation in this proceeding…"

Hafner offered an "I gotcha" smile as he produced a signed and notarized waiver from the patient and also his mother, allowing the medical records to be used for this specific proceeding. He handed this to Gilliam.

To the juror panel, he said, "What I gave Mr. Gilliam is a notarized letter from the patient involved, Mr. Ramos, as well as his mother, that gave us permission to review and share the information in these medical records with you solely for the purposes of this judicial review."

He pulled out a second letter and opened it up. "This is a handwritten note from the patient's mother, who insisted that I read this to you. I will do so and ask that it be placed in the record of these proceedings. She says, very simply, 'Dr. Strader saved my son's life. Bless him, and please make sure he is there for others.'" Hafner handed the second letter to Gilliam while quickly scanning the jurors. He could tell that Dr. Meller was moved. Dr. Kalim gleamed, attentive and smiling, while Klein and Alvarez slinked back in their seats. Rosero seemed nonchalant.

Hafner used the few seconds it took to walk back to his assigned seat to reassess the proceedings. He was extremely confident that he had Meller's vote and Kalim's and was just as confident that Alvarez and Klein were lost. Rosero hadn't been seriously involved in the proceedings since it started. Why would he vote for Strader? Under what circumstance could he break the tie to exonerate the good doctor? Rich socialite's plaything, playing the MD to mix with the elite crowd, yet willing to risk it by fooling around. Hafner reached his seat and jotted two notes, one about Rosero and the other, three words to Strader—watch me work.

Hafner exaggerated the clarity of his voice, speaking slowly, distinctly. "Mr. Morgan, you just told us that on that night it may have taken you only ten minutes to reach the hospital, right?"

Morgan was silent, fighting for an answer. "Give or take."

Hafner jumped in. "I'd say it was a bit more give. The ER record showed that you were called at 1:35 AM but you didn't arrive at the ER until 2:30. Can you explain what took an extra 45 minutes, give or take?"

Morgan, taking his time: "Well, as I said, I couldn't reach my tech…"

"And?"

"And I had to set up the GI bleeding cart and bring it to the ER myself."

"That's right—sorry, I forgot. The GI tech didn't show up. And just so I don't get it wrong, I'd like the court reporter to read back what you said earlier about what your responsibilities are and what you do."

Turning to the court reporter, he asked, "Could you please read back Mr. Morgan's earlier statement, starting with 'I'm responsible...'"

Hearing no objection, she complied. "I'm responsible for all of the endoscopic equipment being in operational condition, and I send equipment for repairs and order new equipment when necessary. If I'm assisting with a case, I make sure the tech or I set up all the instruments and medication before the case starts and that everything is cleaned by protocol after each case and at the end of the day. Either the tech or I set up and maintain the GI cart when we have to do a case in the ER or OR, you know, for a bleeder or a foreign body. I function as the head nurse in the GI lab, so I do lots of different things both in dealing with patients and their problems…which is why I chose this field."

"Thank you very much." Turning back to Morgan, Hafner continued, "I guess that clarifies the missing time. Can you tell us just how the GI cart is set up?"

"I'm not sure what you mean."

Gilliam: "May I remind you that this witness is not the subject of the proceedings here."

Hafner, ignoring Gilliam, continued. "I'm just trying to make everything as clear as possible for the doctor panel. It seems like you had at least 30 minutes to set up the cart and get it to the ER to work with Dr. Strader.

What exactly did you do? Was the cart already ready to be used, and you found some other problem that took time? Did you have to actually set up the different tools that make up the cart, or check the endoscopes, or what? And was there anything different that night from any other night when you had to come into work on a bleeder? You said earlier that you made sure the cart was set up at the end of the day, and checking the records, there were no other procedures performed after the lab closed. So please, clarify all this for us."

Morgan: "If it's okay with you, Dr. Hafner, let me back up a bit.'

Hafner: "I'm not sure where you're backing up from but go ahead." Hafner was surprised that Morgan seemed to be gathering himself, catching his second wind.

Morgan: "Maybe I didn't make it clear before. Usually, the tech sets up the GI cart in case of any emergencies after hours. I'm responsible for making sure that it's done before we close the lab at the end of the day. If we get called in, like that night, to the ER, usually the tech will get the cart from the GI lab and set it up in the ER or the ICU or wherever we're going to do an emergency procedure. On that night with Doc Strader, I couldn't reach the tech so I had to do everything myself. So I went to the GI lab and brought the cart to the ER. I thought that everything was on it the way it was supposed to be…but I guess it wasn't. I'm sure this wouldn't have happened if the tech had been there like he should have been. But I apologized to Doc then, and I apologize again now. Sorry, Doc." Just like that.

Gilliam chimed in. "Well, that explains it. The tech didn't show. Let's move on."

Hafner waved Strader quietly with one sideways hand gesture while approaching Morgan.

Hafner: "So it seems you are saying, despite having about thirty minutes to check and set up the cart, you assumed that the tech had left it set up correctly and you didn't check it, but instead used those 30 minutes in some other way, and you're apologizing for that? Or, are you apologizing for mislabeling Doctor Strader as being disruptive, or maybe for both?"

A bewildered Morgan responded, "No, I mean—I guess I just mean I'm sorry."

Hafner continued. "And—I forgot, you had to mix up the medication and bring it with you to the ER, right?"

Morgan: "Right."

"And that's usually, what, midazolam and Fentanyl?"

"Right."

214

"A very important part of your job, I'm sure. For the panel, can you describe how much you usually take, how you record what's given, and how you reconcile the medications used?"

Gilliam, "Hafner, what does this have to do with anything?"

"I'm showing how some of the time may have been used by Mr. Morgan. Keeping accurate track of the meds is a critical part of his job, I'm sure. Mr. Morgan?"

Morgan responded warily, not looking at Hafner or the panel. "Depending on the type of case and where it's being done, we usually will sign out 5 mg of midazolam and 50 micrograms of Fentanyl. The midazolam is usually in unit dosage vials, but occasionally we have to use larger vials with separate syringes. As we're doing the case, we mark down the dose given and the time it was given…"

Hafner interjected, "And after the case is over, you transfer this data into the electronic report that's typed on the GI EHR?"

An unhappy "Yeah."

"And after the case, you empty the syringe in a receptacle and reconcile the meds present at the start of the day with those at the end of the day, and the amount used to make sure all the numbers were in agreement. Right?"

"Right."

Hafner, "I'm sorry we went off track, but I did want the panel to know how careful the policy is with these meds and that it could have taken a fair amount of your time."

He beat Gilliam's inevitable interruption before it began. "In the interest of time, let's move forward. So you got to the ER to assist Dr. Strader with the bleeding Mr. Ramos." He glanced at the medical record. "Tell me if I have this right. When you arrived, the patient was hypotensive, had a heart rate of 160, was fighting, and had already thrown up blood all over Dr. Strader. Is that accurate?"

Morgan nodded.

Hafner: "Speak up, please."

"Yeah, that's right."

"And Doc, as you call him, didn't yell at you for being late?"

"Correct, not then."

Hafner kept it flowing. "Let's remind the panel, and Mr. Gilliam, that this young man was critically ill, fighting for his life. You and Doc and the ER nurse, Angie, worked together to transfuse him, give him fluids, a touch of sedation, and then Dr. Strader began the endoscopy. Is that the way things went?"

Morgan nodded and followed with, "pretty much."

Hafner let it go. "And Doc, as you call him, found a bleeding site, an ulcer in the antrum of the stomach, even with the patient bleeding and struggling. Seems pretty cool to me."

Another nod from Morgan.

Hafner: "And in a patient actively bleeding like this, your job is to intervene to stop it. And correct me if I'm wrong, but that usually involves a combination of therapies, starting with an injection of epinephrine into the bleeding site with a needle through the scope, followed by either a thermal approach with a bicap, heater probe, or maybe a laser, or the use of clips that are deployed through the endoscope and are designed specifically for bleeding. Correct?"

"Correct."

"And that night, you and Doc worked together, and you injected the ulcer with epinephrine." He looked up and Morgan nodded. Hafner asked, "Right?"

"Yes."

"And knowing that epi is inadequate alone, Doc asked for the hemo-clips, right? And you said you didn't bring them? And then he asked for a heater probe or a Bicap, and you said you didn't bring any of them? Is that what happened?"

"Yes, they weren't on the cart."

Hafner asked, "And at that time didn't Doc express the fact that you were experienced and he couldn't believe that you would not have these available and that the patient was in a perilous condition?" He noticed Morgan was getting a bit anxious, rubbing his hands together and moving side to side in his chair.

"Yeah, he said something like that, and then he cursed me. Used the f--- word."

"Ah, the f--- word. Fuck. There you were, you, Doc, the patient, and the ER nurse. Now, I'm going to paraphrase that conversation, as relayed to me not by Doc but by the nurse. I want you to tell me if anything I say is different from what you recall from that conversation. Okay?"

"Okay."

"Good. Doc asked for clips and you said you didn't have them. He got upset and reminded you that epi alone was inadequate to stop the bleeding. He then asked for a heater probe or a bicap, and you said everything was in the lab and you would go to the lab. You asked him if he wanted the clips or the probe. Doc was clearly perturbed and reminded you of the risks of not being prepared and that he was surprised at you. When you then asked if he wanted the clips or the heater probe, like it was one or the other, he became more vocal. He didn't curse you but was greatly upset that you were giving him a choice, that you would bring one tool or the other when both should have been on the cart. That's when he said, 'What the fuck do I want?' He said to be back in three minutes with the heater probe to make sure this never happened again, and if you were unable to set things up right in the future, he'd get someone who could.' Now is that consistent with your recollection?"

"You know, it was the middle of the night, I was trying to do my best, and with Doc so excited, I'm not sure what he said."

"I'd like the panel to note that the witness has not refuted anything that I said. I could go on and on but I think we've heard enough. I'm finished with you."

Gilliam: "Dr. Robertson, any further questions? We have time if you want to re-examine the witness."

Robertson only wanted to re-examine his car and then his bedroom. He couldn't wait for this to be over. "No further questions."

Gilliam looked at the panel. "Let's take a short break and we'll hear the witnesses from the defense side if there are any. I apologize that Dr. Hafner has prolonged these proceedings."

To everyone's surprise, Dr. Meller called out, "No need to apologize. That examination was important. If you don't mind, I'd like to speak with the panel outside."

Gilliam gulped, "Your call."

Hafner noted that Meller seemed to be canvasing them on the way out but didn't seem to get what he was looking for. They all drifted out to the hall.

Hafner turned to Strader. "We did fine with Morgan, although he's pretty quick on his feet." Strader was bleary-eyed, slumped a bit in his seat, his hands folded in his lap. Hafner was surprised at the change in Strader, who looked like he was giving up, reconciled to defeat. Hafner thought they had more than held their own. Hafner tried his best to boost him. "I think Meller canvased the panel, maybe looking for a unanimous verdict so they could just tell Gilliam that we didn't have to present our case. That tells me that he is on our side. Kalim was with him, but not the others. So nothing has really changed. It looks like whichever way Rosero votes will swing the decision."

Strader tried to joke. "If only you had Kalim's legs." It fell flat.

Hafner said, "If they come back and say it's over, then they convinced Rosero, and we won. I don't think they could end this thing against you without hearing our defense. Assuming they decide to continue, we'll bring Porter first if they let her appear, which I doubt. Then Angie, and then, if you insist, you. We'll make that decision at that time. Okay?"

Strader stiffened. "I'm speaking."

CHAPTER THIRTY-SEVEN

Hafner used the ten minute break to sharpen his focus on their defense. He put the probability of Porter appearing as less than 20%. Angie would be solid and would clarify the Gil Morgan episode. She'd speak of the favorable ER experience with Strader over the years. No votes but valuable material if this became a civil lawsuit. As for Strader's testimony, what could he say, that he was sorry he wanted the best for his patients? That someone from the hospital had poisoned his cat? That he was up all night dialyzing his cat and was really disgusted at this whole thing? That he was sorry for what he said to the nurses, and was insensitive? Hafner was convinced that the cat's poisoning was linked to tonight's proceedings, but of course they had no proof. No, Hafner figured. Neither Strader's testimony nor their speculation was going to change any votes. Rosero—concentrate on Rosero.

****

The panel reconvened and the proceedings were to continue. Hafner noted that Alyce Wagner had delivered a large manila envelope to Dr. Robertson, who didn't open it.

Gilliam continued to stoke Hafner after glancing at his watch. "Gosh, it's already 7:15. Dr. Hafner, call your witnesses—and let's try and get these good doctors home by 8:00."

Hafner responded, "We can end this charade now, apologize to Dr. Strader and to the good doctors for wasting their time, and go home. Right now."

Gilliam: "Call your witnesses."

Hafner: "I'd like to call Dr. Joe Morales."

Gilliam stepped outside the room for a few seconds, then returned.

219

"He's not there; must have gotten stuck somewhere. Next witness."

Hafner moved on. "We'll call Chief of Nursing Porter, who has agreed to appear tonight."

Gilliam did the outside inside bit again, except he took a bit longer. He re-entered without Nurse Porter but with info on her absence.

"Unfortunately, one of the Nursing Supervisors got sick and had to be sent home, and with no other backup, Nurse Porter had to fill in. She can't appear tonight."

Hafner looked disgusted at Gilliam and shrugged his shoulders at the panel. "What a coincidence. Go figure. Mr. Gilliam, how about if we adjourn for this week and reconvene next week so that our witnesses can appear?"

Gilliam suppressed a slight smirk as best he could. "Let's finish up with your remaining witnesses tonight, and I'll decide whether any extension of time is necessary."

Hafner: "Don't bother. Let's call Angie Franklin, our ER head nurse."

Gilliam repeated his act but Angie did appear, dressed in her working scrubs. Hafner was a bit perplexed. Why did they work it so that Porter wasn't here but didn't interfere with Angie testifying? Red flags went up.

Angie was sworn in, and Hafner began his questioning.

"Head nurse Franklin, can you tell the panel about your credentials and work experience here at Palms Hospital?"

Her voice was soft and crisp. "I have RN and MSN degrees. I've worked the ER at Palms for twenty years, the last eight as head nurse."

"And you have worked with Dr. Strader during those twenty years?"

"Many, many times."

"During those twenty years have you had any incidents where you found that Dr. Strader was not responsive to the needs of the ER or its patients?"

"Never. He always comes promptly when called, takes expert care of the patients, and takes time to talk with both the nursing staff and the patient's family."

"So, based on your extensive experience with him professionally, you would not label him as a disruptive physician?"

"No. Quite the opposite. If everyone was as responsive and practiced like Dr. Strader does, this hospital would be far better off."

Hafner noticed the easing of furrows on Strader's brow. The panel was attentive—even Rosero seemed to be listening. So far so good, Hafner thought. The lack of objections left him a bit uneasy, but he trucked on.

"We've had Gil Morgan appear as a witness for the hospital…"

Gilliam jumped in. "Hafner, this is a confidential proceeding and this witness should not be briefed on who any preceding witness was or to what they testified. Understand?"

A minimally chastised Hafner replied. "Sorry, your honor. I'm not up to snuff on all of the legal procedures. Let's go about this differently. Were you present recently when Dr. Strader performed an endoscopy on a critically ill patient who was hemorrhaging, Mr. Ramos?"

Franklin: "Yes."

"Was there an incident between Dr. Strader and the GI nurse?"

"Yes."

"Can you briefly describe your involvement and what occurred?"

"Sure. Mr. Ramos was critically ill and hemorrhaging. He actually threw up blood all over Dr. Strader." She glanced at Strader, smiled and continued.

"Dr. Strader and I were at the bedside, trying to restrain and resuscitate him, giving him fluid and transfusing him. I had called the GI bleeding team about an hour earlier, but nurse Morgan finally came without the tech."

"Usually, there are two people who come in?"

"Yes, the nurse and the tech. This time it was only nurse Morgan."

"And Dr. Strader was eventually able to endoscope the patient?"

"Yes."

"And what happened?"

"Dr. Strader found the bleeding site. It was a gastric ulcer, and he injected epinephrine into the ulcer area to decrease the blood flow. He asked nurse Morgan, I believe for hemo-clips, which are clips to seal off the blood vessel and stop the bleeding, but nurse Morgan said they weren't on the cart."

"And then…"

"Then I believe he asked for a heater probe, something else he could use, and was told that there was nothing like that on the cart. Dr. Strader told the nurse to go back to the lab and get them quickly, and nurse Morgan asked him to choose which one he wanted, suggesting that he wouldn't bring back both."

"And?"

"And then Dr. Strader scolded Nurse Morgan for putting the patient at risk by not bringing the right tools on the cart, told him not to let it happen again, and I think he told him to come back very quickly."

"And in your opinion, did nurse Morgan put the patient's life at risk?"

"Yes. We had to stop the bleeding—the patient was hypotensive and in danger of bleeding out."

Dr. Robertson broke in. "I object; this is speculation and calls for expert opinion."

Gilliam: "Sustained. The panel should ignore the statement of putting the patient's life at risk."

Hafner: "I'm sure the members of the panel who actually take care of patients are well aware of the potential mortality of someone hemorrhaging blood, with a BP of 70 and a pulse of 170. But I'll go on. Did he curse nurse Morgan? Excuse me, but did he say 'fuck'?"

"My recollection is that he used that word but not as cursing the nurse. I believe that he got upset when the nurse asked him which of the two devices he wanted when it was obvious he could need both. I believe he said something like, 'What the f--- do I want?' I think he found it hard to believe that the nurse was acting this way, especially since this was an experienced nurse."

Robertson: "Objection, calls for speculation."

Gilliam: "Sustained. The panel will ignore this statement."

Hafner: "Whatever. I know it was like 3:00 in the morning—was anyone else around to hear this?"

Franklin: "No, the area where we were taking care of Mr. Ramos was off to the side, and he and the three of us were it."

Hafner: "So, you believed that the nurse's actions jeopardized the patient, Dr. Strader raised his voice in calling out the nurse for his actions, cursed, but not at the nurse or the patient, with no other bystanders listening, and was able to save the patient?"

"Yes."

"Do you consider Dr. Strader a disruptive physician?"

"No. Not at all; I think he's a great doctor."

"Thank you. No further questions."

Hafner sat down and Robertson stood up, the manila envelope resting on his desk in front of him.

Robertson spoke in a low and civil tone.

"Nurse Franklin, you and I have worked together in the ER for a long time, right?'

"Yes, for many years."

"And I selected you for head nurse?"

"Yes, you did."

"And you'd agree that in all of the years we worked together, we never had a problem with Dr. Strader's professional performance."

"I agree. We never had a problem with any part of his work."

"And over these, really too many years to count, you and I have worked together professionally and from time to time have had to attend hospital social functions together?"

Hafner's antennas rose.

He broke in. "What does this have to do with the charges in this case, may I ask?"

Gilliam: "Can you answer that, Dr. Robertson?"

Robertson: "Sure. I think we all know, human nature being what it is and that sometimes our personal judgments can influence our professional judgments. Ms. Franklin, have you also had a social relationship with Dr. Strader?"

Franklin looked to Hafner.

Hafner jumped up. "I object – this is completely irrelevant to anything. This question should be withdrawn."

Gilliam: "Objection noted and overruled— this could speak to the witness's credibility. Please answer the question."

Franklin tried to pick her words carefully. "Yes." And she left it at that.

Robertson was on the hunt. "Would you say you were in a relationship with Dr. Strader?"

A pause. "We see each other socially. Nothing serious. Nothing that would keep me from telling the absolute truth at this meeting."

Payday. Robertson jumped on her response, opening the envelope to reveal pictures of the July 4th Fireworks party, Strader and Franklin snuggling, and a subsequent photo showing Strader leaving Franklin's condo early in the morning. Hafner was stunned.

Robertson read from his script. "I think these photos call into question the 'serious' nature of your relationship with Dr. Strader and should disqualify you as a credible witness. I submit that her testimony be stricken from the record."

Gilliam pondered a bit, looked at the photos, and announced the decision that was obviously made in advance of the meeting. "I really have no recourse but to strike this testimony from the record and instruct the panel to ignore it."

Kalim shook her head in disagreement, Meller grumbled as he made notes, and even Rosero frowned.

Strader jumped up and before Hafner could quiet him, he let fly. "This entire proceeding is a joke. To put this good nurse through the wringer is unconscionable." Looking at Robertson and Gilliam, he continued. "You make me ashamed to be associated with a hospital that would create this whole thing. This is pure bullshit…"

Gilliam was really rolling now. "Dr. Hafner, control your client. I'll tolerate no outbursts here. Let's take a quick three minute recess before you call any other witnesses that you have."

Hafner looked at a trembling Strader. He thought about Strader's ordeal with Tomas, the extent to which the hospital was playing dirty pool, and the testimony which he was about to give. He thought about the lack of effect any testimony would have on Rosero. Trying to figure out what to say that would make a difference in the outcome seemed futile.

He put his hand on Strader's arm. "Don, listen to me. I think that they've made up their minds. It's still 2-2 and we are not going to move Rosero one way or the other. We'll have to figure something else out for him. You should have told me about Angie. I might have told you…nah, I don't know. But for your testimony now, I say fuck it. Let's tell them like it is and be done."

****

Recess ended and Hafner spoke.

"This has been a most unusual experience for me, and I trust for the panel as well. I have one final witness, Dr. Strader. Before calling him, I'd like the panel to indulge me for two minutes. The final testimony will only involve one question, so we won't be delaying your time to get home." Hearing no objection, he went on. "The panel all know what a fine doctor and person Dr. Strader is, and the high standards he sets for himself and everyone else. He's acted the same for the last twenty years. I suspect that this proceeding is not about any of the three incidents brought forward but something entirely different, which I won't go into. You've seen the bias shown here, the sudden lack of availability of witnesses, the sneaking around in the private lives of good citizens and photographing them without their permission, casting aspersions where none exist. Yet the coup de grace happened yesterday, and since it may influence Dr. Strader's ability to testify, I need to bring it to your attention."

Gilliam admonished Hafner. "Your job here is to call your witness. The panel and I can make any judgments on his testimony. Bring on the witness."

From the panel, Dr. Meller spoke up. "Mr. Gilliam, with all due respect, this has been an eye opener and the panel would like to hear out Dr. Hafner."

Gilliam grumbled and sat down. "Proceed."

Hafner: "Thank you, Dr. Meller and Mr. Gilliam. I'll make it super brief. Yesterday, someone poisoned Dr. Strader's cat with radiator coolant. It wasn't an accident –there was kibble different from what the cat eats mixed in with the coolant, and it was not placed in an area where cars or any vehicles travel. It was in his own backyard. The police and the appropriate animal control authorities have been notified, and an investigation is underway. There are suspicions raised about the timing of the poisoning and tonight's testimony. Dr. Strader, in fact, was awake all night performing peritoneal dialysis on his cat, Tomas, and I'm pleased to report that as of this afternoon, the animal began responding. So Dr. Strader was subjected to this trauma as well as to the ordeal of working all night and all morning. That's all I have to say about that. My final witness is Dr. Strader." He waited for Don to get settled again.

"Don, this has been some experience for me as well as for you. Knowing you and working with you in the hospital for the last several years, I have the highest respect for you, and I don't think you have to defend yourself in front of your peers. They know who you are and what you're about."

Gilliam: "Is there a question coming? Hafner, this isn't closing arguments."

Hafner: "I have only one question. Don, after all you've contributed to your patients, the community, and this hospital, what is your opinion of the people behind this charade and of the hospital allowing this to go forward?

Strader: "It's a fucking disgrace."

Hafner: "Thank you, Dr. Strader. I have no further questions and no further witnesses."

A bewildered Gilliam didn't even ask Robertson if he wanted to cross-examine Strader, to Robertson's great relief. "Meeting adjourned."

CHAPTER THIRTY-EIGHT

Rare grey clouds adorned the crown of Mount Jacinto on Thursday morning as Vialotti huddled in his office over papers, books, and a whiteboard with diagrams. The AC was racing its hardest to keep ahead of the advancing morning heat and sweltering humidity. Mr. Dominguez and three of Florita's family waited under Bea's watchful eye in the outer room where her neat and clean desk was ready for battle.

Frank was immersed in the quagmire of his gargantuan problem: Florita's death—no, as Strader put it, her murder—was uncorroborated by a squeaky clean medical record with no evidence to suggest malpractice. Frank wrung his hands as his forehead furrowed and his bushy eyebrows rose and fell. He'd have to tell the family that they had no case. They were not going to have the chance to take it to the bank. His hands bookended his head, and he sighed, waiting for a sign. It came. Boom, thunder closely followed a long flash of lightning that briefly illuminated the window in his room. And then rain, pellets of rain and what looked like hail, knocking on the glass. He didn't remember such a fierce display in all his years in the desert.

He didn't consider himself a superstitious man, except for his common sense approach to black cats, ladders, careful handling of mirrors and picking up pennies. But this sudden rain, the booming thunder and lightning, was this a sign? Doc Strader didn't say no when he asked him about Florita; the hospital was trying to shut down the good doctor, and they had tried to keep Florita's medical records under wraps—why? Frank grimaced, got up and paced as he reasoned with himself. *If the records were right then Strader was wrong, but if Strader was right, then the records were wrong. And why would Strader be wrong and heap all this trouble on himself—no way. Just as Vialotti thought, Strader must be the key. And he was troubled by whatever happened—he wanted to talk, Vialotti could tell. Maybe just not now.*

Frank threw open his office door, with vigor in his smile and his voice, welcomed in the Dominguez family. Bea set up the necessary chairs, so the three of them sat facing Frank.

The husband spoke first. "Senor abogado, what can you tell us? We hope for good news. Will the hospital pay us for the death of my wife?" His family murmured their agreement.

Frank spread his hands out in front of him. Looking at each of them with a decisive focus, he responded slowly, honestly.

"I'm pretty sure that something happened to Florita that shouldn't have happened, but the expert who reviewed her medical records found absolutely nothing wrong. In cases like this, when we think there is malpractice, we get the records and have them reviewed by an expert, and if the expert says that nothing was done wrong, then we can't really file a case.

The unhappy faces registered with him.

"Lots of people get sick and die even when everything possible is done and done right. Sometimes people have a complication from an operation or a procedure that may even cause them to die. But doctors aren't perfect and complications occur, even when things are done right and the law allows for them. That's why before a procedure, the doctor gives the patient a form to sign, telling them of all the things that could go wrong. It's what we call informed consent, and although it tells the patient all of the bad things that can happen, it really protects the doctor. The doctor can say, 'well, the patient knew that it was possible she might die, but she accepted that risk to have the surgery or procedure done.'"

The family's hush was palpable, as were their expressions of confusion and disappointment.

Frank had been here many times before, in so many cases where there was a bad result but no malpractice, just a crushed family. But his instinct was that this one was different. He stood up, his hands and arms conducting a symphony to guide his words.

"Mr. Dominguez, Florita's loved ones, I know how sad you are and how angry. I know you have probably talked with friends, with your neighbors, and maybe they have told you to go to a big law firm, maybe in LA. And if you want to do that, I'll be happy to give you my file and the expert's opinion. No charge. But I can tell you that after they read the record and the opinion, they will tell you to go home, that Florita was very sick and died, and that no one was at fault. No lawsuit. And I can also tell you that they would be wrong. I need help from Dr. Strader, but I have to wait a week or two before I can speak with him. I ask you to wait two weeks and come back and see me then." His arms and hands stopped in unison, hands in front of and framing his face as if a camera was taking a headshot. "And I can tell you we will have a case, we will get justice, and we will take that to the bank."

Mr. Dominguez spoke for the family. "Okay Senor Frank, two weeks."

CHAPTER THIRTY-NINE

While Strader made a beeline to the Vet hospital to see the recovering Tomas, Hafner, who needed a release from the pressures of the trial, donned his alternate identity garb and hit the casino. He peered inside the poker room and saw an empty cutoff seat at a nine-person, $2/$4 no limit hold-em table and settled in just to the right of the dealer.

He bought $400 in chips and nodded to his adversaries, most known to him as regulars at the Wednesday night game.

"Ralph, Gordo, how are you guys doing?"

A grunt from Ralph and a "Joey" from Gordo was all he got. Ralph, a rotund ex-cop with an astonishingly short neck, was short-stacked, while Gordo, a mouse of a man with facial hair resembling a Schnauzer, guarded three small stacks of his own.

The two regulars sat to Hafner's immediate right; to his left, a thin Asian lady he didn't know occupied the dealer's seat. All nine players threw in their ante. Joey got dealt two diamonds, a jack and five. All the players called to the Asian lady who raised to $75. Everyone folded except Gordo, Ralph and Hafner, who called the raise. On the three community cards flopped, two more diamonds appeared, the 6 and 8, along with a deuce of spades. 34.97% - Hafner didn't even have to think – with four cards suited after a flop, his chance of making a flush was slightly over a third. His eyes scanned the remaining table for the tells that most amateurs had, gestures or actions that betrayed their hand. It wasn't math and it sure wasn't science, but he was confident that Ralph and Gordo would be giving it up. With Ralph, it was almost too easy. Every time he straightened up in his chair and showed good posture—he had a good hand. Right now, he remained slouched, so no worry. With Gordo, it was even easier—his half smile and call bet without raising told Hafner he had nothing. The woman was a mystery, her eyes hidden behind large black shades, her posture covered by a dark blue sack dress from which her bony arms and delicate hands emerged. She hardly moved as she raised to $150. No voice, no emotion, no unnecessary movement—no telling. Ralph and Gordo folded. Hafner called the raise.

His mind wandered to the faces and figures at the hearing. He didn't have to be an expert in body language to read Klein and Alvarez, or Meller or Kalim, for that matter. The former two were immutable pieces of stone, the latter empathetic, supportive, and attentive in their demeanor. And then there was Rosero—what could he make of him? Hafner didn't know whether it was the chase or the conquest that stoked Rosero's fire. How were they going to get to him? One last face was recalled. Alyce Wagner— he saw her in the corridor right after the session had ended, looking his way. Her smug expression said it all, 'I gotcha.' To Hafner, it also tipped her hand. She was the hatchet man. Good to know.

Back to the game, he thought. The fourth card, Queen of clubs – no help. He checked. The mystery woman raised again, this time $250. The board didn't offer much. He figured her maybe for a pocket pair— two diamonds like he had—maybe with a Queen or king high. Maybe with the flop she had a set— three of a kind. He had a lot invested, so he stayed in. As he waited for the dealer to turn the last card, he saw Holiday just outside the poker room door entrance, wildly waving and gesturing for him to join her. He gave her the one minute sign.

The river card was dealt—king of diamonds. He made his flush and checked. His opponent didn't hesitate. She was all in. Looking at the board, he had her pegged for a set of sixes or eights, possibly a flush. If she did have a flush, only the Ace or Queen of diamonds in her hand would beat him. The probability of his winning the pot was now much higher.

Pushing all of his chips in, he calmly said, "I call."

The Asian lady less confidently turned over her cards— she couldn't leave her three fives. The cards spoke. His flush beat her three of a kind. Joey committed the gambler's sin, leaving without giving the others a chance to get even.

He stood, pointed to Holiday, and said, "Sorry, but when a beautiful woman calls, I fold. See you next week." He grabbed his chips and left.

****

"Where to?" She asked. "How did it go tonight?"

"Anywhere. Lousy. One question at a time."

"Sorry." She squeezed his arm and added softly, "Gee, it really must have gone bad."

"How about a late dinner? Have you been to Melvyn's?"

The melodic ring of Holiday's cell interrupted. She looked at the number, and her face tightened. She motioned that she had to take it and disentangled their arms. He didn't protest as she walked away and answered. She seemed distraught when she returned.

"Dylan, that was the home my dad's in. He's acting up a bit. He's hallucinating and being belligerent. They can't reach his doctor."

"So they want you to go and calm him down."

She awkwardly nodded.

He went on. "Actually, that's a good idea. Let's go."

****

Fifteen minutes later, they dismounted from his bike in the parking lot of the Celestial Homes Memory Unit, a single floor, sprawling Spanish style building housing thirty residents and many more untold stories. The moonlight contrasted against the darkening sky threw a foreboding frame to the home, while the five minute wait for the matronly aide to open the locked door added to the secrecy within. The sign above the door read, "Welcome to Celestial Homes, where our residents live in peace."

The woman's voice was warm as she greeted them.

"Hi, Miss Holiday. Hello…"

"Dylan." He looked around at the deserted main room, clean and neat, round tables, each with four cushioned seats, four well-situated rockers, and last year's Christmas tree, under which slept Jeets, a seventy-pound mutt turned service dog, light brown coat shiny even in the poorly lit room. He lifted his head to receive Dylan's petting.

Dylan smiled as he pet him. "Don't get up, Jeets. Just like last time."

Holiday was too occupied to notice. She spoke hurriedly. "Hi, Cassie, the nurse called about dad."

"Come this way. Mr. Grove is—he's just not well tonight. Having those hallucinations—rats, wolves, Lord knows what else. We couldn't calm him down. And we know you don't want him restrained." She looked at Dylan, then back to Holiday.

They marched quickly to a shriek-filled room at the end of the hall,

231

where a sweating Mr. Grove stared at the ceiling in disbelief. He clutched the nurse, who was trying to comfort him.

He half-yelled, half-screamed, "Oh, my God. Get those rats." His gaze careened from the ceiling to the corner of the room, pupils dilated. Sweat dripped from his forehead, causing him to blink repetitively as he panicked from the horrors he perceived surrounding him. "The wolves. Timberwolves in the corner. Eating that little girl's head. Run." He tried to get up but Holiday embraced him in a wrestler's body lock. He squirmed and screamed even louder, "Run, get me outta here."

Holiday wiped the sweat off his brow, held him and gently kissed his forehead. "Dad, it's me, Holiday. There are no rats, no wolves, and no little girls. You're having a bad dream."

He looked at her, felt all her strength against him, and yielded for a second. He looked at the ceiling again, unable to separate what he was seeing from reality.

"Dad, it's just a dream, a nightmare, like I used to have when I was a kid. Remember when I would cry out and you would come and hug me? You're safe, dad; we're all safe."

His belligerence waned, the warrior at battle's end. He found Holiday's arms more soothing than her words. He shuddered and closed his eyes, afraid to re-open them. Somehow, he allowed himself to settle in.

Hafner made mental notes of the visual hallucinations, the dramatic sympathetic response Mr. Grove had expressed, and the degree of terror that engulfed him. Hafner noticed the remnants of a weeping bandlike eruption on one side of the man's face.

Hafner turned to the nurse, a fortyish, heavyset woman.

"Nurse," Hafner said. "How long has he had shingles?"

She glanced at Mr. Grove, but didn't answer. Instead, she used a dressing to wipe his face as best she could, given Holiday's hold on him.

Hafner was patient. "Nurse?"

She was forced to look up. "Sorry, but I can't tell you. HIPAA."

Holiday pulled her head back, still holding on to her dad tight as her eyes passed over the violaceous, crusting lesions that cruised down the left side of his face in a curved line. "Irma, Is this shingles? You can tell me—I'm his daughter, as you well know."

"Yes," came the sheepish reply.

Hafner interjected. "How are you treating it? And how long has he had it?"

Irma was hesitant. "I can't tell you without the doctor."

"Well, then why don't you call him? And you can tell him it's Dr. Hafner, and I'm here with Mr. Grove's daughter."

"But it's so late. And no emergency. The doctor will be mad at me." She took a few steps from the house phone and towards Holiday, like a child getting her mother's reprieve from dad's scolding.

"The doctor's name?" Hafner asked, unmoved.

"Er, Dr. Jonas, he's on call, but…"

Hafner asked Holiday, "Do you know this, Dr. Jonas? I don't—he's not on the hospital medical staff."

"I never met him but I think I've spoken with him a couple of times. He seemed nice."

"I'm not sure nice is what we need right now." He turned to the nurse. "Irma, what are you going to do with Mr. Grove now that his daughter has calmed him down a bit?"

"Put him to bed—give him a sleeping pill?" More of a question than an answer.

"And when he starts hallucinating again?"

Irma shrugged.

Hafner said, "You never told me or Mr. Grove's daughter how long he has had shingles and what are you doing to treat that."

"A few days. I'll check and be right back." She rushed out of the room toward the small nurse's station and medication room.

When she left, Hafner turned to Holiday, who had loosened her grip on her father but still held his left hand with hers. Her other arm cradled his shoulders. His agitation had markedly decreased, and he looked at her profile rather than the demons in the ceiling.

"Holiday, Holiday," he repeated softly.

Hafner said, "Holiday, I'll do whatever you want. But if your dad has had shingles for a week and they just started treating him with valacyclovir one or two days ago, it's not likely to help but may well be causing his hallucinations and should be stopped. If they can't or won't reach Dr. Jonas tonight, you can sign a form that makes me his doctor of record, and I can write orders. I had a patient who was here about eight months ago so I have privileges to practice here, and it shouldn't be a problem. It's your call." He saw her hesitancy and added, "We certainly can try to reach the doctor first and I'll talk to him if that's what you want." At that moment, she reflected a vulnerable beauty that transfixed him. He wanted to be part of her, not just a doctor taking care of her father.

Irma returned with some news. "I spoke with the doctor. He said I should put Mr. Grove to bed and give him a sleeping pill. He said there was no need to bother you."

Holiday nodded to Hafner, who took over.

"Irma, I want you to get a change of doctor form which Ms. Grove will sign, making me the doctor of record. Then I'll look at her father's record."

****

It took twenty minutes to finish the chart, write orders and put Mr. Grove to bed. Hafner reminded Irma to call him with any problems. He emphasized that the valacyclovir had caused the hallucinations and was discontinued. Since it was started too late to really help the rash, Burow's solution and calamine lotion would be all that was needed. Hafner had also changed Mr. Grove's medication, discontinuing the current sleeping pill.

He told her, "You'll have to watch him carefully tonight and maybe tomorrow, but after that, he should return to his usual self. Remind him if he gets agitated that he's just having a bad dream and that there are no animals chasing him. And call me anytime."

With that, Holiday kissed her dad goodnight, and they were off, arm in arm, feet barely touching the floor. It took a flashback to Strader's meltdown earlier that evening to tumble Hafner back to earth.

CHAPTER FORTY

While Mr. Grove was being put to bed at the Celestial Home, Strader was caring for his own patient—he had taken Tomas home. His kid was thrilled by the cat's recovery, but Will was boiling.

"They did it. It's so obvious. Fucking hospital criminals. Poisoned my cat—our cat—mom's cat." He faltered for what seemed a minute. "Tried to kill him for what? They're the animals. Thank God you were there, dad. Those sons of bitches. We're gonna get them, aren't we?"

"Yes, we will, son."

The cat had made a remarkable recovery; his last lab had been almost normal, allowing Dr. Doug to discontinue his IV and dialysis catheter and send him on his way. He sipped at fresh water from the tap, as he loved to do, but avoided the kibble and Fancy Feast treat Strader offered. His very needy meow cautioned Strader against leaving him even for a second, so they went to bed. Strader stroked him while reliving the past thirty-six hours of hell. Tomas kneaded softly on Strader's chest, thinking, who knows what. Both exhausted, they welcomed sleep together.

****

At five AM, Strader gently slid out from under Tomas, leaving him asleep on the bed covered by a yellow cat comforter knitted by one of Strader's patients. Strader watched him for a few minutes, relieved by the cat's easy, rhythmic breathing. He made himself a quick cup of coffee, drained it, and sat at his kitchen table. His neck hurt from tension, as well as the physical work with Tomas. Not so much a pain but a continual muscular contraction that forced his shoulders closer to his head. He took two aspirin and slopped some Bengay liberally on his neck and shoulders. *Good old aspirin, the name first dubbed by the Bayer boys in 1899, though its salicylate* *component had been in use since antiquity. Salicylates were derived from plants such as willow and myrtle and were touted by Hippocrates in 400 BC as a means of reducing fever. Now not only a pain, inflammation and fever reliever but a potent weapon in the fight against strokes and heart attacks, and with cancer prevention properties to boot. At pennies a pill. The benefit and economics against some of the newer anti-cancer drugs that might prolong life for a short few months in a small percentage of the patients who took it, at a cost of $400,000 or more—well, do the math. Yet he would have paid five times that amount if there were something that offered a glimmer of promise when Rosemary was sick.*

Rosemary. He realized he hadn't relived his agony for the last year or so and guessed that today it was his loneliness, the loss of contact with his patients, peers, and the hospital staff, that freed his brain to remember.

****

Four years ago, he'd held her hand gently, dabbing her lips with a glycerin swab to keep them moist. She looked disapprovingly at him as she reached out with her untethered hand for her tube of lipstick, reapplying it without a mirror. She would not see anyone, much less Saint Peter, without her lipstick, its redness sharply contrasting with the pallor of her face. He inwardly cringed at the downward curve to her lips, the barely perceptible fasciculations in her arms and legs representing electrical shocks and unimaginable pain as the crusading leukemic white blood cell monstrosities invaded her spinal cord and nervous system. She actually scolded him for messing up her lipstick and causing her more work.

"Oh Don, I can't teach you anything." And yet he felt the faint squeeze from her hand.

He smiled but inwardly cried, feeling breathless, hopeless, and angry. He had just come back from his meeting with the Chairman of the Department, discussing potential experimental or even alternative approaches that didn't exist. Bottom line--nothing to offer, his wife would die. He was sure that she knew and equally certain that she would not let him comfort her; she would do the comforting. Her favorite nurse came in with an artificial smile but real morphine, which Rosemary acknowledged as the final dose with a parting wave of her fingers. Strader was moved when the nurse gently kissed Rosemary on the forehead before she left. Rosemary had already given him his marching orders as to what to do when she was gone. She closed her eyes and her sleep deepened in sync with the increasing shallowness of her breathing until it was all sleep and he was alone.

Stella joined her dad at the bedside, and now tears could flow freely. Strader knew that Will wouldn't join them; he was too angry. Acute myelogenous leukemia in someone Rosemary's age, who had failed first-line therapy, was undefeated. Strader understood, and he wasn't going to force Will to do anything—much less be in the room at that moment. Will was a strong-willed boy, no, man. Besides, Rosemary said that he was entitled to have his own feelings. Why not be mad when your mom gets leukemia? She said that time would change his perspective regarding his dad. Strader sure hoped so.

Strader was amazed at how many of the nurses, interns, residents and fellows joined their vigil with solemn faces, hugs, tears, and expressions of profound sorrow.

Brushing against his leg, Tomas inched him back to today, with all the losses still mounting. His wife, his son, now his practice and reputation. He almost lost Tomas, and Angie was humiliated because of him, the Florita shit-show. He felt crushed beneath this avalanche of loss, sorrow, and disillusionment. He couldn't breathe; he needed to claw his way out. Raising Tomas to his lap, he was grateful to have a companion.

Earlier today he had said what he thought about the whole thing, 'It's a fucking disgrace,' which, of course, it was. He wanted to rip into Klein and Alvarez for their deafness and complicity. He would like to kick Rosero in the balls, not once but several times, for his one-track mind. He wanted to thank both Meller and Kalim for taking this onslaught seriously, paying close attention throughout, and hopefully being supportive. He wanted to thank his kids, who had both shown up for him, even Will. And lastly, he wanted to thank Vialotti for sniffing out the evil and advocating for the family when their case seemed non-existent. He would thank the intrepid lawyer when this was all over. As to his own lost cause, at least he told Gilliam, the jury, the court reporter, and everyone who would see the transcript. *It was a fucking disgrace.*

By ten a.m., he had filed away his thoughts: Doug was a reassuring friend, Angie an understanding supporter, and surprise, Stella gave him the news that both she and Will were coming out this weekend to be with him next week. And Will said he found a way to help in the Florita case. Maybe Rosemary had been right—maybe Will was coming around. *Strader thought, 'lose one, win one,'* as he returned to his bedroom to deposit Tomas.

CHAPTER FORTY-ONE

Friday was celebration time in CEO Hendrickson's Board room, where Alyce Wagner paraded around the Boardroom table, dropping her executive summary of Wednesday night's judicial review session for the CEO, Appel, Gilliam and Dr. Robertson.

The CEO viewed the first page and his eyebrows shot up. "Did he really say fuck in front of the panel?"

Gilliam and Robertson shared a nod.

Appel said, "I told you we were going to get him. Alyce, give us the two minute summary."

Alyce was happy to assume center stage.

"At Wednesday's night session, session two, it was established that Strader cursed the GI nurse, and we discredited the ER nurse's testimony by showing pictures of her being all cuddly with Strader."

The CEO broke in. "And where did you get these photos?"

Alyce responded on cue. "By good fortune, they happened to be sitting near me at the Fourth of July event and found their way into a few of the photos I took that night. I thought it was important to establish that the witness was not impartial, so I gave them to Mr. Appel."

Appel interjected. "I think we all get the picture. So Strader curses the GI nurse, his only witness is discredited, and to top it off, he takes the stand and curses again. Cursed about the entire proceeding. Great for us. Alyce, now update us on your interviews with the jurors."

"I had casual conversations with Dr. Klein and Dr. Alvarez, both of whom were very upset by Dr. Strader's behavior. They each agreed that there was no better description of his behavior than disruptive. I happened to run into Dr. Rosero at Employee Health and when I asked him his take on the judicial review to date, he stated that he's always been a supporter of the hospital, and he winked at me."

The CEO asked, "And the other two?"

Alyce responded, "Dr. Kalim was very busy and told me she found the

239

proceedings very interesting. That's all she would say. And Dr. Meller was too busy to talk with me. So we have three votes secured, which is all that we need."

The CEO continued, "Well, what's next?"

Appel took the reins. "We have the votes, Dale. All that's left is to write a good summation for Dr. Robertson here to deliver next Wednesday and have Mr. Gilliam count the votes to end Dr. Strader's career."

The CEO stood up. "Appel, no screw-ups. Let's get this over and behind us. You know what's riding on this." And he left.

Alyce shot an inquiring look to Appel, who smiled at her.

"Great job, Alyce. I think your work is done. The rest is up to us." The meeting adjourned.

CHAPTER FORTY-TWO

Hafner finished his Friday office hours at eleven, only 20 minutes late. He loved the early morning office, scheduled each Friday for his chronically ill patients, where he could tune them up and keep them out of the hospital over the weekend. He had switched to his motorcycle gear and picked up Holiday, who had visited her greatly improved dad at Celestial Homes. Hafner and Don had agreed to put off their next meeting until Monday since Strader's family was coming in from the East Coast.

Holiday never disappointed. In tight black leather pants and jacket, she jumped on the back of his bike, pressing against him. He gulped as she tucked her soft blonde hair into her mike-accessorized helmet. With both his and his cycle's engines revved, they were off. A fun, two hour drive to San Diego, where he, no, check that, they, had afternoon rounds with the residents. On the way down he filled her in on the details of the Wednesday night review and his thoughts on Strader's chances, which were low without divine intervention.

By three o'clock, he and Holiday had heard the intern, Dr. Lang, present a case of a young woman with a persistent cough and dramatically abnormal chest x-ray, with an infiltrate in her right lung, enlarged lymph nodes, and multiple tiny nodules. They talked about quirks in the case, the uncertainties of medicine, the need for reflection, and the time to think. Hafner coaxed the correct answers from them and the final diagnosis of a fungal, treatable pneumonia was comforting to the patient and enlightening to the young doctors, who marched out of rounds, chirping like baby chicks fed a voluptuous worm.

****

Evening descends in Ocean Beach in discrete mini-epics of pelicans, vertically plunging to their spotted ocean prey. The sun doesn't set but plays light games, hiding behind clouds until it finds the horizon, adored by crowds on the shore, on the dangerous rocks, in their cars, on terraces, or peeking out windows, all looking for the magic of a green flash as the sun disappears. Dylan and Holiday enjoyed the show from the remnants of a trail connecting Pesky Point to the Newport Pier, a path partially upended by the sea, home to the homeless, the adolescent drinkers and pot users, adventuresome dog owners on their evening runs, and occasionally, lovers. Holiday leaned against him, enjoying the slapping of waves against rock, the spectacle of seagulls rummaging to and fro in the air, and the single line formation of pelicans looking for their next ocean restaurant. She closed her eyes and sniffed the tangy salt air, almost tasting it, and lay her head on Dylan's shoulder.

She said, "Don't you just love that smell? The ocean is so amazing."

"Do you know where that smell comes from?"

"The ozone?"

He shook his head.

"Something from the Gulf Stream or some other current from the ocean?"

"Nope."

"Tell me." She poked him. "C'mon, tell me."

"You'll never get it out of me."

She pressed against him. "Tell me."

"You won't like it. The smell of the sea is actually from a gas, called DMS, or dimethyl sulfide, that bacteria convert from DMSP, a compound produced by single-celled sea dwellers called phytoplankton."

"Tell me something nice about it."

"What's really great is that birds love that smell because it means what's called a plankton bloom. Fish feed on these plants and provide food for pelicans and other birds."

She laughed and kissed his neck. "You're such a know-it-all, trying to impress a small-town girl. I'm not sure you're even right. I remember similar smells far away from the ocean. Riddle me that."

He stroked her hair and whispered into her ear. "Probably in the grocery. They actually add it to some processed foods to give a certain flavor —tomatoes, cabbage... even cream and roast chicken. It's in soy sauce, truffles — lots of foods. I can go on…"

Her mouth smothered his. They kissed and laughed… the coast was clear as they looked around them.

An hour later found them at OB Noodles, a local goldmine with great pho and a raucous crowd. Sitting at an outside table among the tattooed dog lovers, she let him order: a number 12 (rare steak pho), dumplings, the house special fried rice, a local beer and a glass of chardonnay. They talked about the events of Wednesday, of Dylan's disgust with the whole process, and of the extent to which the hospital was going after Strader— the cat, the pictures with Angie, the whole thing.

Holiday shifted a bit on her bench, "I can't believe they actually followed him around like a parolee and took pictures of them together. Did he really say to everyone that he thought it was a fucking disgrace?"

Dylan answered. "His very words."

"I agree with him."

"Me, too. We're kind of screwed, and I can't think of a way out. We need three votes—we got two. They got two, no doubt. And the deciding vote, this guy Rosero, I don't think he's heard a single word in the two sessions. He spends his time trying to score with Kalim, one of our intensive care specialists. Doesn't seem like he's having much success, from what I see, but I think that's just driving him more."

Holiday's popped up from her seat, hitting her leg on the table, the sound causing others to look at her. She rubbed her knee and sat down.

"Dr. Rosero, that young doc with an office on Sunrise?"

Dylan nodded.

She couldn't help herself. "Very handsome, dressed to kill?"

Dylan felt a twinge of jealousy until her eyes gave her away. He nodded. He said, "Actually, he's so good-looking I'm kind of falling for him myself."

Holiday thought for a few seconds before speaking. "You want his vote, right?"

"We need his vote. His vote decides whether we win or lose."

"What if I told you that I've met him twice, and I think he's taken a liking to me?"

Dylan frowned. Not sure he wanted to hear this. "So?"

"This guy is a major player. You know his wife is very rich. Once, I brought my dad to his office for a checkup— he spent maybe thirty seconds with my dad and fifteen minutes trying to hook up with me."

"To no avail, I hope."

She ignored answering, enjoying his discomfort. "The second time was at his house." She paused.

Dylan's eyebrows shot up his forehead, but he didn't take the bait.

She continued. "To be more accurate, his wife's estate. She asked me to give her some design ideas. She was thinking of switching from traditional to mid-century modern. He followed along like a dutiful puppy, rolling his big puppy eyes, pushing close to me every time her back was turned. Not cool, trying to hit on me without his wife knowing. I did catch one quick turnaround by her, almost as if she knew what he was up to, and she gave him a dirty look, which calmed him down. He's a player, and he takes risks."

Dylan said. "So you know, it's impossible for me to get his attention, let alone his vote. And since he does have a hospital contract for employee health, he's their third vote. They win. Unless…"

She completed his sentence. "Unless I get his attention."

"No, we are not going to do anything like that, have him take advantage of you."

"You've got it backwards. We are going to take advantage of him. The one thing this guy can't afford to do is rock the boat, embarrass his wife, lose his relevance. Listen…"

They spent the next two hours scheming, eating fried rice, and cementing a plan.

CHAPTER FORTY-THREE

Two days flew by. Vialotti had closed a three-year-old malpractice case for twenty-nine grand. Wrongful toe amputation. Too bad, he thought, wrong toe. If it had been the big toe, now there was some money to be made. But his client got vindication, and he got a small check. Not really worth the time and effort, but at least the errant doctor had to foot the bill. Walking down Palm Canyon drive at eight o'clock on this Sunday morning, he missed by one block the Strader entourage, Don and his kids, making a beeline for the Starbucks on Tahquitz, where the Bank of America used to be.

As they crossed the street at Palm Canyon, Strader cautioned, "Let's not talk about it in the store. Small town."

"Who calls it a store anymore?" said Will.

"I think it's sweet," said Stella. "Americana."

Strader jumped in. "As soon as this is over, I'm sure you'll find a nice museum to put me in."

Stella said, "Better than a nursing home."

"Amen."

Stella and Will ordered their exotic caffeine expressions, while Strader chose a humble all coffee, no frap or cap or lattes. They secured a table furthest from the entrance, with two empty tables buffering them from other customers.

"How do you feel, dad?" Stella asked. Like a daughter, not a lawyer.

Strader scratched his nose with his thumb and forefinger, a move that Joey the gambler would instantly recognize as a tell. Indecision; playing a bad hand. Strader looked around to make sure Alyce wasn't around, stealthily taking pictures or eavesdropping.

"Like a flood has washed away my house with everything in it, and I'm treading water, trying to stay afloat, watching it all sail by. My colleagues, patients, profession, and reputation are all gone. I'm drowning." He lowered his head, shoulders slumped, and peered down at his shoes. The sun blasted its way through the window, seeming to spotlight their table. Strader looked up at his kids and continued. "You know me, who I am. I don't try to hurt people."

Will started to respond, then let his dad continue.

"Sometimes I can be a pain—I don't know that mom's docs in New York cared for me, but I made sure they cared for her, respected her, did the right thing by her—and they did. I've tried to do the same thing here with all my patients—you know that." His voice cracked. "I'm rough at times, politically incorrect, maybe even a bit of an a-hole, but this whole case isn't about that. It's about Florita and what I said at that FWP meeting, and the hospital is scared and coming after me."

"Well, they should know not to mess with the falcon," Will said animatedly. "I know in my gut that they poisoned Tomas. They're amoral for that and for what they're trying to do to you. But we're gonna knock them right on their asses, wait and see."

Strader was tired. He reached out a hand to touch his son's shoulder. "Thanks, Will. Dylan Hafner has done a great job as my lawyer, but when the fix is in, what can you do?"

"Plenty," said Stella. "That's why we're here. To clean up this mess and restore your name, restore who you are. And we know who you are, dad. And we love you for being who you are. Don't we, Will?"

A sheepish nod and a firm hand clutching his dad's. "I want to get those fucks who poisoned Tomas, that's what I want. Pardon my language, dad, but I'm pissed."

Stella reached over and grabbed her dad's other hand. "We're going to meet with Dr. Hafner later today. At the tram of all places. I want you to take the day off. Play with Tomas, and watch the game. Hafner, from what I know, is a brilliant guy. Don't worry—we are not going to lose this case. I don't lose cases."

Strader sighed. "I really don't know how I could even go back to that hospital, even if I win. I can't change it--my ways don't work anymore."

Stella downed the remainder of her coffee. "We'll deal with that Thursday after we kick their asses on Wednesday night."

CHAPTER FORTY-FOUR

Hafner was suspicious of the hospital's surveillance tentacles, so he chose the Palm Springs tram to meet with Will and Stella. They rode together in the tram car at the base station, already 2,000 feet up.

Will said, "Man, they really upgraded this ride since we were kids. Remember when mom and dad would take us up? In the winter when all of a sudden we'd be in snow?"

"And you would only wear your flip-flops. I remember mom's huge basket of southern-fried chicken with biscuits and how happy she was that dad's pager couldn't go off. He liked it too, but being out of call range made him so fidgety."

The glass surrounding the tram car offered a view of greening mountains and fading sandy desert as they ascended. The inner car rotated slowly with the ascent, giving them a changing panoramic view. They exited to a secluded wooden bench surrounded by pine trees and dense bushes—the site of so many childhood picnics. They shared the bench, Stella in the middle.

"Man, what I'd give for mom's chicken right now," Will said.

"Me too," Stella said. "But today is no picnic."

"No, it's not. Your dad's a good man," said Hafner. "His patients are lucky. This judicial review has been a pain for me, but I'm honored that he asked me to represent him. The hospital group has done some terrible things to him. Poisoning his cat—I mean, are you kidding me? They've tried to screw him over every which way and I've done my best to get it all on the record. He's been knocked down. I don't know whether he wants to stay and practice here even if he wins."

Stella said. "I have an idea of what an ordeal this has been from our phone calls, just from the fact that my dad asked for help, something he never did when we lost our mom. So here we are. How do we win—how do we get justice?"

"I figured out how to prove that they covered up that drug screw-up in that woman's death," Will said. "I just need to get into their system. We will take them down."

Stella seemed surprised by Will's words. "First things first, Will. We have to win this trial. Right, Dylan?"

"Right. For Wednesday night, I need to get everything on the record in case we lose and have to go to a civil trial. I don't know if your dad would actually do that— right now he's an angry, disillusioned guy. I sense that at times he doesn't want to fight anymore. He doesn't— we don't— really know how to win— it's not a case decided on its merits. I think it's two votes to two right now; pretty well cemented on both sides. The deciding vote, Rosero, has a hospital contract and no allegiance to anything but skirt-chasing."

"So what magic words will get him to switch?" Stella asked.

"Words won't do it, I'm afraid." Dylan paused, letting it sink in. Both Stella and Will leaned forward in their chairs, waiting for the disclaimer.

Stella bit first. "But?"

Dylan leaned forward in his chair. "If we go by the rules as your dad insists, we lose. I've looked at this a thousand times— we lose." He let that sink in.

Will jumped from his chair. "My dad hates to lose. He doesn't lose— except for mom." He sat back down.

"We all lost," Stella said softly. "Even dad couldn't change that. And now this, his other love." She took a deep breath, her eyes meeting Dylan's straight on. "I've a feeling you don't like losing either. What's your plan?"

Dylan switched his gaze to Will, then back to Stella. "First, we must agree that this doesn't get back to your dad, even after the trial is over. Agreed?"

Two nods.

"Remember, they poisoned his cat, stalked and photographed and silenced his witnesses. So, as they say, turnabout is fair play."

Stella broke in. "I hope we're not poisoning anything."

Dylan smiled, "No poison, no physical harm. Nothing like that. We're going to play a game of chance with Dr. Rosero— well really, a game of chicken. I'm a big math nerd, I gamble, and as a doctor and in life, I deal with uncertainty, with probabilities, with risk versus reward, with sizing up patients and people in general. So, if we do nothing, I put on a strong closing argument, the probability that Rosero votes our way is small, less than ten percent. He has no upside but a potential downside with the hospital if he does. He's not a dumb guy. He knows what the hospital can do— he's seeing it firsthand with this debacle. So that option for us is out— if we want to win. So my girlfriend, who you'll meet later today, and I looked at ways that we can create a risk that would make him cringe and make the benefit of voting for us the only prudent way to go." He paused.

"And?" A Will and Stella chorus.

Dylan's smile broadened. "The popular dogma is that you need a certain perception of your given context to change behavior. A bad but realistic example in medicine would go something like this: a doctor orders 10 lab procedures a day from an independent lab, for which the doctor receives no revenue. In this scenario, the context is the need to have lab done, and the perception is that you don't earn any money from lab, so your behavior is to order ten labs a day. Now the doctor puts a lab in his own office, and he makes ten dollars for each lab done. The perception now is that the lab has become a revenue center for him, so he finds himself ordering thirty lab studies a day, for which he earns $300 a day. His behavior changes.

Stella said, "I know we're not setting up a lab for him. Go on."

"Rosero's perception is that he can get away with his current behavior and side with the hospital without there being any repercussions with his wife or his standing as a doctor. He can hit on women and get away with it. We use his own tendencies to compromise him. We let him hit on a certain girl. We take some photos, and then we let him know that we'll expose him if he doesn't vote for your dad. He's a skirt-chaser and we have a very pretty skirt to tempt him— my girlfriend."

Will looked at his sister. "Isn't this extortion? I mean, I don't really give a fuck— er, sorry, but can dad or we get in trouble?"

"It's closer to blackmail," Stella said. "Dad would never go along with this…"

"You have a better idea?" said Dylan.

He watched Stella rest her chin on her fist. Just like her dad, he thought.

She spoke. "Not better, but legal. I can't get my dad involved in breaking the law. Not him. Blackmail is when you threaten to reveal information against a person or persons that could be embarrassing, damaging socially or incriminating unless your demands are met, whether it's money, property or services. It may sound crazy but you still can be charged with blackmail even if the information is true or incriminating." She went on. "In this case, the threat is to reveal photos, and the service you want is for him to vote your way. So, no can do."

"But we're not even talking to him, let alone threatening him."

"The threat is implied. No can do." Stella was resolute.

249

Dylan persisted. "So, if I have information that I threaten to reveal, whether by direct or implied means, that can still be considered blackmail. Right?"

"That's the law."

Dylan thought for a few seconds about the risks Rosero faced if he was found to be screwing around with a patient and the real possibility of ruining his marriage and career. This seemed to Dylan to far outweigh the dubious benefit of his siding with the hospital. He wouldn't give it up. "So how about if we have no information and make no direct threat?"

"Well, if you have no information and make no threat, the elements for blackmail would be lacking. That would be okay. But how would that work?"

"Leave it to me. And trust me. Can you live with that?"

Will looked at Stella, hopefully.

"What can I say? Okay. But I don't want to hear about anything that could be construed as illegal. Get it?"

Dylan nodded, unsure of whether she was emphasizing "hear about" or "illegal." He had been going to have them meet Holiday, but now he thought it best to hold off till after the trial.

"Just looked it up," Will said, eyes on his phone. "In California, the law combines extortion and blackmail into one. It's a felony, punishable by up to four years in prison and a ten-thousand-dollar fine. Hey, now can we talk about the other thing, the Florita case, as my dad calls it?"

Dylan said, "I doubt that it's going to come up on Wednesday. But sure, we can talk about it."

"You know about the picture he took of the nurse's handwritten notes?" said Will. "He— no make that we— don't know when or how to use it."

"I don't know what your Dad has told you about Florita," Dylan said.

Stella recited methodically. "We have the facts. A medical error leads to a death, and there is a hospital cover-up, the only witness to this being my Dad. He's troubled, alludes to it in public, and the hospital seeks to discredit him, ruin his career...his life. Dad is a member of the medical staff, and his taking of the photo may be a HIPAA issue or a violation of medical staff policy, even though he was the physician of record. And without that photo, there is no documentation to support his story."

Will chimed in, "Don't forget the meds. Dad said that at the end of every day, the nurses had to reconcile the meds and count that the amount of drugs remaining matched with the amount given."

Dylan said,"We checked that. They did match. They either just fudged it or diluted the midazolam vial with saline. Either way, they closed that loop."

Will catapulted from the bench. His feet crackled on remnants of pine branches. "Not true. Dad said they used a big vial of midazolam that had 10 mg per cc. So, if we can get a log of the meds used for each patient right before and after Florita, we'll..."

Dylan jumped in. "We'll be able to see the effect of the dilution, with patients after Florita requiring a bigger volume, that is, of the diluted midazolam, until that vial was used up. Very sharp. But how do we access the records? I can't get them, and neither can your dad."

Will said, "You have access to the hospital's electronic health record system, right?"

"Right."

"From home and work?"

Dylan nodded.

"Then I can get in using your password and trust me, I'll find it."

"The problem with that is they can use an audit trail to trace that to me, which exposes me to HIPAA and possible Medical Staff and cybersecurity violations."

Will smiled. "I've done security projects for large corporations, the government, and some of the big hospitals in Boston. There will be no audit trail to you. Once I'm in the system, I'll detach from you, make an anonymous link to the GI lab records, and pull out what I need. The beauty of my approach is that I'll do it simultaneously with you on the system doing your usual work. This, of course is all timed and you couldn't be in two places at once. So we're good?"

Stella and Will fixed their gaze on Dylan, who hesitated for a few seconds.

Dylan shrugged his shoulders. "What the hell. Deal me in."

CHAPTER FORTY-FIVE

By the following evening, the hospital was all set for the upcoming Wednesday finale. Alyce Wagner had spent that busy Monday securing her three votes. Alvarez was locked in.

"We have to protect our nurses, everyone, from this bully, Strader," he had said.

"I'm sure the CEO will appreciate your support of the hospital," Alyce said, smiling.

"Thank you, Ms. Wagner."

She noted that he still had to read her name tag before addressing her.

Her second stop, with the other hospital ringer, went just as well.

She left word at both Meller's and Kalim's offices that the hospital was grateful for the time they had given to the judicial review and hopeful that a just outcome would be finalized on Wednesday.

She had discussed with Appel the best approach to take with Rosero, and she described the result as positive.

****

Twenty minutes had been allotted to their meeting in Doctor Rosero's sparse Monday schedule. He was punctual, an attribute common to the most organized and least busy physicians.

He reached for her hand. "Ms. Wagner, so nice to see you. I haven't seen you recently when I'm at the hospital. How are you?" They shook hands gently.

Alyce said, "Nice to see you as well. I've been very busy, as I'm sure you are. I just stopped by at the request of the CEO to extend his gratitude for your work at Employee Health and your time in attending the judicial review."

"It's not something I enjoy, but it has to be done."

She sensed that he was looking for something more. Smiling, she said, "We all know how precious time is for you busy doctors. We need more fine doctors like you who are willing to give their time for the good of the hospital. We're hopeful of extending your contract you're your role in hospital affairs in the future."

They briefly locked eyes. He smiled. "I understand." Meeting over.

****

Appel relayed Alyce's report to the CEO, who had become more comfortable with a majority outcome for the hospital. Appel would spend the evening polishing Dr. Robertson's summation and reviewing Gilliam's procedural role. They would all meet on Tuesday for a two-hour rehearsal. Appel was upbeat— he could see a step up the administrative ladder.

****

Frank Vialotti wasn't upbeat at all. He was tired of waiting and apprehensive that this could be the end of the line for the Florita case. He told the family to expect some news next week at the latest. He had nothing new, but he hadn't tried to reach Strader again. He felt sorry for the doc. Palm Springs was a small town with a single powerful hospital. Although initially there were emotional and supportive letters for Strader in the paper, they were soon overwhelmed by critical ones. Hospital propaganda at work, he thought. He'd help Strader if he could, and maybe after this was over on Wednesday, Strader would enlighten him on where and how the malpractice really took place. Help him and the Dominguez family. Maybe.

CHAPTER FORTY-SIX

Holiday arrived at the small, lavish office fifteen minutes early. The waiting room seated six, with two beautiful Spanish mahogany chairs and a deep, soft red couch. On a chiseled glass coffee table were three current magazines catering to female readers. On the wall were desert-themed photos, a vibrant blue and yellow Barcelona seascape, and a smattering of European diplomas. Yes, Rosero was a bona fide doctor, and a local headline with Rosero and "best doctors" in the same paragraph was proof positive of his expertise.

Sara, stylish in an off-white blouse and skirt, greeted Holiday as she entered. Sara was around sixty and the doctor's sole employee.

"Good morning, Ms. Grove, so nice to see you again. Is your dad doing okay? If I remember correctly, we only saw him one time."

Very smooth, thought Holiday. And so much nicer than the usual "sign in and sit down" she had gotten used to in the medical offices she visited with her dad.

"He's doing okay, I guess, given his diagnosis. A little rowdy at times."

"Well, I'm sure you keep close tabs on him and provide him with the love and support we all need."

"Thank you, Sara."

"When you called last evening, the doctor insisted that your problem must be important, so we freed up the schedule for this morning. He has clinic this afternoon at Employees Health, over at the hospital, and you know how unpredictable that can be."

"I can imagine."

They were interrupted by Rosero's soft closing of the entrance door.

"Good morning," he offered as he strode by. He didn't wait for the mandatory reply but retreated to his office. Holiday and Sara both took in his perfectly creased black pants and Egyptian cotton shirt. Perfect pants, perfect butt, thought Holiday. When he returned, he added a long, sparkling white coat, Dr. Rosero emblazoned above the chest pocket, with a double-headed stethoscope draped around his neck.

He beckoned to Holiday to join him and accompanied her to the back. The scale and vital signs station were in the hallway between his consultation office and the exam room. Sara shouldered her way between them, placing Holiday on the scale and weighing her.

"One twenty-six. And you're…"

"Five foot eight…and a half."

She finished taking vital signs and Rosero ushered Holiday into his consultation room, styled to coordinate with the waiting room. Holiday remembered how impressed she had been by the ornate blue couch lining one wall. A Remington sculpture of a vaquero on horseback rose from the floor to desk height on the opposite wall. She sat across the desk from Rosero.

"What a beautiful office you have. And you've added that Remington since my last visit."

"Thank you, and there is even more beauty now." A real charmer, she thought. She and Dylan had pigeon-holed him as a hunter, the kind of guy who loved the chase, the challenge, the seduction. Which is why she had dressed in a buttoned turquoise blouse and modest, roomy capris. Let him imagine what was underneath, she wasn't going to gift it to him.

Holiday had seen it all as a companion: the guys who just wanted to be seen with a pretty young thing, those who were there solely for the company (and she was surprised at how many fell into that group), and the rest, who she skillfully let down easily.

She said, "You are very kind."

He ignored his computer, his attention all on her. "How can I help you?" A comforting smile.

"Well, it's really nothing major. I have some stiffness in my neck on the left side and the back of my shoulder. It's been going on for a few weeks and hasn't improved. Usually, I wouldn't see anyone about it but I'll be away for the summer starting Thursday, and you were so helpful to my dad. So here I am."

His smile broadened. "You did the right thing. Now please, I have a few questions to ask. First, did you do anything to hurt yourself…lift something heavy, throw something…any accident?"

"No, that's the funny thing. I don't remember doing anything unusual."

His thick black eyebrows rose to a single horizontal crease on his forehead. "I see. What do you do that you would call usual? You are a designer, right? I remember when you visited my home."

"I have an interior design business that I started back east. But in the desert, I'm in the hospitality area, from setting up events to helping out as an escort." She and Hafner had discussed whether or not to mention her escort work and decided the scarcity of time was more crucial than possibly diminishing Rosero's thrill for the hunt.

Her matter-of-factness caught him off guard, but he wasn't one to miss an opening.

"And in this work...anything...uh...physical that you think would cause this? I mean, and pardon me for asking, have you found recently that you had to do some new activity that could cause this pain you have?"

She was completely unfazed. She crossed her legs and leaned slightly forward, watching his gaze lower to her chest. "No, nothing that I haven't done before."

Rosero hurried to finish his history-taking.

"It doesn't sound serious, a muscle strain, maybe. But we shall see with the examination."

"I'm looking forward to it— I mean to finding out what's wrong with me."

Sara, waiting at the door, led Holiday to the exam room. She took a fresh white cotton smock from a small linen closet and handed it to Holiday.

"Please, just down to bra and panties, and leave the smock open to the back. The doctor will be back in a minute." She looked like a tourist awaiting an encounter between a sea lion cub and a shark. "And I'll be with him."

"Thank you, Sara." So far, so good. She reviewed her planning session with Hafner. Make it Rosero's show; he had to lead. But make it happen. So she changed into her frock and waited. In two minutes, Sara and Rosero returned. Sara seated Holiday on the exam table, then stood at her left side while the doctor did the standard exam of her eyes, ears, nose and throat. She could smell the smooth sandalwood fragrance of his after shave as his face loomed inches from hers. His skin was tanned yet smooth. She felt his face brush hers as he bore in with his ophthalmoscope to visualize the back of her eye, the retina. Dylan had warned her of the potentially vulnerable points in the exam, and she was ready. Rather than recoil, she deftly prolonged their facial contact. She noticed Sara's disapproving look, like those of the nuns from her childhood at the church dances.

The doctor spoke. "Everything is good; let us examine your neck. Please, swing to the side. I'll help." And with a firm touch, he grabbed her knees and swung them to Sara's side, then positioned himself behind her on the other side of the exam table. His strong fingers encircled her neck, searching in vain for an abnormal thyroid gland or lymph node. Satisfied, he focused on the back of her neck and upper shoulder, feeling, kneading, massaging. He spent an inordinate time rubbing in a circular manner at and below the occipital prominences at the lower back of her skull, then on the velvety skin of the ridge between each shoulder. Holiday let her muscles relax and contract in sync with his probing. He continued until Sara's dark stare signaled an end.

Rosero found one spot just behind her shoulder, rubbed it vigorously, then stopped.

"It is as I thought," he said. "A tenseness of the muscles. Nothing more. A daily hot shower, maybe a massage, and you'll be fine." He watched closely as she got down from the table. "Yes, quite fine."

"Thank you so much, Dr. Rosero. I actually feel much, much better already." And with a soft smile, she added, "You'd be a great masseuse."

"Thank you," he laughed. "I'll have to think about that. Come back to my office when you are dressed and we'll talk about what's next." And seeing Sara still on guard, he threw in, "Some medicine if you need it while away."

Holiday wasn't sure what Rosero would do next, but probably nothing with Sara around. Holiday felt the need to act quickly. All their plans and precautions now seemed to hinge on averting this middle-aged woman's vigilance. Dressed, Holiday returned to Rosero's office only to see a concerned frown on his face. She sat down quietly.

"I reviewed my findings, Ms. Grove, and I have concerns only for your travel, that this spasm could return. I would like for you to have one more treatment before you leave. Perhaps I can fit you in tomorrow."

"I'd love that but tomorrow will be crazy for me with packing and getting my father all squared away, and I leave early Thursday."

Disappointed, he looked at his schedule. She didn't know if she was going to lose him, but Dylan had emphasized that she shouldn't be eager.

"I'm sorry to be such a problem." She arched her back as she stretched her neck from side to side, and he caught the swell of her breasts against her top.

He canvassed his calendar with renewed vigor and spoke to himself just loudly enough for her to hear. "Tomorrow's no good, and I have a review at six. This afternoon is Employees Health Clinic and my office is closed. When can we do this? And where? One more treatment would definitely help"

"Oh, please, don't let me be a problem. I'll be okay."

A knowing smile accented his cheekbones and white teeth.

"I have a solution if you trust me."

She nodded.

"We keep a small suite at the Plaza Hotel, just off Palm Canyon. Mostly for my VIP patients. Some go to the plastic surgeon for cosmetic surgery, and some have a same day procedure and need a place to stay overnight. There is an exam room there and some equipment for heating or cooling. I think I could give you a good treatment and some exercises that will help."

"I can't thank you enough. What time and what suite?"

He said, "At the Plaza, Dr. Rosero's suite, suite A, on the ground floor just off the lobby. Two o'clock. And please, don't say anything about this to Sara, I don't want that you be charged for another visit."

"You are so nice. I'll be there." And with a sway in her hips, she left.

****

As expected on a blistering July afternoon, the Plaza lobby was empty, except for a group of unfazed European tourists vying for heat stroke honors after hiking the Indian Canyon trails. A nervous Holiday in tight white shorts and a blue tank top rang the doorbell at Rosero's suite and was instantly welcomed inside by Rosero. The suite was unlike any medical office on the planet, with rich drapes covering the windows, a generous bar, and a king size bed opposite a heavy Spanish wooden chest of drawers, above which was a large flat screen TV. A small exam table stood in one corner. She felt his eyes on her as she looked around.

"I tried to make it a comfortable place, Holiday. Is it okay to call you by that?"

He took her silence as approval. "As I said, most often, this is used for overnight stays after plastic surgery— very demanding patients, you know. Please, may I offer you a drink to relax the muscles for the treatment?"

"I don't usually drink in the daytime," she answered, "but I guess a glass of wine wouldn't hurt."

He was already pouring. "Perfect. I have something even better for you— a bottle of wonderful champagne." He handed her a generously filled champagne glass and managed one for himself.

"Thank you. What a treat." She took a small swallow. "It's so good. I have to warn you, I don't hold my liquor very well. Maybe we should get started with the treatment." Another swallow. He followed suit.

"Yes, yes, but of course. Come, let's jump up on the table."

Holiday checked her watch. 2:08. She had ten minutes. As she followed him, she placed her small purse on the wooden chest, balancing her iPhone upright in front, facing the bed. Being in front of her, he didn't notice.

She sat on the table and he began rubbing her neck and shoulder, just as he did in the office.

"You're still a bit stiff, yes?"

"Yes, but that feels oh so good."

"I studied chiropractic and I've found it quite useful. I'm going to try some oil to relax the muscles."

She felt strong hands spreading warm, lavender-scented oil on her neck and shoulders, rubbing lightly at first, then forging a path between her shoulders with his thumbs. He seemed in no hurry. She figured she had six minutes left.

She forced herself to say, "Oh my God, that feels so wonderful. But this table is so hard. Is there…?"

"The bed?"

With that, she turned and brushed his lips with hers, jumped down, reconnected with her champagne and took a big swallow. She jumped on the bed, lying on her stomach. Rosero, not far behind, oil and all, sat on the bed beside her. Her eyes danced with mischief as she turned towards him, exposing the swell of her breasts. She started to lift off her tank top, then stopped.

Laughing, she said, "I want to give you a massage." She kissed his neck but before he could fully embrace her, she said wantonly, as if slightly high, "No, no, I mean a real massage. Take off your shirt and your pants and lie down." His eyes captured the sensual beauty of her hair, face, chest and buttocks as he unbuttoned his shirt, unbuckled his pants, and climbed into bed with her in his black briefs. They embraced on top of the covers, and his hands were now pawing. She pulled back, saying, "Hold on, I owe you a massage." She stalled him by pouring generously from the oil jar straight onto his chest. She laughed as she spread it evenly about his shoulder and pecs. He had a soccer player's absence of fat and toned muscles. Catlike, he turned and reached for her again—and her phone rang. She jumped up, making sure he noted the phone's position, directly facing the bed before she answered.

"Hello," she said.

In a booming female voice that she was sure Rosero could hear from the bed, came the response.

"Miss Grove, it's your dad. He's really bad. Please come quick."

"I'm on my way. Give me five minutes. Tell him I'll be right there."

And with that, she threw her phone in her purse, slid into her sandals, and sailed to the door.

"I'm so sorry, I have to go. My dad."

Rosero was composed. "Go Holiday. But I'm desperate to see you again. Before you leave for the summer."

"I think you will. I'm sure we will." She blew him a kiss and was gone.

CHAPTER FORTY-SEVEN

As the big day awakened, Tomas clung to Strader's lap. Strader rubbed his pet's head, stroked his back, and tickled his ears. He'd spent the night fielding his thoughts, drifting from the dreary four years of med school to the excitement of residency and fellowship. Proving himself in the early years of private practice, growing his practice and his family with Rosemary. Never saying no, always available— to his patients first, then his kids and Rosemary, pretty much never to himself. His rules nurtured from his residency training days— be available, be accountable, be knowledgeable—and he was.

Last night Will confirmed that the GI lab medication log provided strong evidence that midazolam had been diluted after Florita's case. Just in case they needed it now. It would certainly be useful to Vialotti in the future. Strader didn't ask how that information was obtained but for now, tried to focus on the judicial review and his future. He stroked Tomas's side with the back of his hand, which morphed into the paintbrush move, sliding his hand up and down the back, palms up one way, down the other. Tomas yawned his contentment.

"You knew mom only a little, didn't you, my little Tomas? She brought you to us. She loved you and I'm sure you loved her too. You were still a kitten when she got sick. I tried so hard. The docs were so empathetic, listening to the well-intentioned but unproven treatments I suggested. Rosemary and I talked and talked. I cried, and she tried to laugh. It was so hard to sit by her and watch her deteriorate. She was so brave, elegant even as those fucking leukemic cells overran her bone marrow, liver, spleen and her spinal cord. That last day she gave me orders and advice. She told me to enjoy Stella's accomplishments and be patient with Will. She said that it was fine to spend time with you, but Angie might be a better companion. You didn't shed much, which was a plus because I wasn't so good at cleaning up. She told me how proud she was of me, our family, and our practice. How good she said it made her feel when a patient would say nice things about me, how hard I worked to get them better." He saw that Tomas had closed his eyes. "You're right, my friend, no more babbling."

Strader brought Tomas back inside while he poured himself another coffee. His thoughts were morose, filled with death— Rosemary, Florita, and now his practice. The hospital was immutable, unwilling to change, except when it improved the bottom line. All of the mission statements, tag lines: compassion, care, continuity; because your life matters—bullshit. Money talks. And Rosemary was right; preaching didn't help. Opening his mouth would cost him his position on the medical staff. Even if he could stay, he'd be a divisive person in the hospital. No one wanted to hear the truth or be held accountable, not nurses, not doctors, not anyone. These days preference was to get lost among the team, doing the employee run, the eight-hour day, ample time for recreation, family, and fun. A shrinking culture of excellence and a flourishing one of expedience. Strader recognized his quixotic acts to be ineffectual, producing little change. He had endured the pain of losing Rosemary; now, he faced losing his practice too.

He downed his coffee in strong gulps. He was not one to go gently into the night. Dylan thought he should teach, something he never really had time for with his busy private practice. He recalled talking with Angie about this. Well, now he would have time. He couldn't— make that he wouldn't practice anymore in this town. And he was too old to start a new practice somewhere else. But teaching—teaching had always been an honorable core of medicine, and flashes of the lasting influence on him from his great mentors, Janowitz and Present and many others, made him smile. Teaching, a way out and hopefully a way up. Teaching.

Restless, he decided to take a walk around his complex even though the temperature was already nearing the century mark. In shorts and a t-shirt, mumbling to himself as he buzzed passed the tennis courts, he resembled a punch-drunk former boxer compulsively committed to his workout routine. Two retired tennis devotees briefly glanced his way but didn't wave. His brain was flooded by thoughts of Rosemary, Will, Kayesha and Tiny from the office, of memorable patients alive and dead, of that sonofabitch Morgan and that slimy Alyce Wagner. He thought of Frank Vialotti and his wife, who on her deathbed, had admonished Frank not to sue Strader just because he couldn't save her from cancer. And now Vialotti was in on the Florita case. And somehow, Strader not only didn't mind, but he wanted to help the malpractice attorney. Sweating, a bit short of breath, he found himself back at his front door, Tomas inside waiting for him. He picked up his cell phone, scrolled through his contacts, and dialed.

"Good morning. Mr. Vialotti's service, this is Tina. The office is closed till ten. Can I take a message?"

"Yes you can, Tina. Please tell Mr. Vialotti that Dr. Don Strader called. I'd like to see him in the office on Friday. I think I may be able to help him. He has my call back number."

"I'll let him know."

CHAPTER FORTY-EIGHT

The late afternoon blowtorched its way into evening. By five-fifty, everyone except Dr. Meller had assembled, hopefully for the last time. Strader and Hafner were seated at their usual spots, the five jurors at theirs, and Gilliam and Dr. Robertson were looking over papers and discussing strategy. Alyce Wagner, the bouncer for the event, positioned just outside the conference room door, noticed an attractive but uninvited figure walking towards her. Holiday Grove, dressed in casual business attire, carrying a large manila envelope. Alyce stopped her.

"Can I help you?" she asked.

"No, that's okay. I just have to drop this off to Dr. Hafner."

Alyce reached for it. "I'll take it and deliver it to him for you. You can't go in there."

Holiday pulled it back while deftly sidestepping her to reach the conference door. "Sorry, but I need to hand-deliver this. HIPAA, you know."

"But you can't…"

Too late. Holiday skirted by her, entering the room to the surprise and stares of those assembled. She walked up to Hafner, leaned over to open the envelope, and retrieved several glossy prints. Strader glanced at them, photos of Will and Stella and one of Strader and Rosemary taken when they first came to the desert. Hafner and Holiday looked at Rosero, who looked like he was witnessing the apocalypse. Hafner nudged Strader, who followed the others in gazing directly at Rosero.

Holiday gave him a cheerful "Dr. Rosero" shout out and watched him grimace as he looked first at her, then at the photos and the others staring at him. He was too far to see any detail in the photos but assumed the worst. All he could do was nervously give an acknowledging nod. Holiday waved to him, then exited, all eyes following her as she left. Gilliam had seen the delivery of the envelope to Hafner, Rosero's subsequent uneasiness, but he couldn't figure out what action to take.

He spoke to the assembled group. "Before we start, I want to canvas the juror panel to make sure that everyone is ready to proceed. I know Dr. Robertson is ready and I assume that Dr. Hafner is as well."

Hafner waved the now closed envelope. "We're all set."

Rosero was quiet, not even paying attention to Dr. Kalim's crossed legs next to him.

Dr. Meller looked at the other jurors. "I guess we're set as well."

Gilliam proceeded. "First of all, I want to thank all of the doctors for spending precious time for this important judicial review." Secure that he had the three votes for a favorable verdict, he continued. "We will make this short. We have heard from the hospital's witness list and Dr. Strader's short rebuttal. To the panel, you are charged with whether Dr. Strader is in fact, a disruptive physician, as the hospital has claimed. Tonight we will have summation statements, hopefully short, by each side. Following this, you will be polled for your vote by Dr. Meller, and the results will be tallied. I will participate with Dr. Meller to validate the results. Are there any questions?"

Hafner asked, "How will the votes be polled? I assume it will be a secret ballot, and after all ballots have been submitted, Dr. Meller will tally them up and report them to you. Is that right?"

"Dr. Hafner," Gilliam answered, "We are all pretty tired. A formal secret ballot isn't necessary. We can vote by a quick show of hands, and both Dr. Meller and I will count them."

"Mr. Gilliam, I think that Dr. Meller and the jurors will all feel that a secret ballot is not only more appropriate but will eliminate potential bias, which could be the basis of an ensuing civil trial, which neither the hospital nor my client desires."

Gilliam, again a bit flustered, offered, "A vote is a vote is a vote."

Meller interceded. "As the foreman of this panel, I think a secret ballot is what we'll do, and it should only take a few minutes."

Gilliam was defeated. "Okay, if that's what you want. I was only trying to move things along. Then let's get right to it. Dr. Robertson."

Robertson stood up, folding and opening his hands as he read from his script, not looking up once at either Strader or the panel.

"I also appreciate the time you've given. I didn't volunteer for this, but the bylaws have to be enforced or else we could have chaos." Hafner rolled his eyes and groaned loud enough for the panel to hear. Robertson cleared his throat and plowed ahead. "This is what our bylaws state:

"'The privilege of medical staff membership requires universal cooperation with physicians, nurses, hospital administration and others to avoid adversely affecting patient care. Harassment is. prohibited by any medical staff member against any individual physician, hospital employee or patient on the basis of race, religion, color, national origin, ancestry, physical disability, mental disability, medical disability, marital status, sex or sexual orientation. Any form of sexual harassment is prohibited. Information about the competence, performance or conduct of a medical staff member may be provided by any person. If information deemed reliable indicates a member of the Medical Staff may have exhibited behavior thought likely to be contrary to the medical staff bylaws, unethical, deleterious to the safety or quality of patient care, or below accepted professional standards, a request for an investigation or action against such member may be initiated by the chief of staff, a department chair or the medical executive committee.' The bylaws call for a summary suspension 'Whenever a member's behavior is such that immediate action be taken to protect the safety or health of patient(s) or to decrease a significant or imminent likelihood of harm to the health, safety or life of any patient or other person'."

He paused, just as he had practiced. "Simply stated, a Medical Staff member must be sensitive to diversity among staff and hospital employees, shouldn't use profane language in the hospital, and shouldn't intimidate or make fun of the staff. We have presented evidence that Dr. Strader has repetitively violated these rules, which creates a real threat to our staff and patients. Dr. Strader is a fine doctor, but a disruptive one, and if we follow our own rules, he must be removed."

Never has a doctor been happier to sit down than Robertson.

Gilliam turned to Hafner. "You're up."

Hafner pump-fisted his worn-out client as he stood, no papers in hand. He directed his words and eye contact to the panel.

"I'm not going to recite the bylaws or further disprove the allegations against Dr. Strader. I'm going to talk about this proceeding, briefly and honestly, and then I'm going to talk to you as one doctor to another and about what Don Strader really means for you as practicing docs, and for your patients. Dr. Strader has been a vocal advocate for patients his entire career. Have any of these alleged complaints been of a level to trigger this review? I don't think so. How was our side treated? Our witness, Chief of Nursing Ms. Porter, was forced to work instead of appearing here. Angie, the ER nurse you all know and respect, had her privacy violated. And last Tuesday, the day before Dr. Strader was to testify on his own behalf, his only pet, his cat, gets poisoned. Coincidence?"

Gilliam growled, "Dr. Hafner, you sound like a desperate man. The hospital has impeccably presented its witnesses and its case. In this lawyer's opinion, you have failed to rebut. A cat poisoned? Please. The panel will disregard these remarks. Now I would suggest you fish or cut bait."

Hafner was undeterred. "Mr. Gilliam, the impartial presiding officer— right." He waved Gilliam off before he could respond and continued. "But let's address the facts of this case in its context, the acute hospital environment where you all work to make sick people well. Excuse me; I misspoke before. I do want to repeat the bylaw that Dr. Robertson quoted. He said that the bylaws call for a summary suspension ' Whenever a member's behavior is such that immediate action be taken to protect the safety or health of patient(s) or to decrease a significant or imminent likelihood of harm to the health, safety or life of any patient or other person'. I mean, c'mon, has it ever even crossed anyone's mind that Dr. Strader was imminently likely to impair someone's health? Could you imagine if someone said that about you, Dr. Meller, or you, Dr. Kalim, or you, Dr. Rosero? Could you imagine? I'm positive you would say that's wrong, the very opposite is true. As it is in the case of our longtime colleague here." He gestured to Strader, who sat immobile, silent as if listening to his own eulogy.

"Dr. Strader stands accused of being disruptive. One definition of disruptive is innovative or groundbreaking, and in this context I would not only find him guilty, but my greatest hope for our profession is that all doctors would follow his lead. He protects his patients and holds all involved in their care accountable every time." He walked toward the panel, stopping six feet away.

"What's worse, letting patients suffer, die from medication errors, lack of communication, fatigue and understaffing—or speaking out against the problems in the hopes of making people accountable and making the hospital a safer and better place for our patients." 'Better to light a match than curse the darkness.' Well, maybe Don Strader got that confused, he was lighting a match, and a few swear words may have crossed his lips."

Hafner took two steps toward the jurors, all now watching attentively. He spread his hands apart in front of his chest, looking at each juror in turn before continuing.

"You see something wrong in the hospital that's a threat to your or anyone else's patients. You do nothing. No harm—no foul. Should this be punished?" He paused.

"You see something wrong and you want it fixed, but you call it out in an unartful way. No harm, possible good. Foul? - Should this be punished? I come from a math background; I study probability. Which of these two examples has a higher probability of improving the quality of care for your patients? Saying nothing, doing nothing is easy, no enemies made, but it doesn't move the needle. Calling out medical errors in an unartful way--is that a reason to end someone's distinguished career? Dr. Strader's illustrious career?" Hafner subtly adjusted his position so he was directly in front of Rosero, who nervously avoided eye contact.

Hafner continued. "Compare this case to the following hypothetical: a colleague physician sees a patient and tries to seduce her, abandoning the very trust so fundamental to the doctor-patient bond. The current guidance is that doctors cannot initiate sexual or improper relationships with current patients, no doubt derived from the original Hippocratic oath, which stated, 'whatever houses I may visit, I will come for the benefit of the sick, remaining free of all intentional injustice, of all mischief and in particular of sexual relations with both female and male persons, be they free or slaves.'" Hafner paused, waiting in vain for Rosero to look up.

"Behavior like this I think we can all agree, should be reported not only to the medical staff office but also to the state. This doctor should be exposed and a license review undertaken. In such cases, if physicians keep their license, they are required to inform patients of their transgressions."

Gilliam had had enough. "This isn't law school or an ethics class. I instruct the panel to disregard these remarks. You are wasting our time, Hafner. I'm going to give you three more minutes to finish and then have a vote. Three minutes."

Hafner caught Rosero's eye and quickly continued.

"Thanks for the three minutes. Just to finish that last thought." He had Rosero's attention. "Of course, there may be some overriding situation that would make you not report such an incident." He raised his eyebrows. "But that's not the point. In conclusion, to the panel, those who take care of patients and bear the burden of their outcome, those who work in ancillary ways, like you, Dr. Klein, and you, Dr. Alvarez—what kind of doctor do you want on this staff? If it weren't for Dr. Strader and some of his frank discussions of hospital problems, we would not have a GI bleeding team, a nutritional support team, a better ratio of nurses to patients in the ICU, we would not have the degree of accountability that we do, although we all know we continually need to improve. Dr. Strader at Palms Hospital has been disruptive only in the positive sense, and he should be rewarded for this, continued in the highest esteem of his colleagues and patients, and not smeared by this panel. Thank you." He returned to his seat next to Strader, who quietly patted his arm.

Dr. Robertson left the room, followed by Hafner and Strader. Alyce Wagner greeted them with a smug expression that Strader ignored. Hafner whispered, "You lose," as he passed her. The three doctors were led to a small waiting room to await the decision. Dr. Robertson sat away from the other two, awkwardly banging his feet against the floor and table.

Inside the conference room, Gilliam spoke. "I apologize for the time taken for these proceedings, but of course they're not lawyers. Dr. Hafner, in particular, seemed to get off track near the end, which wasted time. You've heard all the information, and now it's up to you to decide whether or not Dr. Strader fits the bylaws definition of a disruptive physician. If he does, then he deserves to be removed from the medical staff. We can expedite things by voting with a simple show of hands."

Dr. Meller objected. "I thought we decided to have a written secret ballot."

"Why waste the time? As the hearing officer, I think a show of hands is fine. This way, we can all verify the count." He stood up, his towering height a weapon.

Meller wouldn't budge. "No. As the lead juror, I feel accountable that the voting is carried out right, without any peer pressure or fear of recrimination." He removed a blank sheet of paper, quickly folded it into six parts, made sharp creases and ripped the paper into ballots. As an angry Gilliam glared, Meller wrote on five of them two boxes and labeled them yes or no. He folded them nicely and put them on the table.

To his fellow jurors, he instructed, "Pick one. If you favor the hospital's position, removing Don Strader from the staff, check the "yes" box. If you find that the hospital has not made its case that he is a disruptive physician who should be removed, check the "no" box. Yes, for the hospital, no for Don Strader. Is that clear to each of you?"

All nodded their approval and completed their ballots, Rosero being the last to finish. Meller had them placed back on the table and he scrambled them thoroughly.

"I'll take them one at a time, call out the vote and record it, and have Mr. Gilliam verify the vote." Meller began the process.

"One for the hospital."

"Verified," said Gilliam.

"Two for the hospital."

"Verified," in a more relaxed voice.

"One for Strader."

"Verified." And expected.

"Two for Strader." Expected.

A stillness paralyzed the air. All eyes were on the final ballot as Meller unraveled it and read it twice to himself before handing it to Gilliam.

Meller was triumphant, "Three votes— for Dr. Strader. The panel has found for Dr. Strader. All privileges should be reinstated immediately. Mr. Gilliam?"

A stunned Gilliam sat down, staring at the final ballot as if it was a black widow spider in his hands. His mind raced to find an alternative but one word forced its way out. "Verified."

A satisfied Meller and smiling Kalim led the way out, the others following without emotion. As soon as Dylan saw the joy in Meller's step, he bear-hugged Strader.

"We won, Don, we won."

A spent Strader could only sigh and pat Dylan's back while trying to breathe. Appel and Alyce briefly surfaced from the adjoining admin office to witness Meller's smile and Gilliam's slouched, slow walk. Alyce refused to believe her eyes and approached Gilliam, who shook his head.

She shuddered.

An animated Dylan approached her and whispered in her ear. "Hey, Alyce. Fuck you. And you are going to get yours."

****

The celebration dinner at Johnny Costa's was in full swing by eight-thirty. Johnny C, a former chef for Old Blue Eyes himself, served the best Italian food in the city. Hafner had reserved the front room for their party of ten. They laughed, ate and drank.

Nurse Porter chuckled, addressing Strader in front of the group. "You know, Doc, there was a time or two when I wasn't ready to throw you off the staff, but I could have tossed you off the roof."

He nodded.

Will said, "I'm glad she's not our mother. Dad, you don't know half of the trouble we got into in school. Not just me but Stella too."

Stella blushed.

Will continued. "Mom took care of them. She just had to give us 'the look.' And she promised us that she wouldn't tell you. I'm sure she didn't."

Angie confessed about how Don initially intimidated her in the ER before she understood him. Holiday giggled but offered few details of her tryst with Rosero. Kayesha and Tiny, who had carried the office over the last few weeks, described how weird yet wonderful it was working for their doctor. Hafner's easy laughter and feasting diffused the residual angst he

273

had over the lack of decency that colored the whole ordeal.

Doc Morales stole the show. "In the old days, our nurses wore starched white uniforms and hats. They were so clean I was afraid to ask them to do anything. I'd do it myself. In those days, some thought we had magical healing powers and admired us even as we smoked cigarettes at the nurse's station and even in the patient's rooms."

Don Strader ate sparingly. He scanned the table, thankful for his children, his friends and supporters, and his doctor-lawyer advocate who now seemed like family. He held Angie's hand. He thought about Palms Hospital, Florita, and Frank Vialotti, of his own obligation and future. He lifted his glass of Merlot towards the ceiling and toasted Rosemary. He knew what he had to do and felt good about it.

CHAPTER FORTY-NINE

A good clinical teacher is himself a Medical School.
– Oliver Wendell Holmes (1809-1894) "Scholastic and Bedside Teaching"

The human lessons which medical practice teaches are great and should be
passed on to our pupils.
– Sir Robert Platt (1900-1978) Universities Quarterly 17:327, 1963

If they are not interested in the care of the patient, in the phenomena of disease in the sick, they should not be in the clinical department of medicine, since
they cannot teach students clinical medicine.
– Maurice B. Strauss (1904-1974) Medicine 43:619, 1964

The second Donald Strader MD Christmas Party was an unconvention-
al event, even by San Diego standards. A large area was cordoned off
on Pacific Beach, just south of the Crystal Pier, with four barbecue pits
manning the perimeters. Sea scent, mixed with turkey, ham and stuffing
trimmings, atomized the air. Beachgoers with skimpy bathing suits, even
in December, and tattoos depicting undecipherable images and messages,
strolled by nonchalantly. Authored by Hafner and the medical students
on Strader's service, and hosted by Angie and Holiday, the Party had a
friends and family atmosphere, the highlight, other than the food, being
the gentle roasting of the good doctor by his students, by way of a playact-
ing doctor-patient encounter.

It had been seventeen months since Strader's exodus from the desert
to a two-bedroom cottage in Pacific Beach, three short blocks from the
ocean. He returned to Palm Springs infrequently, visiting with Doc Morales and Dr. Doug and lunching with Kayesha and Tiny to keep up with
the local news. Alyce Wagner and Appel had long been jettisoned by the
CEO at The Palms hospital, who himself was clinging to his job. Alyce
was tied up in legal proceedings both personally in the Tomas poisoning
caper and as part of the conspiracy in the Florita case, which was slowly
dragging its way towards justice. Gil Morgan was still working at the GI

lab, pending the trial's outcome. He felt remorse and struggled with the cruelty of circumstance, how the frenzied need to be at his son's soccer game caused him to make such a tragic mistake, only to be compounded by Alyce Wagner's forceful manipulation. Life now was so different, so compromised, but the least he could do was set the record straight, and he would. Frank the Bank, now armed with factual ammunition, was leading the charge to get justice for Florita's family, and yes, substantial compensation for all. Strader hadn't heard from Dolly recently about her bowels, and he wondered whose ear she now hounded. Strangely, or maybe not, he missed those calls.

He had waited until this past summer to sell his Palm Springs condo. Rosemary had told him to wait one year before selling to make sure he didn't make a mistake. He waited and got a decent price for it, which helped in the purchase of his new place. Angie had moved in two months ago and had decorated the cottage in beach style shabby chic, which was growing on him. Tomas happily peeked out from the east-facing kitchen window each sunny morning; afternoons were spent in several newfound hideouts. Weekends were often shared with Dylan and Holiday, who both still lived in the desert, to fulfill Holiday's obligations to her dad.

The pain of Strader's judicial review was rekindled when he had to give depositions on the Florita and Tomas cases, but it was intermittent rather than constant and commandeered less and less of his brain.

Still sporting a summer tan, in cargo shorts and a tee, Strader settled into a beach chair next to Angie, front and center for the show. Angie had somehow obtained matching doctor and nurse faux tattoos, which she had emblazoned on their respective arms. As the master of ceremony, Hafner made the intro.

"This year's virtual case, the second in the Dr. Strangelove series, as we like to call it, features me as Mr. B, the patient, Mary as Dr. Mann, Georgie as Dr. Strader, and Ms. Grove as the nurse. The setting is the city hospital emergency room. The topic is acute abdominal pain."

Hafner dropped to the ground and writhed around on a towel, hugging his abdomen. Holiday couldn't get him quiet enough to obtain vital signs, so she gently slapped him. Hafner held his hands out as if he was going to be cuffed. The audience laughed. Georgie (as Strader) stroked his chin but said nothing.

Mary walked to the bedside (towelside).

"Good morning Mr. B, I'm Doctor Mann. You seem to be in a lot of pain." Glancing at a virtual record, she said, "I see you're twenty-nine. Can you tell me about the pain?"

276

"It hurts." Everyone chuckled except a slightly embarrassed Mary. She shot back, "I know that it hurts. That's why they call it pain."

Georgie, as Strader, chimes in. "While open-ended questions are welcome in the office setting, you need to be more specific in the ER." He looked at Strader, who smiled in approval but wanted more. Georgie read him right. "And there is no reason to berate the patient for your stu... indelicate question."

Mary hid her fluster adequately. "Can you tell me where it hurts?"

Hafner said, "It hurts— in my belly. All over my belly. Holding it isn't helping, and neither are you."

Holiday slapped Harry again. "Be nice to the doctor. She's trying to find out what's wrong with you...besides your attitude, to get you better."

Hafner moaned.

Mary continued. "Where exactly did it start?"

"In my bedroom." Another slap. An audible chuckle from Strader.

"No, I mean, where on your body, check that, where on your belly did it start? Can you point to it?"

Harry pointed to the middle of his abdomen below his sternum but above the belly button.

"And when was that?"

"Yesterday afternoon. But it got worse last night and today it's even worse."

"Did the pain travel anywhere?"

"Well, it seems to follow me everywhere I go," said Hafner. Even the exasperated Mary laughed. "And it's really bad now. Can you give me something for pain?"

Another slap.

"Very soon. Just a couple of more questions. Have you been outside the immediate area lately?"

"No."

"Did you have a fever with this, or nausea, vomiting, or diarrhea?"

Hafner, writhing again, "No, No, No and No. Can I have something for pain now?"

"No. Not yet. Where does the pain hurt the most? Can you point to one spot?"

"Right here." Hafner pointed to his right lower abdomen, touched it himself, and almost came off the towel.

Mary eagerly touched the spot. Hafner jumped in pain. She pushed in a bit and it hurt, and the pain didn't change when she quickly removed her hand from his abdomen.

"Have you had this kind of pain before?"

"I don't know. One time they told me I might have chronic appendicitis."

Mary touched the rest of his abdomen, which was less tender. She listened for bowel sounds with her stethoscope and seemed satisfied.

She spoke in a pseudo-confident manner. "Well, Mr. B, you may have appendicitis. We'll need lab and a CT scan. There are no signs of peritonitis, so we can hold off on a surgeon."

"Great. And that shot?"

"Sure, we can give you something."

Before Hafner could finish the word Demerol, Georgie, as Strader, moved next to Mary's side.

"Dr. Mann," he said. "How much Demerol should you order—five milligrams or ten?"

Hafner jerked his head upward. "Five or ten? What am I, a bird? One hundred barely touches me."

"I see," said Georgie. "So you've had this pain before and required Demerol?"

"I told the doctor that I had it before. Chronic appendicitis. And it's killing me. I need something for pain."

Georgie reached down with his right finger, and as soon as he touched the skin, Hafner hit the sky. Leaving his hand on Hafner, Georgie swung his gaze past him and sighed. "Look at the bikini on her. Amazing." Not quite as impressive as Hafner's recovery as he whipped his head around to take in the sight. And there was a lovely young woman, clad in a white thong bikini, who bent forward as she set down her towel less than one hundred feet from the Strader perimeter. She looked with interest at the doctor actors and smiled. Hafner beamed back his best college yearbook smile but didn't defend against Holiday's smack. Georgie's continual poking of Hafner's abdomen produced no pained response or cessation of his wide smile. Georgie nodded and spoke to Dr. Mann.

"Distraction," he said. "Extremely valuable in the differentiation of organic from non-organic pain. And before we order a CT scan and narcotics, Dr. Mann, what one other test might be helpful here?"

Hafner tried to cover his being outed by moaning again, but he couldn't help himself and said, "I will not take a lie detector test."

"That's not a covered benefit," Georgie replied. "Dr. Mann, what is one simple bedside test to help decide whether the pain is from some acute abdominal process? Georgie was pleased by Strader's nod.

Dr. Mann asked. "A bedside ultrasound?"

"Well, while that might help, I was thinking of a physical finding. Have you heard of Carnett's sign?"

Dr. Mann drew a blank.

Georgie was at his Strader best, "A quick summary. He's twenty-nine, which virtually excludes some acute illnesses, like a ruptured aneurysm. His pain localizing to the right lower quadrant suggests an acute appy. However, the history of prior episodes, the need for narcotics, the knowledge of Demerol dosing, and the distraction of his symptoms by a small bikini gives us pause. Which brings us to Carnett's sign, which I'll now demonstrate."

He turned to Hafner. "Mr. B, how is your pain now?"

"It's killing me doc. I really need something right away."

"Okay, it's been ordered. I know you're hurting but can you tighten up your abdominal muscles? Contract them really tight."

Hafner does it and yells. "What are you, crazy? The pain is killing me."

"When you tightened up your muscles, the pain worsened?"

"Yeah, a lot."

"That is a classic example of a positive Carnett's sign, increased tenderness with muscle contraction, suggesting abdominal wall pain, not internal pain. If we believe Thomson's study in the Lancet in 1977, there is a 95% likelihood that this is abdominal wall pain and not visceral pain. You could stop here, treat locally, with no narcotics and no additional tests. Some optimistic comments, your availability, and Mr. B is good to go." Georgie looked to the real Dr. Strader.

Strader took up the cue with relaxed intensity.

"Well done by all parties. Mary, you were very much in your patient's corner. Maybe a bit too much, but that's always the side to be on. Trust me. Georgie, you were a very good me— but of course, there's always room for both of us to improve. Dr. Hafner, you were so good you should consider a career as a professional patient or comedian."

Hafner took a bow from his seat on the sand.

Strader went on. "The crucial points from this case are to gather old records and check his narcotic history with CURES. Do a drug screen, ask about trauma, family history, and prior surgery. A CT scan is better than an ultrasound if acute appendicitis is the likely culprit, but it's not needed for everyone with belly pain. In this case, I'll accept the diagnosis of abdominal wall pain, I'd avoid imaging or testing except for drug screening, and I'd get the old records. Remember that your goal is to help this patient whether his problem is surgical, medical, or social. There is always uncertainty. If the likelihood is 95 percent that Mr. B has abdominal wall pain and not appendicitis, five percent of the time you'll be wrong. The difference between a competent doctor and an expert clinician is follow-up and feedback. Always follow up. Your decision-making will become somewhat instinctive over time. So, well done. Now let's eat."

Dylan, Holiday and Angie worked the barbecue pits. Burgers, hot dogs, and sausages smoked and popped as they emitted their intoxicating fragrances. Veggie patties, brussels sprouts and onions cooked with more reserve.

Mary, Georgie and the other nine students stood and sat in a circle around Strader, peppering him with questions about cases, real and virtual. Strader held court in his beach chair. He answered each in detail, always with the reminder that they, as physicians, were themselves teachers, patient advocates, and fortunate to be called to the noblest profession.

The gulls, normally voracious, kept a respectful distance, quieting their caws to avoid disrupting the proceedings.

The end.